Prais

Amber Perry's colonial American debut is a stirring story with high drama, romance, and suspense aplenty. From lovely cover to satisfying conclusion, *So Fair a Lady* will win romance readers' hearts!

-Laura Frantz, Christy Award finalist and author of The Colonels' Lady and Love's Reckoning

Amber Perry's debut novel brings to life the days before the Revolutionary War in vivid detail. This fast-paced, historical romance will appeal to colonial enthusiasts and inspirational readers alike.

- Stacy Henrie, author of Hope at Dawn (Of Love and War, Book 1)

A tender Colonial love story, *So Fair a Lady* will sweep you back in time to a nation's turbulent beginnings where love and loyalty wages war against two men ... and the one woman who has captured both of their hearts.

-Julie Lessman, award-winning author of The Daughters of Boston and Winds of Change series.

Heartwarming, suspenseful, adventurous, and romantic ... everything I love in a novel! Amber Perry's elegant prose and deep characters will transport you to pre-Revolutionary War America where tensions were high, betrayal was common, and love blossomed in the most unexpected places.

-MaryLu Tyndall, award winning author of the Escape to Paradise series

When I opened *So Fair a Lady*, I had no idea the emotional turmoil I would endure as I joined Eliza on her tumultuous voyage from her genteel home, through unspeakable heartbreak, and swoon-worthy happiness, all the way to The End. Amber Perry creates a world so real, so intense, that the reader forgets the realm around them and falls down through time into the chairs set in front of the warm fire, ready to join the characters as they try to make sense of the turbulent world around them. This is 'seat of your pants', 'did he just kiss her like that?' reading!

-Jennifer Z. Major,
www.talesfromtheredhead.blogspot.com

So True A Love

Book 2

Daughters of His Kingdom Series

By, Amber Lynn Perry

So True a Love
By, Amber Lynn Perry

ISBN-13: 978-0692367605
ISBN-10: 0692367608

Cover Design by Indie Cover Design (Original concept by Tekeme Studios.)
Cover Photography by Danyell Diaz Photography
Interior Layout by Lynnette Bonner of Indie Cover Design - www.indiecoverdesign.com

Published by Liberty Publishing

CreateSpace Edition

Author/publisher information and contact: www.amberlynnperry.com

Dedicated to all who yearn for liberty.
May your strivings be blessed by God.

Now the Lord is that Spirit: and where the Spirit of the Lord is, there is liberty.

2 Corinthians 3:17

Author's Note

In September of 1774, General Gage initiated a run on ammunition magazines in and around Boston. This was called the Powder Alarm. His design was to secretly remove gunpowder from the colonist's supply and cripple their ability to resist British authority. Though the Powder Alarm ended quickly, the impact imprinted on the minds of the patriots. This action created a firestorm that eventually led to the first official military conflict of the American Revolution at Lexington and Concord on April 19th, 1775.

Gunpowder was highly volatile and difficult to obtain as all supplies were manufactured and supplied by Britain. Therefore, the precious reserves were highly valued by each side of the conflict.

The extreme tensions between Whigs and Tories, and the upheaval of everyday life that colonists experienced is difficult to fully comprehend. The dangers were very real and very present, for Loyalists and Patriots alike.

Chapter One

Sandwich, Massachusetts
April 1, 1775

Kitty Campbell pressed a gloved hand against her stomach to quell the surge of feathers in her middle. *What was I thinking?* She stared out the foggy window of the parked carriage as fat drops of rain plunked against the glass. Tucking a lock of her wayward curls around her ear, she exhaled, reviewing what had brought her to this moment. Perhaps she should have at least tried to send Eliza a note to tell her she was returning. Then, for the hundredth time she reminded herself, there hadn't been time.

With God's grace, they would receive her arrival with jubilation, not woe.

She pressed her legs together as the cool air wriggled up her dress. Too bad she'd resisted Henry Donaldson's invitation to wait for him inside the tavern while he conducted his business. Whatever he must do, it took much longer than she'd expected. She shifted in her seat. At least it wasn't Boston. Though both Boston and Sandwich were on the coast, somehow Boston seemed colder. With its hoards of homesick soldiers and wild patriots, empty harbors and lonely streets—she couldn't be more pleased to leave the city. Her breath plumed against the window. But it wasn't the weather that made Boston cold and loveless. Without her childhood home and loving family to warm her spirits, any place would be equally icy. The year she'd spent in Boston hadn't transpired the way she'd anticipated. She sat back and released a heavy breath. Eliza had been right. Somehow, her sister was always right.

Kitty's shoes tapped the floor and she drummed her fingers against her knees. Where was Henry? Hopefully nothing was amiss, though 'twas surely nothing that a strong captain in the British Army couldn't handle himself. She rested her head on the cushion behind and pinched her lips in a nervous smile, crowding out any worry she felt for her friend. She stared into the street, past the streams of water trailing down her window. Would Eliza and Thomas really be glad she'd returned? She wriggled in her seat. Could they see past their differences?

Or would they only see her as a Tory?

Her smile vanished, taking with it the last degree of warmth in the empty carriage. Had she really done right in coming back? She toyed with the fabric of her gloves. When Henry had learned he had business to attend to in Sandwich, he'd insisted she travel with him, and not return. She'd agreed without a second thought, though if only she'd—

Just then the door opened and she jumped, pressing a hand to her chest with a quick inhale. Releasing the pinch of sudden tension, Kitty laughed. "Oh, Henry, 'tis you."

Rain dripped off his hat and his warm smile eased around her shoulders, but the tension in his eyes revealed a displeasure he reserved behind his gaze. The burden of his position in the army seemed to weigh more heavily on his shoulders with every passing month.

"Did I startle you?" Henry's grin widened, before he cupped his mouth and called to the driver. "We'll go up the road. Take your first left and continue on until you see the house on your right. Stop there."

Henry crouched low and stepped in, shutting the door. His broad shoulders and long legs filled much of the space in the small carriage, though it was his strong character that swelled around Kitty, making that familiar contentment release the nervous twitching in her fingers.

Tossing her a quick look, he removed his hat, revealing his dark blonde hair pulled in a queue. He exhaled and gave her a friendly smirk. "Even the driver had the sense to come inside and wait. I do hope you weren't too lonely. Or cold."

The carriage lurched forward and Kitty clutched her seat. "The silence was welcome. I had much to contemplate." The pinch in her voice revealed more than she'd intended.

"I know what you mean to say." Henry fingered the black felt of his hat. His gentle blue eyes softened, while his brow creased. "Boston was far too dangerous, Kitty. I care for you as I do my own sisters and I would have advised them to do the same."

The cold rain lashed against the window and somehow pelted straight through her. "You're right, and I shall always be grateful to you. I'm simply unsure what to think. I don't believe the way my family does, and it is not as if they reserve their feelings to any degree."

Henry's strong jaw tightened. He pulled his lip between his teeth and stared out the window a moment before answering. "I must tell you Kitty, in confidence, though I support the king as you do, I see many virtues in what people like your sister and brother-in-law are striving for."

Kitty's brow shot skyward. Such words, especially from Henry, were nothing short of treasonous. She shook her head with a questioning laugh. "Henry what do you mean? You shouldn't jest in such a way."

"I do not jest." Henry's expression darkened. "I value my position in the army to be sure. I need it in fact, to support my sisters. I love England. I am subject to the king. But..."

Kitty tipped her head, disbelief knitting her brow. "But what?"

He pushed a quick breath from his mouth and met her gaze as the carriage tottered and swayed. "I'm beginning to understand why the patriots feel to fight for their liberty."

Kitty dropped her hands in her lap, her mouth gaping before she snapped it shut. "Henry, the king is our ruler, our protector. You of all people should know that." Sitting straighter, she exhaled and shifted the reticule in her lap to ease the budding tension. "You must watch yourself. You're speaking as a traitor."

"Harsh words, Kitty." A knowing smile lifted his mouth and he patted her hand with a quiet chuckle. "Just because I believe in someone's right to defend themselves doesn't mean I'm a traitor. You're a wise woman, Kitty. You know no one can be forced to come to an understanding of such things. That comes in God's time. This conflict is crucial, and someday you'll come to see that truth as well."

Truth. The word rammed into her middle making the tea and cream from that morning's breakfast sour in her stomach. Eliza claimed their Father had wanted them to discover the truth, that he had wanted them to embrace the cause of liberty, but Eliza was mistaken. He'd raised them to revere the king.

I'll honor you, Father. I know this is what you would want me to do.

Henry cleared his throat and pointed out the window on her side of the carriage. "See that building there?"

Kitty peered out the clouded glass. "Aye." The small stone building rested in a generous clearing set-back from the road. Two windows near the roof peered at her like large black eyes, and a sturdy wooden door in the center of the stone walls appeared unhinged. Kitty blinked and squinted to see more clearly through the foggy glass and streams of rain. A cloaked figure hunched near the ground beside the door and she strained to make out more than that, but gave up the attempt when Henry started again.

"That's the town's ammunition and arms magazine." He shifted in his seat, looking out the opposite window then down to his hands again, his voice taut. "It seems more and more towns feel the urgent need to defend themselves should the king decide to make his control more pressing. As all powder is manufactured in England, the colonists take great care in protecting what little they have for they believe it belongs to them, although the king believes differently."

Kitty touched the wet sleeve of his red coat and tried to allow a smile to peek from behind the angst. "Nothing will happen, Henry. This trouble will die down soon enough. We must be patient."

"I'm not so certain. Not with the tensions arising in and around Boston. You know that, Kitty, you saw such first hand." Henry's tone dropped and his stare split through her. "Your sister has embraced the patriot's cause with passion, and it *is* a valiant cause, Kitty. Keep your heart open to the possibility that you may do the same."

She jerked back, as if his hateful words roped her to the seat. "I will never come to see why they are doing any of this, Henry. Never."

A brief sigh passed his lips that were twisted in a wry smile. He reached around her shoulder and hugged her as an older brother might—as her dear Peter might have done, had he lived.

"Let's not argue," he said. His warm voice dulled the blade in the air. "You know I support you, as I do your family." The richness of his tone resonated in the small carriage and he cleared his throat as if to purge the undeniable emotions. "Perhaps I'm speaking more for myself than for you. Be that as it may, there will come a time when we will be called upon to act in defense of the cause we believe in. It won't be enough to merely stand by silently and watch others fight for us."

His words acted like pointed barbs, piercing her through to the fragile center of her soul. Watching out the window as they passed rain-soaked trees, Kitty drove a spike of determination into the lid of her resolve. There was nothing anyone could say or do to move her from supporting the king, no matter how desperate or convincing. Her father had raised her honorably, and that was how she would live.

No matter what anyone did to persuade her, she would never conform to the beliefs that ran rampant as pestilence. Kitty Campbell would be a Tory until the end of her days.

Biting spring raindrops plunged from the voluminous clouds, pelting Nathaniel's face. Fists clenched, he raced over the muddy ground. *This cannot be!* His muscles cramped as he rounded the corner and pinned his gaze on the magazine. Clutching tighter to the medical bag in his hand, he ground his teeth and tore ever harder across the rain-soaked road.

Glancing at his friend beside him, Nathaniel spoke between hurried breaths. "How badly is he hurt?"

"I cannot say." Thomas Watson matched Nathaniel's every stride and squinted against the rain. "His father is with him now."

Shards of anger, like pieces of shrapnel, drove deeper into Nathaniel's gut. Caleb was only a boy, no more than fifteen years. He should never have guarded the building alone.

Nathaniel glared ahead as he ran. *Tories.* Growling in his chest, he pushed harder as the realization hit with the same sting as the cold rain. Who else would steal the precious munitions from their own townspeople?

He increased his speed another measure as he neared the stone building. Caleb's father, Roger Oliver, held his son's bleeding head in his lap, his weathered face scrunched in an anxious scowl.

Nathaniel skidded to a stop beside them, spraying mud as he pressed his boots into the ground. He bit his tongue to keep from swearing and dropped to his knees in the sopping ground beside his patient.

The gash across the boy's head trickled rain-soaked blood down his face and across his eye. Nathaniel looked between Roger and Caleb, chest pumping. "Has he said what happened?"

Roger shook his head. The muscles in his jaw flexed as he met Nathaniel's gaze. "I should have been here, Dr. Smith. 'Tis my fault."

Nathaniel yanked open his bag. "We are all to blame. He was too young to guard this place alone."

Brushing a strand of hair from the boy's face, he scanned Caleb's body for obvious signs of injury. No gunshot wound, no apparent stabbing. Only the blood dripping down Caleb's head drew his concern. Nathaniel inched closer and cradled Caleb's neck and jaw as he examined the weeping gash. Immediately his muscles released a portion of distress. Whoever had hit him, hadn't intended to kill, that much was clear. The superficial wound had knocked the boy unconscious, but not injured his skull. Nathaniel reached into his open medical bag and removed a strip of linen that the rain instantly doused. Lifting the boy's head, Nathaniel continued to make visual assessments as he wrapped the cloth around the wound. "Wake up, Caleb. Tell me what happened."

Roger squirmed and Nathaniel looked up when the man spoke. "All I can gather is that someone attacked him and stole some of the powder."

Nathaniel frowned as he knotted the bloody bandage. *That much is obvious. But why?* He gave his patient one last evaluation before he pushed off his knees and squeezed Roger's shoulder. "God be thanked, your son's wounds are not serious. I believe he will soon recover fully."

Roger bowed his head and sighed, mouthing a silent prayer. With a grunt he scooped his boy in his arms and stood in a single, swift motion. He glanced down before meeting Nathaniel's stare as the heedless rain continued to fall. "We are indebted to you, Doctor." A tight smile pulled at his mouth as if he wished to say more, but couldn't.

Nathaniel smiled and nodded toward the road. "Take him home and get him dry. Wrap a new bandage around his head and have Martha prepare a bowl of warm liquid for him when he wakes. I'll assess the damage here and return within the hour to inquire after him."

Roger started to move, then stopped. His strained voice attested to the heavy burden he carried in his arms. "I shall be at my post tonight."

Nathaniel cupped Roger's shoulder and prepared to protest, but Roger turned and started down the abandoned street, speaking over his shoulder as he left. "Martha will care for Caleb. I won't neglect my duty."

God bless you, Roger.

Nathaniel squinted against the rain and stared after them. The weight of his watered-down greatcoat matched his heavy spirits. Who would attack an innocent boy, then—

"Nathaniel. You'll want to see this." Thomas's hollow voice echoed from inside the small stone building.

Nathaniel turned and rushed forward. He swung the door open and charged in, scouring the ravaged scene. The pungent scent of black powder permeated the damp air. Muskets were strewn across the floor and all but three powder barrels rested on their sides, though most of them remained sealed, still protecting their precious contents. The largest barrel in the far corner stood upright and slightly open, as if dispatching its report of a lost battle.

Thomas stared motionless as the rain continued to drum on the roof. "I cannot believe this."

Restrained wrath cankered Nathaniel's twitching muscles. "Leave it to the British. I have no doubt this is General Gage's doing. He has attempted such around Boston, has he not? He will stop at nothing to fulfill the King's demands." Nathaniel's boots clanked along the wood floor as he judged the damage. "The last thing they want is for us *rebels* to store munitions. The munitions we *need* to defend our freedom against the very people who wish to destroy it."

Thomas rubbed his chin. "But someone from Sandwich has done this. Not the military."

"Of that I have no doubt. The British have spies in every corner of this colony. Marvelous way to start the morning, is it not?" Nathaniel gave a sarcastic smile before kneeling down and fingering a small trail of gunpowder that twisted across the floor. He rolled the black powder between his fingers, the light of his spirit dimming as if the very blood of the people of Sandwich had been drained from the building. He stood, following the trail with his vision, until it disappeared in the mud a few feet from the door. Whoever stole the powder should have at least made sure they didn't drop the precious reserves on the way out.

He released an audible breath, motioning for Thomas to help as he righted the toppled barrels and replaced the fallen muskets. The gray morning light crawled in through the clouds, blanketing the abysmal surroundings in the faintest of light while the rain tapped ever harder on the roof.

Nathaniel turned to Thomas, his stomach churning the raw hate that swelled. "I know who is behind this and I intend to bring him to justice." The presence of one Cyprian Wythe lingered in the room like a phantom.

Thomas raised one brow. "We don't know who did this, let's not start casting blame. We must show restraint or we will surely make things worse by pointing fingers until we know more."

The comment fueled the growing fire that billowed behind the temperate exterior Nathaniel failed to present. He all but yelled. "Don't pretend you're not as irate—I see the red in your face. Our munitions are raided, a boy has just been attacked. Where's your passion, Thomas?"

"My passion for this cause is as vital as ever, but I tend to have more sense than you when it comes to matters such as these." Thomas's volume rose as he pointed at Nathaniel's chest, his voice as sharp as his gaze. "Watch yourself or your impetuous nature will do you in."

Nathaniel glared and straightened his shoulders. Impetuous? Nay. Able to make judgments and take command when needed? Aye. Hadn't the town appointed him as Chairman of the Committee of Correspondence for those very reasons?

He clenched and released his fists, choosing not to argue the point. Instead, he picked up the broken piece of chain that rested in a shallow puddle by the door. "I wonder how long it would take for Joseph to repair this?" Nathaniel's childhood friend, Joseph Wythe—himself a valiant patriot—could best anyone in blacksmithing for sixty miles. Too bad he had such an unfortunate man for a brother.

"Not long, I'd suppose." Looking over the reorganized space, Thomas plucked a long musket from a shadowy corner. "Do you think it is still safe to keep everything here? Should we not move the stores immediately?"

Nathaniel shook his head and tenderly ran his hand along the fractured lid of the top of the largest barrel, feeling the same as if human flesh had been mutilated. "Why did they not take it all? From what I can surmise, whoever did this got away with only several bags worth. And all the muskets are accounted for. 'Tis strange. Alarming." He brushed the dust from his hands and locked eyes with Thomas. "Some might assume this was simply a thoughtless act of youth, but I cannot see it as such. This is a threat to our independence and to the safety of the families of this county."

Thomas pressed his tricorn onto his head. "Well, you certainly weren't selected as the Chairman of the Committee for your lack of zeal." Pulling his jacket around his neck, he stepped out into the rain with the hint of a smirk.

Nathaniel grinned and followed him out. "How thankful I am for your *overwhelming* support."

Chuckling, Thomas squinted up at the sky. "I'll stand guard."

"I shall have a replacement for you by noon." Nathaniel smiled and smacked his friend on the back as he left, but the merriment that inched upward quickly receded. A cloud, as grey as the ones overhead, darkened his spirit with every step. Those munitions were vital. Without them they couldn't ensure the safety of their families against the time the British would surely fall upon them.

And that time was coming.

"Nathaniel," Thomas called.

He stopped and turned.

"We will see you this evening at Andrew

Cooper's?"

Nathaniel nodded. "He's asked me to give a political speech and you know how I crave such attention." He took a few steps backward, that refreshing merriment trickling over his back. "This gathering will no doubt attract the patriotic women in town as well, and where beautiful ladies are present, there shall you find me."

Before Thomas could continue the conversation that might lead to avenues Nathaniel wished not to discuss, he waved over his shoulder and marched toward Roger's home. 'Twas then, unbidden, words spoken several days past echoed in Nathaniel's mind, as they had from the moment Thomas had voiced them. *One day, Nathaniel, you will find yourself in the presence of a woman that robs you of all your senses, leaving you tongue tied and acting more a buffoon than a gentleman.*

Nathaniel chuckled to himself and switched his medical bag to the other hand. If he hadn't felt that way about a woman thus far, the possibility of such a thing occurring now was more than remote. Better to enjoy the smiles and flirtations than steady his attentions on finding a wife.

As he made his way down the muddy street, the reality of the morning's discovery socked him in the gut, thankfully smacking him away from his thought's unwanted wanderings. What was he thinking attending a political meeting on the same day the magazine had been raided? There were more important things to do than eat cakes and drink wine. Then again, he could use the affair at Andrew's, and his speech, to focus his energies on rallying the people and finding men to guard the magazine. He humphed. Better to go and make the most of it.

The rain continued to pour, making its way through Nathaniel's coat and seeping into his shirt and waistcoat. He picked up his pace. His responsibilities as Chairman occupied more energy and brainpower with every day that passed. Even though he wished to spend most of his time carrying for his patients, independence was far more crucial. Their lives changed day by day thanks to Parliament and the "high and mighty" King George. He looked down at the dark mud that clung to his boots. This robbery and Caleb's attack brought to light the very fears that forced him to pace his parlor floor night after night. This was no longer a vague, untouchable enemy. This threat was real, tangible and right at their doors.

Nathaniel halted, his muscles tensing as he stared into the rain.

Someone wanted to rob them of their liberties.

He would find out who. And he would stop them.

Cyprian Wythe stood by the window in the office of his detested establishment, parting the curtain just enough to allow him a fair view of Nathaniel Smith as he walked from the magazine toward town. Cyprian swallowed. The rain drummed against the window, driving the emptiness deeper.

He ran a hand over his unshaven jaw, the shivers from this morning's encounter still shooting down his spine. He hadn't meant for anything to happen to the boy, it simply *had*. How did the British expect an untrained man to do the job of a mercenary? What were he and Andrew supposed to do? They hadn't expected anyone to be there and they *needed* that powder.

"Your mission is to secure their munitions secretly over time—not bring attention to it by attacking their guard—let alone a young boy!"

The memory of Captain Donaldson's heated tone burned his ears anew.

Cyprian dropped the curtain and slumped at his desk in the room above the tavern. He snatched the quill from its dock and twirled it in his fingers, trying to ignore Donaldson's warnings.

"This command comes from Major Stockton. If you fail to fulfill his requests then I will be forced to find another man for the job."

Another man for the job?

He lunged from his chair and pounded his fist against the desk, jostling the newly acquired bag of coins Donaldson had tossed at him in anger. The tinkling sound made him clench his teeth until they nearly cracked. Holding his arms rigid on the edge of the wood, he lowered his head.

Camilla needed him. The weakness of her smile and the gray around her eyes haunted his mind like a tortured ghost. A man shouldn't lose his wife like this—not so soon. The money the British paid him for this job would cover the cost of his debts and the medicines that kept her alive. With a snarl, Cyprian looked up. He didn't need that wicked patriot doctor to care for his beloved. He could buy the opium from any source he wished. It kept her heart beating and dulled the heedless pain.

The weight on his shoulders seemed as heavy as the solid oak underneath his fists. He shoved away from the desk and went again to the window, staring past the sheets of rain that watered the earth.

Beyond the deluge, the resulting puddles and mist, the magazine taunted him.

He reserved a quiet chuckle and whispered. "We shall meet again, my friend. Depend upon it."

Chapter Two

The surrounding quiet in the Watson home mingled with the mumbled voices of Eliza and Thomas, seeping not only into Kitty's bedchamber upstairs, but into her spirit as well, chasing away the bitter loneliness she'd borne for more than a year. The sweet scent of lavender-water curled upward as she stared into the mirror atop the table beside where she sat. She smiled at her reflection, recalling the joy on her sister's face when she'd opened the door and found Kitty smiling back at her. Thomas, too, once he'd returned from town, had burst into jubilant laughter. They'd welcomed her with a warmth Kitty could never have imagined, but should have expected.

She closed her eyes as a melancholy rolled over her. Why had she agreed to go to tonight's party? All she wanted was to stay amongst the warmth of home and family, to reminisce with Eliza and stare at the fire while sipping hot cider. Instead, she would have to feign enjoyment at a gathering that would surely bring more discord than merriment. What else could a patriot crowd produce?

A gentle tap sounded at the door.

"Come in." Kitty swiveled in her seat.

Eliza entered, wearing an exquisite cream-colored

gown embroidered with a vibrant array of pinks, greens and golds. Her dark locks were piled magnificently atop her head, making her brown eyes seem almost black.

She stopped, her dainty jaw dropping. "Kitty, you look stunning in that emerald gown." Eliza's smile broadened. "Too bad Father isn't here, I'm sure he would have just the perfect flower for you to tuck behind your ear."

The tender memories whisked to the forefront of Kitty's mind, and she could almost feel Father's rough fingers tucking a stem into her hair. That had been his way of making Kitty feel cherished, and now the recollection made her miss him all the more. She opened her mouth to answer, but only smiled. No words could express emotions so richly sewn into her heart.

Eliza stepped behind Kitty, and spoke to the mirror. "I hope you don't mind me saying, but you have changed so much in this past year, I hardly recognized you."

"Hardly recognized me? Nay. I haven't changed at all."

Eliza giggled. "Aye, you have. You are so grown up. So much a lady now that it hardly feels proper to think of you as my little sister. But I'm afraid you will always be exactly that." Resting her hand on Kitty's shoulder, Eliza leaned down and placed a quick peck on Kitty's hair. "I hope you don't mind."

Reaching up, Kitty squeezed her sister's fingers. "I should be happy all the rest of my days to be known as Eliza's little sister."

"I'm thrilled to hear it, though I can assure you this evening I shall introduce you as simply, 'my dear sister, just returned from Boston.' And leave the 'little' behind."

Kitty's spirit dimmed at the mention of the dreaded outing. Though she strained to keep it from her expression, Eliza missed nothing. She pursed her lips and glanced away before smiling, though perhaps not as wide as before. "I am so grateful you've decided to come, Kitty, though I know 'twasn't your first choice for the evening. You were a most welcome surprise, I find it difficult not to bring you with me."

Kitty lowered her chin. "'Tis true, I would prefer to stay home. But at least you will be there, and we shall have plenty of time for solitude in the coming days." She looked up and tugged at the unruly waves that framed her face and neck. "If only I could make this mess into something fashionable, I might look well enough to stand beside someone as lovely as you."

Eliza batted Kitty's hand away. "You know I promised to do that for you, and I guarantee you will have the *most* fashionable coiffure of any woman there tonight." Her smile widened as she snatched the brush and several pins from the table. She placed the pins in her mouth and spoke through her teeth. "I cannot allow my sister, whom I have pined for these many months, to do any kind of work her first evening home."

Kitty sat straight while Eliza curled, pinned and tucked.

"Liza, I know you'd petitioned me to stay here and not return to Boston after you and Thomas were married, and I now see your wisdom. I thought I could make things work but... it wasn't to be. I do hope Thomas won't feel I'm intruding upon your home by inviting myself to stay. Especially since you are so newly married."

"Of course I feel you're intruding."

Kitty jumped and swiveled in her seat as her brother-in-law approached. He entered, pushing open the door until it met the wall, a deep scowl wrinkling his forehead. He stopped a foot from her seat, and winked. The flicker of merriment in his blue eyes pulled a smile from Kitty's lips. She never ceased to be impressed by Thomas's handsome features, his black hair and the distinguishing strength of character that shaped him as much as his muscular frame.

His face softened and his voice turned calm, like a deep, steady river. "Kitty, you are always welcome in our home. I can't tell you how pleased I am you've come back to stay. We count it a blessing to have you."

His words took shape within her. "Thank you, Thomas. Liza is very blessed to have you. As am I."

Thomas winked again at Kitty then gazed at his wife, his eyes soft. "'Tis been over a year now that we've been married, Kitty, so you may remove 'newly' from your description of our union. I say we have quite mastered the art of marriage, have we not, my love?" Thomas leaned forward, planting a gentle kiss on his wife's cheek.

Emitting a quiet giggle, Eliza tugged on his cravat, her cheeks blushing. "Aye, I believe you're right." She trailed her hands down his waistcoat, checking his appearance one last time, then grinned in approval before turning back to Kitty. She patted Kitty's sleeve. "You look perfect. Shall we go?"

Kitty quirked a brow and offered a forced frown that surely showed her good humor behind it. "Must we?"

"I have a feeling you will be very glad you joined us." Thomas motioned to the door, a mischievous slant to his mouth. "After you, milady."

Once the sun finally retired after it's doleful descent, Cyprian took one last bowl of broth upstairs with the vial of precious medicine in the pocket of his breeches. Careful not to step on the creakiest spots in the wood floor, he rested the tray on the table beside the bed and scooted a small stool closer to Camilla. He stroked her arm, pained at the thought of waking her. If only he needn't attend the ill-timed patriot gathering he could stay by her side and read to her until she once again rested in blissful sleep. But he needed to talk to Andrew. Tonight.

He took her hand. "Camilla, 'tis time to take your broth."

She blinked her eyes open and tried to smile, though she offered no words. Somehow her eyes looked more sunken and the circles around them darker.

His heart pinched. Why must she suffer so? He continued stroking her arm, and leaned closer, reaching for the vial in his pocket. "How are you feeling, my love?"

Her eyes instantly misted and her voice came out in a thin whisper. "Like I'm dying."

Cyprian gripped her thin arm tighter as his throat thickened. "You are not dying." He brought the vial up to the bed and uncorked the top. "Now, be a good patient and take your medicine. I don't want to force your pretty mouth open."

A full grin on Camilla's face showed him her teeth, bringing back memories of their first years together—when they both were so young and death seemed an eternity away.

"I'll try not to be so difficult for you," she said.

He clutched her hand and kissed her frail fingers. "You never are."

I'm doing everything I can for you. I promise.

After spooning her the first dose of medicine, Camilla gave a weak squeeze to his hand and slipped back into a heavy sleep with her next breath.

His eyes burned as he clutched the vial in his fingers, his knuckles white. "I will keep you alive, Camilla. I will. I promise."

The quick walk to the stately home on the bank of Shawme Pond seemed twice as long as it should have been, thanks to the weighty anxiousness that made Kitty's feet stick to the muddy ground as if it were two feet thick, instead of only slightly damp from the morning's rain.

"Tell me again whose home we are visiting?"

Eliza peered over her shoulder. "Andrew and Mary Cooper. Andrew is a wealthy merchantman, and strong proponent of the patriot cause. He holds these gatherings every month and invites all who are favorable to the idea of liberty to mingle with those of like minds."

Her voice was so mild Kitty almost thought her sister had completely forgotten their differing views until she continued. "I don't wish for you to be uncomfortable, Kitty. There will be many guests who will be more than delighted to discuss anything you like. And I do believe the Whitney girls will be there. I am eager for you to make their acquaintance."

Kitty craned her neck to take in the regal entryway with its large double doors as the three of them walked up the stone steps. An inviting orange glow radiated into the street from the expansive windows. The fine draperies and furnishings peeked out at them, as if hoping to sneak a glimpse of the outside world. From the safety of the front stoop, Kitty stared at the many silhouettes of the merry partygoers.

Suddenly, a servant opened the tall doors even before Thomas could knock.

"Welcome." The thin gentleman greeted them with a slight bow and gestured for them to enter, his white wig hanging a little too low around his ears. "Forgive me for being over-quiet," he said, a smile on his lips. "The speaker has just begun and I might say, he's very animated. You are welcome to enter and find a place to stand near the back."

Kitty's palms sweat in her lacy gloves and she licked her lips. *Calm yourself.* She followed Eliza inside, and inhaled the spicy aroma of cider and candle's smoke that mingled in the air. Sighing, Kitty scanned her surroundings, determined to acquire a glass of cider and procure a quiet corner where she needn't speak to anyone. She almost giggled as she stared at the magnificent dark-wood molding that crowned the ceiling and the large portraits and marble busts that decorated the entry. Not such a miserable place to spend an evening. She might in fact enjoy it. A mite of anxiety lifted. Scrolling bronzed sconces holding tall white candles lined the walls of the long empty hall that extended in front of them. A red and gold rug hugged the smooth wood floor. She kept her teeth together to keep her mouth from hanging open. She'd hardly seen a home in Boston to match such majesty.

She nodded at the servant who took her cloak at the door, and Thomas motioned for her and Eliza to enter the large hall. Skirting the fringe of the crowd, Kitty brushed arms with well-dressed ladies and men, all enraptured with the speech in progress. The three of them quickly found an obliging spot near the windows in the back, and Kitty swallowed, struggling to fit in, as if somehow her political leanings were as obvious as the emerald green of her gown. Glancing around, she reminded herself they would never have to know her true beliefs. She stood straighter. Though, if they did, they would likely ridicule her and throw her into the streets. How bad could that be? She stifled a grin at the ridiculous vision. Well, at least then her feelings would be out in the open. This time an easy smile washed over her face and a jovial sensation shot though her nerves like a brush of wind against a lonely meadow. Inhaling a relaxed breath, the sound of the speaker's voice tugged at her ears. Stopping, she gathered her senses, her heart suddenly racing as if it remembered something more than her mind. Leaning quickly from side to side, she strained to look past the sea of white wigs and feathered coiffures to find the owner of the voice.

Could it really be him? She glanced at Thomas and Eliza who whispered to each other as they listened. They didn't seem to be surprised. But then, why should they?

Kitty licked her lips and lifted on her tiptoes. Perhaps her memory played tricks upon her heart. It had been over a year since she'd last seen him.

Perhaps, it wasn't him after all, and was only—

The group parted slightly and Kitty's heart stopped. She dropped back on her heels, and sucked a quick breath through her lips.

There, on the far side of the room Nathaniel stood, his chiseled features made even more alluring by the yellow glow of candle-light. Kitty's mouth went dry. She tried and failed to focus on his words. His commanding presence dominated her will. She couldn't pull her gaze from his eyes that danced with passion as he spoke, and the muscular frame that filled the fabric of his burgundy suit.

Extinguishing her irrational excitement, Kitty brushed a long curl from her neck and did her best to keep nothing more than a moderate measure of surprise in her tone when she cupped her mouth and spoke into Eliza's ear. "You didn't tell me Nathaniel would be here."

Before Eliza could answer, Thomas bowed toward Kitty, the glimmer of a chuckle lighting his eyes. His tone remained low. "He *is* the most out-spoken of patriots."

Shrugging, she tried to show her nonchalance, not the thrill that heated her neck and ears. Kitty exhaled through tight lips and looked down at her dress. *Why didn't I wear a nicer gown?*

Leaning forward, Thomas whispered something to Eliza and she nodded before he ducked away toward the refreshment table.

"Nathaniel will be thrilled to see you." Eliza turned her attention back to Kitty, keeping her volume low. She winked. "He speaks of you often, you know, asking how you fare and if we've heard from you."

Kitty's heart leapt at the news, but she pretended

not to feel it, hoping the pleasure of her sister's words didn't make their way to her face. "I'm sure he is all politeness." For surely 'twas nothing more.

A motion to the side drew Kitty's attention and she turned. A tall man stood alone in the corner, wine glass in hand, his gaze floating across the crowd as if he were looking for someone. His icy-black stare then landed on Kitty and her blood chilled. No matter how her inner-self reacted, she forced her outer appearance to remain collected. She raised her chin coolly, and turned to her sister speaking close to her ear. "Liza, who is that man in the corner to my left—don't look too quickly."

"I needn't look." Eliza's face lit with a silent laugh as the actress came to life, completely masking the real subject of their conversation. "I already know who you mean. I saw him when we came in."

"Who is he?"

"His name is Cyprian Wythe, and a more loathsome man you will never meet. At least that's what Thomas has said. I've never formally met him. His wife is gravely ill, poor dear. That's all I really know." Eliza motioned to the front of the room. "If I were you I would focus my attention on someone *much* more interesting."

Kitty followed Eliza's gaze and her breath halted. Nathaniel's expression was lit with the same passion that filled his voice, and though she did her best to focus on his words, Kitty's heart had been snatched by a flurry of delightful and dangerous emotions. Would he be pleased to see her? What would she say? What would *he* say?

Kitty! Get hold of yourself.

The fleeting attraction she'd felt for him those months ago had been folded and neatly put away like a gown she was too fond of to wear. So why were these emotions now emerging from their place of security?

Nathaniel continued his spirited speech and the hushed room seemed absorbed in his presence. The more he spoke, the more his face brightened and his voice strengthened. A few rounds of "huzzah" and "hear, hear" were the only sounds, other than the periodic swish of skirts and quiet tap of shoes.

"Freedom is ours for the taking," he said, scanning the crowd. "Can we much longer stand by and succumb to these oppressions as an ass would submit to an unruly master? Nay! Who can stand these afflictions and not be soon shaken into a realization of our awful state? The king wishes us to believe that we do not struggle; that your existence is not made more difficult by his hand; that your day-to-day living is not challenged by his rule. But our lives *do* change daily and we *do* feel it, and we will *not* ignore the truth!"

The room boomed with applause. Men rapped their canes against the ground and women clapped gloved hands in wild agreement.

"I for one cannot remain idle," he continued. "It falls upon each of us to stand up in the cause for which our futures depend. I will not forsake my country. Will you?"

Another more passionate ovation exploded from the group. Kitty sank back against the wall behind her. How could these God-fearing people believe that discord and arguments were sanctioned by the Lord? These patriots should submit to their leaders and be peace loving. Wiggling her toes in her shoes, she squirmed and took a side-ways glance at Thomas who stood near the refreshment table. Had he wanted to bring her here in hopes of changing her mind? Kitty quickly glanced to Eliza. Her sister's face shone and she alternately nodded and smiled as she listened with rapt intent. Had she brought Kitty here for that reason as well? The thought left a painful prick in Kitty's heart.

Her posture slumped as the pressing realities trapped her between idealism and fact. Being home with family was a blessing indeed, but the challenges that lay ahead rose like a storm on the horizon. She shook her head. If she kept silent, as they all should, then there would never be a reason to argue issues that should not even be entertained in the first place.

After a cleansing sigh, Kitty lifted her chin and choked on her breath when Nathaniel's gaze locked with hers.

Nathaniel struggled to keep the words flowing. He blinked to clear his vision. From his position it was difficult to see to the very back of the room where the lights were more dim, but he would know those radiant eyes from a hundred miles away.

Kitty.

Why was she here? Wasn't she supposed to be in Boston?

Her slight smile unraveled his carefully woven strands of focus and for a moment he nearly walked straight to her. He would never forget the moment, over a year ago, that he'd first seen her in that emerald gown. It still hugged her perfect curves the same way and emphasized the rich auburn ringlets that dusted her neck.

Pleasant thoughts from those many months ago emerged from a forgotten pocket in his mind and his pulse jumped. The scent of her hair and feel of her hand against his arm ignited his memory. Had it really been so long since they'd spoken? Somehow it seemed like only yesterday. Yet in the same moment, it seemed like a lifetime.

With a quick shake of his head, he found his pace again and continued with more earnest. The excitement of her presence increased his zeal and the crowd responded to his energy. When he finally concluded his speech, his entire body hummed with passion for the cause he cherished. And, if he would allow it, from the pleasant thought of Kitty's company.

Applause thundered through the room and he offered a polite bow, impatient to make the journey across the room to the back where she stood. Keeping his eyes fixed on his destination he struggled to make his way through the crowd.

"If you have a moment, Dr. Smith, I'm anxious to speak with you about the—"

"Forgive me, Mr. Barker, but there's someone I must see." He pushed past three others, but the group kept pressing.

"What a rousing speech, Dr. Smith," another one said. "Patrick Henry himself couldn't have been more stirring."

"Thank you, Sir." He kept moving.

"There you are, Doctor." Caroline Whitney, a tall, regal blonde snatched his arm with a polite grin and a gentle tease in her voice. "You promised me a dance and the music is about to begin. Will you go back on your word?"

"Forgive me Miss Whitney, but—"

From the side three more women surrounded him like an enemy force, their weapons of low-necklines and flirtatious smiles at the ready.

A brunette sidled-up far too close for propriety. "I believe you promised me the same."

"And I," a short one pouted.

"You have caught me, ladies." He shot a quick look in Kitty's direction. "I fear I must beg your forgiveness for I will be unable to keep that promise at the present moment."

"I cannot pretend I am not wounded," Caroline said, producing half a grin. "Though, I understand that you are a man in high demand. I shall hope for a dance later on. Thankfully the evening is just beginning."

Yes, thankfully. Hopefully Kitty would be there for the whole of it.

Then his peripheral vision caught the movement of a familiar figure and Nathaniel's subconscious unsheathed an armor of defense jerking him to full alert. Tall and loathsome, Cyprian Wythe walked straight toward Eliza and Kitty, his air of superiority resting on his shoulders like a coat of thorns. Nathaniel's ire flickered to life.

Caroline continued talking though Nathaniel could hardly make sense of her words as his vision reached out to strangle the enemy. "Is everything all right, Doctor?"

"Hmm?" Had she said something? *I'll drag that devil away from here by his queue and—.*

"Doctor Smith?"

"Forgive me, Miss Whitney. I must take my leave." Tension barreling down his limbs, Nathaniel darted toward the back of the room.

Cyprian trapped Kitty and Eliza as if they were

under investigation for high crimes. What could that man possibly have to say to them? Nathaniel's neck corded. If only this were his home and he could do as he pleased with his *guest*. Where was Andrew? He should know about this...

Nathaniel pressed through the crowd, moving skillfully between partners and avoiding full glasses of wine as he hurried to the rescue. From the set of Eliza's shoulders and the roundness of Kitty's eyes, Nathaniel could almost guess Cyprian's conversation.

As he neared the threesome, the general mumble of voices behind him cleared and he honed his hearing on the conversation in progress.

"I'm sure I don't know what you mean." Kitty's feminine voice remained stoic, though the flash of color on her face revealed her surprise.

"You're a Tory, Miss Campbell." Cyprian raised his chin. "I recognized the look of disgust in your face when we were forced to endure Dr. Smith's traitorous drivel. I too share such sentiments. You do not wish to be here among people such as these, I believe."

"Forgive me, sir, but you cannot possibly—"

Cyprian raised his glass. "You do a great credit to our king, Miss Campbell. Unlike those in your family who have chosen to take the path of treason. They'll pay for their deeds, but you and I shall be rewarded for our loyalty."

Nathaniel reached Cyprian just as he finished his slander. With reserved rage, he coolly placed a hand on Cyprian's shoulder and squeezed, speaking through gritted teeth and a hard smile that barely masked the fire of emotions that blazed beneath his waistcoat.

"I'll thank you to keep your *opinions* to yourself, Mr. Wythe, and to leave these women alone." It was all he could do to not shove the man away and kick his sorry breeches into the road.

"Coming to the rescue, Doctor Smith? How chivalrous." Cyprian grinned and sneered down at Nathaniel's hand that still gripped his shoulder before he turned toward Kitty. "If you ever care to converse with someone of the same mind, please call upon my wife. She is bedridden, and in terrible need of company. We Tories must stick together." He nodded and smiled as if they were all the most amiable of friends.

Nathaniel released his grip and clenched his fists so hard he feared his bones would shatter. "Leave these women alone and find someone else to torture."

"The only person I care to torture would be you, Doctor, but it appears I must postpone that enjoyment for another time." After a swift bow Cyprian disappeared into the crowd.

Working to soften his breathing, Nathaniel turned to Kitty and touched her arm. "Are you two all right?"

Eliza nodded, indignation written into the soft lines of her face, while Kitty's lips remained tight and her expression drawn though she offered a weak smile.

With a light chuckle, Nathaniel assumed a more relaxed stance, though inwardly his anger popped and fizzled like meat on a spit. He nodded in the direction Cyprian had gone and lowered his voice, relying on his charm to brush away the tension that lingered. "That fellow can make even I, the most courageous and stoic of gentleman, quiver in my boots."

Kitty's stirring smile sprung to life, somehow

bringing light to the entire room. "Quiver in your boots, Dr. Smith? I don't believe it."

A carefree laugh tumbled out from deep in Nathaniel's chest, chasing away the remaining bits of unease. "Aye, fair maiden, you have caught me. I never quiver." Nathaniel glanced behind to make sure the man had truly left them before allowing his gaze to wander over her. His words slowed. "Kitty, this is quite a surprise. I had no idea you were in Sandwich."

The candlelight shimmered in her blue-green eyes like the sun on a summer sea. "Eliza and Thomas surprised me as well. I didn't know you would be here, though I suppose I should have gathered as much. This is a—" She stopped and dipped her chin, the unspoken words made clear thanks to the flush in her face.

Nathaniel sent Eliza a quick look before placing his fingers against the soft lace around Kitty's elbow. "You are welcome here, Kitty. I know Andrew and his wife would say the same. You can't know how pleased I am to see you and I plan to flog a certain brother-in-law of yours for not informing me of your arrival."

Kitty grinned. "He didn't know I was coming."

"Either way, I shall find a reason to punish him just the same."

She nodded with a mock expression of agreement. "Well, I'm sure he deserves it for some unrepentant crime."

"No doubt of it." He smirked and refused to lift his eyes from her face. Knowing she could feel the heat of his gaze, Nathaniel made the most of the moment and winked. Her mouth toyed upward ever farther and she stared at him in return. An unfamiliar warmth began in his chest, but instead of extinguishing the sensation with reason, he allowed it to simmer.

Thomas entered their small circle, relieving Nathaniel of the spell Kitty cast upon him. "So I see you have been acquainted with our guest."

"A remarkable surprise indeed, and 'tis a mercy you hadn't known of her coming or I might be forced to punish you for not informing me." Shaking his head, Nathaniel thumped Thomas on the back with a grin that widened his mouth. "I should have made it my business to drop by early and arrive with you. What gentleman wouldn't want to have the loveliest woman in Massachusetts on his arm?"

Kitty shook her head with a wry smile. "Nathaniel, you do tease me."

He exaggerated a hurt expression though the emotions that burst to life in his chest were surprisingly real. Keeping a tone of jest in his voice, he chuckled. "You wound me, Kitty. I speak only the truth."

"I know how you are, Nathaniel." Her eyes beamed, toying with him, as a stifled grin perched on one side of her mouth. "Do not think I didn't see your harem following behind you as if you were an Arabian prince."

"We shall argue about this another time." Nathaniel pointed a finger at her, using a slight laugh to hide his unusual embarrassment at her having witnessed such a display. He motioned to Thomas, his blithe spirit dipping. "While you were sampling the fine food, your wife and Kitty had their first encounter with the infamous Cyprian Wythe."

Thomas winced. "That's an unpleasant experience for anyone." He released an over-exaggerated grunt when Eliza tapped him in the stomach with her elbow.

"Thomas, you must watch what you say." She tried to appear insistent, but the way her eyes grinned, Nathaniel could see she found the humor in Thomas's statement.

Kitty remained subdued, slowly spinning the almost empty wine glass against her gloved fingers. The shine in her smile faded. "Is he really a Tory? Or does he simply say that to cause a scene."

"Nay, he's a Tory of the worst kind." The disgust in Nathaniel's deep response weighed heavier than he intended. He hoped the gentle melody of the minuet playing behind them would help assuage his tone. "Cyprian has informed me many a time that he prays continually for the demise of the patriot cause."

Thomas's expression darkened. "Aye. 'Tis not a secret to anyone who has the displeasure of being acquainted with him. Mr. Wythe makes his sentiments very well known. The man is a snake."

"Well said." Nathaniel nodded, failing to stem the surge of irritation bleeding into his good humor. "He is uneducated and thick-headed. Impeding our progress at every turn. Anyone with half a brain can see the need for freedom is paramount."

"'Tis because of Tories like him that we cannot more fully defend the freedoms that are rightfully ours." Thomas raised his glass and took a sip. "And why we must put all our energies into guarding the magazine."

"Hear, hear! 'Tis only too bad we don't have more of an audience to applaud our brilliance." Nathaniel laughed. "Then again I *did* just give a rousing speech. Are you trying to steal my glory, Thomas?"

"I may try, Nathaniel, but I fear I shall never have

your magnetism." Thomas smirked and took another sip.

"The magazine?" The innocent question in Kitty's tone matched the wideness of her eyes. "Donaldson pointed it out to me on our arrival. Has something happened?"

Thomas swallowed the drink in his mouth. "Oh, yes, I suppose we didn't have a chance to mention it before now." He humphed. "The town's ammunition magazine was raided this morning."

"What?" Eliza shot a hand over her mouth.

"Mercy!" Kitty's petite jaw gaped. "Who would do such a thing?"

"Our friendly neighbors the Tories. Who else?" Nathaniel answered. "Under the direction of the British army, I have no doubt. There is ample evidence of their actions in this regard in provinces around Boston. It doesn't surprise me that they've decided to extend southward." His muscles grew tighter at the memory of Caleb's bloody face. "That powder and those muskets are all we have to defend ourselves and it seems that our system of guarding it is no longer sufficient against our strengthening enemy."

With her lower lip between her teeth, Eliza shook her head. "Are you sure? Could this not be an isolated incident?"

"Hard to say," Thomas answered.

Nathaniel pulled his shoulders back. "The British want to squash all rebellion and what better way than to steal our means of personal protection."

"That's deplorable." Kitty stared downward shaking her head and blinking. "Why would they want to take away your means of protection? Isn't that your right?"

Nathaniel raised his brows. "It most definitely is." He nudged her with his elbow. "I'm proud of you Kitty, you're beginning to sound like a patriot."

Kitty turned her head away as if the comparison was not appreciated.

Eliza looked around the room, scowling. "Do you suspect anyone?"

Nathaniel rubbed the back of his neck, regretting that his words had made Kitty uneasy. "Nay, we have no suspects." *Not officially...*

"We aren't ready to place blame or make accusations." Thomas stepped forward. "However, we are certain the perpetrator is a Tory."

"Thomas is right. We have plenty of those loathsome fellows in town to pin our suspicions on." Nathaniel sighed, succumbing to the glowering mood that stole every thread of his earlier levity. "In earnest, I shall echo your earlier proclamation, my friend, and state that in my mind the acquaintance of not only Cyprian Wythe, but *any* lover of King George is a grave displeasure."

Thomas raised his glass. "Hear, hear, my friend."

"Then I am surprised that you are able to abide my presence."

Kitty's stiff response blasted a hole through Nathaniel's middle and the resulting silence choked the merriment from their little circle like thick black smoke. He looked up only to be censured from the shock that drained the light from her eyes. Her lips pressed tight, turning them colorless.

The blood drained from his face. *Idiot!*

He couldn't bring himself to look away from her wounded expression, aching for words that would soothe the pain he'd inflicted. The pleasant tune from the quartet and the quiet hum of voices continued around them, each guest blissfully unaware of his thoughtless remark.

Thomas reached out to her, his brow pinching. "Kitty, you must know our comments are no reflection on you."

"Are they not?" She handed her glass to Eliza. "If you'll excuse me, I shall take my leave so as not to injure you with my presence any longer." Kitty brushed between them before facing them one last time. "Forgive me, Eliza." She darted from the room, holding her skirts as she wove through the tangle of party-goers toward the exit.

The hollow chill her absence created smacked Nathaniel on the back of the head like an irritated father. He exchanged a narrow glance with Thomas before slamming his eyes shut. How could he be so foolish? How could he have allowed himself to say something so hurtful to someone so gracious? The temperature of the room went hot, then instantly cold. *So much for your famous charm, Nathaniel. You've proven your lack of it with amazing skill.*

"I'm ashamed of you, Thomas." Eliza's quiet tone slashed against Nathaniel's ruptured conscience. Though her expression revealed only a fraction of the emotion that bubbled beneath, it was enough to pry apart the already gaping crater in his shame. "You as well, Nathaniel. You *both* know how desperately she yearns for harmony in these political matters. She is strong, yet she is tender—and you *both* should know better than to say such derogatory things with her present." She looked toward the doorway where Kitty had exited. "Now that she will be staying with us you will have to find a way to temper your statements."

"Staying?" Nathaniel turned his head. "You mean this isn't a visit?"

Thomas ran his tongue over his teeth as if trying to recover from the wounds he continued to receive from his wife's chastising glare. "Nay, she... she has moved back from Boston. Permanently." He pushed out a heavy breath. "Please forgive me, Eliza. It was very wrong of me."

"Aye, it was very wrong. But 'tis not I to whom you should be apologizing." The wrinkle in Eliza's brow softened and she eased her fingers between her husband's. "I'm not asking you to stop speaking of politics in her presence, rather keep your position on Tories away from her ears."

Thomas gazed at his wife, humility and adoration in his eyes as he kissed her forehead. "I'll go speak with her."

He turned to go, but Nathaniel grabbed his arm. "Let me. 'Twas I who started the conversation."

Thomas glanced at Eliza and quirked his brow. "Do you mind?"

She shrugged. "This is between the two of you."

Without waiting, Nathaniel started toward the hall, smiling over his shoulder as confidence lightened his step. "I'll bring her back, and have her smiling the rest of the evening. Mark my word."

Chapter Three

Kitty peered up at the dark ceiling just outside the ballroom and blinked, trying to make the tears seep back into her eyes.

She should never have come back to Sandwich. With her unpopular political beliefs, her presence would only cause greater disharmony as the months went on. But what to do? There was nowhere else to go.

The continual humming of voices from the ballroom grew quiet as she walked down the dimly lit hall toward what must be the library. A stream of light filtered through the doorway and she drew near to it as a butterfly draws near to a sun-kissed bloom. 'Twas what she needed—a quiet place where she could compose herself before having to return to the room where she was as wanted as a burnt piecrust.

Almost at the door, the whisper of hushed voices trickled into the hall and she stopped.

"You idiot. You should have left the boy alone."

"It wasn't my fault!"

"We need to try again tonight."

"Tonight? Are you mad—"

"We have a job to do and we *will* do it."

The two men emerged from the room and jerked

to a halt before her, their glares boring holes into Kitty's skull.

Her breath caught as the sneer of Cyprian Wythe made her shrink backward. The other unfamiliar man glared, but lacked the same poison in his eyes.

Cyprian looked up and down the dark hall before nailing his gaze upon her. His voice grated against her like a fork on a metal charger. "What are you doing here young miss? Come looking for company? Were the patriots too much for you?"

Her heart beat so quick it held her response captive. She tried to force a smile on her lips, but the heaviness around her consumed every muscle.

Turning to his companion, Cyprian motioned to her. "Mr. Cooper, this is Miss Campbell, the young lady I was telling you about. She, too, is a Tory. Since there are so few of us, we must band together."

As if Cyprian had said nothing, Andrew stepped up and made a quick bow. "Good evening, Miss Campbell, 'tis a pleasure to meet you." He stood straight and darted a quick look to Cyprian, his expression hard. "You must forgive me. Though you, gentle lady, are welcome in my home, *this* Tory is not. Thus, I'm escorting him from this gathering. Please excuse us."

Cyprian leaned toward her, his breath stale. "Whose side are you on?" The frightening hatred that oozed from his black eyes pushed her backward until her shoulders pressed against the wall. He tossed a quick glare to Andrew before they walked toward the large front door at the end of the hall.

Kitty pressed a hand to her throat, trying to catch her breath when another set of footfalls neared and several voices echoed in the hall, but all she heard were the bold words whirling in her mind. *Whose side are you on?*

"'Tis almost as if you're searching for trouble." Nathaniel's rich timbre jerked her from Cyprian's ominous query. She pushed off the wall and brushed her hands against her skirts, hoping the action would soothe her ruffled nerves.

She shrugged and smiled. "Would you believe me if I said I wasn't?"

Nathaniel's eyes brightened in jest. "Nay, I would not." He looked behind him toward the two he'd just passed and his expression turned dark. "Was he bothering you again?" He stepped nearer, the dim light of the hall casting perfect shadows across his face.

Kitty raised her chin slightly and looked away. "Nay. That other gentleman, Mr. Cooper, said he was escorting him out."

She looked back at Nathaniel and nearly lost her breath when her gaze collided with his. The caring in Nathaniel's eyes, the way his tenderness encircled her, seemed to lift her from the floor. His jaw lowered slightly and he tipped a single brow upward as a smile teased one side of his mouth. Her heart thudded against her ribs. Should she tell him what she had heard between the two men? Blinking, she made a quick shake of her head and smiled to hide the surge of questions. Of course she shouldn't mention it, 'twould be folly, surely. None of this was her affair and it was best left alone.

Nathaniel lifted his head with a glint of warmth in his face and gestured for her to enter the library. She struggled to keep the heat from her cheeks when his hand rested against the small of her back.

Once inside, she scanned the welcoming room. A large fire crackled in the fireplace in the center of the library's far wall and illuminated the modest rows of books surrounding them. Two large chairs and a settee lounged comfortably in front of the hearth as if soaking up the warmth from the flames.

Nathaniel stood in front of her, thankfully keeping a healthy distance. If he came too close she might be tempted to let her gaze memorize his rugged features, as though she didn't already know them by heart.

He planted his feet beside the nearest chair and folded his arms, staring at her with those all-searching eyes.

Her stays tightened the longer he stared and she wriggled to ease the discomfort. Would he not speak? She tried offering a gentle smile to coax some kind of response from him, but the glowering look remained. Why was he so quiet? *She* had been belittled by him. Shouldn't she be the glaring party?

The silence grew so loud Kitty could endure it no longer. She shifted her feet. Fiddling with the embroidered rose on the bottom of her stomacher, she chanced a look at him again. Her pulse jumped. Why did he look at her as if he peeked into the locked rooms of her heart? Kitty looked back at the flames, reminding herself that Nathaniel's allure affected all women.

"What made you come back?"

Kitty jerked at his sudden question. She sputtered for a moment then laughed. "What made me come back? What do you mean?"

He shrugged with one shoulder, never moving his gaze away from her. "At Eliza's and Thomas's wedding last year you were convinced that returning to Boston and living with your aunt was the best course to take. But it appears you have changed your mind. So, what made you come back?"

"Is that why you followed me? To ask me that?" Her face burned, but she feigned composure and looked at him with as much ease as she could marshal. "Boston is too dangerous, you know that."

"'Tis true, I am well aware of what Boston and its residents suffer. But I cannot believe that was the only reason you returned."

Training her mouth to reveal nothing more than a slight grin, she strained to keep her pulse quiet. She stepped toward the fire, resting her hand atop the chair, acting more casual than she felt. "If there were any other reason, do you think that I would share such information with you? Surely, Nathaniel, I cannot share all my secrets."

"Secrets? Well, now I *am* curious."

Kitty rubbed the lace on her gloves and emitted a warm, genuine laugh that eased the strain in her voice. She offered an impish smile. "I came back for several reasons, if you must know. As I mentioned, 'twas for matters of safety that Henry Donaldson insisted I return as well as—"

"Donaldson?"

Kitty peered over her shoulder, hiding the grin that surged at the undeniable question in Nathaniel's eyes. Could he be... nay, not possible. She kept her focus. "Aye, Henry Donaldson. You remember him, do you not?"

"Aye, of course. I just... I just hadn't known he was still... around. He was always a good friend and I admire him, despite his poor choice of allegiances." Nathaniel's interested expression stayed lifted, but the light in his eyes went flat. "Are you... have you been seeing much of him of late?"

"I have," she said. "He's a close friend and I

admire him very much."

Nathaniel's expression didn't change, but his Adam's apple bobbed and he cleared his throat. "I see."

She once again toyed with the fabric of her gloves, unsure what else to do with her hands. Quickly focusing on the subject of their conversation, she stared back into the fire. "Henry said it was too dangerous for me to stay despite my protestations. With Father gone and Eliza here—*and* since our home was destroyed that December... well, my home is here now."

The scent of smoke wafting from the fireplace in front of her snatched the horrid vision from its hiding place in her mind. Instantly she witnessed anew the roaring flames that devoured her treasured childhood home, taking with it all her cherished memories and replacing them with ash.

She turned to Nathaniel, his face drawn as if he too relived the tragedy. The bond they'd shared that night had forged a friendship that could never be shaken.

Nathaniel stepped forward, the look of tenderness so rich in his eyes it wound around her shoulders like a warm cloak. "I can well understand that, Kitty. Donaldson was right in advising you to return." Then, as if the heaviness were too much, he shrugged and sighed with added gaiety to his tone. "Well, I will admit that Sandwich didn't feel the same with you gone, that's for certain."

She tipped her head with a smirk. "You pined for my return?"

"With the pains of an anguished soul."

"Lying is a sin, Nathaniel," she teased.

Nathaniel laughed, his broad smile exposing his

straight teeth. "All right, if you want the truth I pined more for your cooking, and more specifically for your carrot pudding. Are you satisfied?"

"I knew it." She laughed then sighed as the weight of the evening's earlier troubles tapped against her memory. "Truth be told, Nathaniel, I'm beginning to believe it might be better to risk returning and staying in Boston rather than making the people of Sandwich uncomfortable with my presence. Tories are not welcome in these circles. I don't belong here."

"Don't speak foolishness, of course you belong." Nathaniel's dark brow lowered and his pointed gaze softened. He stepped forward and brushed her elbow with his fingers. "Kitty, you and I were always very good friends. I have never been ignorant of your political leanings. Neither have Thomas and Eliza." He paused. Strength and caring framed his character while the fire framed his face. "Nothing will ever change the way we feel about you. Thomas and Eliza will love you without fail—and you and I shall always be friends."

"I'm sure we shall." Kitty smiled and tamped her ballooning emotions down with the same force as a fist to a rising lump of dough. *Friends*. She drew in a long breath. "I wish you to know that even though I believe differently, I won't go against your cause, despite my reservations about your beliefs."

"Very generous of you, milady." Nathaniel's mouth tilted into a droll grin. "Though I hope you know I won't stop trying to convert you to our grand cause. That is my mission for every person whom I meet who is not yet a believer in the values of freedom."

Kitty crossed her arms. "You may try, Nathaniel, but I fear you will not succeed." She smiled, enjoying the volley of wits. "I shall never abandon the teachings of my father. He was a true, honest man and I know—no matter what Eliza has come to believe—the way he raised us is the *right* way. I can never leave the safety of the king's rule, no matter what anyone may say to persuade me otherwise."

Nathaniel stepped closer and leaned in, the reflection of the fire burning in his gaze. "Now *that* is a challenge I am most ready to accept."

Frozen under his hazel stare, Kitty swallowed to try and wet her suddenly dry mouth, but quickly recovered her senses, kindling the ire that sparked at his challenge. "You may look at this as some sort of game, Nathaniel, but I do not."

His expression crunched and he stepped away. "Game? Not in the least. The cause of freedom is vital. Every colonist is entitled to their liberty and we must have it. This very evening you yourself said we have a right to protect ourselves, a very freedom-loving statement. We need everyone, Kitty. Because freedom is *for* everyone."

His words burned. She raised her chin. "So I am merely a possible conquest? A number to add to your forces?"

"When someone as intelligent as yourself is so embroiled in the wrong I find it my duty to enlighten them."

"Enlighten me?" She scoffed and stiffened her arms at her sides. "Nathaniel, you may think I'm wrong, but I am not."

"I don't *think* you're wrong, Kitty." His expression, and his voice, darkened. "I *know* it."

The conviction in his eyes sank deep into Kitty's chest and she recoiled. Nathaniel didn't remove his gaze and her breathing accelerated. Her jaw flopped open as shock drenched her. He thought she could be converted to his cause. He thought she could be dissuaded from her deep convictions despite their unyielding roots. Did he and Thomas and Eliza really view her as a valued friend, or only pretend it for her sake? The reality of such a thought took the strength from her limbs.

A cutting pain slashed deep. Tears threatened and before the frightful emotions could make themselves visible she darted from the room, but Nathaniel grabbed her arm.

"Where are you going? I came to apologize for earlier and I can't allow you to leave more upset than before." The kind sincerity in his eyes wedged the hurt deeper as he continued. "Allow me to speak that which I came to say."

"Nay. This conversation has ended." She yanked from his grasp and marched to the door, mumbling under her breath. "Perhaps I should have accepted Higley's proposal after all."

"Higley? Who's Higley?" He marched after her and tugged on her elbow. "You mean you're not courting Donaldson? Has someone proposed to you?"

"Nay, I am not courting Henry, and aye, someone has proposed." She stopped at the door and whirled around. "I should reprimand myself for not having thought more of the arrangement. At least he accepts me for who I am instead of hoping to change me to meet his expectations."

She started toward the exit but Nathaniel darted in front of her. "Kitty, you're talking foolishness. No one wants you to change."

Ha! Kitty tilted her head. "Really?" Had he completely forgotten what they'd just discussed?

She dodged sideways to make her escape but he

blocked her flight, gripping her shoulders. Holding back an unladylike growl, she glared. "Nathaniel, let me pass."

"Not until I can make you believe that I don't want to change you—and not until you tell me who this Higley fellow is. I am most curious." His chin lowered and he looked at her with the condescendence of an older sibling, ready to scold her for stealing a sweet.

How dare he! She let out a sharp laugh refusing to dignify his question with an answer.

Yanking from his grasp, Kitty marched down the hall.

Nathaniel followed directly behind. "Where are you going?"

She stared forward, her breath heating with each exhale. "Home."

He pulled on her shoulder to stop her. "By yourself?"

She jerked to a halt. This time she did look at him, praying the barbs she threw from her eyes made their mark, but from the irritating smirk he failed to hide, her invisible weapons did nothing. "Aye, by myself."

He shook his head. "If you're leaving, then I'm escorting you home."

"You are not."

"You may be stubborn, Kitty Campbell, but I cannot allow you to walk home—"

"You absolutely will. I am at *liberty* to do as I please, am I not? I have the *right* to refuse to be escorted by a thick-headed patriot missionary."

"Kitty wait!"

Dumbfounded, Nathaniel started after her then dropped his hands to his sides and watched as Kitty hurried down the hall and escaped through the front door. *Headstrong girl.* What was she thinking going home at night by herself? Was she really so angry that she would refuse his gentlemanly offer to see her safely home? Ridiculous. He should run after her and see she made it home no matter how she snarled and scratched.

Wiping his hand across his jaw, he shook his head and went back into the library to collect his scattered pride before having to enter the party as if nothing had happened. Staring into the fire, he hoped to commiserate with the only witness of the scene, but instead the flames scolded him with every popping spark. He balked as if the reprimand were audible. What could he have done different? He'd come to apologize, but she wouldn't give him a chance.

Indignation burrowed into his chest as another cheery melody began in the ballroom and fluttered its way down the hall and into the library. Blast. Where was his buoyant spirit, his unyielding vim? Glaring at the fire that still chided him, he pressed the palm of his hand into the smooth wood of the mantel. Of all the women in Sandwich, why did it have to be Kitty who riled him so? Traitorous emotions.

"There you are."

Nathaniel spun at the sound of Thomas's voice and glared. "Where else would I be?"

Thomas entered, looking around the room, his brow slanted. "You seemed to be taking an excessive amount of time so I thought I'd come to make certain you two weren't arguing." He motioned forward. "So—did you make amends?"

Nathaniel stood motionless, mouth agape, producing only small, stunted grunts as he struggled to find the best way to describe the bloody mess.

Thomas's timbre dropped. "What did you do?"

"Me?"

"Of course, *you* must have done something or you wouldn't be standing there like a bumbling fool." He looked around again. "Where is she?"

Thomas's incriminating tone flicked away the last remaining thread of Nathaniel's good humor. He brushed past Thomas and stomped toward the door. "The same place I'm going. Home."

"She went to your home?" The shock in Thomas's voice would have been amusing if Nathaniel had been in the mood.

"No," he said, whirling around. "She went to *your* home, and I'm going to mine." Pausing, he ground his teeth and released a rough exhale. He had to get out of here. He had to try and figure out why his conversation with Kitty had both his head and his heart spinning like a child's toy. "Give my apologizes to your wife."

He made a quick escape down the hall before Thomas could protest and before being witnessed by any unwanted attention in the ballroom. Plunging into the clean night air, he took long breaths to cool his heated blood. Did Kitty really think he saw her as only a "number"? Gads, it was as if she didn't know him at all.

Nathaniel kicked at the dirt as he stomped toward home. Even though he knew her convictions were misplaced it didn't give him the right to make her feel uncomfortable. He growled. Besides, it wasn't as if he'd said anything wrong. She *took* it wrong.

Once home, he slammed the door behind him and lit an oil lamp, making both light and shadows dart across the floor and up the walls.

As he marched up the stairs to his room, the faceless Higley invaded his thoughts. Did Thomas know anything about this fellow? Nathaniel should have probed for more information while he had the chance.

Blast! Why did he even care?

He set the lamp down a little too rough and removed his jacket.

Kitty needed to be with someone of her own mind, and Nathaniel needed to rein in his ludicrous emotions before they sent him to an early grave.

He stared into the shadowy corner of his room and fingered the base of the lamp. If his upbringing had taught him anything, 'twas that finding a spouse with the same beliefs and ideals was paramount. He'd witnessed enough heartache in his youth to understand that. Too much fighting, too many tears. Rubbing his temple, Nathaniel groaned as the memories of his parent's discord assaulted him. He knew better than this—this foolish attraction to a woman so different than he. Then why couldn't he escape the image of Kitty's pink cheeks and adorable angry mouth as she'd stomped away?

He kicked off his shoes then slumped on the edge of the bed. Dragging his hands down his face, Nathaniel dragged his gaze to the musket on the wall. Like a surging wave, the weightier matters of the day crashed against him. This was no time to ponder over some fickle woman. His vow to keep the people of this town safe poured through his veins with every pump of his heart. Not only did he need to provide care for their physical well-being, but their very livelihoods may depend on him should their safety be threatened. Untying his cravat, he growled and corrected himself. Their safety *had been* threatened. Standing, he yanked the fabric from his neck and wadded it before launching it across the room. Breath surging, he stared at the shadows. He *would* keep the people of Sandwich safe at any cost.

Chapter Four

Drinking in the cool night air, Kitty shook her hands at her sides as she trudged down the deserted road in the blackness. It had been less than a day and already the tensions between her and her family were as burdensome as she'd feared. She expelled a shaky breath. Perhaps she'd misunderstood her answer. Perhaps coming back to Sandwich had been a mistake and God had desired her to stay in Boston. Even though the city was dangerous for some, surely it wouldn't have proved to be so for her. Would it? She was a Tory after all.

The temperature dropped another degree and she hugged her arms as a strong chill coated her skin. Was it the air, or the struggle in her soul?

Give it time.

The comforting whisper of God chased away the bite in the air and she stared up into the heavens. Where was her faith? *Forgive me, Lord.* It *had* only been a day, and she wasn't about to throw away the chance to stay with Eliza because of a petty argument with a headstrong man.

She looked up at the expanse of stars, inhaling the sweet scent of lilac that caressed the air and suddenly the past swirled around her, transforming the trees and shadows into the beloved front walk of her childhood home. The memory enfolded her like Father's comforting embrace. Closing her eyes she relived it as if it had only been yesterday. Father draped his arm around her shoulder and pointed to the stars.

"You know, my child, every time a star twinkles, 'tis God giving a blessing."

Kitty opened her eyes and stared at the sky above her, yearning so much for Father her bones ached. Remembering her response to him, she swallowed to press down the lump in her throat. "But the stars twinkle all the time, Father."

"Aye," he'd said, crouching down to her. He plucked a moon-kissed flower and tucked it behind her ear. "That is because God is always blessing his children, Kitty. Always."

Inhaling a shuddering breath, Kitty flicked the tear from her eyes. She shouldn't cry. These were happy memories.

Father, I miss you. I wish you were here to help me—to stand beside me in this time of turmoil.

She shook off the oppressive melancholy and started forward again. Only a few more steps down the road and Kitty halted, scattering rocks across the dirt as goose bumps splashed her skin. She held her breath. The sound of footsteps scuffled behind, and she strangled the gasp in her throat. Was someone there? Spinning around, she stared into the shadows.

Her heartbeat tapped quicker with each breath. Had she only imagined it? An eerie quiet draped the deepening night. She pressed a hand to her head. Mercy! Was she simply exhausted? She must be, to be imagining such things.

Another rustling in the bushes snatched her attention like an icy hand around the neck. She spun to glance behind, but again, nothing. Struggling to placate her trembling heart, she breathed out through tight lips. Foolish girl. She need only return home and finally get a good night's rest.

Turning, she stepped back and slipped. With a sharp yelp she tumbled backward and rolled down a small embankment into a clump of trees. Kitty rushed to her feet, and brushed off her skirts, feeling the crunch of dead leaves and small twigs as she moved her hands along the fabric.

"Bother. My fine dress." As she moved her hand over her arm, her finger slipped into a gash in the fabric then slid over something sticky on her skin. She closed her eyes. *I'm bleeding.*

Her stomach knotted but she took a deep breath to try and ease the rising alarm that coursed down her back. An invisible companion seemed to whisk its protective wings around her shoulders, admonishing her to hurry home which only made her fears ascend to greater heights. Where *was* home?

Panic attempted to buckle Kitty's knees. She clutched her chest and whirled around, trying to find her bearings in the unfamiliar surroundings. Mercy, where was she? The unfamiliar terrain taunted, shapes and shadows reaching out to her with their long, spiny arms. She scanned the far road through the trees, desperate for familiar landmarks but the dark masked everything she might have known.

She was lost.

Her hands shook. *Lord, help me.*

Kitty took a few steps toward the opening in the trees as a flurry of hoarse whispers darted toward her. She snapped her head in the direction of the sound and held her breath. A small stone building rested in the clearing and suddenly her memory burst to life.

The magazine.

Her limbs went numb. She ducked behind the trunk of a tree, praying it would shield her from view. Moonlight illuminated the small clearing with its silvery glaze as two men, one large and one small, came from behind the corner. Clutching the bark of her wooden shield, she couldn't swallow, couldn't blink.

The men moved toward the door, one holding a ring of keys, the other a large satchel. The bottom half of each of their faces was covered with a dark cloth, masking their identities. The smaller man looked around, tapping the empty bag against his leg, while the larger one fiddled with the lock until finally he shoved it open with a forceful heave. With his body half in and half out, he peered from left to right then ducked inside the blackness.

Kitty thrust her trembling hand over her mouth to keep from crying out. *Another raid!* She had to warn Thomas.

She pressed her quivering hands to her chest to try and clam her racing pulse. One deep breath. Two. She had to be wise. If she ran now, one of them would certainly see her and warn the other. If that happened... she couldn't think of it.

Keeping her eyes nailed to the violated building, she gripped the rough bark of the tree and waited. Finally the small one disappeared inside with the other, and Kitty put fire in her feet.

The thump of Kitty's pulse thundered in her ears as she ran. Halfway out the safety of the trees, her foot dashed against a fallen branch. The unforgiving earth came up to meet her before she even had time to brace for the fall. Her face smacked into the ground, driving dirt and bits of rock into her mouth.

Sputtering, she struggled for her footing, but her skirts entangled her legs.

A mumbling came from the inside of the building and the two men scrambled out. Her heart leapt to her throat when their eyes landed on her.

"There!" The larger one pointed and sprinted toward her like a hungry wolf.

Kitty could hardly move, and yet her body reacted with animal-like fear. She scrambled to her feet, lungs heaving, as the man wrangled her from behind, covering her mouth. Kitty tried to scream but his hand was hot and hard, and pressed with such force Kitty feared she would faint.

The man yelled at his accomplice. "Keep a lookout. I'll deal with this."

Kitty's vision blurred as frenzy stole strength from her limbs.

The man's sturdy grip stiffened. He dragged her to a tree and spun her around jamming her back against the trunk. Instinctively, Kitty swung her arms and scratched at his face, trying desperately to find her voice that remained mute with horror. As her fingers made contact with the fabric around her attacker's face, she pulled and instantly gasped.

"You!" Her voice was little more than a high-pitched whisper.

Cyprian's face contorted and his fingers dug deeper into her arms, as if he intended to leave an imprint on her bones.

The milky light from the moon coated his warped features. "You little spy!"

"Nay! I wasn't spying, I—"

"Liar! That's why you were listening by the library door." Cyprian's gravelly tone grated against her like sand in a swift wind. "You were sent to watch and your accomplices thought you'd go unnoticed since you're a senseless female."

Kitty clutched the tree behind her. No words came to her defense. She could only focus on praying and holding back the tears that singed her eyes.

Cyprian's dark glare turned a wicked black. "You will *never tell anyone* what you have seen here tonight. Do you understand me?"

Blinking, she could only shake her head. "But I didn't see anything, you must believe me." God would forgive her for lying, wouldn't he? The words started flowing. "I left the party early and got lost on my way home. I was trying to find my bearings when I tripped and fell in the dark." The more she talked the more her voice shook as much as her trembling frame until the words were almost too severed to be understood.

"You're a terrible liar." Again his grip tightened. He inched her higher until only her toes touched the ground. "What kind of Tory are you—if you are one at all? I am working to defend the king, and what do you do? You seek to over throw him. Just like the others."

A knife-like pain gouged her middle as his words cut into her already wounded soul. Her throat ached. "Nay, 'tis not true! I do support the king! You don't understand—"

"Cyprian, who is it?" The other man ran forward. His voice was deep and hard when his gaze trailed over her. His eyes narrowed and he pulled his mask higher. "What are you doing here?" He didn't wait for her answer before he turned to Cyprian. "This bodes ill. Very ill."

Cyprian grunted without moving his eyes from Kitty. "That idiot doctor sent you, did he not?"

Trembling, Kitty sputtered, her knees buckling. "He did not! I left the party early and—"

"You've already said that much and though 'tis a clever story, I know you lie."

The other man stepped back and whipped around as if he expected someone to dart from the cover of the trees. "We must finish quickly."

Cyprian's heavy voice slammed against Kitty like a rolling boulder. "You *will* stay silent. Do. You. Understand?"

I cannot. I cannot stay silent—not about this.

She must have spoken the words aloud because the incoming smack sent a shooting pain through her head.

"I can see you are not yet convinced." Cyprian grabbed her face with his hand and forced her to look at him, grinding the flesh of her cheeks into her jaw. The moonlight shone off of his teeth as he sneered. "And I know just the way to make sure you'll never breathe a word."

Cyprian slapped her again and this time her body went completely limp and she tumbled to his feet.

Andrew shoved Cyprian's shoulders. "What are you doing? The boy and now she? This was not part of the plan!"

Cyprian could only stare at the motionless girl, anger rotting his stomach. *Traitor.* Not even her innocent eyes could wedge through the tightly cemented bricks he'd laid around his heart. No patriot spy would stop him from this mission. And certainly not a woman.

He moved back and stared, feeling Andrew's eyes on him.

His threats should be enough to keep her foolish mouth quiet. And if not, he would prove to her he wasn't a man to be dealt with lightly. Not when Camilla's life depended on every cent the British paid him.

"Why do I let you do this to me—to her, to anyone?" Andrew glared, his rage glinting off the whites of his eyes.

Cyprian sneered. "Because this is what I want. And I always get what I want."

Chapter Five

The rapping against the backdoor lurched Nathaniel out of a heavy sleep. He shook his head before trying to read the clock on the dresser. Running a hand over his hair, he squinted. What hour was it?

"Nathaniel! Nathaniel! Get down here now!"

Thomas's frantic voice breached the closed door and hurled upstairs, grabbing Nathaniel by the collar and shaking the sleep from his eyes.

Nathaniel's pulse charged. "Coming!"

He was used to frenzied patients fetching him at all hours, but something in Thomas's tone made his spine stiffen. He put on the first pair of breeches he grabbed from the drawer, yanked a clean shirt over his head, and shoved his feet into a pair of stockings and boots before bounding down the stairs two at a time.

Swinging open the door, he jumped back as Thomas barged in, chest heaving.

"What's happened?" Nathaniel gripped the cold door handle before he slammed it shut.

Thomas wouldn't stop moving. "We can't find Kitty."

"What?" Nathaniel stopped and time slowed as he tried to comprehend Thomas's meaning. "I don't understand. She's not at home?"

"She is not." Thomas's stomping boots echoed between the walls as he paced the length of the study. "Eliza is frantic. We've scoured every inch of the house, the barn. What's worse, we can't even tell that she ever made it home from the party." He stopped and pointed a finger at Nathaniel's chest. "What were you thinking letting her leave alone? I thought you had at least some sense in that self-righteous head of yours."

Nathaniel's volume exploded. "I *tried* to persuade her to allow me to escort her home but she refused to—"

"When have you ever let something like that stop you?" Thomas's tone grew louder with every word. "She could be anywhere, Nathaniel. She could be hurt!"

A firing squad would have been more welcome at that moment. Why hadn't he just gone after her? *Fool!*

"We will find her, Thomas." Nathaniel yanked his hat and greatcoat off the peg, determination driving into his muscles with every pump of his heart. He pulled open the door. "You head into town. I will go the other way around Shawme Pond and up past Newcomb Tavern. If you find her, bring her to your house immediately. I will do the same."

Thomas followed him out the door. "Good. Eliza will be waiting."

"If neither of us has found her within the hour, we'll organize a larger search party."

Thomas nodded his assent and dashed up the street into the shadows, calling Kitty's name.

Guilt pooled into Nathaniel's lungs like a foaming wave. He raced up the street, his body somehow both numb and violently alert. Calling Kitty's name, he tried desperately to keep the frantic edge out of his voice. Whatever had happened to keep her from returning home must have been grave. She might be headstrong, but she was too level-headed to hold a grudge and... what? Runaway? Go back to Boston?

Impossible. Boston was sixty miles north and she could never make such a journey alone much less in the dead of night.

He gripped the back of his neck and spun around. Only trees. Only the lonely, deserted street. The scent of cold ground and green foliage swelled around him and it was then another alarming realization struck his mind. His blood pumped at such a rate he felt nothing but heat, but Kitty would be dangerously chilled if she was in fact still out of doors. The memory of her stomping into the night without her cloak censured him once more and his worry climbed another rung.

He picked up his pace to a dead run. "Kitty? *Kitty*!"

Suddenly he stopped.

He didn't want to pass her by. Perhaps she was injured and unable to respond? His breathing raced. For this, he would need to check his pace and though his legs demanded speed, his mind commanded temperance.

Nathaniel kept his speed in check, scrutinizing every sound, every shadow.

As he neared the small clearing where the magazine rested, a rounded shadow near the trees snatched his gaze and he stopped. His muscles burned and his eyes strained against the blackness.

"Kitty!"

Racing toward the figure, his worst fears

pummeled him like the fists of a trained fighter. He skidded to a halt and dropped to his knees beside her, instantly assessing her condition. She sat against a tree, hugging her knees against her chest, staring ahead, her entire body trembling as she rocked lightly forward and back as if he were nothing more than a shadow.

"Kitty, are you all right? What happened?" He touched her elbow and cringed. Her skin was far too cold. He flung off his jacket and draped it around her shoulders. "Kitty, look at me."

She didn't answer, wouldn't even turn her head. "Are you all right? Are you hurt?" He gripped her shoulders and dipped his head to meet the direction of her gaze.

Slowly she turned to him. Her pained eyes blinked as the realization of his presence seemed to trickle over her. "Nathaniel?" The pale light showed little of her expression, but the small whimper that squeaked from her quivering fame nearly undid him. "Nathaniel, I..." She covered her face with one hand and exhaled through tight lips, attempting to calm her quaking voice. Pressing off the ground she struggled to stand. "Forgive me... I am well, I simply—"

"You are not well." With a hand to her shoulder, he kept her seated and scanned right to left, hoping a spot of moonlit ground would offer some relief from the dark, but she already sat in the most lighted plot. He chewed a curse. His blood surged as anguish and anger made ready allies and prepared to fight for her welfare.

He focused on her face and clamped his teeth. She was not without wound as he had hoped she might be, as evidenced by the shimmer of blood that trickled from her nose. Rage nearly suffocated him. Was that all she suffered? Had she internal injuries? Emotional ones?

Careful to keep his touch appropriate lest she flinch under his examination, he felt down her head and neck, and smoothed her arms to assure him no bones were asunder. His pulse charged faster. He needed to get her home and in enough light to allow him to properly care for her and assure himself her wounds were superficial.

He snatched a handkerchief from his pocket and gently held it to her nose. "Hold this."

Kitty took the offering, yet remained still but for the unending tremors her body refused to quiet and the breath that revealed any moment she might succumb to tears. He glanced around, scanning the clearing for any movement should the attacker still linger in the shadows, but he saw nothing. He turned back to her and met her anguished gaze. Kitty was not a female who submitted to fits of crying over even a slight disturbance. He struggled to keep hold of his emotions that edged dangerously toward the precipice of panic.

"What happened? Who did this to you?" He gripped harder to her shoulders, attempting to pry a response from her sealed lips while his mind scattered in all directions, desperate for answers. Her round eyes blinked, and her quiet, heaving breaths came in quick erratic bursts.

She shook her head and struggled to stand once again. "I must get home."

He gripped her around the waist to assist her, but she pressed him away. "I am well, Nathaniel."

This is madness! He scooped her small frame in his arms. "I will not have you walk."

Without protest she wound her arms around his neck and clung to him as he hurried toward the Watson home. Holding her against him, his heart burst with every hurried step. Kitty held tighter, gripping the collar of his jacket. She pressed her face into his neck, her heated breath on his skin burning him with regret. He should never have let her leave the party alone.

He quickened his step. It was then her warm tears trickled down his neck and the restraint he'd maintained nearly burst through the bulwarks with which it was bound. A vile remembrance of many months past clouded his memory and he shuddered. If someone had taken advantage of Kitty as had nearly happened to Eliza...

Once at the house, Nathaniel kicked the door open. "Eliza! I've found her!"

Rushing in from the kitchen, Eliza covered her mouth to muffle a scream. "Dear Lord, what happened?"

"I don't know." He started up the stairs, scaling them two-by-two. "I need a bucket of water and clean cloths."

"Right away."

Taking Kitty into the second bedchamber, Nathaniel eased her on the bed and immediately lit an oil lamp.

"You needn't worry over me so." Kitty's tight voice tapped the air and he spun around to see her lean her head against the headboard, eyes squinting as if trying to bear the pain of her injuries.

He almost gave in to irritation and scolded her for such words, but in the light of the lamp her wounds revealed their grim state and he stalled. Her hair was undone with bits of leaves and a dusting of dirt. A long red mark across her jaw crossed paths with several more dirt smudges and a small trail of blood still trickled from her delicate nose.

He set the lamp on the table and spun toward the door, grinding his teeth. "Eliza!"

"I'm here." She rushed in, bucket and rags in hand. "Kitty! What happened?" Immediately rushing to the other side of the bed, Eliza embraced her sister.

Kitty's chin quivered as she fell into Eliza's arms, but still made no reply to the question that had now been put to her more times than a few.

Nathaniel yanked a cloth from Eliza's grasp. "No matter how you protest, Kitty, I do plan on attending to your wounds and I expect you to endure it." He teased. Partly. "Sit back and let me examine you properly."

Kitty pulled away from her sister and sat still, her shoulders slumped against the wood. "I've told you, Nathaniel, I'm—"

"Enough."

Kitty stared, her mouth still half open.

Nathaniel hadn't meant his response to bite. After inhaling and releasing a heavy breath, Nathaniel met her red-rimmed gaze. With a soft smile he hoped would mitigate the tension that abounded, he quieted his voice. "You will allow me to examine you, Kitty, or I fear I shall need to tie you to the bed."

Kitty looked down without even the whisper of a smile, as he'd hoped his continued teasing might produce. *Why won't you say what happened?* He ground his teeth and wetted the fabric before starting to clean the gash on Kitty's cheekbone when he noticed the trail of blood on her arm. Blast! How many injuries did she have?

"Will she be all right?" Eliza's typically even voice wavered when she questioned him as if Kitty were not present.

Nathaniel looked back at Eliza and felt his worry spike at the concern in her face. He couldn't voice the full measure of his worries. Not yet. For that, Thomas would need to be present. For if indeed his worst fears were realized, and she had been violated, they would discuss privately how to find and exterminate the demon.

He continued to gently dot the cloth against Kitty's face and breathed deeper. No stitches were required. Thank the Lord.

Kitty rested against the headboard once more and pressed her eyes shut. Taking slow, deliberate breaths, she clutched her sister's hand while Eliza gently brushed her fingers back and forth along Kitty's grip.

Finally he could take the quiet no longer. He dropped his hands in his lap and leaned forward until his closeness forced her to look at him.

"You must tell us what happened. Now."

Kitty looked away, unable to bear the way Nathaniel's gaze seemed intent on extracting the truth from her whether she relinquished it or not.

She shut her eyes once again. Throbbing pain. Everywhere.

Kitty reached up to press her palm to her head, but stopped when the slash in her arm protested. She scrunched her eyes then pulled them open, blinking to try and clear the pain enough to make sense of the ordeal she'd just endured. She grimaced as her teeth crunched on the remaining bits of bitter dirt in her mouth. Had it really happened? She pressed her lips tight to stop her chin from quivering when the reality slapped her memory just as Cyprian had slapped her face.

"Please, Kitty," Eliza pleaded. "We want to help you, dearest."

Nathaniel inched closer, dabbing the cool rag under her eye. He didn't meet her gaze this time and kept silent, though the tick in his jaw and the harshness of his breath witnessed his concern. Her stomach flipped upside down when his fingers brushed against her cheek. Looking straight ahead, Kitty focused on the folded blanket at the end of the bed, so her wayward vision wouldn't be tempted to trace the determined lines around Nathaniel's eyes.

He tipped her chin upward, examining her nose. Even though his volume stayed quiet, a loaded anger rumbled past the calm. "Whoever did this to you had a heavy hand."

Heart racing, the terrible memories bludgeoned her anew and she stared, fighting against the emotions that threatened to strangle the breath from her chest.

Iron hands.

Threats. Demands.

Every thought choked her like the enemy's haunting grip.

"What is it?" Nathaniel leaned closer, the lines in his brow deepening as he cupped her shoulders with his strong but gentle fingers. "What happened, Kitty?" His voice held back the urgent question that exploded in his eyes.

Kitty darted a look at Eliza, whose lips were

drawn, but pulled up at the sides as if the presence of a smile would somehow bring comfort and ease the words from Kitty's lips. *Dear Lord, what do I do?*

Her body trembled and a tear trailed over her cheek, but she pressed her lips tight, guarding the truth that struggled for release. Cyprian's words thundered. *If you expose our plan, the consequences will be—*

Slamming the door to the memory, Kitty cut off the horrid words before they could bring more tears. She closed her eyes and covered her face, wishing she could as easily shield her mind from the wrenching reality. Her chin quivered ever more as the horror of the night's attack swirled around her, consuming the room and transforming it into the cold, black clearing where the magazine looked on like another helpless victim.

Nathaniel and Eliza spoke to her, but their voices melded into a strange cacophony, jumping around her and weaving in and out. Pressing back against the bed, her mind worked desperately to locate a solution, but there was none. None except deception.

Trembling, the unbidden threats seeped into her memory. *Every Saturday at two in the afternoon, there will be a package waiting for you on the back porch of Newcomb Tavern. You must retrieve it, and deliver it to the specified location within the hour. If you do not, someone you hold dear will happen upon an untimely accident. If I suspect you have spoken of what you know, the consequences will be beyond comprehension.*

Reaching to her, Nathaniel removed a leaf from her hair, drawing her away from the frightful memory. The kindness in his eyes drew another tear down her cheek. *He will surely hate me now.*

She pressed a hand to her mouth as an added guard against the words that crouched on her tongue, ready to spring from her lips the minute she opened them. Moving closer yet again, Nathaniel removed the hand from her mouth and clutched it between his. His voice rippled around her like the gentle laps of water along a riverbank, soothing and cool against the burning pain in her chest.

Brow creased, he lowered his chin. "Whatever has happened you needn't be ashamed to say."

Eliza leaned in, her tone quiet and smooth. "Has someone... has someone used you ill, Kitty?"

Blinking, Kitty tried to place her sister's meaning when suddenly her understanding cleared. "Nay, nay, 'tis nothing like that. I..." Tears burned and her throat ached. How she wanted to tell!

A look of disbelief etched into Nathaniel's brow, as if he was unsure whether to accept her tale. "So no one took advantage of you?"

"No one." *Not in the way you think.* Kitty bit her cheek to keep from sobbing. How could she possibly keep such a secret from the ones she loved? Yet, the ramifications for divulging what she knew were too great. Cyprian's threats were real. She had seen the poison in his eyes, tasted the gall of his hatred.

Clearing her throat, Kitty swallowed the words she yearned to share and focused on the bits of truth she *could* divulge. "I stumbled down an embankment and became lost in the dark."

She stopped, flinging a quick glance at her companions. Did they believe her? Unable to distinguish any affirmation from their expressions, she continued. "I must have hit my head because... because I don't remember any more."

"Kitty, please. We are not so foolish as to believe

that." Nathaniel shook his head and his breathing turned rough. "You don't get those kinds of marks on your face from falling. Someone hit you. Who was it?" The anger in his voice didn't match the welling concern that turned his hazel eyes deep brown. "Don't be afraid to tell. Whoever did this, I vow, will never harm you again."

Kitty's throat swelled until she feared her emotions would flow out like a toppled vessel. *Perhaps not I, but he might harm Thomas or Eliza—or you.* Kitty tried to smile and pumped her voice with sincerity. "No one hurt me, Nathaniel."

He jerked back and his face scrunched. "Do you think I can't distinguish between the mark of an intended injury and an accident?"

Eliza reached over Kitty and touched his arm. "Nathaniel—"

He pushed off the bed. "Eliza, I'm a doctor. I witness these types of injuries more often than I care to admit." He pinned his searching eyes on Kitty once more. "I know you've been hit. And I want to know who did it."

The ropes of panic pulled tight around Kitty's chest. "Nathaniel, please, you must believe me!"

"This is ludicrous." Nathaniel threw the bloodied cloth into the water bucket and marched to the door. "Someone's attacked you and I'm going to find out who it was." Turning to Eliza, he gripped the doorframe. "Her wounds are stable. Stay with her and finish cleaning and wrapping her cuts."

"Where are you going?" Kitty's voice cracked, tears dripping from her chin. "Please Nathaniel, don't. You won't find anyone."

His jaw hardened. "We'll see about that."

Chapter Six

Nathaniel marched down the stairs and plunged outside just as Thomas raced to the house. Even in the darkness, Nathaniel could see the look of dread on his friend's face.

"Did you find her? Is she all right?"

"I found her. But she is not all right."

"What do you mean?" Thomas froze then dashed for the door.

"Hold on." Nathaniel shut the door, leaving them both on the stoop. "I need to talk to you."

"Well?"

"It appears she's been attacked."

"Attacked?" The drop in Thomas's tone revealed he too was struck by the images of Eliza's horrible injury last year. "How bad? Why won't you let me go to her?"

"If it were too terrible I would be with her." Nathaniel craned his neck to look toward the upstairs window. "There's something she isn't saying, and I don't like it."

"You think she's been threatened?"

"No doubt."

Thomas growled. "Who? Why?"

"That I intend to find out."

"Nathaniel!"

A voice echoed through the dark trees and jerked Nathaniel toward the sound of approaching footsteps. "Roger? What are you doing here?"

Panting, Roger Oliver crouched and grabbed his knees for support before pointing in the direction he'd just come. "Another break in at the magazine."

"What?" Thomas and Nathaniel spoke in unison.

Nathaniel stepped forward and grabbed Roger's arm, his blood already at a steady boil. "Are you certain?" Rage, confusion, regret—all piled in his gut like a poisoned meal.

Turning for the road Nathaniel sprinted toward town with both men striding beside him.

Thomas glanced at Roger as they ran. "A second raid in less than twenty-four hours?"

"I fear it may have... happened at the changing of the guard." Roger spoke between breaths. "When I came to relieve Billy... he'd already gone and the lock on the door was unlatched."

Picking up his pace, Nathaniel charged down the road to keep the building anxiety from ripping his muscles in two.

Billy. Nathaniel's breath heated. Had he been paid off to leave the watch early? The bachelor was new to town, and though he claimed to be a patriot, perhaps he practiced deception like so many of the Tories they knew.

When they reached the scene Nathaniel kicked in the unlocked door. His shoulders cramped and the sound of his hard breath bounced against the walls of the violated building.

It was impossible to see anything with the room as black as charred wood, but there could be no doubt someone had been inside. The lid to one of the barrels was ajar and two of the muskets had fallen to the floor. Not the same state of disarray as before, but equally alarming.

"Where is Billy now?" Nathaniel whirled around, a bitter curse slamming against the silence. It didn't matter where the idiot was—probably home and in bed. He would get an early visit from Nathaniel.

He spun toward Roger. "How much did they take? Do you know?

"'Twill be too hard to tell in the dark." Thomas stood in the doorway, his broad frame illuminated by the moonlight. "We won't be able to make a proper assessment 'til morning."

"What?" Was Nathaniel the only person who cared what had happened here? "We *can* do something about it and we will do it now!"

"Thomas is right, Nathaniel. We can't risk an explosion by bringing any kind of flame in here for us to see by. We have no choice but to wait until morning." Roger stepped away from the open door, his hands on his hips. "I'll keep watch until dawn. We can decide then what more we can do."

Ducking as he exited the building, Nathaniel froze when his vision narrowed on the exact spot several yards away where he'd found Kitty. Bits of awareness fitted along side the questions still resonating in his mind. Could Kitty have...?

"Roger?"

"Aye?"

Nathaniel patted the man on the back and drove out a harsh sigh. "You did well. I commend you for doing your part and for fetching me the minute you saw something amiss."

"Of course, Doctor." Roger straightened as if the compliment added inches to his small stature.

"Now," Nathaniel continued, "I need you to return home and be with your family."

Roger protested. "But, Doctor 'tis my turn to keep watch—"

"You've done enough, my friend. I shall keep the watch tonight."

"As you say, Doctor." Nodding his farewell, Roger glanced between Nathaniel and Thomas before disappearing into the trees beside the road.

Thomas neared, keeping his voice above a whisper. "You've discovered something."

Nathaniel stared at the ground a minute longer before drawing toward the spot near the trees and resting on his haunches. He pivoted back toward the magazine, his arm across his knee. "I wonder if this is related?"

Thomas knelt beside him. "Related?"

"Kitty's attack."

"You think Kitty's attack is related to the raid?"

Tapping the ground with his fingers, Nathaniel locked a fervid gaze with his friend. "I found her in this very spot. Though we don't yet know how long she was lying here before I came upon her—we may never know—she could have witnessed something and the perpetrators don't want her revealing what she saw."

"That's possible."

"What do you mean 'that's possible'? I believe that's what happened and we must find out with certainty."

Thomas punctured Nathaniel with a glare he'd endured far too many times. "I can see what you're planning, Nathaniel, but take care. Pressing Kitty for a confession will do more harm than good."

Standing, Nathaniel rubbed his thumbs over his

fisted fingers. He burned the ground with his glare, fighting the urge to run back and sit at the edge of Kitty's bed until she disclosed the truth that rested just behind her lips.

Nathaniel raised his eyes to the heavens, conceding that then again, Thomas could well be right.

"If she's as distressed as you say," Thomas continued, "then we must proceed with tenderness and let it come out in time. Kitty has never been one to keep her thoughts to herself for long."

Nathaniel joined Thomas in a fleeting chuckle before his jaw turned solid and his biceps flexed. "I'll stay here. You go home to Eliza and Kitty. They'll be wondering where you are."

"Aye." Thomas nodded. "Take care to stay awake. This is the most trying watch of the night." With a hard pat on Nathaniel's shoulder, Thomas made his way back up the road at a modified run.

Staying awake would be no trouble at all. Walking back to the magazine, Nathaniel's body burned with unqualified rage as he stared into the room that contained the town's life-blood. Who would do this? Who would steal from their own people and threaten an innocent woman?

He slammed the door shut before smacking his palm against the stone.

Turning back to the woods, he stared at the small spot of earth where Kitty had sat wounded not an hour before. She knew something—had been made to suffer something wrenching and though he would need to tread carefully, he had to discover what she knew.

The fate of their freedom might depend on it.

Sunlight filtered in through the window of Kitty's bedchamber, beckoning her to push it open and allow the songs and scents of spring to caress the stale air. Across the room, still abed, Kitty leaned forward, straining to hear Eliza's light footsteps downstairs, but only silence whispered back. She quirked her lips to the side and gauged the distance to the dresser and the open door. If Eliza found her up, Kitty would never hear the end of it. With a huff, she sat back against the soft pillows. She'd been abed for just over twenty-four hours though it seemed like days. The low throbbing of pain had all but vanished and only a dull ache remained in her jaw, the lone remnant of the awful encounter.

The gnawing reality that chewed on her conscience drove every pleasant emotion from her spirit like a breath blows steam from a bowl. Her soul ached as Cyprian's threats rang through her head.

She pressed a hand to her forehead. *Lord, what am I to do?*

"You're up early."

"Thomas!" Kitty jumped at the sound of his voice. "I didn't hear you come up."

He grinned, leaning against the doorframe with his arms crossed. "Awake before nine? Astonishing feat, I must say."

She pulled the shawl tighter around her shoulders, forcing her mouth to stretch upward. "You startled me." She hadn't spoken to him since the incident, or since their ill-fated conversation at the Cooper's party. Her nerves jumped like a rowdy child.

"You look as if you're afraid of me." Thomas

winked and pushed off the wall before coming to sit beside her on the bed. "I'm so sorry about what happened. Both at the party and with..." He motioned to her head where the wound had already begun to heal. "I'm glad you are well. Nay, more than simply glad, Kitty, I'm overjoyed." He paused. "We intend to discover who it was that attacked you, Kitty. We will bring them to justice, I promise you that."

"Thomas, you are too good to me. But I have already made it quite clear. I wasn't attacked."

He thinned his gaze and ran a hand over the cleft in his chin. "Nathaniel is convinced otherwise."

"Well, Nathaniel's wrong." She startled at the strength in her voice. Never had she employed more energy in the production of deceit than she did now. And she would surely be forced to do so again in the days to come. Flooding her features with sincerity, Kitty met Thomas's gaze. "I should never have left the party alone. 'Tis my fault and mine alone."

Looking down, Thomas took her hand and gently gripped. "You must know, Kitty, though you and I may argue from time to time, and I may say some things I ought not, it will never change the way I feel about you. The welcome that we offer you in our home is unconditional. Though Eliza has chosen to support the cause of the patriots, that does not mean we will insist you do the same. We pray you will feel safe here. Both in body and heart."

Tears pressed at the backs of her eyes. Her voice cracked, though she strained against it. "Thank you, Thomas." So many words begged for revelation. So many strivings yearned for unveiling. *I will do my best to keep you and Eliza safe.*

She released her grip and sat straighter. "Speaking

of Liza, where is she?" By this time yesterday she had already been up to plait Kitty's hair and talk of the happy duties they would acquaint themselves with as the day stretched before them.

Thomas's cheeks reddened, but he quickly smiled and turned his head toward the door. "She... she isn't feeling herself this morning, but it's nothing serious. I've taken it upon myself to make sure you are well enough to get out of bed. *If* you are well enough."

"Oh I am, most definitely." Worry needled into her stomach and she ached at Eliza's absence. "You're sure nothing is the matter. She isn't ill?"

"Nay," Thomas said, "I assure you, your sister is quite well." A dreamy look captured his eye before he blinked it away. "If you are feeling recovered then, I suppose you may get out of bed and make yourself useful."

The tease in his voice coaxed a laugh from Kitty's throat. "So *that's* what this is about. You wish to put me to work." She giggled again as he got up from the bed. "I do promise to make myself useful, Thomas. If there is ever anything I can do, please let me know."

Thomas stopped near the door. "Now that you mention it, there is something I am in need of."

"Aye?" The idea of finally escaping the confines of her bed and getting her mind away from the dreadful memories revived Kitty's lagging spirits. Saturday was still four days away, perhaps in that time she could come up with a solution, a way to avoid the deed that Cyprian pressed her into performing.

Thomas pointed downstairs. "There's a bundle that needs to be returned to Nathaniel. Eliza mends his shirts. He says he is down to only two wearable ones—and, I fear she won't be able to deliver them any time soon."

Kitty fumbled desperately for an excuse not to execute his request. The last person she wanted to see was Nathaniel. “Thomas, I’m not sure…”

Half of Thomas’s mouth lifted while his eyes squinted. “Only a few moments ago you couldn’t wait to help. Not going back on your word, are you?”

Kitty pursed her lips when every rebuttal fled her mind. Finally, she shrugged and displayed a grin. “As you wish.”

“Excellent.” Thomas motioned behind him with his thumb. “You’ll want to go to the back door. Nathaniel reserves the front for patients or strangers. If you knock several times with no answer, you may be certain he’s left for the day. He usually gets an early start so I expect the house will be empty. Eliza has made a habit of leaving the bundle on the kitchen table. Rest assured there is nothing untoward about you entering his house in his absence.”

Mercy! Go into his house? “I understand. Thank you.”

Thomas started out the door then paused and pivoted, looking over his shoulder. “You know, Kitty, ‘tis about time someone else started mending Nathaniel’s clothes for him.”

He winked and darted down the stairs before Kitty had time to respond, or to smother the dream of a future her heart so longed to nourish, but one that would never be. Foolish, foolish heart.

Chapter Seven

Bundle in hand, Kitty marched down the street and around the corner, her grip tightening as Nathaniel's home came into view. Mercy! She hadn't known her heart could beat like this. She pressed a hand to her breast and felt the rapid thumping. *Gracious.* No need to be so nervous. Yet, she was.

Approaching his home as one might a den of lions, Kitty's palms began to sweat. 'Twas a simple task. Knock, leave the clothes on the table and escape to the safety of the road. He would not even be home, so why worry?

The clean spring air infused her lungs with a solid coating of courage as the scent of blossoming trees brushed past. Not a single cloud cluttered the brilliant blue sky. The warmth of the sun gently massaged her back and the cheery song of the birds almost made her forget her worries, until her shoes rested on the back step of Nathaniel's two story home.

A minute passed. Then two. The longer she stared at the door the more it seemed to loom higher and wider as if it hoped to frighten her away.

Kitty inhaled and shook her head until the childish imagining vanished. With bravery securely in place, she rapped her knuckles against the door and waited. Tapping her fingers against the bundle in her arms, she looked around. No answer, not even a sound from within. She knocked again, this time warily peeking into the partially open window beside the door. After another full minute passed and when she was sure not a sound emerged from the house, she sucked in a deep breath, twisted the door's cool, bronze handle in her clammy palm and entered.

Instantly the scent of a day-old fire and fresh soap stole her attention. So this was how Nathaniel lived? The tidy house was warm and inviting. The richness of the furnishings startled her almost as much as the way her heart seemed to find rest the moment her feet tapped against the floor.

A peculiar tickling sensation started in her chest. What did the rest of the house look like? How did he keep his parlor? Did he hang paintings of family on his walls? Clutching the bag closer, Kitty sighed. Curiosity was natural, but hazardous. *Focus, Kitty.*

Instead of heeding her own wise counsel, she stepped further into the room, her eyes scanning the masculine space. A few moments wouldn't hurt. How could it when no one was home?

Gathering her surroundings, she surmised the room she stood in must be his study. A large bookcase hugged one wall, while a stern fireplace occupied the other. Medical books of every width and breadth were strewn hap-hazardly atop a large desk, as were diagrams of human anatomy that reminded her of the ones she'd seen as a child on Father's desk. A large chair waited, ready to receive its master. Her imagination began a healthy exercise and she smiled. How many hours in the evening did Nathaniel read in that chair with his cravat untied and rugged whiskers scattered across his jaw? A robust fire in the fireplace, a glass of cider on the table perhaps? Did he like living alone? Did he ever get lonely?

Did he ever wish for a wife?

Silly girl! Quickly locating the kitchen, she deposited the bundle on the table next to a sack of dried apple slices and silently made her way to the back door through the study, then stopped.

Nathaniel's desk whispered to her in Father's own warm tone. Her throat thickened at the bittersweet memory. How many hours had she spent at Father's side asking him about conditions, why the body did this and that and what would help? So many. The desire to study medicine and assist patients had burned within her like an unquenchable fire from the earliest days of her youth. But she knew she would never attain her wish. Medical school was not a place for a woman.

She blinked back the surge of emotions that flooded forward.

"Sweet girl," Father would say with a smile as he tweaked her chin, "you needn't study medicine to practice it. You can heal others with nothing more than your smile."

Father, I miss you more than words can say. I promise to make you proud, to live worthy of what you taught me. In every way.

Mindful of her surroundings, Kitty ran her fingers over the thick books on the corner of the desk and cocked her head when one familiar book peeked out from under a rather precariously placed oil lamp. Excitement bubbled. It looked just like a book her father had studied. Curiosity snuffed out the last remaining urge to leave, and after a hasty look around the room she lifted the lamp and slid the book from its resting place.

The clomp of footsteps thumped on the ceiling above. Kitty gasped. The lamp slipped from her hands and crashed to the desk, the glass slicing her finger as it fell.

"Who's there?" Nathaniel's deep voice drove through every nerve in Kitty's body and screamed at her to flee.

He was supposed to be gone!

Kitty stumbled backward, dashing for the safety of the back door just as Nathaniel ran down the stairs.

She caught only a glimpse of him as she escaped. His shirt, untucked and untied revealed his sculpted chest. His hair, though held behind his head, looked so handsomely disheveled her stomach turned weightless. She should never have come! If Thomas had anticipated such an encounter he would get more than an earful come supper.

Kitty darted down the back steps and toward the road, but not before Nathaniel's strong hand grabbed her arm, spinning her to face him.

"Kitty!" His fingers held firm yet gentle, and his hazel eyes scanned her in one quick sweep. "What in heaven's name are you doing here? Are you all right?"

Nathaniel peered at her with such unreserved concern her knees turned weak. His freshly shaven face looked smoother and more angled than she'd ever seen it. His gaze threaded with hers, striking down any power she might have exerted to resist him.

Once her mouth opened to respond it refused to shut and her words strung together into a giant, tangled mess. "Nathaniel, please forgive me. Thomas promised you wouldn't be home and he asked me to deliver your shirts for you since Eliza wasn't able to do it—and I assure you I wasn't snooping, I was simply intrigued by your medical books and then when I heard you upstairs I was so startled I dropped your lamp—oh! Your lamp! I'm so sorry, I promise to replace it and your medical books—"

"Slow down, Kitty." Nathaniel's disarming smile reached out and bathed her distress in its gentleness. "I don't care about the lamp or the books. I was just surprised when I heard—" He stopped mid sentence and tugged at her hand. A frown pulled at his brow. "You're bleeding."

Swallowing, Kitty did her best not to think about the warmth of his skin against hers. She felt not even the slightest pain. "'Tis nothing. I shall bandage it when I get home."

"No. We shall bandage it now."

The feel of Kitty's delicate skin against Nathaniel's rough hands stilled the earth as he took in her wide eyes and red cheeks. The last thing he'd expected to hear was someone in his study, but the *very* last thing he expected was for that person to be the woman who had occupied his mind ever since the patriot party at Andrew's.

Her wounds from that night's attack—the cut on her head and the redness of her jaw seemed improved already, and if the ever-heightening color in her face was any indication, she felt much better, thank the Lord. He wanted to laugh, but kept it tamped down. Kitty looked so bewitching when she blushed.

He took her elbow and led her inside, directing her to the small room off the study where he conducted procedures.

"Sit down and allow me to have a look at that cut."

Helping her to sit, he grabbed his stool and scooted it in front of her before reaching for his ample supply of ready-made bandages. "So," he said, allowing a smirk to grow across his face. "You claim you weren't snooping, and yet you were deliberately looking through articles on my desk. Very suspect, I must say."

She refused to meet his gaze and he strangled the chuckle that wished for escape. He had to tease her a bit more. "I'm surprised at you, Kitty. I thought you were above such things."

Kitty tried to tug her hand away and her tone tightened. "I really wasn't, Nathaniel, I—"

"Quiet now and stay still."

Keeping a stern look in his eyes he allowed a small quirk at the corner of his mouth. She pulled her bottom lip between her teeth and looked away, and suddenly the desire to scoot his stool closer swelled beyond the bounds of its levy. With a quick shake of his head, he ignored it. Nearly.

Nathaniel pulled her injured hand closer. Lost in the feel of her skin against his, every sense of teasing faded. He took a long inhale of the scent of cinnamon that always seemed to follow her and regained focus on her injury. Fairly deep, and though the blood oozed steadily, 'twas nothing serious. With a flick of his wrist he opened the bandage with one hand, applied pressure, and started wrapping.

Wriggling, Kitty sat straighter. "I'm... I'm so sorry, Nathaniel. I feel simply terrible about the lamp, and soiling your books and papers with all that oil. I do hope you can forgive me." Her silken voice draped around him like a fond embrace.

Must she be so charming?

"Forgive you?" He pulled back, fighting the yearnings with a strong measure of humor. "I'm not sure I can."

He almost regretted taking his jesting so far when her chin popped up and her dainty brows pinched low. "Nathaniel, I..." She started to protest, then humphed back in her seat with the most delightful twist on her lips.

Nathaniel erupted in laughter while Kitty's pert mouth curved sideways into a smile that stroked his masculine pride.

He sighed, calming his jubilant nature. "Think nothing of it, Kitty. There is very little damage done."

He finished wrapping her hand, and almost released her fingers. Almost. They were so delicate and soft, he wanted to memorize the feel of her hand upon his should such a moment never again present itself. Reluctantly, he let go and brushed his palms against his knees in an effort to sweep away the disarming sensation of her touch.

Kitty kept her mouth tight. "I promise to find a way to replace what I have damaged, Nathaniel. I remember how my father treasured his own books and how often he referred to them." Her gaze trailed toward the study as a wistful look brightened her eyes. She rubbed at her bandaged hand. "I would sit by Father's side for hours on end as he made notes in his journal and told me about the patients he'd seen, and..." Her voice faded and she looked at him with a wistful smile. "I decided I would follow in his footsteps, but of course such a thing could never be."

Nathaniel stood then leaned back against the table, staring at the woman who continued to reveal herself in pieces. And he continued to be enchanted. "Kitty, I hadn't any idea you were so interested in doctoring." Just as the words left his mouth, a rushing flood of vivid memories poured into his mind. She'd cared for Eliza after her tragic attack so skillfully, how had he not noticed? And after being shot in the shoulder two winters past, Nathaniel might have suffered far worse had Kitty's natural instincts not led her to care for him so handily.

Unconsciously, he rubbed the site of the scar on his shoulder. "You have an excellent talent for healing, Kitty. 'Tis unfortunate it is not accepted that women study medicine."

She stood and turned away with a shrug and a petite laugh, stepping toward the study. "Aye, 'tis too bad I'm a woman I suppose."

"I'll wager Mr. *Pigley* would say otherwise."

She peeked over her shoulder with a smile in her eyes that teased as much as her words. "I will forever regret speaking his name in your presence. And it's Higley, not Pigley."

He leaned forward and squinted. "I'm sorry, I didn't hear you. What was that?"

She shook her head with a breathy laugh and started toward the back door. Nathaniel followed her down the steps.

"Thank you for caring for my hand," she said.

"Of course."

She stopped and turned into the sunlight, her dark hair glowing with touches of deep red. "And I *will* find a way to make up for the damages Nathaniel, I promise."

"Aye, you must." As if pulled by an ethereal rope,

he moved closer. "And I know exactly how you will do it."

"Do you?" Her large eyes blinked and her voice whispered of unspoken wishes. "How... how is that?"

Negligent of the warning that rang in his ears, he moved another step closer as the urge to pull her near made his hands ache. His eyes grazed her lips as he kissed her already in his mind. *Fool! What are you thinking?* Blinking, he retraced the conversation to find his place. He cleared his throat. "I will be at supper tomorrow and I request a dish of your delectable carrot pudding."

Her eyes danced as the sun kissed her face and her exhaled breath almost sang of relief. "'Tis not the season for carrots, you know that." A sweet feminine laugh floated around his shoulders, beckoning him another step closer until their shoes nearly touched. She blinked again and continued though her words came slow and measured. "But, I shall try to find something I can make that will be equally enticing." She paused and swallowed, her voice airy. "Will you require more in payment?"

"To be honest, there is more."

She stalled. "There is?"

A kiss.

Once again his vision narrowed on her mouth. But before writing a passage in the story of his life he would most certainly regret, he pushed that persistent thought away and kept his expression blank, knowing she would detect the jesting lilt in his voice. "I expect you to make carrot pudding every time I come to supper, when carrots are plentiful, and deliver my mending every Saturday."

Kitty's face suddenly went white and she stilled as if her blood had turned to ice. She crossed her arms and looked toward the street. Had his comment been so upsetting?

He reprimanded himself for becoming lost in the moment and tried to bring back the levity. "Of course if that is too great a request, I might be willing to consider negotiations."

Her expression didn't change. *Blast*. He flicked his fingers against his leg. It hadn't even been two days since her attack and she was likely still suffering the effects. He should have sent her home long ago.

She hugged her arms closer and glanced at the street again then smiled as if she were trying to restore the former merriment between them, but the air sat so heavy Nathaniel could have snipped it with sheers.

"Your requests are reasonable, however..." With a small nod, she looked down. "I'm sure you would not want the people of this town knowing you have befriended a Tory." The pain in her voice pierced his chest and wormed its way into his heart.

With a small curtsy she started toward the road.

"Kitty, stop." Without thinking, he took her elbow and pulled her to a halt. He lifted her chin until her gaze met his. "I've hardly slept since that night, knowing the way I spoke to you."

He brushed the backs of his fingers against her soft cheek and his heart slammed against his ribs. *Stop!* But he couldn't. Her pull was too powerful, and the look of yearning in her blue-green eyes drew him into their enchanted depths. "I promise that you being a Tory makes no difference to me—not to our friendship. I shall do my best to keep my mouth quiet on such issues from this time forth, but I can make no promises. You know me well enough to understand that."

"I understand," she whispered. Kitty's breathing shuddered and she licked her lips until they resembled dew-kissed strawberries just waiting to be sampled. Suddenly he wanted nothing more than a taste of her mouth. He leaned forward, entranced, desperate to know if her kiss would be as sweet as he imagined.

Kitty's limbs went numb and she parted her lips as her breathing turned erratic.

Nathaniel's warm hand moved from her cheek to the back of her neck and his eyes focused on her lips.

Her mouth went dry.

He leaned closer, moving his other hand around her waist and pulling her to him.

Could this be real? Kitty's heart twirled in her chest and she closed her eyes, feeling his warm breath on her face. The emotions she'd carefully concealed so long ago hurled from their hiding place and basked in the sunny-warmth of desire. She need only lift to her toes...

Foolish, girl! What are you thinking?

Gasping, she pushed away as if she had just escaped a whirlpool. Heaving, she stared at Nathaniel's wide eyes and parted lips. This couldn't happen. Nathaniel attracted every available woman in town. Kissing him would change Kitty forever—but it would do nothing to him.

She stepped backward. "I... I need to be going."

When she stepped away, Nathaniel's expression pushed down and his lips pressed together almost as if he regretted the distance.

Nathaniel shifted his weight, speaking in such an even tone and with such a wry smile, 'twas as if he had not nearly touched his mouth to hers. "I'll be expecting something delicious tomorrow night."

A nervous giggle tickled her throat. "You shall have it." She nodded her good-bye and started toward the road.

It took ridiculous concentration to put one foot in front of the other. She could feel his eyes at her back and picked up her pace. Why did he watch her?

Reaching the road, she almost ran for the bend where the trees would mask her from Nathaniel's view when a raspy voice called for her from behind.

"There you are, Miss Campbell. I've been waiting for you."

Cyprian's malice-laden tone scraped across her like pointed nails.

She jerked to a stop and spun, holding her arms at her sides. Glaring, she kept her mouth tight as she spoke. "I have nothing to say to you."

Flicking her gaze to where Nathaniel had been, she exhaled. Thankfully, he had gone back inside.

Cyprian's dark gaze thinned and he laughed. "Aye, but I have much to say to you."

Courage rising, she pinched her lips. "Nothing I care to hear, I assure you."

"I fear you have no choice." He led her forward as if they were good friends, but his rock-like fingers gouged into the tender under-flesh of her arm. "There may be prying eyes, so act as if all is well. Walk beside me, and listen."

Kitty's heart thrashed in protest, but she did as commanded, focusing on the small rocks and clods of dirt in the ground as she walked.

"You have only a few days left," he said. "As I

already instructed, I will expect you to pick up the basket I leave for you at my tavern and deliver it to a small cabin across town."

"But I don't know where—"

"I will take you there now."

Her hands trembled and she held her jaw together to keep from screaming.

Cyprian tipped his hat at a passing rider. "Good day."

As he took her through town, every passing shopper, every carriage seemed to slow and their glaring eyes latched onto her as if they suspected her impending betrayal.

Cyprian continued speaking as they passed the shoemaker's at the opposite edge of town. "No one will suspect what you will be carrying in your little basket, now will they? That is the excitement of it."

Pushing her forward onto a hidden path, Kitty scanned the wooded area for any sign of the cabin, but it wasn't until they'd walked in painful quiet for several more minutes that it finally came into view.

Nestled amongst a scattering of trees, the forlorn cabin begged for attention. The windows were void of glass and the narrow door was ajar, beckoning anyone who may, to come inside and soothe its loneliness.

"I will expect the basket to be taken no later than a quarter past two in the afternoon and be delivered within the hour." Cyprian paused. "If you fail to do this, I will make certain you never forget again."

Unbidden, the question tumbled from Kitty's mouth before she could stop it. "Why can't *you* deliver it? Your threats upon my family are enough to keep me silent. Why force me to do the work you could do yourself?"

His wiry lips curled upward. "Because this is what I want. And you, Miss Campbell, are in no position to question me."

Cyprian stood in the doorway of the abandoned cabin and watched the terrified girl dash through the trees toward the road. Satisfaction twitched at his mouth. Good. She needed to be afraid of him.

The birds twittered in the trees and the sun glimmered off the newly birthed leaves. Like an apparition, his past whirled around him until he could almost believe it was twenty years ago and he and Camilla had just finished building this cabin.

He turned and looked around the abandoned one-room shelter and his spirit groaned. All the happy memories they had created in this place. All the smiles and pleasant evenings spent in front of the fire, reading or listening to Camilla sing. His throat thickened. Jacob had been born here, had toddled and babbled here, and had given his parents more joy than they'd believed capable in a world now so full of sorrow.

A breeze brushed past, rustling a pile of dry leaves in the corner and the memories vanished as the present gripped his throat. Cyprian pressed out a quiet, bitter laugh.

Brushing a hand along his unshaven jaw he struggled to choke back the emotions that attempted to suffocate. Camilla was his life's breath. She'd loved him when no one else ever truly had. Grinding his teeth, Cyprian groaned. Anything—any sacrifice, any crime, any sin was worth what it took to keep her with him a little while longer. He needed his wife, and Jacob needed his mother.

Cyprian moved out the door and down the steps looking behind him one last time. At least he could come here every Saturday—and relive the happy memories. For surely only mournful ones awaited him.

Chapter Eight

Why did dinner at the Watson's have his insides turning upside down and then back up again? Gads. And 'twas as if his fingers were the size of potatoes from the way he had to keep fussing with his cravat that refused to tie properly. He glanced at the clock on the dresser again before fastidiously fastening his hair behind his head for the tenth time. They would be expecting him within the hour.

Sighing, he shook his head. The kiss he'd almost shared with Kitty yesterday had robbed every thought since. The nervous excitement that circled his limbs kept every muscle weightless and somehow simultaneously heavy. He pushed out a quick breath and stepped back from the mirror to assess his appearance from a distance. Well, not the picture of masculine perfection that he'd like, but it would do. He always seemed to receive the greatest amount of smiles from passing ladies when he wore this navy suit, so perhaps Kitty would... Blast!

He spun for the door and started down the stairs as the bothersome thoughts continued to tickle his mind. Had she wanted it too? The kiss? It seemed so. Thankfully she'd been the stronger one and moved away before their fate was sealed. For surely if he *had* kissed her, it would have been the end of him.

Snatching his tricorn from his desk he marched out the backdoor and started down the road. *Get a hold of yourself, man.* The last thing he needed was to pin his desires on a woman that would only bring heartache. He'd promised himself he would wed a woman who believed the same as he—that his marriage would be united. Unlike his parents had been. His heart still cringed at the memories of his father's heated words and his mother's quiet rebuttals. The pain such recollections pulled from the depths of his past assaulted him, the immature Nathaniel being quickly placated by the man he'd become. Never again would he have to endure the lack of love caused by hearts that refused to become one. He intended to keep that promise for the sake of his present, and his future.

Once on the stoop of the Watson home he stomped his heels to kick the dust off his shoes. He straightened his jacket again before swinging the door open and entering, flooding his tone with his usual zeal.

"Good evening, all."

The warm room was empty. Only the crackling fire and waiting furniture greeted him. His perfect posture dropped half an inch. So much for a triumphal entry.

He closed the door and removed his hat. "Did you all hear I was coming and decide to hide?"

"Good evening, Nathaniel." Kitty stepped into the parlor from the kitchen, removing her striped apron to reveal a yellow, rose-dotted dress that molded to her curves in a way Nathaniel hadn't thought possible. Simple ringlets bobbed at her neck and an alluring grin threatened to topple his well-placed line of defense.

"Good evening, lovely lady." Extinguishing every spark of emotion with the skill of a perfect marksman, Nathaniel draped himself in his cloak of dramatic charm and bowed deeply. He closed his eyes and inhaled through his nose. "Aw, Kitty, you have done it again. All I must do is savor that aroma to know this evening's meal will very likely be the best I've ever tasted." If he stayed jocular he wouldn't be at risk of succumbing to the emotions that toyed with him so carelessly.

Kitty rolled her eyes and started toward the fire. "Oh, Nathaniel. You're always full of exaggerated compliments, though I thank you just the same." The grin behind her eyes toyed with his humor.

"Are you calling me a liar, Miss Campbell?" He stepped forward.

Her lips twitched as if she held back a smile that yearned for exposure. "Should I be?"

Before Nathaniel could respond, Thomas descended the stairs, followed by Eliza.

"Ah, Nathaniel, there you are," Thomas said.

Nathaniel exchanged shoulder smacks with his friend. "Did you begin to think I wasn't coming? I'm early."

"Aren't you always?" Eliza produced a smile to accompany her slight giggle. She sat in the chair opposite the small table between she and Nathaniel. Her typically fair complexion appeared more peeked than usual and Nathaniel's medical training shoved to the forefront.

"Forgive me Eliza, but are you well? You look pale."

Eliza peered up at Thomas who stood beside her. She nodded at him and he nodded in return.

Thomas reached for her hand and rubbed it between both of his. "We... we've been reluctant to share this news until we knew for certain, but it seems enough time has passed."

Eliza sat straighter in the chair, a grin on her face to brighten even the darkening sky that peeked through the windows. "I am with child."

Kitty's jaw dropped and her hands flew to her mouth as a delighted squeal peeled through the room. She flew to Eliza's side. "Oh Liza! I'm so happy for you! Praise the Lord!"

"Well done, my good man." Nathaniel thumped Thomas on the back.

Thomas shook his head and chuckled, looking back briefly at his wife. "Thank you. I do believe this is only the beginning of our joy."

"I should say it is, Thomas."

Kitty pushed to standing and knit her fingers over her stomacher, a dreamy smile painting her bright face. "A baby." She beamed and sat in the chair nearest her sister. "So this is why you didn't come to see me the other morning." Sniggling, she pressed her hands into her lap and glanced at Thomas. "I suppose it is a very good thing I returned when I did. When the baby comes Thomas will be so beside himself with glee he won't be worth the two hands he has to offer."

Eliza and Thomas chuckled, and Nathaniel's chest warmed. He stared at Kitty as she exchanged sly looks and blithesome smiles with her sister and brother-in-law. The room melted away and all he could see was Kitty. Her dark hair and yellow dress, her wide smile and blue-green eyes shining like a summer sea as she laughed. If only her convictions weren't so... so wrong. He'd never known a woman of such beauty and gentle grace to have such a spark of life. She possessed a passion that simmered within her like the embers of a fire that never fully die, and when revived, bring flames as high as the heavens.

Just then her eyes landed on him and his heart cantered, spilling out the unwanted emotions. They would be a terrible match. Despite his penchant for a hearty debate and his tolerance for those of differing views, his zeal for freedom could never acquiesce enough to allow a binding relationship with a Tory.

Friendship. That would have to be enough.

Nathaniel cleared his throat. "'Twas only a matter of time until you came back, was it not, Kitty? Who can stay away when there are friends and family like us to be had? We *are* the most delightful people in all of Massachusetts."

"That we are." Eliza nodded and tossed a playful smile at Kitty.

Kitty opened her mouth, but a knock at the door stopped the conversation where it stood.

Thomas raised his brows and shrugged before he went to the door and opened it.

A young man in a weather-battered jacket and breeches stood at the stoop, his hair wild under his dust-covered hat. "Is this the Watson residence?"

"Aye, I'm Thomas Watson."

"Excellent." He offered a quick, slight bow. "I am here to deliver a letter to Miss Katherine Campbell."

Kitty jumped at the sound of her name. *Me?*

Thomas nodded a thank you at the man and took the letter. The courier stepped away from the door and was astride his horse once again, thundering into the dusk.

Kitty couldn't move. All eyes converged on her. No one said a word, but they didn't have to. The unspoken questions in their faces—brows high, mouths lined with the hint of what might have been smiles—expressed their curiosity far better than any words could have done.

Thomas neared and handed her the note. "Were you expecting a letter?"

"Nay." For truly, she wasn't.

The instant the paper rested in her hands she battled the blood that rushed to her face. The handwriting was unmistakable. *Higley.*

She looked up and smiled, tucking the letter in her pocket. Maintaining a composed manner when she spoke proved more challenging than she'd expected. "'Tis nothing. I will read it after supper."

"Nay, Kitty, read it now. We shall wait for you." Eliza's one raised brow made Kitty's stomach flip. Did she suspect? She must. There were no relations with whom communications were expected.

Feigning indifference, the three witnesses converged in front of the fire, leaving Kitty alone near the door of the kitchen to read the missive. With a quick snap she broke the seal and unfolded the paper. Her hands turned clammy and her stomach refused to cease its tumbling, forcing her to take refuge in the nearest chair.

Dearest Miss Campbell,

I have only just heard the news that you have left Boston. I am both pleased and saddened. Pleased, because I wish for nothing but your safety and happiness; saddened for I wonder why you would have chosen to leave when you know I am away and cannot kneel before you and plead with you, with all the energy of my heart, to stay.

Kitty's cheeks burned. When had he learned of this? She'd planned on sending him word of her return to Sandwich as soon as she could, but there hadn't yet been time. Releasing a breath through circled lips, she stole a quick glance at the others and breathed a mite easier. They were well engrossed in conversation, thank the Lord. Assured the moment remained private, she continued on.

You must know that my feelings for you have not dimmed, rather in your absence have grown and filled my heart with such longing it pains me to imagine a life without you by my side. That evening not so many weeks ago, as I held you in my arms, I knew I belonged with you, and you with me. I plead with you, dearest Kitty, let me know that your heart reflects my own so that you and I may be husband and wife and find everlasting joy in each other's embrace forever.

Yours, James Higley.

Kitty rubbed her brow. Another proposal. *Dear James. What am I to do?*

"Is everything all right, Kitty?"

The sound of Eliza's voice forced Kitty to spin on her seat and she dropped her hand to her lap instantly refolding the letter.

"Aye, indeed." She stood and almost spoke again, but perhaps protesting overmuch would bring even more unwanted attention.

Eliza's expression piqued to her hairline and she held in reserve a smile that surely meant what Kitty suspected. She held back a growl. Her sister would receive a scolding if her probing caused the conversation to continue. Kitty forced her shoulders to relax and her neck muscles to soften. Feigning serenity would be her only salvation this evening. Smiling, she made a point to meet Thomas's gaze. He had only one brow quirked in question. She braved a glance at Nathaniel. His features were more drawn even though an encouraging grin lifted one side of his mouth.

"No need to question so deeply with your eyes, all is well." Giggling, she plunged the letter in the pocket of her skirt hoping they would join the repartee. "Should we not begin supper?" She motioned to the kitchen and held her breath.

The three exchanged fleeting glances. Did they not believe her?

Thomas cleared his throat and nodded with a step toward the kitchen, but Eliza would not be so easily persuaded.

"Have you... have you had word from someone? Someone you knew in Boston?"

Once again Kitty's face began to burn and the grasp she had on her composure released a fraction. Oh, why didn't she possess the ability to hide one's true emotions?

When she didn't answer Eliza stepped closer, a tender softness in her eyes at last replacing the teasing. "I won't press you to tell something you wish to keep secret." She patted Kitty's arm and crossed to the kitchen door. "That is unless it has anything to do with a young man."

A sudden edgy laugh erupted from Kitty's chest.

No!

Thomas tugged lightly on her elbow. "Has someone been courting you, Kitty?" The question was both merry and sincere, matching the brightness in his eyes.

Kitty stared, wilting under the heat of every pair of eyes that rested on her. The embarrassment clung to her like a wet chemise. If only she could sprout wings and fly from the room—from the house even—and find a quiet place to shed her humiliation in peace.

Nathaniel stepped forward, his hazel stare stealing her ability to move. His mouth bowed wide. "I do believe I might know the name of this mystery suitor."

"Truly?" Eliza stared first at Nathaniel then at Kitty. "Is it true, Kitty? Someone has been courting you?"

Kitty pinched her lips and glared at Nathaniel just long enough for his face to express a satisfaction she wanted to smother. She flooded her voice with calm when she turned to Eliza. "I had planned on telling you—"

"This is such a surprise!" Eliza flung to her side. "Who is he? How long have you known him?"

Kitty licked her lips and shrugged. Better answer her sister's question now and have done with it regardless of who was in the room.

She quickly met both Thomas's and Eliza's questioning glances before beginning. If she looked at Nathaniel she might fire more imaginary arrows, and that might make him more self-satisfied, so she artfully averted her gaze.

"I met James Higley the day I returned to Boston after your marriage. I was getting out of the carriage in front of Aunt Grace's home when I slipped on the ice and would have fallen had he not been there." She turned to Eliza. "I will admit I was smitten at first. He was such a gentleman, and looked so dashing in his red uniform. He asked if he could come to call the next evening. Somehow after that he managed to come by every Sunday afternoon." She should have been more reserved, but somehow she included those details, not wanting to believe she did it to bring a bit of discomfort to Nathaniel, no matter how true it was.

Thomas lifted and lowered his shoulders. "So he's a soldier then?"

Kitty nodded. "Aye."

Eliza squeezed Kitty's hand. "He came by every Sunday for a year? I should say, if that doesn't indicate his affections, I don't know what does." The smile-lines around Eliza's mouth deepened. "Are you still smitten with him?"

Kitty could feel the cut of Nathaniel's razor-sharp stare. What did he think of all of this? Of course she shouldn't care what he thought. Yet she did, and certainly didn't want to look at him, but somehow her gaze collided with his, sending heat of another kind cascading down her skin. No emotion rested on his angled face, but the coded questions in his eyes burned and she fumbled over her words.

"Nay, I... I'm not. He is... he is a very good man, truly, but he tried too hard to impress me with his money, his status and relations—things that matter so little. And he pressed his attentions upon me too quickly for my comfort."

Nathaniel's jaw muscles flexed and he shifted in his seat, sharing a pointed look with Thomas.

Thomas wriggled in his collar as if trying to calm

a rising emotion. "Did he act without propriety?"

"Nay," Kitty said, "never anything like that. He was a perfect gentleman. He simply shared his affections more openly than I cared to do."

"Did he kiss you?" Eliza's giddy smile matched the sparkle in her voice.

"Liza!" Kitty jerked back.

"Oh forgive me, I shouldn't have asked such." Eliza's expression softened. "We can speak of this later."

Eliza's confession was well meant, but the damage was done. A sheet of humiliation dropped over Kitty's head and draped her frame until she thought she might droop under the weight of it. She darted a quick look at Thomas before daring a glance at Nathaniel. His elbow rested on the arm of the chair with his chin perched in his palm. Eyes round, his eyebrows shot upward as if repeating the question Eliza had just asked.

"Well, did he?" Thomas said, dropping his hands to his sides.

Kitty pulled her shoulders back and opened her mouth to defend herself, but Eliza spoke first.

"Don't press her, Thomas. I should never have asked such a personal question." Eliza took Kitty's hand and lowered her voice. "Don't be distressed. We are family here and we care for you, that is all."

Nathaniel certainly wasn't family. And he certainly didn't need to participate in such a personal exposition of her affairs. A splash of irritation coated her heated skin.

Thomas's accusatory stare hardened, but he let the embarrassing question fade. After releasing a long breath, he shifted his feet. "So, who were the relations this man hoped to impress you with?

Thomas Hutchinson and family?"

The former governor of Massachusetts would be a noble relation indeed. At least in the mind of a Tory. However, Thomas and Nathaniel certainly wouldn't think it any sort of honor. Had he intended to tease her or did he ask to extract more serious information about James?

Kitty tried to take a deep inhale, but her stays pulled tighter as the conversation progressed. She lifted her chin, trying to summon the courage behind her heart. "He is the nephew of General Thomas Gage and a lieutenant in His Majesty's Army."

A tremendous silence owned the room. Thomas and Nathaniel shared shocked expressions before Thomas's face coiled in disgust. "You can't be serious."

"I most certainly am." Kitty tried to breathe, but the task grew ever more daunting. "Do you think that's something about which I would jest?"

Eliza shifted her feet and looked between the two men, demanding with her eyes that they remain silent. "Kitty, do you know who General Gage is?"

Kitty flinched and scowled before regaining composure. Why did everyone insist on speaking to her as if she were completely unaware of the political goings on? "I am perfectly aware of who General Gage is, and it seems as though you are more impressed by him than I."

"Impressed? Hardly." Nathaniel pushed out of the chair and paced the length of the room. "That man is as repulsive as they come, Kitty. He's King George's personal puppet and more eager than any to smear the colony with the blood of his own countrymen." He shook his head, pounding his feet harder with every step. Suddenly he stopped and pointed at

Thomas, his voice raw and deep. "I wouldn't be surprised if Gage is somehow coordinating the robbing of our powder."

The powder.

Suddenly the room swayed. Kitty grasped the seat beside her. Was Gage the one giving orders to Cyprian? She breathed through her mouth to try and keep herself from fainting. Though she would never agree with the patriot's cause, how could she possibly be involved in something so horribly wrong—by force or no?

Yet, how could she *not* with such threats against those she loved? *Lord, what am I to do?*

Thomas stepped back and dropped into his seat, rubbing his forehead. "All I can say is I am grateful beyond my ability to express that you are no longer smitten with this James Higley."

The malice in Thomas's voice snapped Kitty back to the present. "Why? Because if I were you would be forced to refuse my staying with you? Are my political sentiments equally *repulsive*?"

Fists clenched, Nathaniel pulled his broad shoulders back. "The matters at hand are much more grave than you think they are, Kitty."

An unpleasant spinning sensation turned her stomach to rock. How dare Nathaniel speak to her that way? He had no idea how much she knew and how it pained her. "I know more than you think, I simply choose to recognize my place and honor the way I was raised."

"Nay. By ignoring what is happening around you, you release yourself from having to accept something you might actually believe, because if you believe it you would be forced to acknowledge your mistakes and change your position."

"Nathaniel, I—"

"Open your eyes, Kitty. While we patriots strive for freedom, the king and his subservient Tories look to destroy our liberties, and General Gage is at the center of those actions in these colonies."

The accusation in his face stabbed through Kitty like a dull table knife. Struggling to cling to the remains of her fading confidence, Kitty lifted her chin and clutched the chair. "I've already told you, but I will say it again. I may hold to different beliefs, but I will not go against your cause because that is the way my dear father raised me." Rallied by her own words, Kitty stood taller. "In short, while you scamper about and struggle to secure your *freedoms*, I in turn, will abstain from involvement and will have peace in my decision."

"That is where your ignorance is most painfully apparent." Nathaniel's angled features hardened and his eyes turned dark. "For apathy, dear Kitty, is the greatest enemy of peace."

Not even Kitty's sudden intake of breath or the flash of pain that turned her bright eyes a lifeless blue could convert Nathaniel's pulsing frustrations to regret. How could she possibly be so ensnared by falsehoods? Kitty was too wise for that. Her father had been one of the bravest patriots in Boston, completely devoted to the cause, and yet she refused to believe the truth.

Without another word, she covered her quivering mouth and dashed upstairs. A loud wham of the door resonated through the otherwise quiet room entombing them in silence. Eliza shot up from her chair. Her eyes drilled through Thomas first than Nathaniel before she too darted upstairs.

Nathaniel's chest heaved and he marched the length of the parlor. He opened his mouth to speak, but Thomas's downcast stare and rounded posture blocked off his words like a gag. Stopping, Nathaniel wiped a hand over his face. The weight of the missing powder grew until it seemed every small black spec stolen from the magazine weighed as much as the stones from which it was built.

He sighed as the unshed tears in Kitty's eyes smacked him away from his dreary thoughts and back to the parlor. Turning, he looked at Thomas. "I didn't say anything that wasn't true."

Thomas slumped into the chair behind him. "I know."

"She took my words too personal."

"Did you not mean it to be personal?" Thomas peered up at him from beneath a raised brow.

Pride was a most difficult thing to shed. Nathaniel dropped into the other large chair and groaned. "She's an educated woman and her lack of passion for this most vital cause makes my stomach turn."

"You can't force someone to come to this. They must accept it in their time." Thomas leaned forward and rested his elbows on his knee. "Eliza changed. Kitty will too."

Nathaniel shook his head and breathed out a mocking laugh. "I admire your faith in her, but you seem to forget that Eliza *wanted* to know. Kitty does not."

'Twas then Eliza emerged, her lip between her teeth and her head slightly bowed. Nathaniel and Thomas stood the moment she entered the parlor.

"What's wrong?" Thomas asked.

"She's beside herself. She won't even speak to me."

Thomas offered Eliza his chair and Nathaniel joined him in front of the hearth.

Only the popping sparks and the occasional brush of clothing sounded in the silent room. Nathaniel's still pumping pulse scooped the unpleasant realities from his memory. "General Gage is an enormous threat. She has to know how dangerous he is."

Thomas shifted his weight. "Powerful, yes, but I'm not sure about dangerous. The man's a fop."

"That may be true, but the threat he creates is undeniable." Nathaniel moved around and stood behind the empty chair, pressing his hands against the top of it. "Our munitions are vital. I believe that man is behind the raids at the magazine and it is distressing to see someone like Kitty take so little interest in something that affects us all."

"She cares." Eliza stared at the floor and her voice was sullen. "We must be patient and have faith that in time she will come to see the truth as we have."

Sighing, Nathaniel gripped the back of the chair even harder. He looked toward the stairs then refocused on his clenched knuckles. A strange feeling of relief—and at the same time, distress—nestled in his spirit. If Kitty never accepted the cause, then he never had to worry about losing his heart to her and risk the associated pain. If she did, all the better for the cause, and all the more dangerous for him.

Hot tears cascaded down Kitty's cheeks and

plunked onto her hands. Though the muffled voices from downstairs were all but whispers, the truth chopped like a freshly sharpened cleaver. They were talking about her.

Pushing up from the bed, Kitty clenched her fists and marched to the small table in the corner. She pulled out the chair and sat, then snatched James's letter from her pocket and flattened it against the cool wood of the desk. The candle flickered, illuminating James's elegant penmanship. His handsome face hovered before her as she read the words again. Resting her elbow on the table she leaned her head on her hand.

It was clear, wasn't it? Accepting James would be impetuous, but keeping that window open, should situations here prove unbearable, would be wise. She slumped her head down into the crook of her arm. Father would have liked James. He supported the king, and his rank in society was highly favored—by those who cared for that sort of thing any more. *Father, what would you have me do?*

Her gut wrenched. Everything was changing. All around her the world she'd known had flipped on its head. Leaving Eliza would tear Kitty's very heart from her chest. But if her presence brought such grief to all parties, perhaps it would be for the best?

She shot up and stared at the wall, her pulse crashing to a stop.

She couldn't leave.

Cyprian's vile threats slammed against her.

She had no choice but to stay. At least for now. The bondage wouldn't last forever. It couldn't. If she simply complied for a while, perhaps even showed some acceptance, Cyprian would release her from this horrid enslavement and she would once again be at liberty to do as she pleased with her life.

Staring toward the door, she blinked away another rise of moisture and prayed her company in the Watson home wouldn't bring Eliza and Thomas any grief. At the moment she didn't care what it did to Nathaniel. The thought of him dried her tears, replacing regret with healthy anger. The man had belittled her to such a degree that if he ever spoke to her again she might not be able to stop herself from slapping his perfect face.

Scooting back, Kitty opened the drawer of the table and pulled out a piece of paper, inkwell and quill. Dipping the white feather in the black liquid, Kitty began to write as tiny fragments of unease and fear crumbled away.

Dear James,

How pleased I was to receive your letter. You must forgive me for not writing sooner. Allow me to explain my hurried departure with the hope that you will understand that my reasons are not as they seem...

Chapter Nine

The late-spring sun beat upon Kitty's back as if it were nearly August, not mid-June. She stared at the heavy basket in her arms, before shifting her focus to the dull clomp of her shoes against the hard dirt, willing her mind to find distraction in anything but the dreadful action she was minutes from executing.

Her fourth delivery.

Clutching the rounded wicker as if it carried her very heart, Kitty marched across town, heedless of the many shoppers and riders making their way up and down the wide road. Her lean shadow stretched out in front of her, looking as pitiful as she felt. Every painful second that passed drove another nail into her splintered soul. *Lord, forgive me. I abhor being a party to this. What else I can do? Wilt thou not show me another way?*

Once on the fringe of town past the shoemaker's, Kitty glanced behind to be sure she wasn't followed. Her pulse cooled when it appeared all was well, and she darted onto the overgrown path and hurried the rest of the way, as though angry wolves—or perhaps patriots—were on her heels.

The cabin came into view and she raced faster, stopping just in time to place the basket carefully on the front step. She paused to revive her breath, heaving deep through her mouth. Hands at her middle, she clung precariously to her courage and scanned the surrounding woods for the first time since she began this servitude. The sun broke through the skein of tree branches that shadowed the reclusive dwelling as she turned and stared at the checkered cloth that covered the three sacks of powder.

A fathomless ache pushed down through her stomach until it reached her feet and she wriggled her toes to keep it away. How much longer would she be forced to do this? She groaned as she stared at the heavens through the shimmering green. *Please Lord, let it be soon.* Certainly this couldn't go on forever. She hadn't once been negligent in her dreaded charge. She'd even forced herself to smile at Cyprian the one time she'd seen him, praying the simple kindness might soften his iron heart.

So far, there was no emancipation in sight.

A rustle from the inside of the cabin jerked Kitty from her momentary interlude.

Mercy! Someone was inside!

Grabbing fistfuls of skirt she shot down the path, refusing to stop until she reached the safety of the road. Skidding to a halt, Kitty held to a tree with one hand and pressed the other to her chest as she struggled to catch her breath.

Looking behind her, she trembled. Who had been in the cabin? Had she been discovered? A sickening feeling swirled around her, the actions and secrets she held so deep threatening to drown her with dark and consuming regrets. She rested her back against the tree and put her face in her hands, somehow smelling the precious black commodity on her gloves, though she'd never even touched it.

"Kitty?"

The sound of Nathaniel's voice buckled Kitty's knees and she flung her arms to the tree behind her. Panic jumped to her face in the form of heat and she could neither respond nor force a relaxed expression. Quickly regaining control of her wayward fears, she pushed from her place of safety and stepped forward, pretending more than actually feeling the tranquility she painted on her features.

"Nathaniel. What a surprise." She casually glanced at the trail and smiled. Blessed be. No one followed.

Medical bag in-hand, Nathaniel's broad shoulders and impressive height loomed, as did the memory of their last unpleasant encounter. She darted a look at his face, making contact with his vision just long enough to assure him of her civility, but quick enough to assure herself there was nothing there she need long for. However, her heart didn't seem to remember what her pride still clung to. Those warm eyes, the ones she dreamed of more often than she should, narrowed as if concern flickered somewhere within him.

A feather-light cloak of longing flitted down her shoulders. The comfort that nestled in her heart nearly made her forget why she'd been angry. Did he care? In some way? Would he be pained at the knowledge of the demands she was forced to execute against her will? She brushed a hand over her bodice, trying to smooth her ruffled emotions and focus on the embers of anger that still flickered somewhere beneath.

"I must be going." Offering a no-more-than civil smile, Kitty brushed past him. "Good day, Doctor."

Grabbing her arm, he stopped her mid-step, his

eyes bright and his tone as rich as his brown jacket and breeches. His mouth twitched at one side. "You are harsh, Miss Campbell." He pressed a hand to his chest and shook his head. "I have not seen you in a month and yet you wound me with such coldness."

She dared a look at him and reprimanded herself. His eyes looked almost brown in the shadow of his hat and his tan complexion stole her breath. A half-smile lifted one side of his mouth, making her forget where she was. Why must he tease? He knew how it undid her.

Smiling back, she clasped tight to her remaining frustration lest she be lost forever in his charms. "Has it really been a month?" She fiddled with her sleeve. "I reasoned you had chosen to retreat from me since you find my apathy so revolting, Doctor." With that she met his gaze.

His smile-lines grew deep. "Retreating would suggest defeat would it not? And only a fool would retreat from your company, apathy or no. And I, dear Kitty, am no fool." He pulled his shoulders back, causing the fabric of his waistcoat to tighten around his muscular chest. "My duties have been keeping me far too busy for diversions with friends, I'm afraid. And when did you start calling me Doctor?"

Kitty could feel the flames of her anger drowning under the pleasant rain of his kindness, but she fueled it again. "You slandered me in front of my sister and Thomas and wish to think we are still friends?"

A rustling from the path made her heart jump to her throat. Kitty tried to remain casual despite the way her pulse almost blinded her. Taking swift strides, she started toward town and Nathaniel easily matched her step for step. Her heartbeat returned to a more pleasant rhythm when the fortification of buildings once again guarded her on either side.

They moved in silence, though she could feel Nathaniel's eyes on her. "Are you well?"

A nervous laugh bubbled out of Kitty's chest before she had time to mask it with a more genuine one. "Aye, I am well." She looked up. "I thank you for your interest in my well-being." Swallowing she stared ahead, begging God in heaven to shut his mouth from further question.

"What were you doing just now?"

"Doing?" She questioned, praying he didn't hear the wailing in her head.

"I saw you dart from those trees as if the devil himself was on your heels. What were you doing in those woods? I doubt Eliza or Thomas would approve of you going to the outskirts of town alone."

Without losing a step, Kitty shrugged. Compelled by the imperative need to dissuade him from asking any more probing questions, she gave him a warmer smile than she would have wished and offered at least a partial truth. *Lord, please let my answer satisfy his curiosity.* "I was making a delivery and... I heard something that frightened me so I ran until I came to the safety of the road. That is all." She stopped in front of the blacksmith's shop and Nathaniel came beside her. She pulled her lower lip between her teeth as his gaze held steadfast. Had she said too much? With a soft shrug of her shoulders, Kitty practiced her most believable laugh and mixed it with a heavy dose of banter. "I believe you are becoming over-anxious, Doctor."

His gaze never once wavered, in fact grew deeper as if he could see through her charade and into the hidden parts of her heart she wished to keep concealed. He stepped closer, a cant to his voice that stirred a tender place within. "You do not give me adequate credit, *Miss Campbell.* I am never anxious. Only ever concerned."

Kitty couldn't move. Couldn't even feel the ground beneath her feet as Nathaniel's eyes roamed her face again, searching. He stepped closer. "Should I be concerned?"

Aye, he should be. Her heart corroded more every week that passed. Painful regret plunged straight through her. He would never look at her with such kindness if he knew what she'd done.

Kitty met his stare and masked the need for help her own eyes yearned to signal. With a tilt of the head, she smiled. "Nay, you need not be concerned. I am well."

He breathed out hard and looked to the side, almost as if he were trying to hide his disbelief. "As you say, Miss Campbell." He turned back to her, a light in his eyes that toyed with the soft center of her heart.

She stared, stunned under his tender gaze before once more remembering how to move her feet and she continued walking. He stayed perfectly in step.

Nathaniel rubbed his jaw and peered down at her from the corner of his eye. "You haven't forgiven me yet. For what I said to you that night."

Startled by the sudden change in subject, Kitty almost stuttered her reply but answered openly. "In truth I have not."

He shook his head with a frown. "'Tis a shame, considering I am such a loving and forgivable sort of person." The way the lines lengthened around his bright eyes and the slight tilt to his mouth nearly pulled a rich laugh from Kitty's throat, but she kept still. He bit the inside of his cheek then flung her a sideways look. "I must make amends."

Peeking at him from the corner of her eye, she allowed a wisp of a smile to raise one side of her mouth. "I fear you cannot."

"Hmmm." He shook his head and frowned. "That will not do. I shall find a way. Believe me."

A gentle breeze danced around them and Kitty glanced up at him as they walked side by side. Bits of afternoon stubble dusted his jaw. Strands of rich brown hair strayed from his queue and brushed his cheek. Quickly she stared back at the street. Staying angry with Nathaniel was as difficult as keeping ice from melting in August. Not only had he a handsome face and fine physique, he had an alluring charm and a gentle strength that added depth to his character and a pull to his magnetism that Kitty was helpless to resist.

When they reached the other side of town, Kitty's muscles eased and she pushed out a breath that held weeks of anxiety. Shawme Pond glistened in the sun as a group of ducks glided down to the water and a cart laden with hay passed across the road in front of them.

"So." Nathaniel adjusted his hat on his head. "To whom were you making the delivery?"

She whipped toward him. "Delivery?" Her voice cracked. *Stop asking so many questions!*

"Aye, you said you were making a delivery, so who was it for?"

Kitty took a step back, her limbs suddenly cold. "Oh, 'twas nothing... I was simply..."

"She was making the delivery for me."

Kitty gasped and spun around as Cyprian neared, his eyes tender on the edges and poison in the center.

Terror blinded her until Nathaniel took her elbow and gently tugged her closer. She could sense his muscles grow tight as the sound of his breathing turned slow and measured.

Offering a small bow, Cyprian removed his hat then put it back on again. “Forgive me for overhearing.”

Kitty could hardly remain still and clutched her fists so tight her nails bit into her hands. She glanced between the two men as they exchanged venomous glares. What had Cyprian done? Did he plan to expose her now? Like this? The blood in her limbs congealed.

Cyprian shifted his feet then gave Kitty an uncle-like smile that made her stomach harden. “Miss Campbell has been helping me these past several weeks now, and I must say her generosity has been a blessing to us all.”

“Is that so?” Nathaniel gripped tighter to her arm and nudged her backward, increasing the distance from Cyprian. “Remarkable how I find that hard to believe. We bid you good day.”

“Tell him, Miss Campbell.” Cyprian’s gravelly tone stopped them like a fallen tree.

Tugging her to a halt, Nathaniel stood partially in front of her, shielding Kitty from their evil opponent. Every second that passed drained more blood from her head as she feigned ignorance. “Tell him what, Mr. Wythe?”

Cyprian motioned to Nathaniel. “Tell the good doctor how you’ve been delivering those baskets to the needy.”

A foreign emotion, hot and ugly surged in Kitty’s chest. Hatred, pure and seething. Clenching her teeth to keep from breathing fire, she only nodded in agreement.

"Is this true?" Nathaniel questioned.

She couldn't move her tongue, couldn't bring her lips to form the words. Finally, she produced a quiet aye, and stepped backward. "If you gentlemen will excuse me."

"Don't let me detain you another moment." Cyprian tipped his hat, backing away. "'Twas good to see you Miss Campbell, and I do thank you for your continued service. We Tories must remain united."

With that, he spun on his heel and marched toward town, tugging away the remains of Kitty's courage as he left.

Nathaniel's jaw slackened and he turned to her, a thousand questions flickering across his face. "Why didn't you tell me?"

"I—"

"Why are you working for him, Kitty?" His expression crunched and he jerked back. "There's plenty of good that can be done without aligning yourself with such a man."

Tears threatened and her voice quivered. "He... I..." She folded her arms across her chest and looked away. Kitty swallowed the pain in her throat. "I fear I can produce no satisfying answer."

He stared, motionless as if straining to assess what truths evaded him. "You don't have to answer." Then with a sudden shift of mood his voice brightened. "I'd love to assist you on these deliveries, Kitty. I didn't know a family lived in those woods and I attempt to acquaint myself with everyone in town should they ever be in need of a physician. Besides, I really don't like the idea of you doing that alone. Not after the attack you suffered."

Assist her? Kitty's neck cramped until she almost

couldn't breath. "Nay, 'tis fine really. I'll be fine—everything is fine... But thank you." She stepped back, masking her surging fear with a small, tight grin. "I best be going."

Nathaniel didn't remove his gaze, only blinked with ever deepening lines between his eyes. He nodded, his voice deep and smooth like a calming river. "You're a good woman, Kitty." No hint of mocking. Only a sincerity in his tone that threatened to jerk the unshed tears from her eyes.

If only you knew...

Chapter Ten

Nathaniel exhaled a long, low breath as he watched Kitty walk toward home. Her attempt to make him believe she was "well" would have made him chuckle if not for the shadow that hovered over her. No, "well" would not describe her in the least. Her abrupt good-bye and the tears she battled to hide made his muscles twitch with the desire to pursue her and unearth the buried truth once and for all. Teeth clenched, Nathaniel turned in the direction Cyprian had walked as fresh disgust rose within. Perhaps Cyprian was the one who had attacked her the night of the party. Nathaniel tapped the bag against his leg and snarled. Many a time he'd come close to questioning her again, but Thomas's caution kept his eagerness in check.

Rubbing his thumb against the handle in his grasp he vowed that next time—next time he would find a way to confront her, for this secret she carried needed bearing before that persistent shadow turned to ever-present blackness.

"Nathaniel, I'm so glad I found you."

Nathaniel spun around just as Joseph Wythe ran toward him, his face red and his breathing labored. "You must come quickly."

Muscles suddenly taut and awareness sharp, Nathaniel scanned him for signs of injury. "What's happened? Is someone hurt?" Nathaniel knew Joseph well enough to recognize the hard set of his jaw, indicating the news of something severe would soon meet his ears.

"Nay, no one is hurt." Joseph stood erect and stared in the direction he'd come. His face contorted. "'Tis almost worse."

"Worse?" Irritation exploded and Nathaniel grabbed his arm. "What is it, man? Get it out!"

He met Nathaniel's frustration with red-faced anger. "Our powder is dwindling."

The impact of Joseph's words blasted into Nathaniel's chest like a musket ball, socking the air from his lungs.

"*What*?" Nathaniel shot down the road with Joseph beside him. He raced around the pond and across the small clearing, stopping before he stomped into the small stone building. Thomas and several others were already inside, shuffling back and forth and speaking in hushed voices.

The whisperings stopped and all eyes turned to him. Nathaniel marched forward, commanding attention. "Well? Enlighten me."

Billy Curry and Roger both turned to Thomas, apparently waiting on him to disclose what they'd discovered.

The hard line of Thomas's jaw and the blackness of his eyes yelled of fury, but his demeanor continued restrained. "If only we could. Our supply is lessening that much is certain. But how? That's another question entirely."

Surveying the scene, Nathaniel spoke through clenched teeth. "Who is the devil behind this treachery?"

He walked to the forlorn-looking barrel in the far left corner and lifted its lid, peering inside. His stomach sunk to his knees. Completely empty. Gripping the wood, he leaned back and launched the lid into the far wall. His rage exploded as the lid splintered to pieces and fell to the ground. Glancing behind him, the grim faces of the men testified of their similar sentiments.

No one spoke. The small windows of the magazine allowed for little light, but what bits of sun meandered through revealed nothing that might aid in discovery of the offender.

Nathaniel stepped back and tried to keep a tighter hold on the waxing madness. "Did anyone see anything? Anything at all?"

Joseph stepped forward, his height and breadth nearly consuming the corner in which he stood. His deep timber sat heavy. "I checked the locks and hinges. Everything appears untouched."

Nathaniel looked over his shoulder. "What about you Billy, did you notice anything amiss last time you were on watch? Or did you leave early again?" He hadn't meant the accusation to spit so quickly from his lips, but he didn't care.

"Nay." Billy Curry shook his head, his youthful features turning pale. "Upon my word Doctor, I saw nothing and if I had I would have reported such immediately."

The poor lad looked tortured at the accusation of negligence and Nathaniel flicked a quick look to Thomas, brushing his hand along the empty barrel as if he were dressing a wound. "I believe you, Billy."

Then, obvious reality struck from behind and stabbed its ugly truth through Nathaniel's soul.

Turning, he motioned to the door, barely able speak. "Everyone out."

The four of them turned and stared, each with raised brows and tight lips.

Nathaniel gestured out the door, this time with less patience. "I thank you for your concern. I will inform you when I have determined how to proceed."

None of them moved, their reluctance palpable. Finally, Thomas cleared his throat and stepped into the sun. "We shall call an urgent gathering tonight or tomorrow. Be assured we will get to the bottom of this."

Roger ducked out the door, followed by Billy. He replaced his tricorn and nodded, the stern tone of his voice saying as much as his words. "I am at the ready." Billy touched the front of his hat and bowed in assent before they both started back toward town.

Joseph stepped beside Nathaniel, watching as the other men continued down the road. He sighed and glanced quickly behind him. "Do what you must. I shall continue my watch."

Nathaniel acknowledged his friend's comment with a bob of his head when his mind whirred to life. "Joseph, I've a question for you."

He turned, squinting against the afternoon sun. "Aye?"

Nathaniel neared. Placing his hands on his hips, he stared in the direction of the Cooper's home, visible just beyond the pond on the other side. "Have you seen Andrew of late?" It wasn't until that moment he'd realized he hadn't seen Andrew in weeks, in fact he hadn't seen him since that night at the Cooper's home those many weeks ago.

Joseph looked away, his mouth twisting to the side as he thought. "I can't recall. But as you know, he takes the watch every Monday, Wednesday and Friday evening. He's quite busy with the shop. Doesn't do much else these days, though I know he wishes to."

Straining to keep his expression void of the emotion that crawled up his spine, Nathaniel raised both brows casually, while around him howled a startling probability. He hadn't thought of such until this moment. "Three times a week? I only request one of each of you. There are enough of us to make sure no one need spend an excessive amount of time away from their families."

Shrugging Joseph slid his hands in his pockets and followed a cart with his vision as it passed on the road before meeting Nathaniel's gaze. "Wouldn't you spend that much time guarding if you could?"

Point taken. Nathaniel was so often called away by patients, he was gratified when he could serve on two watches a week. In truth, if his trade allowed, he would never leave the magazine until the villain was found and his neck stretched. The way Nathaniel's blood spun in his chest, he could no longer remain still. He flicked his finger against his leg. Andrew had made it clear numerous times how much he despised the king. So perhaps it wasn't so strange the man made it his duty to guard as much as he could. And yet...

Joseph continued. "Andrew wants this blackguard discovered as well as anyone."

Nathaniel wiped his hands down his face and expelled a defeated sigh. He tried to answer with words, but could only nod.

"We can speak with him about it as soon as we meet." Joseph cupped Nathaniel on the shoulder and gave a strong tap before he walked back toward the magazine.

Nathaniel snatched his medical bag and started toward Shawme Pond with Thomas right behind him. Once a good distance from any ears, he allowed his frustrations to crest. "The truth is vile enough to make me ill."

Thomas stepped beside him, but kept his vision forward. "I suspect I know your thoughts."

The birds chirped once again, but this time Nathaniel wanted to scold them for their irritating cheeriness. "'Tis a contemptible thought indeed, but I fear 'tis the only plausible explanation."

Thomas frowned and brushed a hand over his jaw. "But who could the traitor possibly be? They've all taken turns at the watch—blast it, Nathaniel!" He stopped and stared, lowering his voice while his eyes turned from blue to black. "It could be several of them for all we know. This tangle of devilry extends farther into the ranks of our beloved town than either of us care to admit."

Nathaniel's teeth ached from the clenching he forced on his jaw. He sent a side-ways glance to Thomas. "You know what must be done."

Thomas didn't move. "How? When?"

"Not right away." Nathaniel continued to whisper though he had plastered a look of complete indifference over his features as he continued up the road, should anyone be watching from afar. "If we keep the barrels as they are, then slowly empty them, replacing the—"

Thomas silenced him with a look so striking Nathaniel felt like a reprimanded child.

"This is not the place to discuss such things." With a coarse exhale, Thomas put on his tricorn. "I'll come to your home this evening. We can arrange what needs to be done then."

"Nay." Nathaniel cleared his throat. "I will come to your home."

"Mine?" Thomas stopped and his expression lightened. He chuckled. "I might wonder why you are so eager to spend time in my humble dwelling?"

The assertion stopped Nathaniel with a jerk and he glared. "Whatever foolish ideas you have swirling in your head you may dispense of them immediately."

"'Tis too bad that Kitty has kept to her room during your past few visits. I wonder if she will accompany us this evening?" A mocking smile widened Thomas's face. "I have seen the way you look at her."

Nathaniel started walking again. "At Kitty?" Gripping the bag harder to ease the tension away from his tone, he chuckled. "Of course I look at her, but not in the way you imply." He moved his bag to the other hand as they passed Shawme Pond and walked up into town, hoping Thomas would let the comment lie. "While we're speaking of Kitty, there's something you should know."

"So you do fancy her." Thomas's voice echoed with self-satisfaction.

Nathaniel ignored his friend's banter, and continued as if the irritating comment hadn't been uttered. "I spoke with her just before Joseph came to fetch me."

"She was in town?"

"Aye." He recalled the flush in her cheeks and the few times she flung worried glances to the small trail in the woods before they walked through town. "I saw her just past the other side of town opposite the shoemaker's."

"She may have been enjoying a stroll." Thomas tipped his hat at a passing rider.

Nathaniel shook his head, squelching the rising irritation. Did the man not see what was so plain? "'Twas more than that, we saw—" He shut his mouth and kept it closed until they reached the sanctuary of Thomas's print shop. He followed Thomas in and closed the door.

Thomas spoke as he took off his hat and placed it on a peg on the wall. "You saw who?"

The memory turned Nathaniel's stomach. He leaned against the table and pushed out a rough breath. "Cyprian happened upon us on the road. He claimed Kitty was delivering goods to the needy under his direction."

Thomas spun where he stood near the large press. His brow pushed down and he scoffed. "Nay, I don't believe it."

"Neither do I." Nathaniel massaged his forehead and scrunched his eyes shut. The sight of Kitty's tear-laden eyes had so pained him, and wrestled with his need to remain reserved, he had almost lost control and nearly reached out to stroke her cheek. "She looked terrified of him."

"'Tis a natural reaction I suppose." Thomas crossed his arms, a scowl darkening his face. "Kitty tries to appear brave—and she is, but her heart is tender."

"So you believe his claim to be false."

Thomas rubbed the cleft in his chin and looked at the ceiling. "She would not make deliveries for him, but for his wife perhaps. Some time ago I overheard Eliza and some of the women in town discussing Camilla's needs. She used to make regular deliveries to the poor before her illness forced her to be bedridden. It might be that the women organized a group to carry on her service." Thomas shrugged and turned his back to the press. "I wouldn't worry overmuch, but 'tis good to be aware. The concerns at the magazine are far too vital to allow ourselves to be concerned with anything of lesser import."

Lesser import?

Nathaniel ground a retort between his teeth and pushed off the table. Did no one remember Kitty's attack? Did they not remember she had never spoken of the events that had left her so battered? He opened his mouth to respond, but snapped it shut again and swung open the door so he could escape the suffocating frustration.

He stepped out and spoke over his shoulder. "Until tonight then."

"Aye, tonight."

Nathaniel left the press with its heady smells of ink and inhaled the scent of warm dirt roads as he stepped into the sun. Horses clomped past, harnessed to over-laden carts and children darted across the street. He started down the road. Perhaps Thomas was right. Nathaniel tended to over-think. Perhaps he'd made something out of nothing and Kitty had only been— He grumbled under his breath and for the hundredth time reprimanded himself for not softening his frustrations the night Kitty had received that letter from Higley. A breeze brushed past, soothing the heat that ignited at the thought. *Higley*. Had the letter been from anyone else, or if the man had been simply a merchantman or a farmer, Nathaniel's ire might have remained dormant. Might have. Knowing the man had not only proposed, but was the nephew of General Gage made it all the more revolting. Once again the indignation pulsed rough and raw when blessedly the wind cooled his neck. No matter his reasons for speaking such to Kitty, he should not have accused her. It would take concerted effort to make amends and help her feel his sincere affection.

He stopped as if the word were a boulder in the road. Affection? What was he thinking? A woman such as Kitty Campbell would bring more complications to his life than he dared to imagine. There were plenty of patriot-minded women in town whose company he enjoyed and who would—if he were ever to be so inclined—be a fine match for him.

Starting to walk once more, Nathaniel relished the touch of air that soothed his still-heated skin. He could never align himself with a woman who embraced something he did not.

Though finding a way to convince his heart was another matter entirely.

"You're late." Captain Donaldson's tone grated the air as he reined in his spirited mare.

The darkness thickened, adding to the nervous energy that encased Cyprian's spine. "But I am here." Handing over the three large bags of powder, his chest pumped as if he had been the one racing to meet his overseer and not the horse. "I got here as quickly as I could."

Donaldson held onto the bags as if he were gauging their weight and found them wanting. "This isn't much."

Isn't much?

Cyprian shifted in his saddle and clutched the

reins, unable to keep disdain from seeping into his voice. "'Tis extremely difficult for me to get that powder. If you would like to steal it yourself you may."

The instant the words poured from his mouth he wanted to yank them out of the air and shove them back down his throat. Idiot. In a flash, the frightened face of the young Campbell girl turned his blood to ice. He had Andrew just where he wanted him, but the girl seemed unsure, weak. How easy it would be for her to ruin everything he'd done to keep Camilla alive.

Shaking his head, he turned his attention to Donaldson who sat unmoving on his mount, his eyes clamping around Cyprian's neck with the force of an iron restraint.

"Forgive me, Captain, I spoke out of turn." He had to crawl out of the hole he'd dug. "I won't be late again, and I will do my utmost to get more."

Donaldson's expression didn't change. "I am not ignorant of the challenge, nor of your need." He tossed a small bag of coins at Cyprian. "But 'tis not I who commands this operation. If my superiors are dissatisfied, I fear I will be forced to call upon someone else."

Donaldson pulled hard on the reins, turning the horse around completely before kicking its flank and darting into the darkness. The animal kicked up clods of trampled earth that fell back to the ground with a splat, reminding Cyprian how easily he too could be trampled and forgotten. The misty ocean air rested heavily around Cyprian's shoulders like an unwelcome consort.

I cannot fail.

He tapped his heels into his mount's flanks and

tried not to sink into the weight of his affliction. Somehow he had to prove to the British he was good enough for the job.

Nay, not merely good enough. Perfect.

Chapter Eleven

The feel of cool dough against her fingers, the crack of egg against bowl, made Kitty almost believe all was well in the world. She worked the egg into the sticky mixture and inhaled the sweet breeze that blew in from the open kitchen window. Her hair tickled her neck and she smiled. Peace, like a dear friend, wrapped its arms around her and rested its head against her shoulder. Where had it been for so long? Brushing the back of her wrist against her forehead, she pushed a quick, happy breath from her lips. Forgetting the chains of bondage in which Cyprian enslaved her, and becoming lost in something she loved, gifted a precious serenity she had forgotten even existed.

Kitty turned back to the fire to fuss over the pudding. Perfect. The golden brown was just beginning to kiss the edges and would soon be ready to be relieved from the heat. As she stared at the rounded mass, the woes that plagued her crawled upward, its claws scraping into the walls she'd erected and she winced. *I will not endure this now.* She knocked the thoughts away as she focused on the biscuits that would soon enjoy a warm fire.

Just then Eliza stepped into the kitchen and

stopped with a gasp. She pressed a hand to her chest and her gentle features lifted as she smiled. "Kitty, did you invite everyone in town for supper? You've made enough food to feed a hundred people, I'm sure." Her green and cream striped gown swished as she walked toward the table and sampled the crust of a still-warm pie.

"Have I?" Kitty giggled and turned to survey the spread of goods decorating the table. Four pies, two loaves of bread, three cakes of various sizes and a tray of corn muffins. Mercy! How long had she been baking? As she had been blissfully lost in the art of forgetfulness, time had flown by. And oh, that she could do this every day—every moment—until another loathed Saturday arrived.

Kitty shrugged and motioned to the table. "I suppose I have made a great deal of food, forgive me."

"Not to worry. The garden is overflowing now and 'tis good to make use of what we have."

Eliza's meticulously prepared coiffure and well-set gown attested she was ready to leave for the latest gathering at the Coopers. She looked past Kitty toward the fire before meeting her gaze. "You're certain you don't want to join us?"

Not if you dragged me by the hair.

Kitty giggled, tempted to tease her sister with the statement, but thought better of it. "Thank you, no, Liza. I'd prefer to spend the evening by this fire. I can't tell you what kind of soothing power all this baking possesses, and I have surely been in need of it."

The loamy scent of the pudding reached her nose and she spun around, using her apron to snatch it from the heat. Placing it on the table she examined the dish and smiled. Perfection.

Eliza neared, her slender brows lifting. "Carrot pudding?"

Kitty turned to the biscuits, her words spilling out in a hurried stream. "We had so many carrots, I needed to do something with them ere they turn rotten."

"Indeed." Eliza stepped closer. The sisterly teasing in her dark eyes grew more potent until Kitty could hardly stand the weight of it. Eliza smiled. "I must say I find that quite remarkable."

"Remarkable?" Kitty swallowed.

"Thomas and I do not care for carrot pudding. And neither do you." The hint of accusation in Eliza's tone met its mark.

"If you're implying I've made it for Nathaniel then you're wrong." Her cheeks grew hot. Mercy, why must she always be so transparent? She dipped her fingers in a bowl of water and wiped off the dough, praying the meager acting skill she employed would mask at least a portion of her emotions. "I've developed a taste for it, despite what you might think."

With a shrug and a smile that made Kitty's embarrassment bleed into her cheeks, Eliza snatched a slice of apple peel and took a small bite.

"I don't know if that's true about the pudding, but I do think you have grown to like a certain *someone* quite particularly over the past few weeks." Eliza's eyes flashed open as if she planned to say more but remained mum when Thomas strode into the kitchen.

Kitty's shoulders dropped and she exhaled. For now the interrogation had been thwarted and she could breathe unrestrained.

Grinning, Kitty leaned her hip against the table. "You look quite handsome, Thomas, if I may say so."

"I must agree with you sister, I do have a very handsome husband."

Kitty watched as Eliza straightened Thomas's cravat as Mother had done for Father countless times. Suddenly Kitty's imagination produced a domestic scene that made her stomach both fly and plummet. What would it be like to straighten Nathaniel's cravat?

Mercy, Kitty! Why must her heart yearn for something she knew she could never have?

Lifting on her toes, Eliza kissed Thomas on the cheek. "This suit carries treasured memories of our wedding, my husband. I'm so pleased to see you wear it."

He dusted a kiss against Eliza's hairline. "Then I'm glad I chose it." He walked farther into the kitchen whistling a long note as he glanced at the table. "Heavens, Kitty. You've done enough baking for one day—or two or three." He looked over at her and winked. "But it's time you cleaned up, we are expected at the Coopers."

"Oh no, Thomas, but thank you." She turned back to her dough, pulling it onto the floured table. "'Twill just be you and Liza tonight, I fear I don't feel much like being social." Especially around a crowd of patriots.

Kitty pretended not to notice the unspoken conversation of Thomas's and Eliza's back and forth glances. Irritation wriggled through Kitty's chest. She couldn't help but think their motivations for desiring her company weren't driven by personal conviction. Did they honestly believe that by making her attend these ridiculous gatherings every month she would eventually give up her stand?

Thomas broke a piece of crust off the apple pie and snuck it in his mouth. "We would love you to come, truly. And not for the reasons I see swimming in your head."

Kitty swallowed a growl. If only she could keep her emotions from living in her face! "Thomas, please, the townsfolk are beginning to know me as a Tory and I don't wish to—"

"Nonsense." Eliza sighed. "You have yet to be introduced to many of the delightful people of Sandwich, and I am eager for my friends to become better acquainted with you as well." She peered up at Thomas then gazed back at Kitty, the creases in her brow turning deep. "Kitty, I don't know if you are simply unhappy here, or longing for your acquaintances in Boston, but something is... different. You're more withdrawn and there's a sorrow about you..." She stopped and came around the table, taking Kitty's shoulders in her hands. "I think it would be good for you to get out, to meet some more people and see that even though you're a Tory, you will be among friends. I promise."

They would despise me if they knew what I've done.

All the serenity she'd enjoyed suddenly abandoned her, whisking out the window on the next available breeze. So her sister *had* noticed. Eliza's gift of insightful concern made it difficult to hide anything, no matter how trivial. If only Kitty could tell what she knew...

Biting her cheek, Kitty stared down at the steam swirling upward from the pudding. *Lord, be with me.* She forced a hard breath followed by a smile. After sharing a pained gaze with Eliza, Kitty nodded her surrender. "I will go." Perhaps the gathering wouldn't be as bad as she feared.

Eliza brushed Kitty's cheek, her dark eyes soft. "I am pleased, Kitty." With a wink, she grabbed Kitty's hand and led her from the kitchen. "Come, let us clean you up."

Thomas led the way, but promptly stopped and pointed at the table. "Is that carrot pudding?" The glee in his face made Kitty want to toss the infernal pudding in the fire.

She pursed her lips playfully and glared. "Aye, I *adore* carrot pudding. Or didn't you know?"

Removing her apron, Kitty followed Eliza toward the parlor ignoring Thomas's jesting as she walked upstairs.

"Are you sure it's the pudding you like—and not the man that will come to eat it?"

His gentle laughter rumbled behind her as she and Eliza hurried upstairs. Nay. She wasn't sure how she felt about Nathaniel. And for that reason she hadn't cared to attend another patriot gathering since that first night. *He* would be there.

Kitty unfastened her bodice and pulled off her petticoat while Eliza looked through the gowns in the armoire. A groan formed in her throat, but she swallowed it away. Her stomach turned. Seeing Nathaniel did terrible things to her insides.

Terrible? Or, wonderful?

Dotting on a bit of her flower-scented water to cover the scent of cinnamon, she stared at her reflection in the mirror.

Kitty didn't know, and she had no desire to find out.

The rich cacophony of mumbled voices mingled with the music the musicians continued to play, light and merry. Well-dressed men and women in colorful gowns and suits swayed back and forth on the dance floor, while other partiers crowded around the dessert table, clutching half-full glasses of wine in their gloved hands. The pungent scents of dessert and drink, candle smoke and cologne wafted from person to person, until the whole room nearly reeked of gaiety.

Standing in the corner behind the refreshments, Kitty's nervous stomach continued to turn, though in truth the gathering had turned out more delightful than she would have imagined. She smiled and nodded at the few revelers that looked her direction, but it had been hours since she'd conversed with Eliza's friends, and they were now all pleasantly entertained with either male company or other females with whom to converse.

Kitty picked out the clock on the wall near the exit and squinted to identify the time. She twisted her mouth to the side. It had been too long. Where was Eliza? She had taken her leave more than half an hour ago, complaining of an irritated belly. Not surprising, as that happened much of late thanks to the babe that thrived within her. But still, Eliza's lengthening absence did not bode well. Had she taken ill? Had she gone outside to cast up her accounts and was now weak and unable to move? The unknown held too many questions, and Kitty started for the exit. 'Twould be best to discover the answers, both for Eliza's sake and for the sake of Kitty's fragile sanity. Fighting the urge to peek over her shoulder every few minutes to discover if Nathaniel would possibly look her way had all but depleted her sound judgment. She had almost walked over to him several hours past, but sensibility had prevailed and now 'twas three in the morning and they would likely be on their way home within the hour. *Really, Kitty.* She shook her head ever so slightly as she continued toward the exit. And now, with an urgent reason to make her escape, there was no possibility of having to speak with him. Thankfully.

Nathaniel had arrived just a few minutes after the three of them had, and her heart hadn't stopped twirling since. Just as her mind hadn't stopped thinking of him—wondering where he was, who he was talking to. Though she knew 'twas foolish. Every time she peered across the room, pretending to make a casual perusal, there he was surrounded by at least four or five women all giggling and beating their fans hard enough to create a windstorm.

Carefully moving along the perimeter of the ballroom, Kitty found Thomas at the edge of the doorframe, another tall, handsome man at his side.

She curtsied low when she reached them, and they bowed.

The tall, blonde gentleman grinned. His eyes danced over her, and a pleasant smile lifted his face.

Keeping her attention on Thomas, she touched his arm. "Forgive me for interrupting—"

"Aw, Joseph this is who I was just speaking of." Thomas grinned at her as he tapped the broad-shouldered man on the back. "Allow me to introduce my sister-in-law, Miss Katherine Campbell."

Joseph bowed, never taking his gaze from her face. "'Tis a great pleasure to finally make your acquaintance."

Kitty's face grew hot as she curtsied. "Thank you,

Mr...?"

He stood straighter. "Wythe. Joseph Wythe."

Horror clutched Kitty's windpipe until she almost couldn't breathe. The room faded in and out and for one terrible moment Kitty thought she might drop to the floor. Wythe? Shifting her stance, Kitty rallied every thread of strength and remained erect. Forcing a grin, she strained to keep the crack from her voice. "Wythe? Are you any relation to Mr. Cyprian Wythe?"

His features turned instantly taut, though his tone remained cool. "Aye, though I must admit I'm sorry to say it. He is my brother."

His brother. Blood trickled away from her face. She stared out the door, eyes wide, head reeling, until Thomas tugged her elbow. "Kitty, is everything all right?"

She touched her head, and forged a fraudulent laugh she hoped would ease the sudden tension that threatened to stifle her. "Aye, forgive me, I am well. But I have great concerns about Liza."

Thomas straightened and his brow plunged. "What do you mean?"

Kitty shook her head. "I fear she is not well. She excused herself over half an hour ago and I haven't seen her since."

Lips pressed tight, Thomas nodded and scanned the room before touching Joseph on the shoulder once more. "Please excuse me, I need to find my wife."

He darted away and was out of sight before Kitty could follow.

"You are not fond of such gatherings?"

Kitty jumped as Joseph's deep timbre awakened her from her inner dialogue.

She breathed a quick laugh and smiled, embarrassed for having forgotten her manners. "Is it so obvious?"

His smile grew wide, brightening his entire face as if her answer amused him. "I'm afraid so." His height and the solid cut of his features made Kitty yearn to peek over her shoulder. Did Nathaniel see with whom she spoke? Would he wish he were by her side instead of Mr. Wythe?

She breathed away the sinful, yet desirable thought and placed a gentle grin on her lips.

Joseph gestured toward the dancers with the glass he held in his gloved hand. "Many people receive great enjoyment out of fancy parties and endless merrymaking, but I do not."

"You do not?"

"Nay."

The easy way he spoke, and the unpretentious sparkle in his striking eyes put Kitty at immediate ease, allowing her breathing to move slow and soft.

He took a sip of his drink. "I feel more comfortable beside a tower of flames and with a hammer in my hand."

Kitty tilted her head. A hammer?

He must have sensed her unspoken question, because he answered with a pleasant chuckle. "I'm a blacksmith."

"Blacksmith? I would never have guessed."

The moment the words tripped out of her mouth she cringed. *Never would have guessed.* What an inconsiderate—

"Do I not appear as such to you?" Joseph's jolly laugh pulled a giggle from her chest before she had a chance to constrain it. He smiled so wide, Kitty could see nearly all his straight white teeth. "Do not worry,

Miss Campbell, you have not offended."

Being the town's blacksmith would certainly answer for the muscles that pushed against his waistcoat and jacket. But were blacksmiths often so wealthy? Joseph's suit was one of the finest she'd seen on any gentleman all evening. Against her will, her gaze dashed across the room, finding Nathaniel near the large fireplace on the opposite wall, still surrounded by a gaggle of women. His dark gray jacket and cream breeches had pulled her attention all evening. Now, thankfully, she had someone else to occupy her time and thoughts, just as Nathaniel had plenty of ladies to occupy his.

An uncomfortable quiet settled between them before Joseph cleared his throat. "You are acquainted with my brother?"

Blinking, she could only nod her response.

He looked forward and shrugged. "Cyprian and I have never been close, not even as children." The shocking statement made Kitty's brows shoot skyward, but she kept silent as he continued. "But I am very fond of Jacob, Cyprian's son. I do my best to keep the peace between us."

Kitty stared forward, knitting her fingers at her waist as relief and worry battled within her chest. What would this kind man think if he knew what his brother was forcing her to do?

She quickly forced the thought from her mind and focused on the conversation. "I have not met Jacob, but I am sure he is delightful."

A blissful smile split his face. "Aye, he is." He looked up briefly and laughed. "He wishes to be my apprentice and works at my shop any spare moment he can." Joseph stopped and suddenly his vision seemed to memorize her face. Not once did he move his eyes from her. "Miss Campbell, would you think me too forward if I—"

"Joseph!"

Nathaniel's voice and sudden presence made Kitty gasp. Her eyes shot open wide and she clamped her teeth together to keep her mouth from following suit. What in mercy's name was he doing here?

Unfazed, Nathaniel smacked Joseph on the shoulder and nodded approval as he scanned the man's suit and breeches. "You are always my inspiration for proper fashion, Joseph, I must say. You are dressed far finer than any other gentleman here, including myself. I'm surprised you don't have a chorus of women clamoring for your attention."

Joseph grinned as if well acquainted with Nathaniel's humor, then his smile rested slightly and he looked toward Kitty. "That honor is reserved for you Nathaniel, for I am much more content with only one."

Kitty's heart tapped against her ribs. Raising her lips in the most tantalizing smile she could create, she turned her head. Flirtatiousness was never her strong suit, but somehow at this moment the ability proved almost innate. And not, she told herself, because it might make Nathaniel wish he'd come to speak to her sooner.

The music began again and Joseph bowed, offering his hand. "It appears another dance is beginning, Miss Campbell. Would you do me the honor?"

Kitty stepped forward, brushing her fingers across Joseph's, bursting to life with all the charm she knew how to use but so rarely did. "I'd be honored, Mr. Wythe." Quickly shooting Nathaniel a smile she hoped would broil him, Kitty followed Joseph onto the dance floor.

Nathaniel dodged in front of them, his expression drawn. "Forgive me but I'm afraid your brother-in-law sent me looking for you, Miss Campbell."

Kitty frowned. "Is Eliza unwell?"

He shook his head. "Thomas is with her at the fainting couch and asked me to see if you would be available to bring her something to drink."

Worry replaced every other emotion as she gently gripped Joseph's firm hand. "Forgive me, Mr. Wythe, but I need to see to my sister. May we postpone this dance until a later time?"

Joseph nodded, his mouth tipped at one side. "Of course, Miss Campbell. Another time then, and I shall look forward to it."

Chapter Twelve

Nathaniel tried not to glare as he watched Joseph's gaze follow Kitty as she exited the room. Joseph's boyish smile grew wider and he let out a long breath. Nathaniel bit his tongue when Joseph looked back and spoke, his sound tainted with an airy kind of music. "I should have gone out of my way to speak with her long ago."

Offering a polite stretch of the lips Nathaniel counted the many ways his past-self had been a fool. He'd tried to keep himself occupied all evening, tried to keep his mind from tilting Kitty's direction, but no matter how he employed his thoughts otherwise, she consumed him. He'd looked her way a hundred times or more—her shimmering coral gown, creamy skin, and that bright, alluring smile beckoning him—but not once had she peered in his direction. All those smiles were gifted on other, less appreciative recipients. Nathaniel blinked and gave a quick shake of the head. Women were a mystery no man would ever unravel. Thankfully, he could at least maintain his glowing reputation as one who attracted ample female attention. With that reliable diversion, he would protect his heart from the one attraction it wanted.

Joseph let out another breath, snapping Nathaniel from his daydream.

After another sip of his drink, Joseph continued. "Do you know her well, Nathaniel? I assume you see her often at the Watsons." His gaze remained on the door where Kitty had gone. "I suddenly find myself impressed upon to find a reason to visit Thomas and his wife."

Nathaniel cleared his throat and grabbed his suit jacket at the waist to staunch his rising irritation. The only one welcome to make regular visits at the Watsons was Nathaniel. He inclined his head with a frown, and Joseph leaned in, his expression pinching as if he expected the news Nathaniel prepared to share would be grave. "Visits might have to wait. Eliza is with child and needs much rest. Guests might make her more tired than is safe, under the circumstances."

Nodding, Joseph's mouth quirked to the side as if he understood, but wasn't pleased with the answer. "Well, I could always ask Miss Campbell to take a stroll with me around town. That way—"

"Have you seen Hannah of late?"

Joseph turned, his eyes wide as if the sudden question lurched something concealed from his heart. He blinked, shock etched into his features, but Nathaniel didn't uproot the question he'd planted between them.

Seconds passed. Joseph looked down, a frown pulling his eyebrows together, and for a moment Nathaniel regretted his hasty change of subject. He'd wanted the conversation away from Kitty, but hadn't known the mention of Joseph's first love would prove so painful.

Joseph straightened and shook his head, emitting

a sigh. “Nay. I have not seen her. I understand she is still in Plymouth.” Pulling his posture higher, Joseph tipped his head back and drained the rest of the wine in his goblet before he continued. “I doubt she and I will ever again cross paths.” He stopped and stared at the bottom of the empty glass. Rubbing his thumb against the goblet, he offered a smile that went only skin deep. “Which is why I find it a pleasant distraction to meet someone like Miss Campbell, someone so lovely and gentle and sincere.”

Nathaniel squirmed against his tightening waistcoat. “I heard tell she might have a beau.”

Joseph snapped a look at Nathaniel. “Someone is courting her?”

Not about to tell what he knew of the infamous Mr. Pigley, Nathaniel shrugged his response.

Joseph’s sudden boisterous laugh filled the air where they stood. “You don’t have designs on her, do you?”

“Of course not, silly notion.” The answer spilled from his lips too fast, and Nathaniel brushed away his blunder with a quick chuckle.

“Then I don’t see the trouble in pursuing—”

“Oh, there is something I meant to tell you this morning as I made my rounds.” Nathaniel scrambled to fling together something—anything that would cease this infernal conversation. “The uh... the watch for the magazine has been reorganized. We are requiring two men in the evening hours, not just one.”

One brow slanted up on Joseph’s forehead. “I know. I was at the meeting when that was decided.”

“Right, of course.” Laughing again and this time with less natural ability, Nathaniel turned around and scanned the table behind him in hopes of finding his own drink to cover his anxious nerves, but there were none within snatching distance.

"I do have one question about Miss Campbell."

Nathaniel spun back, and quirked his eyebrows in question while inwardly he wanted to shove a cake in the man's mouth to keep him from talking of her. "Aye?"

Mouth twisted, Joseph swallowed before speaking and when he did his volume had dropped to a whisper. "I hear she is a Tory."

A grimace worked its way to Nathaniel's face, but he killed it en route. Did Joseph mean such a thing as a slight against her character? "And if she is?"

"Well, I should like to know her position so when I next speak with her, I may tread gently regarding the subject."

So foreign was the concept, that Nathaniel slowed his mind to dissect what his friend had just spoken. "You would align yourself with a woman who believed so vastly different from you?"

Joseph grabbed his empty drink off the window ledge and clapped Nathaniel on the back. "If a woman is God-fearing, and devoted to her family, I care not what political side she takes. When I marry, I ask only that my wife loves me until the end of my days."

Nathaniel's jaw hung open as he watched Joseph walk to the other side of the room. How could Joseph possibly think that way? Marrying one who didn't hold to the same vital beliefs had proven time and again how destructive such a union could be. How painful. The ever-present scars on his past began to throb and he looked again for a drink to coat his memories when from the corner of his eye a motion near the exit roused his attention. His heart lurched.

Kitty.

He lunged forward to find Thomas, Eliza and Kitty making their way out the door.

Nathaniel followed. "Is everything all right?"

Kitty slowed to answer him as Thomas and Eliza continued down the front steps to the road.

"We are taking Eliza home to rest." The night air toyed with the curls around Kitty's ears and the glow of the candles flooding from the windows kissed her soft cheek.

Trying to focus on anything but the slope of her neck and the tantalizing scent of cinnamon on her skin, Nathaniel aligned the words he'd just heard when blessedly his reason snapped back into existence. "What's wrong with her?" He stared after the pair as they huddled together, his concern for Eliza and the child in her womb beginning to flare.

Kitty moved down the steps. "She is well enough, simply over-tired and needs to stop moving so she can keep food in her belly." She peeked over her shoulder and her full lips pulled into a smile that lured him further from sensibility.

Nathaniel hurried beside her. "I shall go with you. If Eliza is unable to keep meals in her stomach, 'tis no wonder she is weak."

Kitty continued along the road, several paces behind Thomas and Eliza and only gifted Nathaniel with a quick look before she responded. "I believe she will be well. No need for you to leave your throng of women to care for a patient who needs only a good night's rest."

Her words dropped to the road and nearly tripped Nathaniel as he walked. Throng of women? He stared at her. No, 'twas not his imagination. Indeed the tone of jealousy had been there, but why? She hadn't concerned herself with him all evening—had she? Did she really harbor feelings for him as Thomas had long suspected? Nathaniel continued on in silence. Why did he have this sudden longing to be near her, to touch her? 'Twas too dangerous to even consider. And yet, he could convince his heart to do little else.

Suddenly Kitty stopped and faced him. She lifted her chin and searched his face with her large eyes that in the moonlight looked like dark pools of midnight speckled with stars. "Nathaniel, I appreciate your willingness to help and I know Eliza and Thomas do as well. I know just enough about such things to be assured Eliza will be well in a few days time. Do not trouble yourself with us. You may return to your *admirers*." The emphasis she placed on the last word and the tilt of a smile in her gaze undid him.

"The only admirer I'm interested in, Kitty, is you."

Kitty's pulse charged when her gaze collided with his. He couldn't possibly mean what he said. She tried to wet her throat, but the way Nathaniel stared down at her...

With a light laugh, Kitty struggled to recall how to place one foot in front of the other but all attempts failed. She stared back at him, motionless, floundering to keep the jest in her tone. "What makes you believe I admire you?"

He didn't answer. Not right away. His hand slipped around her neck, slowly trailing his firm, soft fingers into the curls behind her head. Pleasurable tingles trickled over her skin at the sensation, slowly winding into her chest where her heart beat like it knew what was to come—and wanted it.

He stepped nearer, words warm and caressing. "Do you not?"

Kitty couldn't breathe, could hardly force her eyes to blink. *Mercy!* Nathaniel's nearness and the dusty moonlight turned everything into a heavenly dream, the kind of dream she'd yearned to embrace, but never allowed. Crickets chirped their blissful melody and the leaves rustled in the breeze. But the only sound she heard was the breath they shared only inches apart.

Licking her lips, Kitty couldn't stop her vision from straying to his mouth. His breath smelled of cider, and the ivory light from the moon shaped perfect shadows against the contours of his nose and jaw. She blinked. It wouldn't happen. Would it?

Nathaniel stepped closer, his own eyes moving down until they landed on her parted lips and she licked them once again. Cupping the back of her neck he leaned down, just as Kitty swept her hands up his waistcoat. She closed her eyes...

"Kitty, are you coming?"

Jerking back, Kitty pushed away at the sound of Thomas's call, breath heaving and body tingling. She should step farther away—much farther—but she couldn't. The sudden shock of what had almost been ripped down her spine. Nathaniel's chest pumped wildly as he gazed back at her, his mouth parted as if he too struggled to make sense of what they'd nearly done.

Finally able to look away, Kitty blinked. She had

to answer Thomas's question, but she couldn't make her mouth move. With effort unlike she'd ever known, Kitty began moving again and somehow found her voice. "I need to be going."

Nathaniel didn't follow, though his gaze did, wide and wanting. "I understand." His quiet answer pulled at the longing that still lingered in her heart.

Rushing now, Kitty hurried to fall into step with her sister and Thomas. Though her mind had finally found its place, her heart had been left behind.

Cyprian knocked gently on the door of Camilla's room before pushing it open. He tried to keep the vines of worry from inching higher around his heart, but he couldn't stop them. Camilla looked as if she hadn't moved at all in the few hours since he'd seen her last. She still lay on her back, her arms straight at her sides as if she were already dead. A curse mumbled from his lips. If only he didn't have this drowning tavern to manage he could stay by her side every minute and see to her every need.

Nearing the bed, he checked to make sure her chest still moved up and down. It did. He closed his eyes and let out a ragged breath.

He bent low and kissed her soft forehead before turning his attention to the dying fire and adding another log.

A tap on the door caught his attention and he straightened when his son opened the door and peeked in.

"Jacob, what are you doing? I thought you were sleeping."

Jacob stared at his mother from across the room, as if afraid of what his father might say if he stepped any further. “Forgive me, Father. I... I couldn’t sleep.”

Cyprian stepped to the door and pressed it open completely, his heart shredding at the recollection of how he’d treated his son in recent weeks. How did one father a child? After twelve years he still didn’t know.

He fought the urge to scold his son for not sleeping. Instead he followed the boy’s gaze. “Did you see your mother today?”

Wiping his hand over his mouth, Jacob sighed. “Aye.”

“Was she awake enough to speak with you?”

Jacob swallowed. “Nay.”

The pain that swelled in Cyprian’s soul squeezed until his lungs struggled to rise. The boy was eaten by sorrow, Cyprian could see it as plain as the freckles across Jacob’s nose. He had to find a way to keep the boy’s mind off Camilla or it would destroy him.

Cyprian clamped his eyes shut. He had to keep the boy busy so there wouldn’t be enough time to grieve over something that would surely haunt him for the rest of his days.

Jacob stared, moisture filling his eyes. “May I see her?”

Cyprian’s throat pulled so tight it ached. “Nay. You need sleep, son.” He nudged Jacob backward, but the boy wouldn’t move his gaze.

The pain was too much. Cyprian pushed harder against his shoulder and closed the door behind him when both he and Jacob were in the hall. “Get to bed. There’s work to be done and I can’t do it alone.”

Jacob nodded and looked behind him at Camilla’s

door before crossing the hall to his bedchamber. He turned and opened and closed his mouth a few times before speaking. "Uncle Joseph says I may come help at the smithy tomorrow. He's teaching me to—"

"Don't you dare mention that patriot's name again." His nostrils flared and he kept his tone quiet, but hard. "I've warned you of people like him."

Mouth pinched, Jacob shifted his feet and lifted his chin as if coaxing his courage upward. "I like Uncle Joseph, Father. He says that—"

"I have warned you once and I'll warn you again. While you are under my roof you are not at liberty to speak the name of that man in my presence."

Jacob lowered his head and slunk back into his bedchamber, shutting the door with a quiet click.

Cyprian shoved his hands through his hair.

Were patriots to overrun his life? Nay! He would not allow his only son to succumb to such treachery.

A smile twitched on his lips. The powder supplies continued to slip from the rebels' grasp. Wicked delight warmed his spirit like ale on a winter's eve until a chuckle bubbled from his chest. Doctor Smith was frantic to know what was happening to the town's precious munitions.

He laughed again. Wouldn't the good doctor be surprised to know that little Tory friend of his played such a large role? Staring down the stairs, Cyprian reveled in the way such knowledge lifted his drooping spirits. Fulfilling the king's command was only part of the pleasure he took in relieving the patriots of their prized powder. Not only did he acquire what he needed for Camilla, he also created havoc for his enemies in more ways than he could have ever imagined. This liberty they clamored for was nothing but a drug, something they believed they needed for survival but would only cause them to destroy themselves and everyone else. They *needed* King George, and the sooner they discovered that, the better for all of them.

Chapter Thirteen

Trudging along the lonely dirt road beside Shawme Pond, Kitty drew in a long breath, savoring the warm scent of early summer and watching the leafy-green branches sway at the command of the breeze.

Closing her eyes, she groaned. Why must it be Saturday? Another two weeks had come and gone—dragging painfully slow like a boat along the sand. She breathed through tight lips to keep her chin from quivering as she squinted up at the sun. 'Twas noon. She had but two hours until the loathed task would once more be laden in her arms and in her heart. At least walking from one side of town to the other would help pass the remaining time. Too, 'twould keep her away from home where possible questions might pry from her the truth.

Her stomach churned with hunger, but the mere scent of food made her want to retch. A terrible torture indeed when making delicious vittles for herself and family had lost nearly all of its pleasure. How could she much longer endure listening to her family belabor over the travails of their dwindling munitions and not speak of it?

Kitty swallowed the ache in her throat and glanced at Shawme Pond as it glistened in the sun.

Several boys played on the banks at the other side, throwing rocks and digging sticks in the mud. The merry breeze brushed passed her cheeks and caressed the wildflowers. The world had always been so beautiful. Now, no matter what went on around her, it was dull and devoid of joy.

Kitty stopped and stared forward as her spirit dimmed. Where was God? If He knew her every thought then He must know how much she regretted this chore. How much she wanted to tell her family what she knew. Why hadn't He provided a way for her rescue?

She glanced at the dust on her shoes. This *had* to be the last time—the last delivery. She couldn't take the oppression much longer or she might burst.

Lord, where art thou? Canst thou not hear me?

"Good afternoon, milady."

Kitty spun around. Devoid of the energy needed to plaster a relaxed smile on her face, her eyes rounded and her insides buzzed. This could not be a more terrible time to cross paths with Nathaniel.

Regaining her shattered composure, she forced her lips to bow upward. "Nathaniel, what a pleasant surprise." Though of course it was not.

He approached, a smile in his eyes that reached out to soothe the tremors in her spirit. "'Tis that indeed."

Clasping her hands at her waist, Kitty forbid her vision to drink him in. But it defied her commands, satisfying a thirst she suffered but consistently ignored. His brown jacket and tan waistcoat played perfectly with his dark complexion. The crinkles around his eyes deepened as his smile grew and she tried to remember how to breathe. Her mind and her body reacted with the same dichotomy of forces, yearning for his nearness and at the same moment needing to escape and never turn back.

Did he ever think of that night outside of the Cooper's home? Of the way their lips had nearly touched and changed them evermore? She thought of that moment every day. Though every day, she scolded herself for such folly.

Nathaniel reached her and offered a gentle bow, his usual bold charm subdued, replaced with a rich sincerity that beamed in his broad smile. "It has been too long since we've seen each other, has it not? At least a fortnight or more in my estimation."

He'd been counting? "Aye."

Glancing around, he then looked her up and down with his eyes squinting as if trying to decipher a puzzle. He tilted his head slightly, and motioned toward her hands. "Making deliveries again? Where are your goods?"

"Deliveries?" That nervous high-pitched laugh surfaced and Kitty wanted to cringe when it escaped. She smiled instead. "Oh no, no—no goods. Simply enjoying the summer air." She waved her arms and flopped them down at her sides. He had better leave promptly. She could not endure being distracted in any way that may cause her to miss her all-important task.

Nodding, the sides of Nathaniel's mouth pulled down in a contemplative expression as he considered her, but said nothing.

Licking her lips, Kitty scrambled to assemble an excuse in the barren desert of her brain. "'Tis good to see you, Nathaniel. As always." She cleared her throat, upset at how her words expressed more longing than she'd wished to expose. "But, I certainly do not wish to detain you, I know how busy you've been. I'll let you be on your way."

Kitty turned and started up the street again, but he was instantly at her side.

"I'm in no hurry, and since it appears that you have no fixed engagements, allow me to walk with you a while. I've missed our conversations, Kitty."

This cannot be happening.

She stopped and guarded her breathing to keep her rising anxiety at bay. "Really, Nathaniel, I'm going nowhere, I'm simply—"

"You're trying to be rid of me." He jerked back and pressed a hand to his chest in exaggerated shock. "I cannot believe it."

Kitty failed to snuff-out the smile that burst to life on her face. "Nay, I'm not, I'm—"

"You're angry with me." He shook his head. "What have I done *this* time?"

Now she giggled. "I am not angry."

"Oh dear. I know what it is," he said, his mouth twisted to the side. "You're going to meet another gentleman."

"Nay!" This time she laughed out-loud. "I am not. I am doing nothing but taking a leisurely stroll." She sighed through her smile. If anyone could make her forget her sorrows, it was Nathaniel.

For the first time in two weeks, the ugliness around her heart receded and the beauty of the world radiated around her in all its color and brilliance. "I speak truthfully," she said, shrugging. "I am merely walking."

Nathaniel's handsome face lit as if the sun shone from within him. "Good." He cocked his elbow. "Come, this day is far too beautiful to stroll without someone with whom to enjoy it. I promise to be on my best behavior."

Taking his arm, Kitty suddenly plunged back into the pit of melancholy. How long would this take? She had two hours before she had to carry out her hated task. Plenty of time to bask in some much-needed happiness. God knew how she hated the terrible wait and the dread that nipped at her heart like a salivating wolf. Perhaps this was a blessing. *Thank you, Lord.*

Glancing at her grinning companion, she pulled her shoulders back and shed the cloak of sorrow, welcoming the distraction as the horizon welcomes the breaking dawn.

"I thank you for your persistence, Nathaniel. I'm pleased you wish to accompany me." She dipped her chin slightly, and added a thread of severity to her tone while she continued to smile. "And I will be watching you, since you promised to be on your best behavior."

He winked. "Aren't I always?"

Nathaniel warmed from the beams of delight that brightened the world around him. He glanced at Kitty then looked back up again and tried to be satisfied with the long looks he'd enjoyed moments before, though he couldn't satiate the craving to gaze at her without end. The rosy complexion in her cheeks made the red in her lips seem to bloom like a summer rose, and his fingers itched to touch that soft strand of hair that danced around her ears.

Peeking down once more, his vision detected and confirmed the concerns he'd noted earlier but promptly dismissed. Her collarbones were more pronounced. Worry pricked. Kitty was thinner.

He cleared his throat and practiced his most nonchalant tone. "Eliza says you haven't been eating much of late, and that you've complained of increased fatigue. Are you feeling unwell?"

Kitty looked up briefly before staring with pointed attention at the road. She pressed her lips, shrugging one shoulder. "Eliza worries over-much."

"She cares about you, as do I." Nathaniel bit his tongue. "We... we are all concerned about you. It is apparent you have lost weight, Kitty."

Kitty stopped walking. She thumped her hands on her dainty hips and offered a teasing smile that hinted at deception. "Is this an examination? I thought you were going to be on good behavior, but so far I'm not impressed." Nathaniel heard her talking, but he couldn't listen. The way her mouth pinched together. The way her eyes shone like the glistening water behind them...

Inhaling to make himself return to the moment, he took her arm and started walking again. Gads. He'd better keep his head or this walk could be more devastating than a shipwreck. To both of them. "I'm a doctor, Kitty. You can't expect me not to notice such things."

Shaking her head, Kitty looked away. "I am well."

Nathaniel locked his jaw to keep from glowering. Terrible liar she was. A wriggle of concern inched deeper into his chest. He wanted to help, wanted to ease the burden she carried. Why wouldn't she disclose what had happened that night? Had it really been as innocuous as she claimed? Surely her hidden pains pointed back to that horrid evening. What was it she wouldn't tell?

"Doctor Smith!"

He stopped and spun at the feminine sound. Kitty did the same.

Up the road floated Miss Caroline Whitney, her statuesque frame looking unusually tall underneath such a loud hat. Beside her, little Charlotte cradled precious "baby Emmiline" in her arms. A smile burst to life on Nathaniel's face when his gaze landed on the four-year-old. The blonde curls crowning her head bounced as she walked, her round face dusted with pink as she gave Nathaniel a shy smile in return.

Kitty flung him a desperate look. "Perhaps I should go—"

"Nonsense." Nathaniel kept a firm grip on her elbow.

Caroline approached and offered a generous curtsy. "Good afternoon, Doctor Smith." A gracious smile lit her face as she glanced down at Charlotte. "You remember my cousin Charlotte, do you not?"

"Why of course." Nathaniel removed his hat and swung it around in a large arc as he bowed low. "What a pleasure it is to see you again, Lady Charlotte." He winked.

The young girl put a hand to her face as a sprightly giggle chirped from her lips.

Replacing his hat, Nathaniel took a step back. "Miss Whitney, Lady Charlotte, allow me to introduce Miss Campbell."

"'Tis a pleasure to meet you, Miss Campbell." Caroline's eyes softened. "I know your sister well and she mentioned you'd recently returned from Boston. I'd wanted desperately to meet you at the Cooper's several weeks past, but I understand you had to leave early. 'Tis a pleasure to at last make your acquaintance."

"A great pleasure indeed." Kitty curtsied.

Charlotte lightly tugged on Nathaniel's coat and he peered down just as she began to relieve her precious wooden doll of its swaddling clothes.

He crouched to the ground and rested an arm over his knee, gesturing to the well-loved toy with his brow raised in question. "Little Emmiline seems to be well recovered, is she not?"

Charlotte nodded and a cherub-like grin revealed two perfect dimples in her round cheeks.

Nathaniel reached out. He tilted his head slightly and kept his voice laden with sincerity. "May I see how her arm has heeled? I should like to remove the bandages if all is back to normal."

Charlotte continued to grin as she slowly handed over the love-worn toy. Cradling the doll as if it were a real child, Nathaniel carefully removed the tiny bandage he'd placed on the doll's arm several weeks past. Prodding gently, he made his expression grow serious as he checked the arm that had "broken". With a quick look to Kitty, he winked and the warm smile she offered in return coated his heart. He stilled, lost in her fathomless eyes until she raised her brows and with a slight gesture glanced toward Charlotte, reminding him of what he'd been doing. Quickly regaining his mental clarity, he lowered his chin and donned the stern turn of his mouth. The young girl's dimples retreated, her gleeful expression replaced with such concern Nathaniel almost regretted the charade.

With a nod, he returned the doll to Charlotte's outstretched arms. "She is well and fully recovered." He dotted Charlotte's nose as a grin rose from the depths of him. "She is very lucky to have a mother as caring as you."

The young girl beamed, her innocence and trust

pulling at something untried in the farthest passages of his soul. Would he ever have a child of his own?

Flinging away the thoughts, he stood. Caroline bowed her head toward Charlotte and offered a knowing giggle before looking back at Nathaniel with unspoken gratitude in her face that tugged a grin from his lips. But it was Kitty's gentle eyes, her slightly open smile and the cant of her head that made Nathaniel's heart prance within his chest.

"If I may, Miss Campbell..." Caroline stepped forward and motioned to Kitty as she moved right along in the conversation. "I must say, I have found such enjoyment in your sister's company and in our conversations about these turbulent times. Isn't it wonderful that we are all part of the same patriot group? Such an important cause in which to unite—especially when so much rests upon our courage."

Kitty's face flushed, a tight smile her only response.

Caroline looked back at Nathaniel then to Kitty once more. "And now we have you to join us. We patriots must rally together, do you not agree?"

Kitty stuttered. "I'm... I'm not actually—"

"She's undecided at the moment, where her homage lies." Nathaniel didn't look, but he could hear a quiet breath escape Kitty's mouth. He wanted to take her hand and caress her delicate fingers. She needn't be so hesitant to share her beliefs. Though after the way he'd snapped at her, her reaction was justified. He swallowed a self-directed reprimand. Would he ever learn?

Always genuine, Caroline nodded as if she understood the implied struggle. "There's much to be considered. 'Tis understandable." She stepped back and pinned her gaze on Nathaniel. "I failed to thank you for joining us for supper Sunday last."

Nathaniel kept his face forward, but from the corner of his vision he could see Kitty's head tilt ever so slight as she took another subtle step away from him.

"Aye," he said, as cool as he could, "'twas a very nice evening, Miss Whitney. I thank you."

Her eyes flitted again to Kitty then back to Nathaniel before she took Charlotte's hand. "We really must be going." She nodded her good-bye while Charlotte waved the tiny hand of her doll. Caroline laughed. "'Twas a pleasure to meet you, Miss Campbell. Good day, Dr. Smith."

She started down the road, leaning slightly to speak to Charlotte of her doll's good fortune as they disappeared around the corner.

Nathaniel sighed and turned to Kitty, yearning to place her slender hand on his arm where it had rested before the untimely meeting. As if sensing his gaze, Kitty glanced up then twisted her mouth to the side in a playful smirk. "So that's where you were last Sunday." She glanced forward and started walking. "I'd wondered."

He matched her leisurely stride, hoping his answer would smooth the creases in her brow as he offered his arm once more. Surprisingly, she took it. "Mr. Whitney is a good friend," he said, "I've known him for years. I only spent Sunday in their home to discuss politics. Mr. Whitney is in charge of setting up the watch for the powder. We've had some difficulties in that respect and I'm in need of more help with the guard now than in the past."

Kitty removed her hand from his elbow, leaving a cold space where her touch had been. "I'm sorry for the struggles you are enduring. I'm sure 'tis quite a burden."

Nathaniel tried to catch her expression. She kept her face forward, but the tight set to her soft jaw and the way her throat bobbed made explicit the one question he'd hoped wasn't true. Kitty didn't wish to speak of politics or any related subject with him—that, or her sudden sullenness meant her unrevealed struggles related to this very issue.

He pressed out a hard breath. It wasn't as if he could simply ignore the conversation. If he couldn't talk to Kitty of such things for fear it might upset her, 'twas the same as ignoring the existence of the sky.

Glazing his tone in gentleness, he continued the undesired conversation, praying somehow he could decode the missives her expressions tried so hard to suppress. "'Tis distressing. More distressing than anything else of late. But I pray God will lead us to the culprit. I know we must discover them soon, and when we do they will certainly pay for what they've done."

Jerking to a halt, Kitty pressed her hands to her stomach and peeked up at him. Her mouth pressed tight and the color again left her face. That gnawing angst chewed into his stomach and if not for a lone passer-by on the street he would have taken her hand in his and stroked her velvety skin until she looked at him—now and long after. *What is it, dear Kitty? Why will you not tell me?*

He opened his mouth, ready to coax the reluctant words from her lips, but he snapped his jaw shut. Now was not the time. Perhaps when they were at home, with Thomas and Eliza near to help ease the tensions that so obviously beset her, they would once and for all unearth the burdens she'd buried in her heart. With a quick look to the sky, Nathaniel acquiesced. There would be no revelation today. Best to change the subject.

"We have arrived." Nathaniel touched the small of her back and motioned toward the picturesque resting place. Leaf-laden branches waved toward the water like green ribbons as the soft breeze brushed past. The warm sun kissed the water and shimmered like flecks of gold, pairing beautifully with the patch of grass that rested just inches from the bank.

Kitty's eyes twinkled like the water at the banks of the pond. Her mouth parted slightly and she inhaled a quick breath. "I've never seen any place so inviting."

"You can't find anything like this in Boston."

An airy laugh huffed from her lips. "Nay, you cannot." She moved forward then jerked to a stop. "But is it at all proper for us to be here without a chaperone?"

Nathaniel kept the smile away from his expression, though it ached for exposure. She couldn't be more charming. "Chaperone? I believe such a formality would only be necessary if we were courting." He leaned forward, finally allowing that grin to expand on his lips. "Are we?"

Her cheeks flashed red and she looked away.

Stifling a chuckle, Nathaniel nudged her forward and sat on the grass at a respectable distance from where she seated herself. If only he could inch closer...

The gentle wind toyed with the curls around Kitty's neck and seemed to blow the additional color from her face until just the perfect hue of pink dusted her cheeks. She straightened her skirts over her daintily folded legs and untied the straw hat from her head, revealing a crown of rich auburn hair that glowed in the sun like embers in a fire.

Nathaniel swallowed. A mad yearning to brush his fingers against her cheek forced his hands to the grass. Kitty rested her hat on the ground and gazed out over the water, closing her eyes as if the very sounds and scents of nature soothed the pains from her soul. He could do it now, touch her hand while she wasn't looking. He reached then halted when another, more desirable daydream flashed to life. He shouldn't even think such a thing, but the image loomed until he could contemplate nothing else. What would it be like? One kiss, one small touch of the lips? He would not ask for more. Yet, the longer he surrendered to the desire, the more the shape of her mouth consumed his vision.

He looked the other way and kneaded his hands together. This foolish affection for her was like the shape of a cloud, one moment there and the next dissolved. A relationship with Kitty couldn't happen. In fact, it *would* not. He'd made that promise long ago. Though perhaps such a kiss, one small kiss, would forever extinguish these childish imaginations from his heart.

Chapter Fourteen

The sparkling water and warm sun caressed the wounds around Kitty's heart. She studied the pond, the quacking ducks gliding on the surface, the song of birds, the brush of the breeze on her face, and relished in the peace of the moment. A peace she hadn't felt in weeks.

Nathaniel peered at her, his head slightly tilted. "You know, I believe this is the first time you and I have ever really been alone."

She laughed lightly to hide the extra thump of her heart. Why must he smile at her that way? Kitty turned her attention to the ground and she plucked at the soft grass, feigning a calm exterior while her insides jumbled. "Nay, we've been alone many a time."

"Not like this." He took a deep breath and wrapped his strong arms around his knees, his muscles straining the fabric of his jacket. "It's nice to see what you are like when you are not in the company of your sister."

"What do you mean? I'm not any different when I'm with Liza."

"You are not different, nay. I simply enjoy... I simply enjoy your company." The richness of his voice nurtured the longing that welled within.

Unsure how else to respond, Kitty's lips tipped up at one end. "Thank you."

He opened his mouth part-way as if he wished to continue, but didn't. He looked ahead, then down into his twined hands.

Kitty ducked her chin as her pulse darted through her limbs and heated her face once more. *I simply enjoy your company*. Had he meant anything more by his comment? Surely not. She brushed the question from her mind.

But it wouldn't leave.

She searched his face and somehow stumbled even though she was already still. Nathaniel's eyes trailed her face and lingered over her hair, her neck and meandered downward, but skirted away before his vision met with her curves.

He coughed lightly and appeared to reawaken his usual swagger. "Tell me something about you I don't know."

"Heavens, Nathaniel, I'm sure you know everything."

"I do not." He rested his elbow on his one raised knee, while the other leg folded underneath it. "If I did, then I would have known all about the infamous James *Pigley*, so I must assume there are more secrets to you that need discovering."

"Secrets?" Her voice cracked. Chest heaving, she turned away. Did he have to use such a word? She struggled to find something within her stalled mind to ease the suffocating silence.

"Come now Kitty, don't play coy with me." Nathaniel's inviting timbre woke her from the shadows. The playful glint in his face pulled a full smile from her lips when he continued. "Here is what

I know of Miss Katherine Campbell formerly of Boston. She enjoys Shakespeare and is a gifted cook. I know she is fascinated with medicine and I know her political standings. She loves God and family..." He grinned wider, a gentle kind of grin that sparkled in his eyes. "But I desire to know more."

The warmth in his stare eased around Kitty as real as if it had been an embrace, soothing away the tension that clung to her neck and shoulders. She leaned one hand on the ground and rested against it. "You're very kind, Nathaniel, but I don't know what to tell. I'm quite ordinary."

"Ordinary? I should say not." Nathaniel reached for a small stick and played with it in his fingers before he snapped it in half and tossed the pieces in the water. He cast his eyes her direction and glared playfully. "No matter. If you choose to be so demure then I shall ask questions. Do you enjoy the ocean?"

"Aye, the seaside is very calming, but I don't care for boats."

He nodded with his lips pursed in thought. "I'll keep that in mind. Do you play an instrument?"

"Nay, much to my mother's disappointment." She sighed and looked heavenward with a tiny laugh, remembering the hours of practice that produced embarrassingly little results. Kitty sat up and hugged her knees. "Do you enjoy reading?"

Nathaniel scowled. "This conversation isn't supposed to be about me."

"Well, do you?" She grinned wider.

He shook his head with a disapproving lift to his brow, but the smoldering grin expressed his merriment. "I enjoy reading. Especially Milton."

"Milton? I adore Milton."

Time passed and their conversation washed back

and forth in a soothing rhythm, like gentle waves on the seashore. Easy, natural.

Nathaniel leaned back and rested on his elbow. A breeze brushed past and several ducks glided down to the water. "I know your given name is Katherine. So why does everyone call you Kitty?" He pulled a bag of dried apple slices from his medical bag. With a few pieces in his hand, he gestured to Kitty but she shook her head to decline.

She sat straight. "Do you not know?"

Holding a piece of apple up to his mouth, Nathaniel prepared for a bite. "I'm waiting." He flicked the morsel in his mouth and began to chew.

She grinned and played with the printed floral fabric of her skirt. "Father was in his study reviewing materials one evening, when Peter—"

Nathaniel raised his hand, his expression tender. "You mean your older brother... the one you lost."

"Aye." The pain of her brother's death, though always fresh, receded as she prepared to share how her dear sibling had given her such a name. She brushed a blade of grass from her knee. "Peter must have been about two and a half years old, perhaps older. Father said Peter came rushing in babbling something about a kitty and pointing vigorously in the direction of the kitchen."

Kitty imitated the motion, making Nathaniel's handsome smile widen. "I'm intrigued. Continue."

"Father followed Peter toward the kitchen where, inside the barrel of flour and covered from top to toe was none other than the baby of the family. So, from that moment on Peter, Father, Mother and Liza all called me Kitty."

Nathaniel pelted the air with that buoyant laugh Kitty loved. "How did you get into the barrel without your mother's notice?"

"'Tis a mystery."

He leaned back onto the grass and rested against his elbow, nodding with mock disapproval. "So you were a wily child then?"

"Am I not wily now?"

"I should say so. And you've enjoyed getting your fingers messy in the kitchen ever since."

"Aye, I have."

He took another bite of dried apple while his gaze narrowed in thought. "I am forever grateful you shared that with me, Kitty." Tracing her face with his eyes, the levity in his expression faltered. Warm and dark like a summer's eve, his voice caressed. "So, the secrets of 'Miss Katherine Campbell formerly of Boston' begin to emerge." Pausing, his voice grew deeper still. "And I can only pray that someday I shall understand all the mysteries that shelter in the precious center of your heart."

Kitty's lungs refused to take in air, then suddenly pumped as if her last breath were seconds away. Her palms grew clammy and her cheeks burned like the sun on her back. The look of desire in Nathaniel's expression, the weight to his voice, the softness in his rugged features, all these familiar hungry expressions had lived in James Higley's eyes, and at the time it discomfited her. But now, it thrilled... and frightened.

To keep from being consumed by the flame within, she pushed up from the grass and walked to the edge of the water, placing all her focus on the way it lapped at the toe of her shoe. Clearing her throat, she tried to remember what they'd last been talking of so she could artfully change the subject.

She licked her lips, and flooded her tone with a serenity she didn't feel. "I figured you had already heard that story from Liza. It seems most everyone has heard it by now."

Continuing to stare at the water, Kitty heard him rise and step near her, but she dare not look around for fear of how another longing gaze from him might melt her where she stood.

"Nay, I had not heard of it." His voice was far too close, far too rich. "Would that I had known this endearing tale long ago." When he spoke again his tone carried more of his hallmark teasing. "Please, I beg you. Do not tell me that even the infamous Mr. Pigley knew that story before I."

Unable to stop it, Kitty tipped her head back as a burst of laughter erupted from her chest, grateful for the way such jesting eased the heat between them. "No, Mr. *Higley* has never heard that story, nor shall he."

Peaceful silence circled. Only the sound of ducks and a few cheery birds accompanied their quiet. But the quiet was short lived and Kitty's nerves flitted again as Nathaniel cleared his throat and began to speak. "So, does this... this Higley fellow have any hope with you?"

Startled at the intimacy of his question, Kitty flipped toward him. She stared before answering his question with one of her own. "What do you mean?"

He stared at her, one eyebrow up as if he were issuing a kind of mock reprimand. "Do not play ignorant with me."

She'd rarely seen him so somber, and the uncomfortable sensation that burrowed in her stomach made her press her hand to her middle. "Truly, I do not know your meaning." Why was he asking such questions? He should be teasing her, pricking her frustrations, not confusing her by alluring her well-hidden longing from its place of security.

He took a step closer, his eyes growing as brown as his jacket. "Allow me to make it clear. He's asked you to marry him." Nathaniel didn't move his gaze from her face. "Will you?"

Kitty choked at the shock of his statement. Her face turned white-hot and she put a palm to her chest. "Such a question, Nathaniel."

"Nothing one could not ask a friend."

Aye, a friend.

That's the way she wanted things between them. Wasn't it?

She closed her eyes. No. 'Twas not the way she wanted it, but it was the way things would be between them, no matter how her heart tried to nourish the growing bloom of something more beautiful.

Reality settled upon her and she struggled to tamp down the hurt that billowed in her chest. Looking away, she sorted through her jumble of feelings but only became more disjointed. One moment he looked as if he *wanted* her as a man wants a woman, the next he spoke to her as a friend?

She exhaled through tight lips. "I suppose love ought to be a deciding factor."

Nathaniel looked out over the water and shifted his weight. His mouth opened and closed several times until finally he stopped his fidgeting and turned to face her, binding her motionless.

His warm gaze cloaked her like the very sun that shown through the canopy of leaves. "Are you in love with him, Kitty?" His low voice rumbled with a kind of desire that turned Kitty's insides to a puddle.

Why are you asking? A quick answer somehow

made its way to her mouth. "Why would I tell you?" The cut in her voice came out sharper than she intended, but the protective shield with which she attempted to protect her heart had rusted clear through.

Nathaniel looked at his feet a moment before returning his face to hers. "Does that mean you are?"

Exasperated, Kitty stomped her foot. "Stop asking me—"

"'Tis only a simple question."

Kitty's jaw dropped and indignation slammed through her. The man had gone daft! How dare he make eyes at her, then talk as if they were "friends" and *then* act as if he had some right to information she'd never told a living soul.

"That is not a simple question, Nathaniel Smith."

"I don't see why not." The roundness of his eyes and the infuriating way he lifted and lowered his shoulders—as if he had no earthly idea why she might be upset—nearly pulled a growl from her throat. He stared at her. "All I need is a simple answer."

The gall! "No!"

"You don't love him?"

"No, I—Oh!" The growl finally surfaced with an accompanying stomp, but it did little to abate the anger that bellowed.

Nathaniel bit his cheek as he tried to hold back the grin that inched across his mouth. The nerve of him! "*No*, I won't be telling you anything!"

"I believe you just did." Nathaniel's eyes lit and he tilted his head just slightly, as if she'd reacted *exactly* the way he'd wanted.

Kitty grit her teeth, wishing she could breathe fire and singe that over-satisfied grin off his face. "You can think what you like, *Doctor*, but I will tell you one thing, Mr. Higley has far better etiquette than to ever ask anything of such a personal nature."

He chuckled, his eyes never leaving her. "You are so enchanting when you're upset."

"Enchanting?" How dare he laugh at her! How *dare* he toy with her feelings in such an insidious way? He was no stranger to women. Was he really just playing with her, or did he simply see her as a friend—nay, a sister—that he could tease and torment?

She pinched her lips and put her chin in the air, still fuming at the way he refused to stop grinning. "Remind me to let Caroline come with you next time you care for a walk. I find I don't enjoy being *alone* with you."

Glaring daggers, Kitty spun around and started toward the road, but she didn't make it two steps before Nathaniel grabbed her arm and pulled her to him, pressing his mouth against hers.

With a quick yelp Kitty tried to push him away, but his hands wound around her back, his lips both gentle and possessive as he tempted her own lips to open. She collapsed into his embrace and shed the remaining anger, no longer able to contain the desire she'd struggled so long to ignore.

She pressed against him and wrapped her arms around his neck as she lifted on her toes, relishing in the way his soft, moist lips molded against hers. The sound of his ragged breathing, the scent of his apple-tart breath, the feel of his strong hands, all imprinted on her mind—and on her heart. Kitty Campbell would never be the same.

He spoke to her between kisses. "I don't think you love him." His warm hands brushed up her back before becoming lost in her curls.

"I *know* I do not." She clutched the soft, thick hair at his neck, savoring how his nose brushed against her cheek.

Nathaniel descended again, devouring her mouth with an intensity that stole Kitty's reason. She clutched him harder, sliding her hands down his muscular arms and resting them on his chest, allowing a tiny moan to escape her throat.

A small voice echoed in the far-away corner of her mind. She should stop. They weren't married. Weren't even courting. This would be scandalous should they be discovered. Only a moment longer. She had plenty of time before she needed to...

Gasping, Kitty shoved Nathaniel away, her eyes suddenly burning as she covered her mouth. She stared at him, her chest pumping as horror filled her lungs. What time was it? *Oh dear Lord, what have I done?*

Kitty tried to step away, but Nathaniel's firm grip held her arm. Lips still glistening from their kiss, his features drooped with worry and he tried to pull her back.

His words came fast and frayed with regret. "Kitty, don't go. Please forgive me, I should never have—"

"Nay!" Wrenching from his grasp, Kitty stumbled back, her body trembling. "I... I can't... I have to go."

Pulling every measure of strength remaining, Kitty dashed toward the street, flinging tears from her eyes as she ran.

"Kitty, wait!" Nathaniel's plea traveled behind her, but no footsteps followed.

If she raced faster, perhaps she could get there in time. *Lord, please!* She'd never been late before. What would Cyprian do?

Charging down the road, Kitty prayed.

Perhaps there was hope.

There had to be hope...

Or the worst had just begun.

Chapter Fifteen

Nathaniel stared after her, his pulse thundering, pumping his heated blood until his entire frame felt ready to ignite. Wiping a hand down his face, he groaned. What had he done? His mouth still throbbed from the passion they'd shared only seconds ago. He hadn't wanted to frighten her. Hadn't even intended to kiss her.

Gritting his teeth, he held his jaw tight and shook his hands beside his legs to rid the powerful regret that flooded him. Blast it. If she hadn't been so alluring with her pert little mouth and cheeks pink from frustration he might have been able to resist her.

He rubbed the back of his neck. Her body felt so natural against his, her lips so soft.

At the sound of light footsteps, Nathaniel spun around, his heart in his throat. Had she returned? His shoulders dropped. Nay, 'twas no one. He closed his eyes and remembered again the look of horror on her sweet face. The memory sliced him with the precision of a surgeon's lance. The kind of passion they'd shared should exist only between husband and wife. No wonder she ran from him as if he were the devil.

He shook his head, his scalp still tingling from the sensation of her fingers in his hair.

But she had kissed him back. No doubt of that. She'd wanted it as much as he had.

Nathaniel stared across the pond, the sun sliding lower in the sky behind him. Things would never be the same now. A curse coiled on his tongue. So much for one kiss being enough. The hunger that such an act had planted in his heart would only grow. Roots of desire and the bloom of passion would flourish now that he knew something more than friendship existed between them. Much more.

Pressing his eyes shut, Nathaniel ground his teeth. Kitty would never embrace the cause of liberty as he did. She held to the very doctrine he strove to combat. *What should I do?* A flutter along the grass caught his attention. Kitty's forgotten hat seemed to beckon him for attention. Stooping, he picked it up and caressed the yellow ribbon between his fingers.

He must forget her and focus on where he was most needed. The people of Sandwich relied on him.

That is where he must put his energy.

Time would take care of the rest.

Kitty pounded on the back door of the tavern. Hands quivering, she spun around, hoping Cyprian would appear and she could explain her reason for tardiness. But what *was* her reason? The answer made tears burn behind her eyes. *Lord in heaven forgive me.*

The slow creak of the door snatched her attention and she turned again, holding her breath.

A young boy, about eleven years old, stood in the doorway. His brown hair and blue eyes struck her so hard she nearly stepped back. He looked so much like Peter had looked. Though bright and gangly, like many boys that age, a sadness in the slump of his shoulders whispered of untold sorrows yearning to be soothed.

"May I help you, Miss?" he asked.

Kitty swallowed and tried to appear as if her heart wasn't about to beat through her ribs. "I'm so sorry to bother you, I'm looking for Mr. Cyprian Wythe."

He opened the door further. "My father isn't here at the moment."

Panic pounded its long nails into her bones. She clutched her skirts to keep her hands from exposing her fear. "I see."

The boy motioned for her to enter. "Would you like to wait for him inside?"

"Nay, but thank you."

Cocking his head, he offered an innocent smile. "My name's Jacob. I know who you are. I've seen you around town."

"You have?" She smiled, but kept it tight. The last thing Kitty wanted to do was engage in idle conversation, but perhaps if she stayed a moment longer Cyprian would appear. Then she could explain her negligence and plead for him not to make anyone suffer because of her foolish mistake and promise she would never do it again.

"Aye, I spend a good deal of time at my Uncle Joseph's blacksmith shop. I've seen you walking past every so often."

"Ah." If he had noticed her, how many other people had?

"You don't talk much do you?"

She pointed toward the road. "'Twas nice to meet you Jacob, I really need to be going."

"What's your name? I can tell my father you came by."

"Thank you, son, you may return inside, I will speak with Miss Campbell." Cyprian came from the side of the house, his expression void of the emotion that resonated in his voice.

Kitty's blood drained out of her head so quickly her vision wavered.

"Obey me, boy." Cyprian nodded toward his son and Jacob obeyed, closing the door without even a smile.

Cyprian's cold eyes speared clean through her. "Do you know what time it is, Miss Campbell?"

Praying for strength, Kitty swallowed and nodded. "Forgive me, Mr. Wythe. I lost track of time—"

"Are you without a pocket watch? Is your home without a clock?" He stepped closer. The blank stare he pinned on her frightened her more than the malice she'd seen in his eyes the night he'd found her at the magazine. "Without you showing your dedication I am forced to believe you have betrayed a confidence and I must stay true to my promise."

Horror welled like a roaring wave, killing her ability to breathe. "Please, please, sir, I swear to you, I have not divulged anything!"

Cyprian blinked, his terrible lifeless expression unchanging.

Hot tears rolled over her cheeks and her chin quivered. "You must believe me."

"Go home, Miss Campbell. All is well." His upper lip twitched into a mocking smile while his eyes remained cold, showering Kitty's skin with the sensation of a thousand wriggling worms.

When she didn't immediately move, he stepped forward. "Did you not hear me Miss Campbell? I said all is well. *Go home*."

She spun away, dashing from her enemy with more speed than she knew she possessed. Racing down the road, tears splashed against her cheeks as his words rang in her mind and his intent sank into her stomach. Suddenly she stopped as the weight of his threats crashed into her like a heavy horse-drawn cart.

All is well meant all was about to unravel.

Chapter Sixteen

Nathaniel pressed his hat on his head and strode out the large wooden doors of Andrew's grand home and into the evening that smelled of salt and earth. The night air sat heavy with sea mist, mirroring the weight that pressed upon Nathaniel's shoulders. He groaned inwardly at the failed attempt to secretly deduce the traitor among them.

Already outside, Thomas spoke from his place at the edge of the stone steps. "Until tomorrow, Andrew." His voice was void of that energy which Nathaniel would have gladly drawn from, had it existed. Thomas touched the brim of his hat and started toward the road.

Nathaniel remained where he stood, the last of the men who'd attended the hastily called meeting. Sensing an inaudible groan from the man whose home they'd once again used as a place of security for their patriotic gatherings, Nathaniel lingered.

Andrew stared forward into the night, his arms crossed over his chest. Almost as if he were looking through the heavy air into their uncertain futures, he turned his mouth and shook his head, his tone as dark as the black sky above them. "'Tis a rotten business, and there's sure to be more anguish before we're through."

Nathaniel tapped Andrew's arm before starting down the stairs. "All will be made right. We shall see to it."

Andrew's eyes followed him, grey and ominous like over-burdened clouds. "I pray you are right."

His gaze held Nathaniel motionless on the first step, as if the man ached for something that remained unspoken. Nathaniel returned his stare, but said nothing, hoping his silence might coax from Andrew what his eyes wanted to share. Could he be... ? Nay. Andrew was more patriot than any of them. Then what bothered him so?

Andrew's chest lifted and lowered. "Perhaps these raids will soon end and we may be at liberty to enjoy the peace we crave, hmm?"

Nathaniel flung a quick look to Thomas before studying Andrew's pensive eyes. "We all wish it. Though I fear Mother England will not grant us such a reprieve. Not until we make it unmistakably clear where we stand on the issue of freedom. Which is why maintaining our reserves is most vital."

Andrew nodded and pulled his bottom lip through his teeth. He quickly looked down and pushed from his position against the door. "Until that time, we shall strive to do the best that is within our power, I suppose. Good evening, gentlemen." With a labored turn he stepped into the house, shutting the thick door behind him.

Tromping down the steps, Nathaniel glanced over his shoulder to where Andrew had stood, studying the conversations they'd shared with the handful of patriot men for the past two hours.

He shook his head, and expelled a taxed breath as he spoke through his teeth. "A blasted waste of time."

Irritation cultivated what meager energy he had remaining and he lengthened his stride down the hard dirt road. "We are no closer to determining the traitor in our midst. How are we so blind?"

He glanced at Thomas whose emotions wore themselves into the tightness of his mouth and the flaring of his nose, but remained speechless.

Nathaniel curled his fists and ground his heels into the road with every step. *Who, Lord? Wilt thou not show us?*

Thomas finally spoke. "Are our plans unchanged? Will we still remove the munitions?"

Nathaniel grumbled and flicked his legs. "I see no other way."

"How shall we do it?"

Kicking a stone from the path, Nathaniel pushed out an exaggerated breath that almost sounded like the bitter laugh he retained. "I don't know." He gnawed on the inside of his cheek. Act too soon and the perpetrator would likely become suspicious. Wait too long and they risked losing more of their munitions. And that they could not afford. "We must act quickly but with caution, that is all I know."

A frog croaked loud in the night air, as if he had heard the hushed exchange and offered his unwanted opinion. Thomas only nodded and rubbed his jaw, remaining silently pensive. Thankfully. Nathaniel craved quiet. He needed it to think of a way to accomplish their designs.

He needed to think of Kitty.

Washed by the warm, silken memories he'd tried so fervently to forget, he succumbed to the memory of the sweet scent of cinnamon he'd smelled in her hair, the cool touch of her hand on his jaw, the way her soft lips—

"Nathaniel?" Thomas's voice boomed.

Nathaniel glanced up with a jerk. "Hmm?"

Brow drawn close, Thomas chuckled. "I've asked you a question. Twice."

Nathaniel sighed and wiped a hand over his mouth to smear away the heavenly sensation that continued to haunt. "Forgive me, I was simply... thinking."

"Simply thinking." A smirk tempted at the edges of Thomas's mouth. "What has you so distracted? A woman perhaps?"

Nathaniel halted, glaring. "A woman? Nay, the threat of war has me distracted." He pointed behind them. "Have I not just been discussing such vital issues? And without the slightest hint of preoccupation?"

Nathaniel's question was answered by another in the narrowing of Thomas's eyes.

Gather yourself, Nathaniel. Don't play the lovesick fool. He rubbed his temples, hoping his friend would leave the subject behind, but when he looked up, Thomas's eyebrows shot to his hairline and an over-satisfied smile expanded on his face. "I know there is something you hide, and I venture to suppose I know the subject."

"Do you? That is remarkable, seeing as how I hide *nothing*." Nathaniel's collar tightened and he grimaced at Thomas's expanding grin.

Nathaniel started up again, walking faster and mumbling frustrations in his mind he wished he could form on his lips but could not, lest Thomas take pleasure in knowing he was right.

Thomas stopped and grabbed Nathaniel's arm. "Speak out, Nathaniel, or I shall be forced to say it for you."

Nathaniel yanked his arm away and kept walking, his words dipped in gall. “Say what?”

“A woman has tied you in knots.”

The words stacked before him like a wall of stones and he stumbled. Staring, Nathaniel gauged the knowing look on his friend’s face, when the truth tripped unbidden from his tongue, both reverent and filled with regret. “I kissed her, Thomas.”

Only a single brow raised, as if Thomas had already expected as much, though his words didn’t match his expression. “Kissed who?”

Nathaniel swallowed, blinking slowly. “Kitty.”

Thomas’s mouth tightened and he turned his head, allowing Nathaniel to see how his jaw flexed before he turned back to face him. The anger in his voice did not agree with the subdued nature of his stance. “Do you know what you’ve done?”

A coarse laugh popped out and Nathaniel rubbed his forehead. “Do not lecture me, Thomas.”

“I must assume you do not, or you would have thought more carefully before doing such a thing.” Thomas stepped forward, his volume rising to meet the frustration in his eyes. “Take care, Nathaniel. Kitty is young as to things of men and women. You cannot play with her heart, ‘tis not fair to her or to you.”

Biting back the indignation that boiled, Nathaniel strained to keep his tone void of the emotions that consumed him. “You will not advise me on such things, Thomas. I will do what I feel, despite your unsolicited warnings.”

Thomas grimaced. “She’s a *child*.”

“Blast it, Thomas! She’s a woman!”

“I know how women flock to you, Nathaniel, but Kitty is sweet and innocent when compared to some of the women you have known. I will not have you using her, not when you well know how she's cared for you these many months."

"I know nothing of what you claim and more than that I am not using—" Nathaniel pulled back and ground his teeth. The words were so disgusting he couldn't bear to repeat them. Using her? Never! Breath heaving in heated bursts, Nathaniel shifted his feet over and again, but found no satisfactory stance. Thomas tread on dangerous soil if he believed he knew something of Nathaniel's feelings for Kitty, when he himself hadn't even begun—let alone allowed himself—to examine the feelings that rooted in his chest. He breathed through his nose, afraid to open his mouth for fear the untried feelings of his heart would spill out like an over-burdened basket.

Thomas put his hands on his hips and looked down at his feet before fixing an irritating glare on Nathaniel. "Does she return your... affections?"

Nathaniel stiffened and laughed toward the stars. "If you're asking if she returned my kiss, then yes, Thomas, she did." He leaned forward and glared, wanting to strip that smirk off Thomas's face with a description of how she'd returned his passion as only a *woman* could, but he pressed his mouth shut.

The muscles in Thomas's jaw flicked. "Do you love her?"

Nathaniel blinked, jaw slack and eyes wide, shocked that such a question would dare hang between them. "I do not." A kiss was simply that, not a declaration of a lifetime of devotion.

Thomas stepped forward. "Eliza feared this might happen, should the sparks between you two become too much to suppress, that you and Kitty would test the bounds of your affection..." He looked away quickly, then back again. "You've likely broken her heart beyond repair."

The regret that had continued to prick Nathaniel from the moment Kitty ran from him, crashed into the tender center of his conscience. Not regret for having tasted her, not regret for succumbing to a desire to hold one so full of strength and beauty in both heart and mind, but regret for the way her eyes welled with tears and how she fled as if he would have stolen her very innocence.

Nathaniel slowed his words, answering rough and low. "I do regret it immensely, but there's no taking it back now."

Thomas opened his mouth, but Nathaniel kept on.

"Do not lecture me of love, Thomas. I recall you struggled in your courtship with Eliza before all was made right."

Thomas didn't respond to the bait of accusation. "You see yourself in a *courtship* with Kitty?"

Nathaniel scoffed. "Of course not."

Thomas's interrogating glower darkened, and his voice grew deep. "I can assure you Kitty does."

"I can assure you she does not. She ran from me as if I were ready to carry her into hell."

Thomas's face scrunched and he opened his mouth to speak, but another voice crashed against them through the night air.

"Doctor Smith!"

The heavy pounding of horse hooves drummed against the hard dirt and in seconds a large, unfamiliar man on horseback stopped before them, straining at the reins of the animal that continued to stomp wildly at the ground.

Nathaniel frowned. "I am Doctor Smith. Who are

you?"

"There's been a terrible accident out at Gray's farm."

Gray? That was some distance away. Who was this fellow and who had sent him?

From the deep lines of worry on the man's sturdy face Nathaniel determined now wasn't a time for questions.

"I'll come." Nathaniel nodded to Thomas before charging the last few yards toward home. He called over his shoulder to the stranger. "I'll retrieve my medical bag and follow promptly."

"I'll meet you there." The stranger dashed away as Nathaniel raced up the road toward his barn.

He grabbed his bag and leapt onto his mount, kicking Astor into a full run. The stars whizzed above him and the trees blurred as he raced to the scene of some accident or illness that was most certainly grave.

The road made a sharp curve. Nathaniel pulled hard on the reins when a thick shadow in the center of the road halted his speed. His pulse pounded, but he clicked his tongue and nudged Astor on at a slower pace. Nathaniel scanned the shadow and breathed harder when the silhouetted figures of mounted men grew clear in the moonlight. Was the injured person among them?

Three large men on horseback sat shoulder to shoulder, blocking the road.

Nathaniel clung to the reins with one hand, and pulled Astor to a stop as he casually reached for the pistol at his side with the other. He grit his teeth. *No weapon.*

Nathaniel sat higher. "Let me pass." His voice boomed through the trees.

The riders shifted on their mounts, not a sound spoken from them, when a realization that should have nudged Nathaniel earlier crashed like a falling tree.

No one was injured. No one needed him at Gray's...

Yanking hard on Astor's reins, Nathaniel kicked the horse's flanks. If he could out run them in the first few seconds he could make it to safety. Roars exploded behind him as the men yelled to one another and in moments the strangers came along side, careless of the horses' dangerous speed.

One man drove his horse into Astor and slammed his body into Nathaniel, gripping him around the shoulders and pulling while another groped for the reins and yanked them from Nathaniel's hands. Nathaniel gripped with his thighs and strained to shake off the attacker but Astor reared and Nathaniel plunged to the ground, slamming against the dirt with a smack that ripped the air from his lungs. He struggled to push up, but the ground swayed as lights flashed in his vision.

Get up. Get up now!

"Don't mess him up too much," someone said. "But make it look real good."

Then the night went completely black.

Chapter Seventeen

Kitty sat on the bed, her knees tucked under her chin, still wearing her day-dress. The solitary candle that flickered on the table in the quiet room had been her non-judgmental companion for several hours already, and would continue to be, until it flickered its last glowing flame. Throat aching, eyes burning from the shedding of so many tears, she watched another drop of wax as it meandered down the ever-lowering stick. She closed her eyes and rubbed her aching head. *How could I have done such a foolish thing?* Dread combed over Kitty from head to foot and back up again, as it had from the moment she tore herself from Nathaniel's consuming embrace. The pain in her joints and limbs continued to lament, continued to deepen. How tired she was, how weak. Her body, her mind needed to rest. But rest would not bring its needed companionship until her servitude was ended.

Cupping her hands over her face, she breathed deep to hold back the sobs that pushed for escape. Cyprian was no simpleton. He would make good, and the only thing Kitty could do now was wait until he did. *Lord, I plead with thee, do not let my actions cause harm to come to those I love.*

A knock at the door jerked Kitty from her prayer.

Her heart plunked against her ribs, but she breathed through her lips to calm her quivering voice before answering.

"What is it?"

"'Tis I, Kitty. May I come in?" Eliza's calming voice eased through the door.

Kitty rubbed her eyes and exhaled, trying to break free from the frightening truths that clung to her like heavy chains. Although Eliza likely knew something was amiss, Kitty might at least be able to blame the changes of personality on subtle illness—which might be more fact than fable, from the way her head throbbed—and keep the darker secrets from surfacing.

Kitty called toward the door. "Come in, Liza."

The door creaked and Eliza entered, a single brown braid hanging over her shawl-draped shoulders. Her white nightgown brushed the tops of her stocking feet as she tip-toed toward the bed. She smiled, and crawled onto the feather pallet, pulling the covers up to her waist as she used to do all those years when they'd shared a bed. Eliza sighed and brushed her fingers along her small, but growing belly.

"You were not with us at supper." The casual nature of the comment didn't match the worry that turned Eliza's dark eyes an even deeper shade of brown.

Kitty's throat thickened and she stared at the end of the floral quilt, hugging her legs ever tighter. How could she eat when the oppression she suffered killed what appetite she might have had? How could she do anything when Cyprian was so angry over her failings? And now to know that because of a foolish kiss her family would surely suffer? A cold shiver raced over her, making her suddenly yearn for a blanket. Was she really so chilled, or was it merely the nipping regrets that cooled the air?

"Your spot in the kitchen has grown lonely of late. 'Tis not like you to be gone so long from your favorite activities." Eliza scooted closer and rubbed gentle circles on Kitty's back, soothing her enough to allow Kitty to rest her forehead on her knees.

Eliza sighed as if trying to keep back a bushel of questions before settling on one. "You are not yourself Kitty, and I cannot help but worry over you. Thomas as well. What troubles you?"

Lord, I want to share this burden, but I fear that revealing such will do more harm than good.

At the thought, the travails of the past weeks pressed harder and clamored for release, but Kitty refused them, breathing tight and pressing her lips together to keep the moisture from her eyes. Kitty shrugged one shoulder and turned away.

Eliza continued the circles on Kitty's back and gave a quick hum in reply, obviously dissatisfied.

"Father taught that keeping our burdens to ourselves is both unhealthy and unwise. You know this, Kitty." The circles on Kitty's back stopped. "From the beginning Nathaniel feared you were hiding something about your attack. I'm beginning to believe he is right."

The mere sound of Nathaniel's name broke the levy around Kitty's tears and they flooded from her. Coursing and purging from the deepest cracks in her heart, she wept the fears and regrets that plagued her like a chronic pain. Her shoulders quivered and she gripped her legs harder with every sob. The more she cried, the more her body revolted—spilling out the tears like a cold winter rain.

Eliza cooed and whispered, wrapping her arms around Kitty's shaking shoulders. "Kitty, please tell me what pains you. I want to help ease your burden but I cannot if I don't know what troubles you."

Kitty wiped her face on her skirt and tried to speak through her whimpers. "I haven't been feeling well, 'tis all."

Eliza tugged Kitty against her and enclosed her in an embrace that soothed the gash in her heart. She tucked a tear-dampened lock of hair around Kitty's ear. "We've been through so much. 'Tis no wonder you have sorrows that beg for release." She placed a gentle kiss on the top of Kitty's head before handing her a handkerchief. "God knows your sufferings, Kitty. He will help you heal. I know He will."

Wouldn't God have helped by now? Kitty wiped her nose on the soft white square, but didn't answer. She refused to give up her hold on her legs, comforted by the small shape she'd molded herself into.

Eliza sat back against the pillows and took up rubbing Kitty's back once more. "I know it may seem as if God does not hear our cries, Kitty. But oft times we are waiting for Him to pluck us from our troubles, when 'tis the very struggle that molds us into the person God intends us to become."

Kitty glanced up, her throat growing impossibly tighter. How could such a thing possibly be? Not for her troubles, surely. God didn't work through blackmail like Cyprian's, and He certainly didn't work in oppression and tyranny such as this. She had learned nothing, except to fear her enemy.

"Good evening, ladies." Thomas's voice echoed through the room. "How are—" He stopped in the doorway when his gaze fell on Kitty.

She turned her face away, but not before she caught the look of concern that painted his expression; the drop of his mouth and the instant wrinkle in his brow. "What's happened?"

Kitty wriggled her toes and focused on the colorful fabric under her feet. 'Twas bad enough for Eliza to witness such a display of emotion, but now Thomas? She couldn't bring herself to speak. Again the waves of fatigue undulated up and down, and the longing for sleep clawed at her eyes.

Blessedly, Eliza answered for her. "She's had a trying day."

Kitty looked up and stalled, hoping the confession would be enough to subdue him, but it was not. Thomas's blue eyes lingered, driving through the shield she'd raised to protect herself, as if he were trying to extract some kind of truth and at the same time heal a pain he knew was there.

"Is this about Nathaniel?"

Kitty's face went from hot to scalding. She closed her eyes, unable to stand Thomas's pointed gaze any longer. Did he know what had happened between them, or had he simply spoken thoughtlessly?

Eliza propped forward on her hands. "Did you and Nathaniel have a disagreement, Kitty?"

Turning to Thomas, Kitty hurled daggers with her eyes. If he *did* know, he had better not say.

Thomas pulled back, his jaw open. "For one who speaks so openly, I'm surprised you have yet to tell your sister."

He does know!

"Kitty?" Eliza asked, eyes round.

Kitty would have thanked Thomas for relieving her of the emotions of moments past, if not for the undesirable, nay wretched subject he chose to discuss. "'Tis nothing, Liza. I assure you."

"Nothing?" Thomas shifted his weight and flicked his gaze between them, as if gauging his next move as carefully as one might a chess piece on a board. Finally his stare landed on his wife and he spoke with enough candor to make Parliament proud. "Nathaniel has kissed her."

Kitty groaned and dropped her head in her hands.

Eliza gasped and tugged on Kitty's arm, her tone carrying equal measures of delight and concern that made Kitty want to evaporate into vapors. "Did he really, Kitty?"

Kitty pulled away and met Eliza's wide stare. Better to confront the truth than deny it. "Aye, but 'twas a mistake and won't happen again. Are you satisfied?" She directed the last to Thomas.

He stepped closer to the bed, the softening muscles in his face reading like the tender care of a sibling. "I cannot bear to see you suffer the pains of a broken heart, Kitty."

The tight muscles in her neck relaxed the longer she stared at him, the anger suddenly fleeing at the concern in his eyes. Though his disclosure was unwelcome, the tenderness was not. "Thank you, Thomas. My tears are not for Nathaniel. I can assure you my heart is fully intact." Once the words flipped out, she snapped her mouth shut. For that *was* a lie. Her heart was in shambles.

Eliza's mouth tipped up at the corners and her dark eyes seemed to reflect the candle's glow even more than before. "I won't press you to share that which you wish to keep to yourself, but I must know if—"

Just then the downstairs door smacked open. "Thomas! Thomas!"

Thomas's face went white as the frantic sound of his name speared the quiet. He spun around and hurried from the room. "Who's there?"

Eliza jumped out of the bed, holding tight to her gray shawl as Kitty sprung from her huddled position and ran for the stairs behind her sister, praying her tearful pleadings had not gone unanswered.

Once in the parlor, the horrid scene forced Kitty against the wall and wrapped around her neck like the cold hands of the enemy.

Nathaniel!

Body limp, head awash in blood, Nathaniel hung between Joseph and Roger as they dragged him through the door and laid him on the rug.

She could not take a breath, could hardly see for the fear that choked and pressed her conscience near to death. *Please, Lord, he cannot be dead.*

Thomas knelt beside his friend, his face ashen. "Eliza go into the kitchen and fetch some water. Kitty we need bandages. Quickly." Thomas looked between Joseph and Roger before returning his attentions to the blood trickling down Nathaniel's face. "How did this happen?"

Joseph started first, kneeling on the opposite side. "I found him crawling from the woods not far from Gray's farm. When I reached him he went unconscious. 'Twas a miracle I was even there."

Kitty pressed her back against the hard wall. The truth punched her in the stomach with as much force as if she had been struck by Cyprian himself.

Dear Lord, no!

Kitty stumbled sideways, trying to keep her legs from losing their strength. She gripped the wall. *Focus, Kitty. Remain strong.* Bandages. He needed bandages...

But she couldn't tear her gaze from Nathaniel's wounds. The blood that oozed from the cut above his eye seemed to call after her, blaming her for its incessant shedding. Kitty looked at her feet, willing them to move. They refused. Blinking, she tried to make sense of such a nightmare. She should have told! She should have warned them what was to come. Vision wavering, Kitty clutched her throat. But how would that have stopped Cyprian's tyranny over her—over them? He would still have had his way.

She was trapped.

And now look what she had done.

Attempting to swallow, she stared at Nathaniel's motionless body when Thomas's clear voice snatched her out of the mire of her thoughts.

"When did you find him?"

"Not twenty minutes ago." Roger stood back, his shoulder glistening from Nathaniel's blood.

Eliza rushed in from the kitchen, a bucket of water under one arm and a wad of rags in the other. Water sloshed to the ground when she hurriedly dropped the heavy bucket and knelt at Nathaniel's head. Her eyes suddenly widened then narrowed and she pushed up and stood in front of Kitty, ducking her head to meet Kitty's drifted gaze.

Eliza gripped Kitty's arms. "He will be well. But in this moment you must be strong. You know more of medicine than any of us, and we need your help. *Nathaniel* needs your help."

Kitty could not keep her limbs from quivering. She pulled her lips between her teeth and peeked over Eliza's shoulder at the man she loved.

Oh dear Lord!

She cupped her mouth. *I love him.*

Eliza continued to plead. "Kitty?"

Kitty sucked in a choppy breath and shook her head ever so slight. "Nay, I cannot. I've never cared for someone so hurt."

Thomas rushed forward, his face crumpled. "Please Kitty, you know more than any of us here."

Tears blurred her vision. *Lord, give me strength.*

Just as the prayer floated from her mind, the terror cleared enough to allow the blood to once again pump through her limbs as if God Himself had touched her with His all-powerful hand.

She inhaled a breath that chased away the remaining tremors. *Thank you, Lord!*

Kitty rushed forward. After what she'd done, if anyone would save Nathaniel, it should be her.

"Bring him to the kitchen."

The men grunted in unison as they heaved him from the ground.

Kitty raced into the dark room, lighting a candle as the men rested Nathaniel's body on the vacant table. Candlestick in hand, she spun around and tried not to whimper. Nathaniel's hair stuck to his face where the blood drained above one eye. Another trickle oozed from his nose.

She handed the candle to Roger. "Thomas and Joseph, remove his coat, we must check his chest for injuries."

Gingerly, the two men pulled Nathaniel's limp arms from his dirt-covered jacket. Kitty snatched a pair of sheers from the drawer in the corner cabinet and cut Nathaniel's already ripped and blood stained shirt. Removing the linen away from his torso, she scanned his chest and breathed more deeply. No bruising. Dare she hope his injuries were not as terrible as they appeared?

She trained her voice to remain even. "Joseph,

remove his boots so I may check for breaks."

He nodded and immediately complied.

She smoothed her fingers up Nathaniel's right leg, then his left. No breaks. *Lord in heaven, I thank thee.*

Moving around the table she tenderly tugged at the blood-matted hair that clung to the open cut above his eye, her heart bleeding the same as his wound. She pushed out a hard breath and straightened her shoulders, encouraging the strength that wavered to remain erect. She met Thomas's pained gaze. "This cut on his head appears to be the worst of it." She leaned closer to inspect the extent of the injury. "'Tis deep. I will need to stich it."

Eliza stepped forward. "What do you need?"

"Your sewing kit."

Eliza darted from the kitchen and returned moments later, the basket over her arm. Kitty pressed a quivering hand to her mouth. How could she do this when her fingers refused to remain still?

A warm hand covered hers, and Kitty turned to her sister. The trust in Eliza's eyes looked akin to Father's, granting Kitty enough strength to calm her shaking. *Be with me, Lord, I pray thee.*

As another, more oppressing wave of pain and weakness crashed over her, she plucked a needle from the basket and threaded the tiny tool, rehearsing in her mind the vow she must now and forever cling to, for the lives of those she loved surely depended on it. She must stay away from the man she loved. She must never again fail at her post.

Keeping him alive, keeping him safe, was all that mattered now.

Chapter Eighteen

Nathaniel yanked the wrap from his head and hurled it to the floor of his bedchamber. "*I* am the doctor, Thomas. I should not be abed. Not when there are patients to be seen."

The afternoon sunlight blazed through the half-open window and the absent sounds of the road not far from his home sung of the Sabbath. If only his friend would leave, he could have his home to himself and be about his regular business. "I am not a child to be coddled."

"Indeed." Thomas produced a satisfied grin from where he sat beside the bed. "But 'twas Kitty's counsel that entreated Eliza and I to insist you remain in bed and rest through today."

Kitty.

He fought away the thought of her.

"I appreciate everyone's well-meant advice, but I shall be the judge of such things." Though a heavy throbbing continued around the cut above his eyes, the pains he would have thought such an attack might produce never lingered, and he felt nearly as well as he had days before. "'Tis clear I am well—"

"Aye, but it has not yet been twenty-four hours since your attack, and as it is the Lord's day, you will follow orders. Tomorrow you may do as you please."

Irritated, Nathaniel touched the wound on his head, once again marveling at the feel of the perfectly placed stitches that kept the deep wound closed. Kitty had attended his wounds for a second time, and as skillfully as any physician would have. If only he could speak to her, tell her how thankful he was for her aid and how sorry he felt for...

He ground his teeth, biting off the thoughts that refused to leave him.

"Very well," Nathaniel conceded, forcing himself back to the moment. He sat back against the headboard, arms folded. "I shall follow *orders*, but please do find me a more suitable companion. I'd much rather have a fair face to look upon for the coming hours, not your unpleasant one."

Thomas's smile burst wide and a chuckle bobbed through the room. "And you resemble Adonis? I doubt you could find a single woman in all of Sandwich willing to sit beside you with your manner so sour and your face a pallet of blues and purples." Humor glowed in the expression that lit his face as he exaggerated Nathaniel's injuries.

Nay, he was not so badly bruised, though evidence of the ambush was obvious to be sure. 'Twas the ache in his head that pained most, and what he strained to focus on, but the unspoken name haunted still.

Kitty.

Surely Kitty would come. She cared for him, though he knew she would keep a safe distance. Nathaniel forced a hard exhale through pinched lips. The effort it took to forget her alarmed him more than it ought. He inhaled deep and focused on the other obvious problems in a fresh attempt to relieve his mind of her.

He gazed out the far window, the warm air billowing the curtain. He touched his head again and spoke quiet, almost thinking more than speaking the words. “I was a fool to allow this to happen.”

“You cannot think of who might have done it?”

Nathaniel shifted his jaw and shrugged.

Thomas nodded and leaned forward, resting his elbows on his knees. “Joseph fears his brother may be culpable.”

Nathaniel fought back a growl and wiped a hand down his face with a rough sigh. “Cyprian’s animosity is strong enough.” He gently leaned his head back against the bed, staring at the jug of cider on the far table, suddenly aching to relieve his thirst.

Thomas looked down at his hands. “Do you think they aim to attack again? Whether Cyprian or someone else, there was a motive in their attack.”

Nathaniel had thought the same. Their intention was not to kill or they would have done so. A warning then? But why and for what?

Thomas leaned back in his chair and folded his arms, voicing the very words that had at that moment flamed in Nathaniel’s mind. “It must be related to the powder.”

“I believe it is.”

“Then we must move quickly.”

“Aye.” Nathaniel continued to eye the far-away jug of cider on his dresser, but ignored the need when such matters required discussion. The hot summer air continued to rush through the window. He glanced at Thomas, and kept his jaw solid. “We will begin tomorrow, as I have both you and I set for that night’s watch.”

Thomas stared, mouth taut, brow wrinkled. “It

will soon be discovered."

"Eventually. But if we remind the guards to keep the barrels untouched for a few days, allowing us enough time to remove it, 'twill appear from the outside that nothing has changed until another attempt is made to take it." Nathaniel forced out a coarse breath. "We must move quickly before anyone begins to question, and we must locate a place to hide the powder before we remove it. After it is done, we may focus on the task of discovering who has betrayed us."

A knock on the back door silenced the conversation. When it sounded again the gentle tap pounded against Nathaniel's heart, but he flicked away the ridiculous, budding hope. It would not be Kitty. She may have treated his wounds, but after their encounter at the pond, any chance of her seeking him out was doubtful.

The knock came once more followed by the creak of the door opening. Thomas stood. His mouth split into a massive grin as he pushed from his position in the chair. "I wonder who that would be?"

Thomas's tone of jest made Nathaniel fire back, lest his previous thoughts had somehow made it into his expression. "I'm certain 'tis one of my many female admirers, come to bring me baskets of goods, with wishes for my quick return to health."

Thomas chuckled. "I would not doubt it." He disappeared down the stairs.

Nathaniel praised the heaven-sent solitude. He threw back the blankets and jumped out of bed. A pair of hushed voices conversed below and he made quick work of the privacy, trying not to allow worry over the whispers to escalate. Who had come? Why did they whisper? Was there another raid on the powder already? Gads! He almost went down in only his shirt and banyan, but stopped.

He yanked a clean pair of breeches and a fresh linen shirt from his chest of drawers and slipped them on, determined to be downstairs before Thomas found him out of bed. Once clothed, complete with stockings and shoes, he examined his reflection in the mirror and tried to focus on the wounds around his eyes and jaw, but all he could think of was a particular pair of blue-green eyes and full red lips that he prayed waited below stairs.

A female voice drifted up the stairway and his stomach floated.

Gathering his hair behind his head with a ribbon, Nathaniel started downstairs and stopped with a jerk when Eliza and Thomas spun to greet him, immediately hushing their conversation. Stamping-out the disappointment from his face he replaced it with a wide smile.

"Eliza. This is a pleasant surprise." He offered a small bow. "I was just telling your good husband how I would much prefer a feminine face to look upon and here you are."

Eliza's typically bright smile didn't appear as it usually did when he teased her. She didn't quite meet his gaze and quickly turned once more to Thomas, lips tight.

Nathaniel's brow dipped. "Something is wrong." Then his assumptions had been correct. They had been whispering ill news.

Eliza's forced smile was too weak to shadow the concern lingering in her eyes. "Nothing is wrong."

'Twas a lie. The urge to insist she explain her trouble died in his throat. He had no right to pry into their personal affairs. If this concerned him in any way they would have made it clear—whether medical or regarding the powder—and since they hadn't, whatever concerned Thomas and Eliza, related to them alone.

"We must be going." Eliza turned to the door then stopped and spoke over her shoulder. "I am pleased to see you have recovered so quickly, Nathaniel. Our prayers have truly been answered." She exited through the door after giving a quick nod to her husband.

Thomas tapped Nathaniel's shoulder, face grim, then followed behind his wife without a word.

"Thomas." Nathaniel tugged on his friend's jacket to stop him, fighting the impulse to press the unspoken issue that so obviously plagued them. He studied Thomas's worried expression, straining to glean any hidden message in his friend's face, but none could be found. He dropped his hand from Thomas's arm, trying to pump a bit of brevity into his voice. "I shall be over tonight, if you're agreeable. We must make ready to act on our plans for the munitions."

Thomas looked after Eliza who had already reached the road. "Uh... come tomorrow. " He turned back to Nathaniel and offered a wan smile. "Give yourself another day of rest. I shall return this evening and we can discuss it then."

Thomas then sprinted after Eliza. Once at her side, he wrapped his arm around her shoulders and she leaned against him before they both hurried home as if fire nipped at their heels.

What could bother them so? Was her condition the cause of such distress? Nathaniel watched until they disappeared around the tree-lined road. An unpleasant niggling in his gut refused to abate. If they still acted strange when next he saw them, he'd press the matter.

Nathaniel closed the door, trying to shut out the foolish disappointment that threatened to rot the bloom in his chest. Kitty hadn't come to see him. He slumped in his favorite chair by the desk and rubbed his temples, eyes closed. 'Twas as it should be. Besides that, the knowledge that she could never, *would* never leave the Tory beliefs, made the decision to forget her that much easier.

And yet...

He stroked the stiches on his head. He could no longer allow his heart to rein over his mind. 'Twasn't fair to him, and certainly not to Kitty. Best to leave the boyish attractions behind and refocus his attentions on the things of liberty and freedom. Things that mattered most to him.

Does she not love her Savior more than life?

God's quiet voice came into his mind like a cool breeze across a hot, lonely dessert. Nathaniel stalled. Such a question. Of what did that matter? Nathaniel looked at the short stack of books in front of him as God's question pierced his spirit once more.

Does she not love her Savior more than life?

Nathaniel answered aloud. "Of course she does."

Then that is what matters most.

His breath quieted. Suddenly overcome with the serenity of the moment, Nathaniel clasped his hands and drooped his head. What was God saying? That freedom was not the most vital pursuit? Of course it was. Without freedom they could not live and worship the way they desired. He needed a wife that could stand beside him in this most vital cause.

Nathaniel should focus his energies in that vein, where the most good could be accomplished for the greatest number. Should he not?

Suddenly Thomas's wife's gentle smile filtered through his memory. Eliza had once embraced the Tory beliefs, and now she enjoyed the strength that came from understanding and embracing liberty's truth. Thomas had been patient with her, had taught her those many weeks and his efforts had proved to be of greater benefit to them both than Nathaniel would have ever imagined. But Thomas would have loved her despite that. His love for Eliza had overcome the—

Nathaniel jerked back at the thought that struck like a falling beam. Was God trying to tell him his prejudices were wrong? Joseph's words from the night of the party echoed. *If a woman is God-fearing, and devoted to her family, I care not what side she takes.*

His head throbbed ever-harder as he rehearsed the verse his Mother had quoted so often. "Can two walk together except they be agreed?" Nay, they could not. He knew that with a conviction that welded his body and spirit. Yet, as his thoughts settled on what he knew, another verse filled his troubled heart. *So we, being many, are one body in Christ.*

Nathaniel pulled back and stared across the room through the particles of dust moving in the light of the window. Could it be true? Could their unity in the faith of Christ be enough to sustain a marriage the way God desired? The way *he* desired?

Shaking his head, he groaned in his throat. He could never think that way. He'd lived through the pains of a family torn asunder by a mother and father who lacked the unity a marriage needed to thrive.

More than that, he didn't love Kitty and she certainly didn't love him, so all this foolish deliberation was for naught.

She needs you.

Shivers trailed down his spine like drops of cold rain. Raking his hand over his head, he winced, not only from the pain of fresh bruises, but from the memories of Kitty's tear-filled eyes, her thin frame, her smiles that lacked the sunshine of months past. Truly, she was not well. But what was it? What had stolen her light and replaced it with shadows?

He wanted nothing more than to help her, but what could he possibly do for her now when he'd destroyed any trust she may have had in him? *Lord, I would do anything to ease her burdens, yet I know not what to do.*

With a growl, he stood. He couldn't think on this now or he risked drowning in the waters of uncertainty. Eager to escape the unrequited thoughts that continued to prick, he snatched his black tricorn off the peg and made his way to the road. Pounding head or no, both his attack and the draining munitions needed his immediate attention.

Joseph may have been right about his brother, and there was only one way to find out.

The desired comfort from the familiar bed and warm quilt never came. Kitty turned under the heavy blanket and pulled it higher around her ears. When had it turned so cold? The chills that had started yesterday eve had become a constant and fitful companion. Eyes dry, she kept them shut, as the light that consumed the room pained her with every peek at her surroundings.

All she craved was sleep. She crunched her eyes shut as another wave of chills, followed by nausea, crashed over her. Breathing long and deep to ease away the horrid sensations, she turned again under the blanket when the sound of shoes tapped against the floor.

Someone touched her arm. She ignored it. For surely she'd only dreamed the gentle nudge.

"Kitty?"

Kitty blinked against the brightness and tried to smile. "Liza?" She swallowed and winced at the stabbing in her throat. Slowly turning over, she trailed her aching eyes toward Eliza who sat beside her on the edge of the bed.

Kitty squinted and braced herself for the pain it would take to speak. "Forgive me. Did I over sleep?"

Eliza's thin, dark brows dropped to her nose when her hand brushed against Kitty's forehead. "Aye, you have, by many hours. 'Tis noon already."

Noon? Mercy!

Kitty pushed up, praying perhaps the forced movement might be the antidote she needed to cure the pains that plagued her. "Forgive me, I should have been up long ago." Once upright, the room swayed and she grit her teeth, focusing on her lap and breathing tight to mollify the nausea that suddenly roared.

Eliza circled a stray curl around Kitty's ear. "Not to worry. 'Twas a long night for all of us."

A long night...

Kitty jerked back and pressed a hand to her chest. "How is he?" The last time she'd seen Nathaniel, his wounds had stopped bleeding and he'd been just conscious enough to allow Thomas and Joseph to place him in the wagon and take him home to recover in his own bed.

She covered her face then swallowed again and winced as the pain sliced down her throat, and into her heart. "Is he well? Do you know?"

"He is well. I just fetched Thomas from his home not long ago, and I can assure you, Nathaniel is much improved."

Kitty lay back against the pillow, the oppressive worry she'd borne suddenly draining from her, stealing with it the last of her energy. *He is well. Praise the Lord.*

Eliza touched Kitty's head again. "You are too warm."

Was she? Kitty clamped her burning eyes shut. Was it fever that made the room feel like fall's chill and not the warmth of early summer? Kitty shook her head. "Nay, I am only tired."

As the words left her lips, her stomach rolled with violence and a cyclone began to push its way up to her throat.

Nay! She could not be ill!

"Liza, the chamber pot!"

Eliza lunged for the empty pot and held it in front of Kitty seconds before she retched the entire contents of her stomach. The burning acid scarred her throat and nose. She sputtered and spit, dabbing at her mouth with her hand. "Liza, forgive me. I don't know what's wrong with me."

"Do not apologize, Kitty." Eliza reached for the cloth that rested next to the pitcher and basin and aided Kitty in wiping her face. Her gentle touch pulled from hiding the tender memories of Father's touch, the kind an ailing child yearns for. Eliza rubbed Kitty's hand. "You are not to leave this room until you are recovered."

Kitty shook her head. "Nay, you cannot care for me, you're not well yourself. I will not put you and the child at risk."

Eliza stood, nudging Kitty back against the pillow and pulled the quilt up around her shoulders. "I'm feeling much more myself these days, so I will not have you worrying on that account."

Kitty clutched the thick fabric and hugged it tighter as another shiver crawled over her skin. "I do worry about you."

"I know you do. You worry about everyone, which is why I believe you are now so ill. If you had taken better care of yourself you might not be ailing." Eliza placed a kiss on Kitty's temple. "I refrained from sharing my worries with him earlier, but I can no longer be silent. I am going to get Nathaniel—"

"Liza no!" Kitty tried to sit up. "Don't tell Nathaniel, I beg you. I shall be fine after a day or two of rest. Do not tell him, please." The blinding light assaulted her and she lay back down, shielding her eyes with her hands. "I need only rest." *He mustn't come here! I mustn't put him at greater risk by being near me.*

"I understand. I had myself wished to keep things from him, had you only been slightly weakened, but now I do so only at your request, and with grave reserve." Eliza sat on the bed and squeezed Kitty's leg. "I will not say anything to him *unless* your condition worsens."

Though she stayed motionless, her bed seemed to sway back and forth like a child's cradle, urging the acid up her throat. She pressed her hand tight to her mouth taking long breaths through her nose. She would *not* get worse! She could *not* miss another delivery!

Glancing at Eliza, Kitty's eyes filled. Who would be next? Who would suffer if she once again failed at her post? How could she much longer live when pressed with such servitude? *Oh dear Lord, if anything happened to Eliza and her baby I couldn't live!*

Nay. She would be better by tomorrow.

Another storm brewed in her stomach and heaved upward without warning. Kitty rolled and retched into the chamber pot. The acid scorched her tender throat, leaving an angry, bitter trail as it left.

Eliza neared, speaking quiet and calm as she held back Kitty's hair and helped her wipe her mouth once more. What did she say? Her words were muddled and echoed through Kitty's head that felt as thick and heavy as a lump of meat. The pain in her neck and head radiated down her spine and into her belly. Even her arms and legs cried-out, aching and throbbing with every movement.

"Forgive me, Liza." Kitty squinted, trying to squeeze the pain from her eyes. "I'm only over-tired as you say." Speaking grew more difficult with every word. The back of her throat felt lined with gravel.

"I'm afraid the idea of that has just been put to rest, Kitty. You are very ill." Eliza's cool hand rested against Kitty's forehead. "I will not be swayed, I am getting Nathaniel."

"Nay!" Kitty summoned the weary soldiers of her strength and clutched Eliza's wrist. "Do not... do not call for him, Liza. I beg of you." Kitty dropped her heavy head against the pillow. "He needs to stay… he needs to stay away."

A spasm in her stomach forced her legs up and pushed a groan from her lips. She covered her face with her hands. This vile illness must leave her body in six days. She had no other choice but to be well.

Another cramp seized the muscles around her stomach and she cringed, crunching her eyes shut as another pain gouged her stomach. Nathaniel must stay away. She loved him too much to allow his nearness. Keeping him from her would secure his safety. *Please Lord.*

With a heavy groan, Kitty hurled herself to the pot.

Chapter Nineteen

Newcomb Tavern bustled with patrons. Surprising, since 'twas the Lord's day. And yet, this *was* Cyprian's tavern.

Closing the heavy door behind him, Nathaniel scanned the crowded room as sunshine glowed in from the windows. Full tables. A fiddler in the corner. A few merry looking travelers, some weary ones. He humphed to himself. No sign of Cyprian, though Joseph had insisted he'd be here instead of home.

"Doctor Smith!"

Nathaniel turned to see young Jacob Wythe approaching, balancing a large basket on his hip, smile broad and eyes bright but weary. Nathaniel beamed a smile in return, in hopes of bringing a measure of joy into a life he knew was filled with sorrow. He tousled the boy's hair. "Jacob! How are you, lad?"

The boy jostled the basket of soiled plates and cups. Small beads of sweat dotted his brow. "I am well enough. Helping Father keep the tavern going." He motioned with his elbow and a grin of satisfaction on his lips. "We are quite busy."

"So I see. A compliment to you, no doubt." Nathaniel winked then glanced behind him and scanned the space, masking the question that tapped at his brow. Jacob could not be the only one working, surely? An older man in the corner filled mugs of ale, but where were the others? The obvious slapped and Nathaniel groaned. Cyprian wouldn't hire other workers. Not when his son would work for free.

Instantly the impulse to relieve the tired boy of the basket and usher him outside to enjoy a day of much needed rest consumed Nathaniel, but he fought the urge, choosing instead to sigh away his frustrations. Such an act might bring embarrassment to the boy who worked as hard as any man.

Nathaniel smiled and spoke with a wide grin. "Joseph said you are now apprenticing under him. He boasts of your talents and claims you will make a fine blacksmith one day."

The lad's face lit as a small grin raised his mouth. "Aye, I am." He looked down and switched the basket to the other hip with a hefty breath. "Father says I may only go there on Saturdays or in between working here, if time allows." He paused before turning back to Nathaniel. This time, all traces of cheer fled at the underlying grief in his tone. "He... Father doesn't like me spending time with Uncle Joseph."

Nathaniel's heart bled. How much would the boy be forced to suffer under his father's unending suppression? He stared, watching Jacob's eyes droop and his mouth tighten as he gazed across the bustling room, as if the pains of a dying mother and the grueling work he must endure, snuffed out any brightness that may have yet burned within him.

When Jacob again sighed and shifted the heavy basket, Nathaniel could stand it no longer. With a quick wink he plucked the burden from the boy's grasp.

"Nay, Doctor, 'tis not for you to carry." Jacob reached for the bundle, but Nathaniel pretended not to notice as he walked toward the kitchen, speaking over his shoulder with a smile in his voice. "I need to speak with your father, is he here?"

Outside the swinging kitchen door, Nathaniel handed the basket to the old man, nodding his thanks, before turning back around and glowing within at the gratitude that welled in the young face before him.

Brows scooping together, smile soft and filled with emotion only his eyes could tell, Jacob pointed to the far hall. "Aye, he's here."

Jacob led Nathaniel through the crowd of tables and chairs, toward the darkened door at the end of the hall. The mumbling of the dining room behind him lingered like a third companion, peeking over his shoulders as if wanting to hear the argument that would likely ensue the moment Nathaniel entered the room.

Jacob knocked then yanked his hand back and stepped away.

The door swung open and Cyprian filled the space, face warped, cravat untied and jacket scarce. "Haven't I told you to—" His angry gaze flew from Jacob and landed on Nathaniel with the weight of a hurling boulder. "What are you doing here, Smith?"

He didn't wait for Nathaniel to answer before smacking Jacob with a rough glare. Cyprian pointed toward the main room. "Back to your duties, boy."

Jacob slunk away, chin to his chest and shoulders drooped.

Nathaniel's jaw shifted. If he only could let his fists do as they pleased...

Cyprian swung the door wide and gestured with a

long sweep of his arm. "Come in, *Doctor*." Seconds after Nathaniel entered, Cyprian slammed it shut then tromped to his cluttered desk and sat. He kept his eyes on the ledgers when he spoke. "Get on with your business and get out."

Nathaniel glanced about the room, calculating his words instead of barking them as he wished to. He'd come here for information, and he'd best take care or his anger might destroy his chances for obtaining what he needed.

Dark and barren, the vision of such a dank and dirty space called from his memory the way his own father had lived before leaving the family—reclusive, angry, careless. Stacks of papers cluttered the lone desk in the center. Unopened crates of ale along the back wall collected dust while empty bottles of beer hugged the cold fireplace behind where Cyprian sat.

Nathaniel took his hat off and patted it against his leg as he stepped toward the desk. "Business seems well."

Cyprian didn't look up. "You didn't come to make idle chatter."

Nathaniel kept on, reason struggling against the rage that still teetered on a cliff's edge. "'Tis hard to keep your own working space in order when you have so much to occupy you." Nathaniel motioned around the room with his hat before pointing his eyes on the man before him. He couldn't keep the hatred behind his teeth and let it seep into his words. "I wonder why you don't employ Jacob's services as housekeeper since he already works so hard with the tavern."

His words met their mark and so did his glare.

Cyprian's head jerked up and his mouth twitched at one side. "I would never ask my son to do such a thing."

"Yet you require him to work endless hours and refuse him the apprenticeship he desires? Jacob is a boy on the precipice of manhood—"

"Do not lecture me, patriot!" Jumping to his feet, Cyprian slammed a fist to the table. "Say your say or get out."

Nathaniel rubbed his thumb over the felt of his hat and ground his teeth. He forced air in and out several times before speaking. "How is your wife?"

Cyprian's face reddened while his fists turned white. "We will not speak of Camilla."

"We will." Nathaniel leaned forward and rested his hands on the table. "For the sake of Jacob's future I would help her, extend her life as much as possible." Cyprian's face contorted, but Nathaniel kept on. "'Tis obvious the boy already suffers the loss of her, Cyprian. Let me help—"

"I would never employ the help of a traitor!" Cyprian's nostrils flared and the muscles in his red face twitched. "State your business before I have you thrown out."

Nathaniel kept his eyes locked with Cyprian's until the man stepped back and sat in his chair. Nathaniel all but growled. "Tell me of the missing powder."

Cyprian's eyes grew wide, when suddenly a hard laugh burst from him, scraping up Nathaniel's spine. "You believe I know something?" He laughed again, tossing his head back. "You came here hoping I'd provide you with information, hmm? You must be desperate."

"Determined."

"Your *determination* seems to be putting you at risk." He gestured toward Nathaniel's face. "Awful business. It seems a miracle you escaped alive."

The flicker of pleasure in Cyprian's eyes cultivated the hedgerow of thorns burrowing in Nathaniel's chest. "Disappointed?"

"Perhaps."

Keeping his fists tight, Nathaniel stepped ever closer. The look of satisfaction in Cyprian's face could not be masked by the indifference he struggled to maintain in his stern mouth and vacant eyes. The man knew something, though proving such would be more difficult than Nathaniel had hoped. "You know who attacked me." A statement, not a question.

"Are you accusing me?"

"Should I be?"

Cyprian lunged. "How dare you speak to me that way!"

"Your protestations testify against you, Wythe, not in your behalf." He replaced his hat on his head and turned toward the door.

Rounding the table, Cyprian followed. "If 'tis information you seek, why do you not ask that little dark-haired sprite?"

Nathaniel spun around. "What?"

Cyprian chuckled again, this time louder and with a smirk that made Nathaniel's fists ache. "She is a Tory, is she not? Why not ask her what's happening to your *precious* munitions. She surely knows as well as anyone."

Nathaniel lunged and jerked Cyprian at the collar, relieving the tension in his fingers as he clasped the fabric tight around Cyprian's throat. Holding the man near his own face, Nathaniel spoke through gritted teeth. "*Never* speak of her again."

Cyprian's expression hardened. "I'll do as I please."

The war that raged in Nathaniel's mind and muscles played out in his hands as he gripped tighter, until Cyprian's face turned a deeper red and his eyes bulged. Nathaniel didn't release. How dare the man insinuate he knew anything about Kitty! How dare he speak of her so flippantly!

When finally reason tore through the curtains of rage, Nathaniel released him with a shove and charged out the door.

Cyprian's voice trailed after him. "She's using you, Smith! Do not trust her, believe me!"

Nathaniel tore through the tables toward the freedom of the front door.

He'd sooner believe the devil.

Cyprian seethed. Smith was all righteous, pious indignation. Telling him how to raise his son, telling him he cared about Camilla. All the while accusing him of the very crimes to which he would never confess, no matter how true. The crimes he committed to protect the people he loved.

He snatched the bottle of opium from his desk drawer and held it up to the light. His nostrils flared. Almost gone. He closed his eyes as a painful sigh left his lips. *Camilla, my love, I will obtain more, I vow it.*

Shoving the precious medicine in his pocket, he bound out the side door of his office and raced toward the house behind the tavern. He charged up the stairs and stopped the instant he reached the room.

Beside the bed stood Jacob, Camilla's hand in his, sorrow and longing in the boy's eyes crushing the very bones in Cyprian's chest. As if he feared what his father might say, Jacob pulled Camilla's hand to his chest and spoke with brows raised in worry. "I didn't want her to be lonely, Father."

Body motionless, Camilla's mouth bowed slightly and the look of exhaustion in her grey face kicked the composure out from under him.

Cyprian pointed at the door behind him. "Didn't I tell you to attend your duties at the tavern?" He neared, and Jacob cowered closer to the bed. Looking between his wife and son, Cyprian quieted. "Can't you see your mother needs rest?"

"Cyprian, please." Camilla's gentle reprimand stayed Cyprian's next words. She cupped Jacob's hand and smiled at the son she'd prayed for, for so many years. "Jacob brings peace to me, as he has done since the day I bore him."

Cyprian's spirit howled in grief as Jacob leaned down and kissed his mother's head, tears rimming his eyes.

Nathaniel's words raked Cyprian's mind, *'Tis obvious the boy already suffers the loss of her...*

He fingered the vial in his pocket. What did the man know of him, or of Jacob? Cyprian knew what was best. Even if what he'd said were true, keeping the boy busy would help stem the agony that awaited once Camilla finally rested beneath the earth.

He swallowed the aching lump in his throat and motioned to the door. "Back to work, son. I will see to her now."

Jacob leaned down to kiss his mother's head, lingering there a moment while Camilla whispered something into his ear. He nodded and looked up, eyes shimmering and without glancing toward Cyprian, slipped out of the room and shut the door.

Cyprian watched, the remains of his heart crumbling. He couldn't allow such sorrow to trespass in his home. 'Twas his duty to keep his wife and child from such things, but it invaded like an unrelenting enemy.

He blinked, still smoldering over the idiot doctor's visit. Had his warning to the Campbell girl meant nothing? Had she whispered of their vital secrets even after he'd proved he would make good on his word?

"Do not be so hard on Jacob, Cyprian." Camilla's voice crawled to him from the bed and he turned.

Pulling the vial from his pocket, Cyprian sat beside her. Throat too thick to speak, he could only offer a small smile as he opened the bottle and pressed it to her lips.

She swallowed and grimaced.

Cyprian gripped her skeletal fingers, hiding his concern with a tight smile. Her skin rested against her bones now with almost no flesh between them. Her once full lips were now so thin, so pale. The woman he loved was leaving him more each day.

He shook his head, shedding the perfidious thoughts. Camilla would not die. She would not leave him and certainly she would never leave Jacob. Not as long as Cyprian could provide this medicine. It had kept her alive until now, had it not? If he could keep that Campbell girl from disclosing his secret, he could keep stealing the patriot's powder and the British would keep paying him.

Cyprian blinked slowly and sighed. "My dear, you must take some nourishment." He glanced beside him and reached for the tray of fresh broth and bread. "It seems Jacob brought this up for you. Will you not take a bite?"

He brushed his fingers over her soft cheek as a weak grin struggled to lift one side of her mouth. "Not now Cyprian, I fear I am too tired."

He gathered the bowl and a spoon, sniffing the bland mixture and stirring it in an attempt to coax an appetite from her. "You're tired because you do not eat. Please, Camilla, you need your strength."

She reached for his hand and moved the bowl away. "You must prepare yourself, Cyprian. We both know... the end is near."

While his mind wailed in protest he kept his voice calm. "The end is not near, and I promise to do everything I can to keep you alive."

And he would. Even if he had to displease God to do it.

Endless chills darted up and down Kitty's back. Blurry swatches of moving color swayed in front of her while distant mumbling voices echoed through the room. Again she shivered. Why could she not become warm?

The cramps and never-ending waves of nausea snipped every thin thread of strength. She could scarce raise her fingers, nor blink her eyelids. Not only were they heavy as sacks of flour, but they scratched against her eyes like hot summer sand.

Another round of heaves pulsed up from her belly, yet she had no strength to move.

From somewhere, hands gripped her shoulders, helping her to heave into the waiting pot but her empty stomach had nothing left to purge. The pressure behind her eyes made her groan. Somehow she ended up on her back again and a cool cloth draped her forehead. She sunk into the pillow, succumbing to the greedy shadows.

Though illness ravaged, her mind refused to stop its exhaustive race. Cyprian's face hovered around her, the basket resting just out of reach, and next to it—Nathaniel, his expression coiled in disgust.

Forgive me!

Chills and flashes of heat took turns draining her will. She groaned and rolled her head against the cool pillow as another surge of pain swept from her head to her feet. She needed to sleep.

Yet, even then Cyprian controlled her.

She would never be free again.

Chapter Twenty

Questions and unrest plagued Nathaniel like a disease. He'd been unusually busy with patients' unending needs and had not a spare moment to call on the ones he cared about most—the ones who could provide the cure for what troubled him. Thomas's print shop had been closed since morning, and the worry over his and Eliza's unspoken troubles refused to abate.

Pulling his backdoor shut after the long day had ended, he eased his hat on his head and started toward the road just as the sun dipped behind the horizon. He drew in a deep breath and gazed at the purpling sky. The quicker he arrived at the Watsons, had a filling meal and a refreshing laugh, the sooner he would regain a bit of his regular enthusiasm. A good talk with Thomas would help put his mind at ease.

He'd wanted to discuss his encounter with Cyprian, but Thomas hadn't come Sunday evening as expected, another reason for the concern that wriggled ever deeper. Thomas needed to know of Cyprian's mention of Kitty. The thought still turned his stomach. If Kitty wouldn't speak with Nathaniel, at least he could tell Thomas his concerns, and

Thomas could then advise Kitty to give Cyprian a wide berth.

As he tromped across the dry road, Nathaniel tried to crush Cyprian's words with every step, but they refused to pulverize. Kitty was a Tory, true enough. She held her beliefs firm, but simply wished to watch the contention from afar. Cyprian's accusation that she knew anything of the missing powder was ludicrous. Just because Cyprian and Kitty were both Tories did not entitle the man to any kind of association with her, let alone authorize him to profess in any way that he knew something about Kitty that Nathaniel did not.

When Nathaniel finally reached the Watson home, he waited on the stoop and rested his palm on the door's cool handle. He needed to calm his breathing and restrain the gathering storm. If the ladies were in the main room, his distress would be obvious and he needed to reserve his unease for Thomas.

Drawing the warm evening air deep into his lungs, he knocked twice before swinging the door wide. Removing his hat, he rested it on the peg and shut the door. "Good evening one and all. I know you have been eagerly awaiting my—" The scene before him snipped the remaining greeting from his lips. He snapped his jaw shut and stared.

Eliza covered her mouth, turned away and rushed upstairs, but not before Nathaniel got a clear view of the tears that painted her face.

Thomas stood motionless in front of the fire, his gaze following after his wife. His own face was drawn and the lack of life in his eyes turned their blue color a dull grey.

Nathaniel tromped forward and tapped his leg as

irritation sought escape through his fingers. It seemed whatever ailed them yesterday had worsened, not improved as he'd hoped. His ire from the walk over acted as a stepping-stone for the brooding curiosity over what caused his friends such grief.

He tried to tamp down his frustration and keep his voice even as he marched to the front of the room. "Tell me the tears on Eliza's face have nothing to do with something foolish you've done."

Thomas jerked as if repulsed by the very thought. "You know I would never do anything to hurt her."

Nathaniel lifted and lowered one shoulder. "Not intentionally perhaps. But men are flawed creatures where women are concerned."

Thomas's Adam's apple bobbed as he trained his gaze on the stairs.

Gads! If Thomas refused to confess what bothered them, then Nathaniel would pry it from him. "Is she suffering with the child? Is it causing her pain?"

"What?" Thomas pulled back as if Nathaniel's words snatched him from the thoughts that lured his mind. "Nay, she is well."

"Is your press struggling?"

"Nay."

His irritation forced its way out through Nathaniel's voice. "Are you in financial strain? Have you received some kind of ill news? Blast it, Thomas, I care for you as I would my own family. Tell me what is the matter, I want to help you!"

Thomas whirled to face him, his mouth taut. "Kitty is ill, Nathaniel. Very ill."

The blood that had risen to Nathaniel's face only seconds before now drained down his neck. "Kitty?"

Time slowed and he blinked as Thomas continued. "She's been ill since yesterday morning."

With another glance upstairs, he sighed. "Eliza is beside herself with worry, and I too can hardly think for the concern that eats me."

The words slapped against Nathaniel like a cold rain and he struggled to think through the haze. Kitty was ill? He stuttered. "Why... why did you not fetch me right away?"

"At first, she insisted that we not bother you. She wished for you to rest and care for your own wounds. Then when she worsened I tried to find you but you were attending other patients and I—"

"So she has improved then. That is why you didn't bother to seek me further."

Thomas opened and closed his mouth several times before sound finally emerged. "Nay, she is not though we had hoped so when she was able to keep down a few sips of drink." Thomas rubbed his jaw. "When she first started vomiting yesterday morning, she insisted she was simply over-tired, but it has not ceased since."

"*What*?" Nathaniel didn't wait to hear more. He lunged then stopped and grabbed Thomas's arm. "Run to my home and grab my medical bag—and my lance and blood bowl."

Thomas nodded with tight lips and dashed for the door.

Pulse charging, Nathaniel raced up the stairs and burst into Kitty's room.

His lungs pumped and his mind raced. Years of medical training and many years more in the practice of his trade could not prepare him for this. He rushed to the bed and Eliza moved aside to let him near.

The grey in Kitty's porcelain face turned his stomach to rock and his breathing seized. The circles around her eyes, and the lack of color in her lips made her appear lifeless, though the blessed sight of the slow up and down of her chest testified she lived. Her skin glistened with moisture left behind from Eliza's moist rag, and her red cheeks screamed of fever. He lowered to the bed and brushed his hand over her forehead and ground a curse between his teeth. Scorching.

"Thomas says she's been this way since yesterday?" He gently pressed his fingers against Kitty's neck and spoke to Eliza. "I would know the whole of it."

"'Tis true." Eliza's voice wavered. "She has been very ill with no improvement."

Nathaniel glanced over his shoulder, fingers still gauging Kitty's pulse. He strained against the fears that assailed him. "You should have sent for me immediately."

"You are right... but I..." Eliza pressed a handkerchief to her mouth to hide the quivering of her chin. "Kitty insisted she only needed rest and that she was merely over-tired. I wanted to believe her." Eliza inhaled a shuddering breath. "We tried to find you when—"

"I know," he answered, touching Eliza's arm. He stood and took Eliza by the shoulders. The sight of tears rolling down her cheeks added to the emotions that flooded into his own heart. "Tell me her symptoms."

As Eliza explained the ordeal—how Kitty had slept unusually long the first day, refused to take nourishment, started vomiting and continued to do so even with nothing more to expel—Nathaniel had to fight the worry that clouded his thinking.

"Her fever began then as well?"

"Aye." Eliza refused to move her watery gaze from

the bed.

Kitty moved her head against the pillow, a grimace twisting her mouth.

Nathaniel looked between the two women then focused on Eliza, gripping her arms again and keeping his tone even despite the way his heart rammed his chest. "You have done well, but now you must rest. You look weary and you cannot put the child at risk."

She inhaled a shuddered breath and nodded, though didn't move. "I... I cannot lose her, Nathaniel."

"We will *not* lose her." He turned to glance behind when Kitty made a quiet moan, praying the confidence he crammed into his voice was believable, at least to Eliza if not to himself. He squeezed her arms and offered what he hoped was an encouraging smile. "You will be no good to her if you become ill yourself."

Eliza craned her neck to take another look at Kitty, repeating his words. "We will not lose her."

Nathaniel shook his head, unable to voice a response. *Lord, please...*

Reluctant, Eliza moved forward and kissed her sister's head before shuffling out of the room.

Nathaniel took his place on the seat beside the bed and blinked. He'd treated hundreds of patients, and many closer to heaven than she. He knew exactly what she needed and how to cure what disease attempted to take her from them.

So why did he feel like a fledgling student, ready to diagnose his first ailing patient?

He quickly stood and pulled off his jacket. Rolling up his sleeves, he combed through the files of diseases and conditions that lived in his memory, ever-ready for consultation.

Dear Lord, guide me. I cannot lose her.

He looked at the clock as the door burst open down stairs. Thomas had returned.

Nathaniel gazed at Kitty's tiny wrist and squared his jaw. The worst hours of his life had just begun.

The candle's flame on the bedside table swayed as Nathaniel moved past. Lonely shadows danced across the vacant walls. He gripped tight to the bowl of crimson liquid to keep his hands from trembling, then set it beside the candle and returned to check the bandage around Kitty's wrist. The faint light accentuated the deep circles around her eyes and the shallow movements of her chest.

Nathaniel tried again to breath deeper and ease the tightness that lingered in his muscles, but to no profit. He pulled his pocket watch from its nesting place in his waistcoat. Three hours past midnight. He looked at her face again, willing that his desire for her improvement would be enough to diminish her fever and allow her to wake and look at him. Yet 'twas not enough. More than five hours of care and not a single sign that she improved.

Tenderly, he pulled the wrappings tighter around her wrist then rested in the seat beside the bed. The rock of emotions that had been lodged in his throat since he'd first seen her hours earlier thickened. With a slight shake of the head he once more reached for the table, dropped the cloth into the small dish of water and wrung it out. He patted it against Kitty's brow and along her neck. Pushing out a rough breath he struggled to mend the pieces of himself that had severed the moment he'd taken the lance to her skin. He'd bled patients hundreds of times before. 'Twas the best way to relieve the suffering patient of undesirable fluids. Still, he could not shake the unsettling sensation that dominated, or the shiver that rippled his spine from slicing through her silken flesh and watching the vital fluid seep into the bowl below.

Staring, he pulled his bottom lip between his teeth. If anything happened to Kitty—and it would not—but if it did...

Nay!

Nathaniel pushed off his knees. He had to move, had to relieve his mind of the images and thoughts that crowded so thick they choked. Pacing the room from the open door to the opposite wall and back, his gaze landed on a folded paper atop Kitty's dresser. He stopped his incessant movement when curiosity flicked his mind. Could it be another letter from Higley? Glancing behind, he looked to the door then to Kitty. Never had he read anyone else's personal communications. 'Twas wrong to do so. But even as the words moved across his mind, he picked it up and flipped the folded paper back and forth in his fingers.

Put it down, you fool.

He placed it back, though somehow his fingers refused to relinquish their hold.

Perhaps the letter was not from whom he guessed. Perhaps it contained information on what had troubled her these past weeks. He turned back again. If this letter carried any bit of intelligence that might aid him in helping ease the burdens Kitty bore, how could he not read it?

Biting his cheek, he rubbed his thumb against the broken seal. With another quick look to the door he opened the letter.

Two words on the bottom socked his stomach.

James Higley.

He slammed his eyes shut and fought the urge to crumple the paper in his hands. Higley still wrote to Kitty? Unable to repress the questions that rallied for answers, he turned away from the door and read.

Dearest Kitty,

I cannot begin to express my relief upon receiving your letter. You were wise to take Donaldson's counsel and leave when you did. Your welfare and safety are paramount, my love. I only wish I could be the one caring for you, protecting you. Knowing you are so far away pains me without end. But I trust your family will give you the best they can, just as I would do, were I in Sandwich with you.

Your response to my proposal is understandable. Though I will admit my heart yearns for a "yes" from you, I respect your need for more time. I would not pressure you into an engagement for which you are not yet ready. But knowing that you have not disregarded my proposal entirely gives me a strand of hope that I will cling to every day until you agree to be my wife. For I pray you will, my love.

I await your answer with every breath.

Yours affectionately,

James Higley

Paper still in hand, Nathaniel dropped his arm to his side and looked up at the ceiling. So she had written to him? Then she hadn't told Higley no, as she'd said?

It took every measure of fortitude not to toss the infernal letter into the fire.

Nathaniel ground his teeth and carefully re-folded the note before replacing it exactly as he'd found it. He pressed out a heated sigh through clenched teeth. Did the man have to be so poetic? *I wait for your answer with every breath.* Gads. 'Twas no wonder Kitty had not refused him. Any woman would find such a man desirable, whose flattering words and family *connections* made a quite irresistible combination. Especially considering the man was a Tory.

The unfamiliar pain that found a home in his chest was a proper consequence for reading a letter he ought never to have touched. He had only himself to blame.

Stepping forward, he stopped at the edge of the bed and stared at the woman whose soul he knew as well as the face he viewed in the looking glass every morning and night. She had become a part of him. How had such a thing happened? The thought of Kitty's kiss trickled past the cut in his spirit, soothing as it washed over him. He closed his eyes. Tasting of her sweetness and savoring that bit of passion had taken all their shared memories—secret looks, shy smiles, laughs, quiet moments at her side—and imprinted her on his spirit as real as a brand on his skin.

He could scarce take a breath when the word for such emotions slowly scrolled along his heart.

Nathaniel shut his eyes. He should not think of such things. Not now. He must train all his energies on her recovery. For she must recover, because if she did not...

He rammed a spike of faith into his quivering

hope. If anyone could make Kitty well, it was he. It had to be. He was the best physician from here to Boston and he knew exactly how to care for her. She would not suffer greater illness, or anything worse, under his watch.

Who is it that is the Great Physician? You or I?

God's tender reprimand folded over Nathaniel's weary muscles. He slumped his elbows against his knees and cupped his head in his hands. God was over all. He knew that. Nathaniel would do all he could for her, but even after all that, God might still desire to take Kitty into His eternal rest and he must trust God's wisdom and perfect love. Yet the effort it took to release Kitty into God's hands made his fingers tremble. He gripped his hair at the roots and battled the pride along with the single abiding emotion he'd scorned for so long.

Forgive me, Lord. I submit to your will, though you know my thoughts, and I could not bear to lose the woman I—

At that moment Kitty's head tossed against the pillow.

He jerked up and scooted closer to the bed, taking her hand in his. "Kitty?"

Again, she moved her head back and forth, and squeaked in pain. Strands of hair pulled away from her braid and clung to her neck where he'd wetted her skin.

Nathaniel gently stroked her arm, praying God would breathe enough health into her weak frame to allow her to tell him what she needed. Her features pulled up as she released another groan. His throat swelled, but he swallowed away the pain. He must be strong, not overcome with emotions that would only steal his abilities when he needed them most.

Brushing the backs of his fingers against her cheek, he spoke through the tightness in his throat as moisture blurred his vision. “I give my all to you, Kitty. And God willing, you will smile at me again. I love you.”

Chapter Twenty-one

The sound of clinking utensils and sloshing water tempted Kitty from her fitful sleep. She blinked her dry, aching eyes and toiled against the weakness that held her body against the bed. The bright light from the window reached for a figure in the corner. Liza? Nay, she was not so tall. The fleeting clarity in her mind flickered like the fragile flame of a candle. She closed her eyes as another surging cramp moved up her body and she fought the whimper that eeked past her throat.

"Kitty?"

She labored to clear the haze in her view and cease the ringing in her ears when suddenly her vision cleared enough to allow a view of the person who had come to loom over her. Kitty's pulse stopped and she gasped. The nausea she'd suffered rolled again.

Cyprian.

"Get out," she croaked, willing her feeble limbs to find strength enough to move her away from him. *Lord help me!*

He took the last few steps separating them and sat beside her on the bed. "All is well, do not be afraid."

He reached for her arm but she smacked his hand away with a yell that came out as a mere squeak. Her arms shook. All is well? Was that not what he had said to her hours before Nathaniel's attack?

Horror consumed her when a terrible thought assailed. She swallowed to coat her dry, cracked voice and spoke through tumbling tears. "Where is my family?" A sob made its way out and she covered her mouth. Again, he moved toward her and she slunk away. "Nay!"

Staring back, he gripped his knees as if striving to keep from striking her as he wished.

Kitty watched his mouth move as he answered, but she could not hear. The flood of tears gushed and though she held back the wails that rammed for release, she had lost all control. The nightmares she suffered for weeks had finally come to life. Cyprian had done something to her family and she was helpless to save them.

Nathaniel had never seen such terror on her face.

He yearned to reach for her again, but continued to grip his knees. Touching her would only frighten her more.

Kitty's sobs grew and she pulled the sheet to her chin, mumbling something about her family through her tears.

Had she not heard him? Stroking her with his voice, as he could not with his hands, he smiled and prayed God would enlighten him on how to ease her fears. "Eliza and Thomas are in town, Kitty, as I said. They are well and will return shortly."

When his answer did nothing to dry the unending tears, he straightened. Was she so upset at seeing him? Had he so hurt her that even his presence as a physician offended?

Her next words answered, spearing him like a dagger. "Get away from me! Get out!"

Nathaniel's blood stalled. "Kitty, I... please forgive me, I never wanted to hurt you—"

"Nay!" Her chin quivered and her voice cracked. She continued to push away until her back pressed against the pillow touching the headboard. "I was a fool. 'Twill not happen again!"

Nathaniel berated himself. Not only had he hurt the woman he loved, he now suffered as greatly, for she would never love him in return. "Nay, 'twill not happen again, I—"

"Leave! Leave me, I beg of you!" Kitty turned away and covered her face, wailing a low, hollow moan.

Though all he wanted was to bring her peace, and though his absence might be what she desired, he could not leave her. "Kitty, you are very ill and we are all worried for you. I will be beside you until you are well. Then, if you still wish me away, I will stay away for good, I promise."

Kitty answered but kept her head turned. Her hands shook as she gripped the fabric at her chest. "I know... I know you are angry with me for forgetting my post, but I beg you, do not hurt Nathaniel again! Do not hurt my family. I'll do whatever you a-a-ask!" Another storm of sobs echoed through the room and slashed its way through Nathaniel's already severed heart.

"Kitty, what are you—" Nathaniel choked on his breath when the clouds in his thinking cleared at the wind of truth. She believed he was someone else! This time when he reached for her, he didn't falter. "Nay, Kitty, 'tis I. I am well, you have nothing to fear from me."

She shook her head, eyes closed, a soft quiet whimper hovering between them. "I can no longer bear this burden." She stopped and cried into her hands. "Release me. Release me!"

Someone *had* threatened her! Indeed the burdens she carried were great, so great that even now in her fever she believed Nathaniel was the one who had hurt her.

He prepared to answer when she hurled forward, hand over her mouth and eyes wide. Nathaniel lunged for the pot and placed it under her face as she retched, though nothing but bits of acid came forth. He stroked her back and cooed until the fits subsided. Tears burned his eyes. The pain she felt, he felt. The unknown sorrows she suffered, he suffered, tearing at his spirit until the need to be near her was too much to contain.

Quickly removing the pot, he snatched the wet cloth from the table and wiped her mouth. Thankfully, she did not push him away. Easing onto the bed beside her, he pulled her quivering form onto his lap and cradled her against his chest. Soft, quiet sobs shook her fevered body as he brushed his hand against her hair. He would willingly take all of her pains, all her fears upon himself. As she wept, he pulled her closer and whispered quiet reassurances, all the while plotting the what's and how's of finding the one responsible for the maltreatment she endured. Whoever had caused her this pain would have it returned to them a hundred fold and more.

Finally, her tears turned to sniffles, then to silence

and her body relaxed against him. Holding her head beneath his chin he looked up to the ceiling as the noonday light bathed the quiet room. Never again would she cry these tears. Never again would she fear. *I promise you, Kitty.*

Chapter Twenty-Two

Downstairs the parlor was draped in quiet though Thomas and Eliza had returned several minutes past. Nathaniel dumped a log on the embers in the kitchen fire and watched the starving flames lick at the wood. He stirred the pot of broth that hovered over the heat and tried to shake off the fresh anxieties. *Who had done this to her?* Nathaniel's fingers twitched as the heat from the growing flames intensified, matching the rising frenzy in his heart. He relived Kitty's cries and tears until he could stand it no longer.

He slammed the side of his fist against the wall and released the pressure in his chest with an audible growl. The stomp of Thomas's footfall entered the room, but Nathaniel couldn't look up.

"How is she?" Thomas came beside him.

Nathaniel spoke to the ground. "I knew it."

"Has she worsened?"

Peering at his friend, Nathaniel spoke through teeth so clamped his head throbbed. "I knew all this time!"

Thomas's brow shot skyward then folded together. "What are you speaking of? Is she improved or nay?"

"She is not improved, but she is not worse. Yet that is not what distresses me." Nathaniel wagged his head, forcing the clouds from his mind. He peered at his friend and kept his tone low. "Someone has threatened her, just as I feared at the beginning."

Thomas dropped his hands and took a step back. His features turned hard as the impact of Nathaniel's words rested upon him. "How do you know this?"

Nathaniel pressed his palms into his throbbing eyes and gripped his scalp. "Her fever is causing her to hallucinate." He turned to the fire and rested an arm across the mantel. "She thought I was someone else. She was deathly afraid of me, or whoever she thought I was, and spoke to me as if I would hurt her family if she didn't comply with my orders." The fresh memories drained Nathaniel's strength and he shuffled to the nearest kitchen chair. "She said, 'I'll do whatever you ask.' "

Thomas glanced toward the door, then quieted his tone as if he feared Eliza might overhear. "Do what?"

"I don't know." Nathaniel pushed off the chair with a heaving breath and marched to the table, pouring himself a glass of cider.

Thomas came to Nathaniel's side, his face contorted. "Are you sure what she's saying is true? If she was hallucinating then she could be imagining half a dozen horrifying things that have no base in reality at all."

Nathaniel tipped his head back and drained the full glass. The liquid coated his dry throat but failed to flush away his anxiety. "Nay. 'Twas real." Kitty's red-rimmed eyes and quivering chin, the way she struggled to move away from him, all testified the truth of her fears. He poured more cider into his glass and took another drink. "'Twas enough to make a man run mad."

Thomas leaned against the table and crossed his arms, his face still coiled in question. "I cannot believe a person would do such a thing to a woman."

Nathaniel slammed the cup on the table. "Can you not? You of all people should know that there are monsters in this world, eager to do whatever is necessary to accomplish their will."

Face ashen, Thomas's mouth tightened. The blackmail he'd suffered at the hands of Captain Samuel Martin burned bright in both their memories. Thomas stayed silent a moment then nodded. "How can we help her?"

"I wish I knew." Nathaniel picked up the glass and turned it in his fingers, staring into the amber liquid. "The first step would be getting the full truth from her, since as of now, we have only pieces."

"We agreed that she must not be forced to speak—"

"I'm no longer sure that's the best course of action."

Thomas stood straight, his voice sharp. "If you compel her, she may pull back and you will be no closer to your goal. If what you claim is true, then I know well the weight she carries and forcing her will only make it worse." Thomas sighed as if the thought of her enduring what he had endured pained him almost more than it did Nathaniel. "I pray 'tis only her feverish mind. I have heard of such things happening. Come now, you are a physician, you have witnessed such episodes before have you not?"

"I do hope you are right Thomas, but I refuse to ignore the warning within me. If I am wrong, then so be it."

Thomas leaned back against the table. "What would you have me do?"

The vexing conversation Nathaniel had endured with Cyprian clobbered his memory. He jerked up. "I didn't tell you—I spoke with Cyprian."

"Aye? When?"

"Sunday." Nathaniel stared at the floor, remembering Cyprian's black eyes and the venom that seeped through his smile.

"What happened?"

"I asked what he knew of the missing powder. He denied any knowledge, as expected. Though he made a point to mention my attack and appeared almost pleased at the sight of my wounds. That was a might *more* than expected." He growled. "But 'twas when he spoke of Kitty that I lost hold of my senses."

Eyes round, Thomas's face reddened. "He spoke of her? Why?"

The vile words he'd arrested since their utterance finally had their freedom. "He said she was using me. That I shouldn't trust her."

"Not trust her? Of what could he possibly be spea—"

"I know not." Nathaniel knew what his friend was about to ask. "His aim is to frustrate and antagonize, nothing more."

Thomas tipped his chin down, and looked at Nathaniel from underneath his dark brow. "You do not think he is the one behind Kitty's troubles?"

Nathaniel wiped a hand over his face. "I do not know, though I admit I had thought as much. And though I would confront him, doing so without knowing all might put Kitty at greater risk."

"Well advised."

Nathaniel groaned. The truth was just within his grasp, but without it in full he was helpless to rescue the woman he loved.

He bit away the curses that crouched on his tongue and redirected his thinking. "Kitty's illness has postponed our plan to move the powder. I would have liked it to be over and done by now, for it weighs upon me." His bones ached and he rubbed his hands over his face once more, trying to remove the fog of worry that clouded his thinking. "Yet as vital the task, I cannot think clearly with Kitty so ill."

Thomas nodded and glanced over his shoulder at the stairway. "'Tis difficult to watch anyone suffer, surely. But it pains most when 'tis the woman you love."

The woman you love.

Nathaniel's heart twitched and he looked away. Having only just discovered such for himself, voicing it to another would make the reality of it rest upon him in a way he was not yet ready to bear.

Thomas smiled knowingly, but his features remained solemn. "I know you try to hide it Nathaniel, but 'tis plain to see. You are more your true self in her presence than I have ever witnessed."

Nathaniel grinned casually, trying to keep the growing heat from his face. Had he been so easy to read? "She is unlike any other woman I have known. I simply hate to see her in such pain." He turned away, clinging to the one truth that would protect his heart. "You know I could never align myself with a Tory."

"Would you risk anything for her?"

Nathaniel frowned. He needn't answer something already so clear.

Thomas stepped closer and gripped Nathaniel's shoulder. The weight of his voice mirrored the humorless question in his eyes. "Would you risk anything for her?"

He flung Thomas's arm away. "Of course I would

risk anything for her, you know that!"

Thomas stepped back, undeterred by Nathaniel's outburst. His tone remained even but dropped deeper. "Would you have her choose Higley over you?"

Nathaniel froze, remembering Higley's tender note. He couldn't help the words from jumping from his mouth. "I would not."

"But what if she loves him?"

He winced. "She does not." *Did she?*

"I don't believe she does either." Thomas shrugged with a slight grin that grated against Nathaniel like a dull kitchen utensil. "Higley is open in his affections and continues to write, asking Kitty to be his wife and join him in Boston. He accepts her for who she is..." His words trailed away, but his gaze nailed Nathaniel to the floor.

What did Thomas imply? That Nathaniel *didn't* accept her? "What are you inferring?" He crumpled the heightening jealousy in his chest and flicked it into the fire.

"You're in love with her Nathaniel, and you must accept your affections or risk losing her."

"I never had her to begin with."

"You would have Kitty marry Higley then?"

"I will not speak of this with you." He turned to leave, then spun and faced Thomas with the army of indignation that consumed him. "I will tell you what you so often told me. Leave this alone. I will worry about my *own* affections in my *own* time."

Thomas nodded. "As you wish. I simply hate to think you might give up on so much happiness."

"Happiness?" Nathaniel pointed a finger at his friend's chest. "What kind of happiness comes from a marriage that is based only on love?"

Thomas tipped one brow, his answer dry. "A fair sum."

"I grew up in a home where my parents married for love despite the fact that my father did not live a Christian life as my mother did, and although he claimed devotion to her, their differing beliefs pulled them apart until he finally..."

He couldn't speak the words. He closed his eyes. The warm kitchen transformed into a frigid cabin and suddenly Nathaniel was 15 again, staring out the door as huge flakes of snow fell in clumps to the ground. The shadowed figure of his father grew smaller and smaller while his mother's wailing cries filled the cold, lonely house.

He shook his head free of the wrenching memory. "I know what unity means, for I lived through the lack of it. I promised myself that I would never marry a woman that did not hold to the same powerful beliefs. And for the sake of my future marriage and my unborn children I *will* keep that promise."

Thomas's expression softened. Stepping near, he rested a hand on Nathaniel's shoulder. "Kitty's devotion to Christ is unwavering. As is yours. You would have nothing to fear on that account."

"Do you not know me, Thomas?" Nathaniel stepped back. "My devotion to Christ is as powerful as my devotion to the cause of freedom. I cannot—will not—align myself to a woman who does not believe the same."

Thomas's mouth stretched into a small smile. "She can change, Nathaniel."

"Aye." His heart groaned. "But will she? I cannot hazard such a great risk."

Nodding, as if he finally understood the fears that rested between Nathaniel and his heart, Thomas peered through knowing eyes, speaking the agonizing certainties Nathaniel had been loath to accept.

“Then, my friend, I fear your heart will pain you with either decision you make.”

In truth, it already had.

Chapter Twenty-Three

The quiet tap of shoes somewhere against the floor reverberated in the room, stirring Kitty from sleep. Eyes closed, she inhaled slowly, bracing for the anticipated pain. When she took a deeper breath and the nausea she expected never assailed, she opened her eyes and gazed at the wooden beams above her. Moving her head against the pillow she tested her fingers and toes before stretching her arms and legs. No longer did her muscles groan or her joints protest movement. Another moment passed and 'twas only then she realized that instead of chilled, the room felt hot. She pressed a hand to her head and felt the beads of sweat that dotted her skin. Knowing well what such moisture meant, she moved her hands together and silently prayed, hoping the simple words carried with them all the depth of meaning she felt unworthy to express. *Lord, I thank thee for healing me.*

A sweet scented breeze flirted with the thin curtain at the open window as Kitty tucked strands of hair around her ear. The light beamed into the room with such ferocity she guessed it must be only a few hours before sundown, for that was when the sun rested just inches above her window ledge as it did now.

Glancing 'round the room, evidences of a caregiver met her eyes. A chair beside the bed, a bowl of water, a dampened cloth and a tray of bread rested on the bedside table. Once more she dusted her fingers over her hair and squinted her tired eyes to make out the hands of the clock on the far dresser. How long had she been ill?

A shuffle near the hall caught her attention. She glanced toward the open door and her heart stalled.

Nathaniel's tall frame consumed the empty doorway. He stopped and stared at her with bright eyes. The sound of his deep voice brushed over her, more welcome than the breeze from the window. "You're awake."

The sight of him made Kitty's heart begin a quicker, lighter rhythm. She swallowed and nodded, unable to produce sound. No matter how the tell-tale flutterings consumed her middle, no matter how her soul yearned for his nearness, she carefully folded the powerful longing and tucked it deep beneath the need to protect.

Nathaniel neared, his eyes combing over her with a tenderness that twined her yearning soul like fine silk. His freshly shaven face and the scent of soap met her senses and she touched her tangled hair, then pulled at the sheet to cover her unsightly nightdress.

She offered a tight grin and struggled to untie her gaze from his, but failed for the desire for him grew with every swell of her chest. He took the seat beside her bed, far too close for Kitty's satisfaction. For the nearer he got, the more the buried emotions pounded for liberation from behind the locked doors of her heart.

Nathaniel leaned back in his chair with a sigh, running his hands down the tops of his thighs. "I should have you punished for the scare you put us through." The humor in his words didn't match the touching warmth in his eyes. "I forbid you to ever become that ill again."

Kitty swallowed. "I shall do my best."

A smile split his face. "Good." He reached for the damp cloth and touched it against her head, his tone growing slightly serious. "Your fever has broken, I see." Moving the cloth along her face and dotting it against her collarbone, his gaze darted around her face as if seeing her for the first time.

Gripping the fabric in her hands, Kitty battled the flight of her pulse and the heat rising to her cheeks. The way he stared, the way he touched her made her almost believe, nay desire, that he saw deep within, past the secrets and beyond the politics that separated them, to the woman within.

The folly of such a desire smacked of foolishness. Once he knew the truth of what she'd done, that she had been the cause of his attack, he would never speak to her again, let alone...

Instead of responding to his comment, she sighed, frowning at the wound above his eye, her spirit cowering at the horrid memory. "You seem to have recovered well." Rolling her head against the pillow, she looked away, her throat thickening. "I'm so sorry for what happened to you." After a deep breath she looked back at him and tried not to be lost in the fields of caring that rested in his eyes. She offered a small grin. "If my father had been here he would have known perfectly what to do." He had always known what to do.

Nathaniel touched the stiches on his brow and tilted his head with a sly lift of his mouth. "Your stitching skills are fair enough."

"Is that all?" She warmed at his jest and a smile bloomed both outwardly as well as within.

He shrugged and struggled to contain a grin that matched her own. "I might concede they are a mite better than fair." Nathaniel lowered his eyes before peeking up at her again, this time all teasing had gone from his expression as well as his voice. "You miss your father."

Kitty looked away, abruptly consumed by a loneliness she hadn't realized had been draping her since the moment she fell ill. She closed her eyes while faint memories from times past whisked inside her. Father's gentle touch, his warm voice and soft smiles rested on her like rays of sunshine.

If Father were here, what would he tell her to do? What wisdom would he share?

Nathaniel continued, as if he knew her very thoughts. "I do wish I could have given you the care he might have, as I know I am lacking in his talent and experience." He looked down and paused before meeting her gaze. "I do hope you know I did my best for you. Though I suspect, given the choice, you would not have had me here."

Regret dumped on her back like a wagon-load of dirt. "I... I hope you do not think—" *How to say it?* "You are a gifted physician, Nathaniel."

"Not like your father."

The temptation to reach for his hand made her grip the sheet. "You are."

"You would trust him with anything."

She nodded. "Of course."

Nathaniel paused, the depth in his voice expanding warm and wide. "What about me?"

"What do you mean?"

His eyes slipped from hazel to brown. "Would you

trust me the same way?"

"You know I would," she whispered.

"You would trust me with *anything*?" The richness in his voice harbored a question that went deeper than his simple words revealed and it cut at Kitty's tender heart.

She licked her lips and looked at the far wall.

The words that vied for freedom trailed away and slunk back into the dungeons of her conscience. The memory of Nathaniel's attack and her involvement replaced her receding nausea with a new wave of torment.

A warm hand encased hers and she turned, staring at Nathaniel's strong fingers caressing her own, almost as if he'd seen into her mind and liberated the yearnings of her spirit. The jolt of heat that shot up her arm reminded her of the tender moments they'd shared. How desperately she'd wanted more. More time together. More laughter and secret smiles. Her throat ached and she forced down the lump of regret.

Kitty played with the soft sheets she'd pulled to her neck and stared at her toes poking up beneath the quilt. "Where are Eliza and Thomas?"

Nathaniel chuckled and rose to the table, pulling a small piece of bread from the loaf on the tray. "I sensed they could no longer stand the sight of me so I sent them into town on a few errands, as I have had to do frequently of late. They should return shortly." He sat again and handed the bread to Kitty. "'Tis been far too long since you've had anything solid in your belly. I'd like you to have a few small bites. I need to see the color back in your cheeks. I've missed it."

She inhaled the fresh scent of the piece he held

before her and tried not to focus on his nearness. Why must he carry such tenderness in his warm stare? Why did his voice have to be so soft? Kitty held her teeth together, but somehow the words slipped free. "I hadn't wanted you to come."

He didn't move. "I know."

"You have enough people to care for, and after just being hurt yourself... it didn't seem right for you to care for me."

"Would you have me neglect my patients?"

"Nay."

"Then how could I neglect you?" He smiled and pulled a morsel off the bread in his hands and nudged it toward her mouth. "Eat."

She swallowed, wetting her mouth. Her body still complained and her head continued to ache, though her stomach grumbled at the smell of food.

Kitty leaned back when his fingers pressed closer. Chuckling, his face bloomed into the kind of smile she loved, bright and uninhibited. "Come now, don't be stubborn. Take a bite."

Her pulse tapped wildly as she licked her lips and opened her mouth.

"Good girl." His fingers brushed against her lips and the fire in his gentle touch spread across her face. He took her hand once more, his angled features drawn. "Kitty, I hope... I do hope you feel that you can trust me, like you would your father." He circled his thumb along the top of her hand, undoing the stone wall she'd so carefully constructed to guard her heart. "We are true friends, are we not?"

Friends. "Aye."

"Friends confide in one another, do they not?"

A frown pulled down at her mouth, for surely he had a motive in asking such questions. But what?

The gentleness in his eyes, though still present, moved aside to allow for deep earnest as the muscles in his jaw flexed. He asked again. "Do they not?"

Kitty nodded, pretending she didn't notice every nuance of his expression. "Aye."

He leaned forward, urgency coating his timbre. Gently holding tighter to her hand, he almost whispered. "I need to know what happened the night you were attacked."

"What?" she breathed. He could not be serious.

"Kitty, I am done pretending I don't know something is wrong. Who is doing this to you?"

Squirming, Kitty fought to keep her breath relaxed. "Who is... who is doing what?"

"Kitty." He moved to the edge of the bed. "I only wish to help you, you must know that. I will protect you, I vow it—only you must trust me."

Tears welled, blurring the wound along his eye. She had been the cause of that and despite her desires to trust, his safety trumped all.

"I cannot tell you." Her voice was flat as the words hopped from her mouth before she could stop them.

He stilled, his posture pulling back. "And why not?"

She tugged her hand free from his, instantly aching from the vacancy that replaced the warmth of his touch. "Do not ask me."

"Why, Kitty?" His brow pinched and his mouth stayed open as if more protests prepared to be spoken.

Her throat swelled until it nearly clogged off the air that reached down for her lungs. She swallowed a groan and turned away. "It is not for you to know."

"It *is* for me to know."

The compulsion to open her mouth and expel the

awful truth she kept hidden was enough to make acid once again inch upward. She clenched her eyes shut, fear and hurt raging in her spirit like a tempest. “Please leave me.”

“As you wish.”

She shot her head in his direction. *No, Nathaniel! I didn’t mean it!*

He strode toward the door, and stopped, his mouth hard but hazel eyes soft as leather. “If you cannot place your trust in me, Kitty, I pray you will find strength to place it in someone.”

With that, he disappeared down the stairs and Kitty’s tears surfaced.

I trust you, dear Nathaniel. But I cannot trust myself.

Chapter Twenty-Four

Despite Eliza's continued prodding to stay abed and despite the protests of her still-fatigued limbs, Kitty dressed and made her way down the stairs and into the kitchen. The savory scents of yeast and nutmeg swirled in the air so heavy she could taste them, and somehow, her body's strength began to rejuvenate amongst the sights and smells of the place she loved so well.

Eliza jumped when Kitty entered and her face immediately slackened. She propped a fist to her hip. "I truly cannot believe my eyes. You should not be out of bed."

"I have more energy, do I not?" Kitty pulled her shoulders back and inhaled deeply, trying to forget the ugly reality that once again, the dreaded day had arrived. "You must admit I have more color and appetite. I should be up. 'Tis healthy for me. You know even father would say as much."

"I will admit no such thing." Eliza twisted her mouth to the side. "I am not happy with you, but I cannot force you to stay abed." She turned back to the dough on the table and plunged her floured hands into the white mass. "I believe were Nathaniel here instead of I, he would not so easily allow you to—"

"I am fine, truly." Kitty laughed playfully to try and buoy both her own spirits as well as Eliza's. She rolled up her sleeves and pulled a large section from Eliza's dough before making it into smaller balls. "You can well empathize with my plight, I know. Staying in bed for so long makes one idle. A terrible feeling." The pleasant stickiness on her hands provided yet more strength to her weary soul. Today's dreaded task weighed upon her like a sack of milled wheat.

"Aye, but you were far more ill than you care to admit." Eliza shook her head and placed a perfectly rounded bit of dough onto the pan.

"I don't wish to speak of it. Nathaniel says I am well recovered, and I *am*."

"Speaking of Nathaniel..." Eliza's voice trailed away but the words she left unsaid were revealed in her eyes.

Kitty feigned ignorance. "I cannot know why you're looking at me that way."

"Can you not? I have never seen anyone so devoted as he." She released a breathy giggle before growing sincere. "You should know how worried Nathaniel was for you, Kitty. He was desperate for you to be well. And since you are up and about and determined to feign liveliness, I shall put your energy to the test." She leaned forward on the table, pressing her hands into the dough. Her voice grew quiet as if she pried for a secret the surrounding furniture should not hear. "You must tell me of this kiss. I have been desperate for details since the moment I heard of it."

Heat blasted into Kitty's face like an oven in August. "There's nothing to tell."

Eliza pulled back and lifted a brow.

Kitty snickered. "You don't believe me?"

When her sister neither responded nor so much as blinked, Kitty shook her head and studied her dough-covered fingers. "I suppose you know I have always cared for him." The memories drifted around her until she could hear his breath, feel the warmth of his hands on her face and the soft cushion of his lips on hers. Her cheeks heated again and she cleared her throat. "We were swept away in a moment of foolishness." A grin tugged at her mouth, but she allowed only half of what wished for exposure. She met Eliza's gaze and raised a single brow. "'Twas nothing, though to satisfy you I will say I... I quite enjoyed it."

Eliza covered her smiling mouth with her floured fingers. A tiny laugh escaped. She bit her lip and took a deep breath as if trying to contain her delight. "Well, since I can tell I shall have to be satisfied with that crumb of information, I shall savor it. However, I will hope for more later."

She reached into the container of flour and dusted the board. "I must say that Nathaniel and Thomas have been distressed about the missing powder. It's produced a worry in them I have never seen." Eliza looked up. "But you seem to have provided Nathaniel with a much needed, and healthy remedy for his concerns. And if I might be so bold, I do hope this budding relationship continues because I believe you two would be a grand match."

A remedy for Nathaniel's concerns? Nay. If he ever discovered her actions...

"I'm sure I don't know what you mean, Liza. Silly notion." Kitty took in long slow breaths and worked the soft dough in her fingers. "You know, I believe a bit of air will help clean my blood. I plan to take a short walk this afternoon."

Eyes wide, Eliza smiled tentatively as if she hadn't expected such a response. "Why, of course. I shall join you."

"That's very generous of you, but I don't think—"

"I should like to get out as well, and you simply cannot find a more beautiful day than—"

"Do forgive me, Liza!" Kitty's volume rose more than she intended. She cleared her throat. "I find I am craving a bit of solitude."

The light in Eliza's face faded. She nodded and looked away, arranging the balls of dough. "I understand. 'Tis good to have time alone." The words didn't match the sorrow in her eyes.

"Please don't think I wish to be away from you."

"I would never think that." Worry dug into the creases on Eliza's forehead as if she somehow knew Kitty's motivations went much deeper.

Kitty glanced at the clock on the mantel above the kitchen fire. Noon. She had two hours before she must perform the dreaded task. Like a torrent, the anxieties she'd reserved rushed upon her, threatening to drown her happiness in its crushing waves.

Snatching the checkered cloth from the table Kitty wiped her hands clean as a warm breeze rushed through the open window. She tried to shadow her pains with a light tone. "As I think upon it, I shall be off now. The weather is begging for me join it." She motioned at the window before she met Eliza's gaze. "I do plan to take my time. Don't worry for me."

"How can I not worry for you when you should not be out at all."

Kitty shrugged as she made her way to the door and offered Eliza a quick wave. "I will be well, I promise."

The questions that veiled Eliza's features couldn't be covered by the tiny smile she offered. Did she suspect?

Before her sister could expose the inquiries that waited in her eyes, Kitty escaped out the backdoor with a smile and a wink.

Her weak legs begged for rest before she'd even reached the road.

She pressed a hand to her chest. In two hours it would be over and she could return home again. Groaning, she bit her lip.

Two hours.

Two years.

Two lifetimes.

This would never be over. Even if she were able to find a way to stop her involvement, the memory of her actions, and her foolishness that caused Nathaniel's attack, would haunt her with every breath.

A lifetime of heartache reached long and wide before her like an empty, colorless horizon.

If only she could find rest. If only she could find someone—anyone who could help her.

Lord, I need thee. Find me, and lead me back to freedom.

The heat of Saturday's afternoon sun retreated at the salty sea breeze that ushered Nathaniel along the street toward Thomas's print shop. Finding the door propped open, Nathaniel strode in, a smirk on his mouth.

"Shirking your work as usual, I see."

Thomas spun around, half a smile on his mouth and one eyebrow slanted up. "No more than you, it would seem." He replaced the several pieces of type and laughed. "What brings you here in the middle of the day?"

Nathaniel chuckled then turned and closed the door. "Well, seeing as I've cured every disease and illness, I'm left to wander the streets." Nathaniel laughed again, reveling in the lightness that humor gifted him and relishing in the peace that at last he enjoyed, knowing the powder would no more be ravished.

Walking nearer to his friend, he lowered his volume. "Everything is finished." He looked behind to reassure himself the door was latched. "The last of the munitions is well and secreted away."

Nodding, Thomas's face lit. "Excellent."

Nathaniel nodded in agreement and stared at the far window, smiling inwardly as the memories of last night's adventure rehearsed in his mind. How easily the transfer had transpired could be regarded as nothing short of miraculous. He met Thomas's gaze. "Now, we wait."

Thomas crossed his arms and stepped back to lean against the press. "The traitor will be discovered soon. Or so we can hope."

"He will be. And when he is, I plan to acquaint him with a quick and proper punishment." Nathaniel stepped toward the door. "I had only come to let you know our efforts last evening were well rewarded and the town's munitions are safe." He tapped the end of his hat. "I'm off to make my rounds. There's a particular patient I must visit."

Thomas chuckled, returning to the corner desk that held the small metal type. "Were you not over only yesterday?"

"Need I remind you that she was very ill? 'Tis best to make sure she is truly recovering."

Thomas peered over his shoulder. "Are you sure you haven't any other motive?"

All expression dropped from Nathaniel's face before he quickly replaced the flick of frustration with humorous defense. "Your wife promised me a mid-day meal, if you must know. And as I am a lonely bachelor I must rely on the goodness of others to feed my empty stomach lest I wilt away to nothingness."

Thomas patted the small metal letters into the galleys, keeping his head down while he spoke. "Take care, Nathaniel. I know you believe your heart safe from infection, but no one has yet found a way to be inoculated from love."

"Inoculated? From love?" A laugh burst from Nathaniel's chest and he grinned to keep the levity of his words from sitting heavy. "Please, Thomas I don't take pleasure in your instruction on matters of the heart."

Thomas shrugged. "I only wish to offer advice that may shield you from a pain that runs far deeper than any physical wound."

"My desire to visit Kitty is the same I would feel for any patient who had been so desperately ill." He grinned, praying Thomas couldn't see past the lie. "Though I care for her, my feelings do not root as deep as you imagine."

Mouth tight, Thomas remained silent, still studying his type. Finally the words on his face found voice. "As you say." He glanced up, eyes hard. "I beg you, do not lead Kitty to believe otherwise, or I fear you will have to be the recipient of my wrath."

Nathaniel frowned until his face nearly contorted as the understanding of Thomas's words found fertile ground. "I have no intention of doing any such thing."

"Our actions do not always imitate our best intentions."

The air in the print shop suddenly grew thick. Rolling back his shoulders, Nathaniel snatched his shield of ready humor. "Perhaps then I should reconsider my *intentions* to bring you a pail of food should Eliza request it of me on my return to town."

Before Thomas could protest, Nathaniel tipped his hat and with a bubbling chuckle stepped out into the street. He kept a clipped pace, hoping the brisk steps would stamp out the uncomfortable niggling in his stomach. Yet, his friend's unasked for admonition blared like the sounding of a trumpet. Perhaps Nathaniel *should* use more caution where Kitty was concerned. Their kiss was evidence of that. But he had been so pleased when she didn't push away from him entirely the day he first found her awake. The knowledge that he hadn't completely frightened her away mended the rift in his heart and made it all but impossible to keep the kind of distance he knew must exist between them.

But somehow he *must* keep that distance. For the sake of his heart, and as Thomas had advised, for hers.

Standing straighter, he tipped his head at the driver of a passing cart and nourished his insecurities on the facts. He and Kitty were friends, had always been, and 'twas natural for him to enjoy the company of such a friend. It mattered not that she was a woman... and a pretty one at that.

A smile tickled his mouth. Pretty, nay—beautiful.

Funny. Brave. Intelligent.

And wounded.

A frown darkened his spirit and slowed his step. Why would she refuse to tell him who had hurt her? Did she not know the depth of his concern? Did she really have so little faith in him?

The questions were too numerous and too ponderous to find the resolution he desired in the short time it took to walk to the Watson's.

Once there, he sucked in a deep breath and knocked lightly before stepping in. As expected, the parlor was empty and the pleasant sounds from the kitchen sang through the room.

"Hello?" Eliza's voice rang surprisingly loud from the kitchen. "Thomas is that you?"

"Nay Eliza, 'tis I."

"Oh, Nathaniel, of course. Come into the kitchen if you like." Eliza's volume continued to carry strong, which gave him hope that his patient was awake. Or even better, resting quietly at the kitchen table.

Nathaniel removed his hat and placed it on the peg by the door and followed the welcoming scents of bread and spices on his way to the kitchen, speaking as he went. "I did mention to your husband that I might be kind enough to bring him a pail of food on my return to town, if you have one for him." Once inside the heated room, he tried to keep the disappointment at not seeing Kitty from etching into his face. "I hope you don't mind."

"Of course not." She looked up with a quick smile. "That would be kind of you, thank you." The pinch in her voice nudged at a hidden worry in Nathaniel's chest.

He tapped his fingers against the top of the nearest kitchen chair and motioned past the parlor.

"How is the patient today?"

Eliza shook her head while she fussed with the dough. "Well enough to get out, it would seem."

"Get out?"

"Aye." She picked up the laden pan and moved it to the fire. "She's gone."

He let out a sarcastic laugh. "I beg your pardon, did you say gone?" Kitty couldn't actually be gone. She was not yet back to complete health. Gone to the privy perhaps, or gone to sit in the sun, but not *gone*.

Eliza pushed up on her knees, her shoulders slumping as she sighed. Turning, she faced him and immediately the concern woven into her features turned his stomach to solid rock.

"She's not here, Nathaniel." Eliza rubbed her forehead with the back of her hand. "She has left to take a walk."

"A walk? She's hardly well enough to leave her room." Angst popped in Nathaniel's chest like oil on a skillet. "Tell me she didn't feel so obligated to make her deliveries to the poor that she put her own health at risk?"

"Deliveries?"

"Aye, the deliveries to the poor that Camilla Wythe can no longer do herself."

Eliza paused. "I'm not sure what you mean."

He tipped his head and spoke slow. "Thomas informed me that you and the ladies in town took over Camilla's deliveries to the poor when she became ill."

Eliza's voice went flat. "We spoke of it, but left that work in the hands of the church long ago."

Nathaniel stalled, struggling against the fragments of information like a wagon struggles up a rocky ledge. "So why would she—" Suddenly his thoughts crested and he could see for miles.

Cyprian.

His heart charged to life, pulsing clarity and pure energy through his limbs. He charged forward. "Did she say where she was going?"

"Nay, she did not." Eliza's expression crumpled. "What's wrong?"

"Do not worry." He raced toward the door, speaking loud over his shoulder. "Whatever is wrong, I plan to make right."

Cyprian stared, blinking and shaking his head to try and untangle the words he'd just heard. "What do you mean it's missing?"

Andrew stood on the back stoop of Cyprian's home, face ashen. "The powder, the munitions—it's all gone."

For a moment Cyprian's mind was blank. All he could see was Camilla's face, and her eyes closing in death.

Yanking Andrew by the collar, Cyprian pulled him inside the kitchen, speaking only inches from the man's face. "How did they know?"

Red seeped up Andrew's neck and his mouth contorted. "If I had alerted them, would I have come to inform you?"

Cyprian looked out the window into the trees. *The Campbell girl.*

Growling, he shoved Andrew toward the door and down the back step. "See if you can get any of your patriot friends to talk, and I will—"

"Cyprian?"

He jerked at the faint sound of Camilla's hoarse voice.

"I am here," he called. Turning back to Andrew he growled. "We need that powder tonight!" He slammed the door as another quiet cry tumbled down to him.

He ran up the stairs to her room and took her hand. "What is it, my love?"

She winced and turned her head on the pillow, but said nothing.

Lowering into the chair beside the bed, Cyprian brushed a strand of hair from her cheek. "What do you need, Camilla?"

Slowly the wrinkles in her forehead relaxed and she blinked as if whatever pain she suffered ebbed away. Her gaze rested on him and the fear in her pale blue eyes nailed him to his seat. "Find Jacob."

Cyprian frowned. "Jacob?" The last thing that boy needed was to see his mother like this.

"Find him now." Her head moved ever so slight as she nodded. Tears welled in her eyes and pooled in his heart. "I must see him before I go."

He shook his head and strained to speak against the thickness of his throat. "Do not speak of such things." Panic stabbed him and his words streamed like blood from a wound. "The medicine is working, it—"

"It is not working, Cyprian."

"It *is*."

With a weak smile, she enclosed his hand with her small ones. "I need to see my boy one last time." Her voice cracked and sent a rift through Cyprian's spirit that nearly stopped his heart. She blinked and a tear trickled down her thin face. "Please, Cyprian."

The reality, the depth of such a statement, shoved

him against the blades of truth he had denied for so long. Struggling to breathe he leaned over and kissed Camilla on the forehead. "I will fetch him."

"Thank you."

When she had closed her eyes he quietly walked to the door and shut it behind him. That Campbell girl would answer for her betrayal. Camilla's life depended on that powder, and if it could not be discovered in time, and Camilla's eyes closed in death, he would be sure that traitorous woman suffered in place of his wife—for a *very* long time.

Chapter Twenty-Five

Kitty rested the basket on the first step and stared. The humid air hung around her shoulders like a damp blanket. Mid-day light shafted through the trees that shielded the tiny cabin. As always, the door of the lonely dwelling rested part-way open. She stopped breathing and strained for any sound that might indicate someone waited for her within. Nothing.

Swallowing away the last morsel of fear that rested in her throat she pressed her hand to the rough wood and pushed it open. A mouse scurried into the corner as the breeze rushed in behind her, sweeping a scattering of dried leaves and dust across the floor.

Inhaling deep, Kitty took her first full look at the place she'd loathed for so many weeks. A wooden chair in the corner. No rug. A fireplace in the center of the back wall, long since forgotten, overflowed with masses of white cobwebs. On the other side rested the remains of a small bed-frame, while a broom leaned against the far window.

With a long exhale she grabbed the chair and scooted it closer to the fire, as if this mournful hearth held welcoming flames. Her weak muscles groaned, but the ache of her heart surpassed every pain. She rested her elbows on her knees and pressed her face to her hands. If the omniscient Lord of Heaven had kept her from dying, then surely he had heard her prayers and would liberate her from bondage.

Where art thou, Lord? Please deliver me!

Just then the breeze blew stronger, slamming the door open behind her.

Kitty jumped up and covered her mouth to keep from squealing.

The basket was gone.

She grabbed the chair for support with one hand and breathed through her fingers of the other. Frantic, she raced to the open door and scanned the forest. No sign of anyone. Not a sound.

She turned and leaned her forehead against the frame of the door, holding back a groan that twisted her insides like a wet piece of wash.

Had someone seen her? Her breathing quickened. Or had someone else followed her and taken the basket? Kitty's blood surged. Nay! Who would Cyprian hurt next?

She pressed her hand to her mouth as a sob erupted.

Lord, I cannot carry this alone.

Another breeze circled around her like the brush of an angel's touch.

Trust in me and I will lead you to freedom.

The words were so clear she jerked around to find who spoke them, but only the trees with their glistening leaves waved back and forth. Swelling with love for her Father in Heaven, she closed her eyes.

God had heard her prayers after all. But... lead her to freedom? What did that mean?

Unshed tears made the light from the trees spray

out in every direction. *Lord, I long to do what is right in thy sight. But what is your will for me?*

Then, as if God touched her memory, Donaldson's words filled her mind, "...there will come a time when we will be called upon to act in defense of the cause we believe in. It won't be enough to merely stand by silently and watch others do the fighting for us."

Slowly, like a bud opening to the dawn, a trickle of understanding illuminated.

God wanted her to act.

She frowned as long fingers of confusion threatened to snuff out the fresh breath of knowledge. Then with what side did God want her to act? Surely he wouldn't ask her to go against what she'd been taught?

Shaking her head, Kitty rested her back against the doorframe. Nay. Father had raised her honorably. Submission, peace, love and devotion to the king was the right way. 'Twas what God wanted.

The peace from moments ago vanished, replaced by a cold, lonely emptiness.

She pressed her lips together.

That was right. It *had* to be. So why did she feel so much... unease? Surely God wasn't telling her that the patriot's cause was—justified?

Kitty wiped her hands down her bodice.

Yet, doing what was right was often difficult, was it not? Again, she shut her eyes. Without Father to guide her, how could she come to such knowledge? If only God would provide some way, *someone* to help her see the truth.

"Miss Campbell, what are you doing so far from home?"

Kitty jumped and nearly stumbled backward on the stoop as her heart leapt with both jubilation and fear. "Nathaniel!" She clutched her chest. "What are you doing here?"

He sauntered forward, never moving his gaze from hers. "I ought to be asking you the same."

She frowned and shook her head. "You need to leave."

"Why?" He didn't stop walking.

"'Tis not safe."

"Not safe to be alone with me you mean?"

He finished closing the distance and stopped just before the first step, close enough for Kitty to see how the dark green of his jacket enhanced the few flecks of emerald in his eyes. Close enough to feel her yearning for him break free from its cage.

His gaze combed her as a weight of sorrow deepened the shade of his eyes. "Worry not. I won't repeat the events of our last encounter, if that is what troubles you."

The finality in his voice pricked her heart, a small stream of pain bleeding out like tears for what would never be. What *could* never be.

Releasing a breathy laugh, she stepped back into the cabin. "I do not fear your companionship, Nathaniel."

"Then what do you fear?"

She spun around and though she painted a vacant expression on her exterior, her insides screamed. *How I want to tell you!*

Nathaniel stepped toward her, his broad frame blocking the light from the door. "I would take away every fear that plagues you, Kitty. You must know that."

The love she tried to restrain pushed from the shadows of her spirit and ran to him, but stalled when God's admonition suddenly poured over her.

Trust him.

Was Nathaniel the one God had sent for her to trust, to learn from? Truly, she had never known so much peace, so much clarity as when Nathaniel was near. Perhaps *this* was God's answer.

Nathaniel's powerful gaze held her motionless. He moved nearer, until only inches away. The power of his closeness stole her every thought. She could hear him breathe, see the throb of his pulse in his neck.

Trust him.

A half-smile framed his mouth. "Eliza told me you'd left to take a walk. Why would you do such a thing?" He stopped and looked around the cabin, then back at her. "You know you are too ill to be venturing any farther than the kitchen."

Kitty forced a relaxed laugh, which Nathaniel would likely see through, but she still must try. Pasting a sly smile to her lips, she pretended not to catch his meaning. "Well, clearly I wasn't as ill as you seem to think, was I?"

"Are you telling me my assessment of your condition was wrong?"

Somehow the commanding quality of his timbre snapped at the brevity she struggled to uphold. Another breeze brushed past and his familiar scent of mint and apple made her close her eyes. *Perhaps... perhaps I can trust him.*

She studied her fingers before meeting his unwavering stare. "Nay. I know that you are never wrong."

She looked down and focused on her hands once more. If he suspected her vulnerability, pulling the unbearable truth from her would be as easy as plucking a drooping flower from its stem.

Nathaniel's voice wound around her as the wind danced through the cabin. "Allow me to ask you again." He lowered his chin. "What are you doing *here*?"

"'Tis true I... I simply wanted to—"

She stopped when his disbelieving stare pinned her lips shut.

One eyebrow lifted. "You wouldn't have left the house unless it was urgent and you certainly wouldn't come to this place alone, unless you *needed* to." He sighed. "Do you not remember I saw you come from here when you claimed to be making deliveries for the poor." He stopped and his eyebrows lowered. "Clearly, no one lives here."

She hugged her arms around her chest and wriggled in her ever-tightening stays. "What are you suggesting?"

Looking away, he ground his teeth before meeting her gaze. "Nothing particular, I just... I worry that perhaps..." He raised his arms then dropped them with a grunt. "Blast it, Kitty, I can't do this."

Her heart rapped behind her lungs. "Do what?"

He stepped closer, grasping her arms. "I can no longer pretend I am ignorant of your sufferings." The pain in his eyes deepened. His voice grew soft and caressed the sorrows in her heart. "Tell me all, Kitty, and I will do everything I can to make it right."

Hot tears welled. "I... I can't."

"You can." He pulled her to him. The spark of indignation in his eyes was enough to ignite the few sticks in the hearth behind her. "You need not fear, Kitty, I vow it."

She stared at him, clenching her teeth as the words crouched on her tongue.

Trust him.

Closing her eyes, she prayed. *Lord, I don't know if I can.*

Then trust Me!

She sucked in a ragged breath and met Nathaniel's tormented gaze. The love in his eyes matched the love that owned her soul and all she wanted was to lose herself in the safety of his strong embrace. How could she not trust Nathaniel? How could she not trust God?

Reaching to her face, Nathaniel brushed the backs of his knuckles against her cheek, his tone warm and wanting. "Please, Kitty."

Licking her lips, she surrendered. *Aye, Lord, I will trust thee. I will trust Nathaniel.*

She took his hand in hers, aching to press it to her lips as she arranged the words that waited to be spoken. "That night after the party as I walked home Cy—"

"Nathaniel!"

Kitty jerked back and Nathaniel sent a worried glance to her before racing out the door.

Thomas's voice peeled through the cabin. "Nathaniel are you there?"

Kitty followed Nathaniel outside just as Thomas reached the steps.

"There's been a terrible accident."

Immediate alertness pulled Nathaniel's shoulders back and turned his bright tone a heavy black. "What's happened? How did you know I was here?"

"There's no time to explain." He shook his head and turned back to the road, running. "There's been an accident at the blacksmith's. Jacob is hurt."

"Jacob Wythe?"

"Aye. Come quickly!"

Nathaniel grabbed Kitty's hand and held tight as

they ran behind Thomas. His strong grip tensed as the words flowed. "Where is he?"

Thomas glanced behind. "We brought him to your house."

Kitty held up her skirts with her one available hand. Her body still aching from fatigue, she prayed she wouldn't trip as she struggled to keep with the pace of the men.

Charging through town and around Shawme Pond, Nathaniel's house finally came into view. The back door flew open the moment they reached the step.

Cyprian.

Kitty gasped and turned to retreat. They had been tricked into coming for naught! But Cyprian's white face and the sudden wail that echoed through the house answered nay.

Cyprian stepped back and motioned to the small room, mouth tight, nostrils flared.

Nathaniel charged in first, followed by Thomas.

Kitty stepped in, stopping just outside the surgery door and pressed her hands to her mouth. Writhing and groaning, Jacob lay on the table while Joseph held his shoulders, whispering in his ear. The muscles in Nathaniel's face twitched as his eyes scanned the boy's leg. Twisted and near unrecognizable, the flesh burst open and the bone stuck out the side while the bottom half of the leg hung at a right-angle.

Nathaniel snatched a small belt from the cabinet and instantly tightened it above the boy's knee. His voice was strong when he peered at Joseph. "Tell me what happened—Kitty go into the kitchen and get a bucket of water, three cloths and a wooden spoon."

She nodded and raced to the kitchen. Her hands

shook as she scanned the room.

There, in the corner! She plucked the necessary items and spun for the door.

"You!"

Kitty yelped and spun when Cyprian hurried in.

She shook her head. Her knees weakened and she braced herself against the wall. "Mr. Wythe, I—"

"If you had obeyed me as you ought, I would not have needed to spend my precious time looking for the powder." He stalked closer, fists opening and closing. "I could have made sure my son was at the tavern instead of tutoring under another traitorous patriot!"

All blood drained from her head. "I don't know what you—"

"Kitty!" Nathaniel's commanding voice tore through the house.

She straightened her shoulders and lifted her chin. "Let me pass."

"The magazine is empty." His voice went sickeningly quiet. "You have broken your vow, forcing me to go on a desperate search when I should have been at my wife's bedside."

Kitty blinked. "Empty?"

This time, Nathaniel's voice blared like a war-cry. "Kitty! Now!"

She didn't even look at Cyprian as she barreled past.

He yanked her arm and pulled her back. His words scraped against her like the underside of a grindstone. "You will tell me where the powder is *now*!"

"I don't know—"

"You lie!" His lips flared as he spoke through his teeth. "Tell me!"

The weeks of forced servitude exploded under pressure of suppressed hatred. Kitty wrenched from his grasp and spoke through a hard whisper. "I am *not* lying and I have *never* lied! I have no idea where your powder is and I refuse to be your slave any longer. Find someone else to perform your evil works."

She lunged for the parlor, but his iron hand held her back and he swung her to face him. His eyes were black and his timbre seething. "You are free to live your life the way you please, all I require is your obedience. I dare you to defy me!"

A tortured yelp from the surgery shot through the kitchen.

She charged from the room.

"Is your sister with child?" Cyprian's words halted Kitty's steps. "I should hate anything to befall her."

Her heart crashed to a stop and she turned to him. "You wouldn't."

He neared, his black eyes matching the color of his soul. "Find. That. Powder."

"Kitty!" Nathaniel rushed out and stalled, his gaze darting back and forth between them. Chest pumping, he stepped forward. Gripping her wrist he led her into the surgery.

Blinking to keep her mind focused on the vital task at hand, the words Cyprian had spoken strangled her thinking. If she didn't find the missing powder he would hurt Eliza! *Nay, Lord, please help me!*

Nathaniel's powerful voice split the air and snapped Kitty away from her thoughts.

"You must all be prepared. This will not be pleasant, but it will be quick."

Joseph's face turned whiter than a summer cloud.

He nodded and leaned down, speaking quietly into the crying boy's ear and brushing his fingers against Jacob's tear stained face.

Nathaniel held out his hand to Kitty. "Where's the spoon?"

"Here."

Snatching it, Nathaniel went to the head of the table and lowered to his haunches so his face was even with Jacob's. A small, tight smile on his mouth, Nathaniel's voice turned soothing as he stroked the boy's arm. "'Tis time. Are you ready?"

Jacob's head bobbed slightly, huge tears flooding down his cheeks.

"You are a brave boy, Jacob. You will do well." Nathaniel stood, and tenderly brushed his hand over the boy's head, his smile softening. With a quick look at Joseph, he placed the handle of the spoon in the boy's mouth. "Bite down hard, Jacob. The pain won't last."

"What?" Cyprian bellowed and charged in, jerking Nathaniel back by the shoulder. "You can't take my son's leg!"

Nathaniel pointed at Thomas then Cyprian. "He is not allowed in this room!"

Thomas came from behind and locked Cyprian's arms with a solid grip.

"You can't do it!" Cyprian yelled. "You're a traitor, a hypocrite, a heathen! Don't you even think—"

Suddenly the backdoor shut and Cyprian's muffled voice struggled to make its way back in. "Miss Campbell, you know better than to let this happen! Don't let him dismember my boy!"

Kitty's mind and strength nearly buckled under the weight of her oppressions when Nathaniel's warm hand rested on her arm. "Don't listen to him." He stopped and sighed. "You know what to do?"

She glanced at the boy's mangled leg, then at the saw in Nathaniel's hand. Clinging to the strands of courage Nathaniel gifted her, she nodded. "I do."

Nathaniel nodded and turned to Joseph. "Prepare your grip."

Jacob wailed as his uncle leaned over him and held him down.

Nathaniel gripped the boy's thigh. "Show me your mettle, son."

Then he put the saw to the flesh.

Chapter Twenty-six

Nathaniel's pulse found its natural rhythm as he wiped the blade clean. Though he'd performed the task numerous times, the execution of such an operation always pained him nearly as much as it did the patient. Especially when that patient was a child. He studied Jacob who slept fitfully, finally overtaken by the pain. It could not have gone more perfectly. *I thank thee, Lord.* Covered with a thick blanket from Nathaniel's own bed, the boy's chest moved slowly up and down, while his brow crunched together.

Focusing again on his task, Nathaniel spoke to Joseph who stood with arms crossed in the corner. "You did well, surprisingly." He looked over his shoulder and offered a half smile, hoping a bit of brevity might lighten the heaviness that clearly rested on Joseph's shoulders. "I almost feared you would collapse."

Joseph didn't offer so much as a glance, his gaze trained solely on Jacob. His throat shifted and he licked his lips as if holding back the emotions that made his muscles flex. "'Tis my fault." His Adam's apple bobbed. "If I had insisted he not assist with that horse..."

Nathaniel swallowed the quick reply he almost

spoke and let the words rest as he formulated a proper response. If he were in Joseph's shoes he would feel the same, and no comment, no matter how well meant would be appreciated. With another quick look at his life-long friend, he sighed. "No matter how deeply you choose to take this upon yourself, the truth remains. Jacob will continue to need you as he always has. You are everything to him."

Joseph's jaw ticked and he stared at the ground. "I will continue to do for him all I can."

Just then, Thomas entered, another bucket in his hands. "Fresh water, as you requested."

"Thank you." Nathaniel took it and sloshed the flesh-covered saw over and over until the tiny fragments fell off the blade's teeth.

Joseph looked up. "Where's Cyprian?"

Moving his gaze from Jacob to Joseph, Thomas answered. "He went home to fetch Jacob a change of clothing."

Nathaniel hummed in response and put the saw in its place in the cabinet. "You've done enough, Thomas. I know you have responsibilities at the press."

Cupping Nathaniel's shoulder, Thomas nodded. "If you need anything more... " He offered a half-grinned good-bye to Joseph and disappeared out the door.

Joseph pushed off the wall and leaned his hands at the end of the table, still gazing at the sleeping boy. "Miss Campbell is incredibly skilled. I'm sure I've never seen a woman do what she did."

Pride warmed Nathaniel like a spiked drink. She *had* done remarkably well. Considering how pale her lips had been, and how her fingers had trembled. He put the last clean instrument on the cloth and glanced out the window, then into the study. Where was she?

He motioned toward Joseph. "Stay with him until I get back."

"Of course."

Though Kitty being in his room was less than plausible, he checked there first, thinking she might have retreated there for a place to rest, then hurried into the kitchen when both the upstairs and the parlor proved unoccupied.

Going outside and around the back, he made sure she wasn't at the well or resting under his shade tree before giving way to the worry that wedged deeper.

Where could she be?

A vision in his mind vanished as quick as it appeared. *The pond.*

Racing down the road on the west of Shawme Pond, Nathaniel rushed past Newcomb to the place where they'd shared that sacred moment. His heart continued a fearsome rhythm. She'd been so close to disclosing her troubles less than an hour before. God willing, he could once again coax her into the comforting securities she needed and would tell him all.

A flicker of movement caught his eye and he halted.

Kneeling near the edge of the water Kitty hunched, scrubbing her arms.

"Kitty?" He neared and crouched beside her, touching her shoulder. "Kitty, are you—"

She squealed and smacked his hand away, her eyes wild. Instantly, she grabbed her chest and released a heavy sigh. "Oh, Nathaniel, 'tis you. Forgive me, I thought you were... I just... I didn't know you were there."

The tremor in her voice pulled a frown from within him that settled on his face. "I didn't mean to frighten you."

Blinking, she turned back to the water and scrubbed at her hands and arms with such fury Nathaniel's own skin began to sting.

"Kitty, you are clean now."

She didn't look at him. "I am not clean." Her voice wobbled. "I will never be clean."

Kitty dabbed at her cheeks with her sleeve.

He touched her again but removed his hand when she flinched. Had the trauma been that much for her? Resting his arm on his knee, Nathaniel stared at the ripples licking the mud at the edge of the pond. Perhaps he'd been too rash in his assumption that helping with such a surgery wouldn't have much affect on her. He'd taken part in amputations dozens upon dozens of times, but this might have been her first. Inwardly he groaned. Considering her own recent illness, 'twas foolishness to have asked for her assistance when he knew full well her fragile state of recovery.

He glanced at the sky. Sending a quick prayer heavenward, he touched her gently on the shoulder. "Let me walk you home, you must rest."

"Nay." Tears continued to fall. "I don't wish to go home. I must finish here."

"Kitty, if you refuse to come, I'm afraid I shall have to carry you and I know you won't like that."

She didn't even look up.

He clamped his fingers around her shoulders, and pulled her to her feet. "You are not well, Kitty. I'm taking you home."

She wriggled to escape his grasp, her volume

rising. "Leave me alone!" Pressing against his chest, Kitty's red-rimmed eyes and ruddy cheeks glistened. "I don't want to go home—I don't want to see anyone ever again!"

She struggled against his hold, but the urgency that pumped in Nathaniel's blood made his muscles flex all the way to the tips of his fingers. What had happened? Just an hour ago she was lucid and calm, now it seemed she was consumed by fear, as she had been the night she thought he was someone else. And yet, now she knew who he was.

Forcing his voice to stay calm he tipped his head to catch her gaze. "Please, Kitty you must calm yourself. You are fine now, everything is fine."

"Everything is *not* fine!" Her shrill cry split the air. "Everything is so much worse than it ever was before."

He shook her shoulders and tried to meet her gaze, but she refused to look at him. "Make sense, Kitty!"

Her melodic voice turned flat. "Leave me, Nathaniel."

Nathaniel dropped his hands and stepped back. Rage mixed with confusion, creating a noxious fume in his lungs. "I refuse to leave, Kitty, until you help me understand what it is that pains you so."

"You will never understand. No one will ever understand." She cupped her face in her hands as a flood of sobs shook her shoulders.

The sound of her anguish tore at him. He could no longer ignore his instincts and swung his arms around her quivering frame, cradling her against his chest. Her muffled weeping tugged at the precarious emotions already treading across his heart. Hot tears bled across his shirt making the fabric stick to his skin. But the only thing he cared to notice was the way she melted into his embrace. Her slight arms wound around him, gripping him as if she were lost at sea and he was her line to safety.

Lord, I would help her, please tell me how.

On and on her tears flowed. Nathaniel nuzzled into her sweet-smelling hair and stroked her back. If only she would confide in him, he would be willing to suffer the very pains of hell for her. His heart had chosen Kitty Campbell, and there was no going back.

But what about unity? What about a family rooted together in truth?

Nathaniel closed his eyes against the warring thoughts. There would be time enough to contemplate such things. Not now. Not when she needed him most.

When her sobs faded to sniffles he eased her away and looked into her glistening eyes. "Darling, you cannot know how my heart breaks to see you suffer. But I can't know how I can help until you confide in me."

Her dainty chin quivered, wavering Nathaniel's already shaky foundation.

She hugged herself and stepped away, moving toward the pond. The afternoon sun spread its warm light on the rippling water, mimicking the shimmering in Kitty's tear-filled gaze.

"I… I cannot tell you."

"Why?" Nathaniel stepped beside her, his stomach twisting. "Why, Kitty? Only an hour ago you were ready to share your burden, and now you will not? I don't understand it!"

A hard breath escaped her lips when she looked away.

His patience teetered on a thin wire. "What's

happened to you? To us? Were we not friends, Kitty? Were we not the most open and jovial of people? And here you are pulling away from me as if I were some kind of stranger. Tell me, are we friends no longer?"

His words found their mark and she snapped her head in his direction. Her tiny nostrils flared and the delicate muscles in her neck corded.

"Friends?" An uncharacteristic sarcasm laced her thick tone. "Do not talk to me about friendship. You kiss me, tease me, flirt as if it is the most natural thing in the world, and yet in the next moment you claim a mere friendship exists between us. And that, Dr. Smith, is not something I can endure."

He leaned into his words until his face was only a few inches from hers. "How can I allow myself to get close to you when I know you are keeping something from me—from all of us."

Her eyes sparked with pain, turning her light eyes inky-blue. "Why are my affairs any concern of yours?"

"Because I *care* about you, Kitty. How many times must I say it?"

"Aye." She straightened her posture and lifted her chin. "You care about me as much as you care about the other Tories in this town, which is frighteningly little. Because I haven't yet embraced the idea of liberty, you choose to view me as less than worthy."

Her words burned like a white-hot iron. He held his jaw rigid. "You know that isn't true."

"Is it not? I've seen the affection in your eyes, but you evade the inconvenient declaration of love because it spoils your perfect future."

He yanked her forward. "Kitty, that is unfair. You know I care about you more than anyone. Ever since I met you I haven't been able to think about anyone else."

"Can you admit we are more than friends, Nathaniel? Can you say that you love me?" Kitty's large eyes blinked. "I know you cannot."

Nathaniel's tongue welded to the roof of his mouth and his voice went mute. Time slowed and he willed his jaw to open and the words to float to her ears.

They would not.

Slamming his eyes shut, he strangled a groan. The woman he held in his grasp brought a joy to his life he'd never known. He would die for Kitty. And yet, he couldn't bring himself to say the words she yearned to hear. Loving a Tory meant despising the cause of liberty that he cherished. A new kind of pain slashed across his heart. If only she would see that freedom was everything.

His gaze twined with hers, and slowly her features dropped as his silence answered clearly what he could not speak.

She pressed her full lips into a thin line and jerked from his hold. The hurt in her face cut across Nathaniel's chest like a freshly sharpened weapon. "I knew it."

He pried his tongue from its holding place and forced his voice into submission. "'Tis not what it seems."

"Your silence says otherwise."

"Kitty, do you not see? You care nothing for the very thing I value more than my own life."

She stared. "And what is that?"

"Freedom."

Kitty swallowed, pulling her arms tighter around her chest. "Freedom? What is *freedom*, Nathaniel?"

"What can I say about something so precious?" He gazed over the pond for a moment before twining his gaze with hers. "There is nothing more crucial, nothing more worthy of sacrifice, Kitty. Freedom is happiness. It is pursuing your dreams. It is liberty to worship and work and find joy as it pleases you. Freedom is striving and failing as many times as required before you finally strive and succeed. Kitty, freedom—liberty—is where you will find the Spirit of the Lord. It is life."

The quiet sounds of nature droned around them. Kitty's tight features relaxed as her eyes searched his face. She blinked and slowly her delicate brows folded together and she looked away.

He moved toward her, anguishing to pull her near. "Kitty you must believe me when I say my feelings for you are—"

"Say no more, Nathaniel." Kitty spun around and started toward the road. "I understand now that it is because of our differences that you refuse to love me."

"I do not refuse to love you." Did she think she was the only one hurting?

Grabbing her shoulder, Nathaniel swung her around to face him. "You are not so innocent, Miss." She tried to wriggle out of his grasp but he held firm.

Kitty scowled. "I don't know what you mean."

"For weeks I have pleaded with you to share your burden." He gripped harder, pinning her motionless with his stare. "Love cannot be free to triumph where there is no trust."

His spirit urged him to say more, pleaded with him to succumb to the desires he'd hidden so long. She must have seen his struggle, for the way her eyes darted between his, the way her breathing turned rapid, testified her need for him matched the longing in his heart. He could not resist. Forgetting his vow, he lowered his head and covered her soft mouth with his. The tightness of her muscles left her body like a receding wave against the sand and she released an audible whimper that sent Nathaniel's pulse racing.

He held tight to her familiar frame, remembering all too well the way her curves molded against him. Her hands swept up his back and circled his neck, making his heart pound at the feel of her cool, slender fingers on his skin. Another quiet mewling sound escaped her throat and he lost himself in her embrace as the world around him faded. All that existed was the feel of her heart entwining with his.

Slowly, reason edged in the small spaces of his mind. He had to stop.

After tasting her mouth one last time, he pushed away. Resting his forehead against hers, listening to their shared-breathing, Nathaniel relished the feel of her breath cooling his lips.

Kitty closed her eyes. "We can't pretend, Nathaniel."

"Pretend?"

She pulled away, her blue-green eyes tearing through him. "We cannot pretend that you and I could ever make the kind of life together that you desire."

He stepped back, the weight of her words crashing against him. "I'm not ready to surrender such a thing. Are you?"

"We cannot surrender something we never possessed." She moved back, her full lips pressing tight. The finality in her tone drove holes through the sails of his dreams.

"Then I fear you and I shall never be one." He shifted his jaw. "And there, my love, lies the overwhelming tragedy."

Chapter Twenty-seven

Kitty froze.

Nathaniel's words were a wintry wind, blowing against her heart that had just been stripped bare. She looked away, her body still humming where his chest and arms had pressed against her. "Nathaniel, I want to trust you." Swallowing the lump in her throat she continued. "But once you learn of what I keep secret you will surely hate me."

He leaned forward, cupping her shoulders. "I could never hate you." He paused, his thumb making circles on her skin while his tender eyes pleaded with her to speak.

She gazed back at him, searching his eyes, and prayed. *Dear Lord, Cyprian has vowed to hurt Eliza. I couldn't live with such a thing. What do I do?*

He took her hand and caressed it between his. "Answer me this. Are you happy?"

Kitty blinked. "Happy?"

"Are you, right now in your life, at liberty to enjoy the true happiness you desire?"

Her throat ached and she couldn't keep back the answer. "I am not."

His brow folded together and his voice dropped low. "Why?"

She frowned, answering in her mind as her eyes darted between his. *Why? Because Cyprian has destroyed my life by forcing me to do something I know is wrong. He's taken away my...*

Suddenly the truth consumed her in a single wave. Her eyes grew wide and her breath quickened.

Cyprian had destroyed her freedom.

Freedom is life.

Kitty tried to breathe as the winds of this newly acquired knowledge blew against her. Could it be that... that the patriots were right?

The touch of Nathaniel's thumb against her cheek shook her from her thoughts.

She stepped back, forcing a smile. "I... I don't know what to say."

Nathaniel stepped closer, slowly moving his hand around her waist. "Say you'll kiss me." His vision narrowed at her mouth before he swooped down. Kitty leaned her head back and opened her lips to accept him as his mouth consumed hers until every wandering thought dissolved.

A slight groan escaped his throat and he pulled her closer, nearly stopping the air in her lungs as his lips roamed up to her ear then down her jaw before landing on her wet mouth once again. His firm hands kneaded up her back and neck, then into her hair until her bun came loose, her hair tumbling around her shoulders.

When her legs finally lost all their strength, she broke the kiss and rested her head against his solid chest and clutched him tight, cherishing the sound of his rapid pulse and the feel of his warm breath against her hair.

He pulled away and crouched down, plucking a white flower from the grass beside Kitty's feet. Slowly he stood, rolling the delicate stem between his fingers. The tenderness in his Autumn-colored eyes seeped into her heart and cupped it as if he held her very soul. His gaze trailed her face as he brushed her hair back and gently tucked the flower behind her ear.

Kitty sucked in a quiet breath as tingles flitted down her back. What had possessed him to do such a thing? Did he know what it meant to her? She fought back the tears that burned her eyes. She reached up and touched the silken petals, unable to move her gaze from his, praying without end that what she revealed would not destroy the longing she now witnessed in his eyes.

Nathaniel toyed with the flower in her hair. "Will you trust me now?"

Twining her fingers with his, she licked her lips. "Please know that, what I am to reveal is—"

"Dr. Smith. Miss Campbell."

Kitty jerked away at the sound of Cyprian's harsh voice, but Nathaniel held her close as the enemy stopped along the road, staring through thin, black eyes.

Panic clutched her heart until it nearly stopped. Had Cyprian been watching? Had he heard her?

"What do you want, Wythe?" Nathaniel's tone dripped disdain.

Hard and lifeless, Cyprian offered a sickening smile and shifted the small bundle of clothes under his arm. His cold eyes coiled around Kitty's neck. "Miss Campbell, I saw your sister in town just now. Poor dear. She looked far too weary to be out when she's so great with child."

Kitty's knees buckled and she gripped Nathaniel's arm to remain steady. The meaning behind Cyprian's words were as real as a knife in her belly.

Kitty pushed away from Nathaniel and sent him a quick look. "I should go to her then." She hastened toward the road without looking back and passed Cyprian as if the dirt near where he stood were on fire.

Cyprian called from behind her, beating against her slave-driven soul. "She's counting on your wisdom, Miss Campbell. I trust you would not wish to disappoint her."

Hatred stormed down Nathaniel's back. *Not again!* He glanced at Kitty as she darted away, his chest aching for the pain he'd seen in her eyes, before pointing all his attentions on the devil in front of him.

Yanking Cyprian by the cravat, Nathaniel pulled him down to the water's edge and shoved him toward the trees with such force Cyprian grappled at the trunk behind him to keep from falling.

Nathaniel's muscles burned hot and his fists itched for the sensation of cracking against flesh and bone. "What have you done to her?"

Cyprian's expression twisted. "I have done nothing."

"You lie!" Nathaniel charged forward, jerking at Cyprian's collar and forcing his back to a tree. Shoving up against him, muscles pooled with blood, Nathaniel yelled through his teeth. "Tell me *now*!"

Black eyes chuckling, Cyprian's mouth curled like a drying weed. "I have nothing to tell."

The punch across Cyprian's jaw happened before

Nathaniel could stop it. He stepped back, chest pumping. Cyprian gripped his face and groaned, then started to laugh.

Nathaniel stepped away. If he got any closer he wouldn't have the strength to stop himself from destroying the man with his bare hands. "Stay away from her."

Cyprian tipped his head back and peeled the air with a revolting laugh. "The only one keeping anything from you is that wench, as you well know." Stalking back to the road, Cyprian continued his repulsive chuckling. "I warned you, Doctor. She's a sly one."

If the man said one more word against Kitty... *Lord, give me the resistance I need or I fear I shall commit a cardinal sin.*

Cyprian slunk to the road and turned, nodding slowly. "One day you will learn what she hides. And when you do, I will be most happy to say that I was the first to warn you."

Cyprian couldn't help grinning as he marched back to the tavern, despite the throbbing pain in his jaw. Why had he not thought of this before? He laughed aloud. The way to get the patriots from questioning him further was nearly too simple. 'Twas brilliant.

And who better than a sworn Tory just ripe from Boston?

Tomorrow, after seeing to Camilla's morning needs, and now the needs of his lame child, he would make a trip to church, and afterward pay the good doctor a visit.

There was something very important he needed to know.

Chapter Twenty-eight

The moon drifted higher, visible through the window's open pane. Atop the covers, Kitty stared and turned on her side, unable to sleep from the weariness in her soul. A genial breeze drifted in from the dark, begging Kitty to share her thoughts.

She sighed and tucked her hand under the pillow.

Freedom is life.

The words wandered through her mind, creating questions as they went. If freedom was so vital, why had Father never spoken of it? If what Eliza said of him was true, that his actions with the Sons of Liberty made him a brave crusader in the fight for freedom, then why had he never taught them the value of such a vital cause? How had Eliza been able to accept the idea so easily, and she herself had not?

With a groan she turned onto her back and closed her eyes, surrendering to the chorus of crickets and frogs until her mind finally relaxed into the peaceful cradle of sleep.

The field was calm and quiet, and the sun just

beginning to rise. Shafts of light shone through the trees where insects danced in circles as if hailing the arrival of the ripe summer morn. Dew covered the grasses and the twitter of birds filled the air as they sang praises to the God who had created them.

Father came from behind and hugged Kitty around her shoulders. She gazed up at him, all worry and sorrow crumbling to dust at his nearness.

The smile in his kind eyes pulled at Kitty's yearning and she turned, wrapping her arms full around him. She hugged him tighter, breathing in deep of the scent of sweet tobacco that always followed him.

"I've brought you something," he said.

Kitty tugged away, a childlike excitement sparking at his offer. "You have?"

"Aye." He smiled and from his jacket pocket produced a delicate white flower. He kissed her head then gently tucked it behind her ear.

Joy filled her so, it seemed to beam from her spirit and shine with the rising sun. She touched the flower with one hand and rested her other ear on his shoulder, hugging him around the waist. "Thank you, Father, I shall treasure it."

She looked up at him and he winked. Pausing, he eased her away and rested his hands on her shoulders. "There is one thing I should like you never to forget. A truth which I hold deep within my heart and one which you should always treasure in yours."

Staring back, she nodded, sensing the gravity his words carried. "Aye, Father."

He gripped her hand. "Your heart's question is answered thus. Where the Spirit of the Lord is, there is liberty."

Kitty's eyes shot open. The sunlight blanketing her feet as the Sabbath morning whispered her awake. She slammed her eyes shut once more, aching for the dream that had seemed so real. But the blissful sleep would not return. Reluctantly, Kitty pushed up and brushed her fingers through her hair then stopped when her gaze rested upon Nathaniel's white flower lying peacefully on the table by her bed. Drawing in a long breath, her lips parted as the meaning behind Father's declaration and his loving action bloomed like the very flower she cherished.

Where the Spirit of the Lord is, there is liberty.

She clapped her hands over her mouth and shot to her feet, unsure whether to cry or laugh or run into the yard with her hands toward the heavens. God could not have orchestrated a more beautiful and powerful answer to the questions she'd wrestled for so many months. Nathaniel's tender act, his gentle explanation of the value of freedom, and Father's poignant words were no coincidence. God had meant them for her. He had meant those very things to sing together in a kind of melody only she could hear—that only her heart could interpret.

She picked up the flower and clutched it to her chest, happy tears flooding her eyes and plunking against her cheeks as a gleeful crying-laugh bubbled from her heart. Father *had* been a patriot! All the questions and doubts were dead, and in their place a field of white flowers. The fight for freedom *was* sanctioned by God. At last she could join the patriots, and the man she loved, in supporting liberty. Why had it taken her so long?

Gazing out the window, she sniffed the soft petals, praying as the terrible realities wedged through, threatening to trample the beauty she'd just savored. *But I am still in bondage Lord. Show me the way out and I promise to champion your Spirit of liberty for the rest of my days.*

Turning, she rushed to her armoire and flung open the doors. What would Nathaniel say when she told him what she'd learned? She giggled, imagining the way his mouth would drop open and his eyes would round. Carefully, she placed the flower on the table and pulled out her yellow, rose-covered dress.

Stopping, her face slackened and she dropped her arms to her sides. The truth ate away at her spirit, covering it with scars. The fact remained. If she told what she had done and what she knew about Cyprian, how could she ensure Eliza's safety? Cyprian had made clear his intentions, and after Nathaniel's attack, there was no doubt he would follow through.

She slumped her back against the open door of the dresser and clenched her eyes shut, rubbing her face into the fabric of her dress.

Trust Nathaniel. And trust Me.

The gentle voice of God overpowered the anguish.

Kitty hugged the fabric close and stared upward. A smile grew across her face and deep into her heart.

Today she knew the truth.

She could trust her God and the man who professed he would care for her no matter what secret she bore.

Today, God willing, Nathaniel would say that he loved her.

Chapter Twenty-nine

Kitty swiveled in her seat, her chemise sticking to her skin from the oppressive humidity that made drops of sweat trickle down her back. She glanced behind her and tapped her finger against her knee. No sign of Nathaniel, but he must be here. He was not one to miss church. Facing forward, she straightened her posture and breathed out through tight lips. What would he say when she told him, both of her horrid secret and of the sacred revelation God had gifted her the night before? A grin lifted her mouth. She imagined once more the mix of glee and surprise on his face when she declared herself a patriot.

She looked behind her again and grabbed the seat of the pew to keep from running to Nathaniel as he stepped in the door. Tall and commanding as ever she'd seen him in his dark brown jacket and breeches, he quietly took the only seat left open on the back row. Resting his hat in his lap, he stalled and must have sensed her vision, for he instantly found her gaze. Even from such a distance she could see his eyes brighten.

She mouthed, "I must speak with you."

The love in his eyes swept across the room and

caressed her cheek. He mouthed in return, "After church."

Kitty turned back to the front, unable to focus on the sermon that had just begun.

After church. She smiled toward heaven and breathed a full breath unlike she had in months. After church, all the ugly and glorious truths would be borne and she would at last be free.

When the church service ended, the crowd shuffled into the stifling humidity outside the chapel doors. Waiting beside the flower gardens on the far side of the church-yard, Nathaniel reached out his hand, sure he'd felt a drop on his neck. He looked up. The thick gray clouds would soon release their flood. He stepped aside and tipped his hat at a family that passed on their way to the road. Chuckling to himself, he waved at the youngest boy who turned as he ran past, his father calling for him to slow down. Visions of the future flurried around him. Would he someday have a boy of his own? The pleasant thought made him spin back around to scan the murmuring group for Kitty's yellow-ribboned hat. She had yet to exit.

Straightening his cravat he gazed across the sea of church-goers and rehearsed the words he'd practiced since the night before. After his encounter with Cyprian he'd decided no longer could he endure it. He and Thomas would sit Kitty down and make her tell them, no matter how much it frightened her, no matter how long it took. Her safety and well-being depended on it.

Just then a tall man in a red officer's uniform exited the chapel, stealing Nathaniel's concentration. His jaw tightened. What was a soldier doing here? The man motioned to a gentleman near the door and spoke something, to which the gentleman nodded and pointed in Nathaniel's direction.

Nathaniel jerked back. The soldier gave a polite bow, placed his hat on his head and started in Nathaniel's direction. His blood charged. Who was this soldier and what did he want with him?

The man locked eyes with Nathaniel, and instead of bayonetting him with a look of disgust, he smiled as if Nathaniel had waved him over for a chat.

With only feet separating them now, the soldier swooped off his decorated tricorn and offered a quick bow before replacing his hat. "Pardon me, but you are Dr. Nathaniel Smith, are you not?"

"Aye." Nathaniel dipped his head in as much of an acknowledgment as his body would allow. "May I help you?"

The man laughed, his broad smile revealing straight teeth and a genuine nature that reflected in his eyes. Quickly his tone turned solemn. "I've just arrived to town and I'm looking for a particular woman with whom I believe we are both acquainted."

It couldn't be. Nathaniel stepped wide to keep from faltering. He pulled his shoulders back and examined the man in front of him. Never one to be impressed by one's status, Nathaniel had to admit, the man had quite a presence. But still, perhaps 'twas not the man he suspected.

Nathaniel flashed a quick, tight smile. "And you are?"

"Oh, forgive me, I am Lieutenant James Higley."

Nathaniel kept his face even, despite the

screaming that wailed in his head. He latched onto the lapel of his jacket to anchor himself in the rough seas of emotion he suddenly endured. *This* was James Higley. He cringed at the memory of how many times he'd called this man Pigley. There was nothing piggish about him. Tall, broad-shouldered, and a strong jaw that matched his commanding air.

The disbelief Nathaniel tried to keep from his face must have sifted past its well-crafted barrier, because James's face lit with a jovial smile.

"Miss Campbell spoke very highly of you in her letters." He looked over his shoulder, a dreaminess in his face that made Nathaniel's stomach turn. "And since I haven't been able to locate her, I thought you might be willing to assist me."

Nathaniel could only blink his response.

James motioned behind him. "I would be much obliged if you would direct me to her place of residence. I've come here on urgent business and I must speak with her directly."

Urgent business?

A horrible thought struck Nathaniel's mind like a blow from a hammer. Could Higley be here to propose? Again? Not possible.

James grinned wide, as if he expected Nathaniel to comply with his request at any moment. Nathaniel kept his lips tightly pressed so the sneer that twitched at his mouth wouldn't be exposed. Why must the man be so jolly? 'Twasn't as if they were friends. Nay, they were rivals. And not only politically... His stomach rolled to a halt at his feet.

Did Kitty really have feelings for this man? From what he'd read in James's letter she hadn't completely disregarded him, in fact, had given him "hope".

"James?" Kitty's startled voice peeled across the

churchyard. She moved toward them with almost as much shock on her face as Nathaniel felt. Her dainty mouth hung open and her sparkling eyes turned a shade of green that nearly matched Higley's own emerald stare.

James swept his hat around in a wide arch and bowed, never taking his gaze off her, then placed the hat back on his head. "Kitty, you are too beautiful for words."

Nathaniel crunched down on his cheek to keep from growling. *Kitty?* How dare this man be so familiar with her?

His chest burned from within and his jaw ached from clenching when James took her hand and pressed it against his mouth. "It seems years since I have seen you."

"James, I... I hardly know what to say." She pressed a hand to her chest and released an airy giggle. "'Tis such a surprise. What brings you to Sandwich?"

James took a step closer, his tone smooth and deep. "Why, you bring me here." James's eyes trailed over her from head to feet and back up again, flitting quickly across her mouth. The spark in Nathaniel's chest turned to a raging blaze and he curled his fists.

"I bring you here?" Her cheeks pinked and she lowered her chin with a coy smile.

Nathaniel pulled his bottom lip between his teeth. Was her smile richer than normal or could it be only his imagination? Had she not smiled such when he'd met her at the cabin? Or after their kiss?

He shifted his feet and twitched his shoulders. Gads. What was wrong with him? He'd never been one to think the worst of people, and here he was judging the woman he loved. Nathaniel brewed over the thought as his gaze trailed over his opponent another time.

James removed the pompous hat and tucked it under his arms. "I've been sent here on business."

Kitty tilted her head. "Business?"

"Quite urgent I must say, but let us not talk of such things here."

Kitty turned toward Nathaniel and her smile brightened. "I see you have met my good friend, Dr. Nathaniel Smith." She motioned between the two of them.

"Aye, I have had the pleasure." James started speaking but Nathaniel closed his ears to all but the sound of the rain gathering in the clouds. How long must he endure this? The stifling humidity not only sucked the sweat from his pores, it sucked the very tolerance from his bones.

While James continued on Nathaniel squirmed, eager for this moment to find an end so he could take Kitty in his arms, lead her away and kiss her again, thereby removing all other men from her mind. Forever.

Suddenly the truth socked Nathaniel in the gut with such force he nearly coughed.

His gaze jumped between the two. Not only was James dashing, good-looking, wealthy and from a well-known family, he was a Tory. Nathaniel's heart stopped until both his soul and his body were void of feeling.

He rubbed his hand over his mouth, breathing through his nose to calm his pulse. So, this is what Kitty had evaded sharing with him all these many weeks.

Her heart did not belong to him. It belonged to James.

He reeled from the blow and tried to control his wild pulse. What a fool he had been. What a blind fool!

James looked down at Kitty, his expression dripping with desire. Nathaniel curled his fists as the muscles in his back flexed. All this time he'd been pouring out his soul, giving the best of himself and she'd only pretended?

He ignored the invisible hand that slapped him for such slander. Deep in the crevices of his cracked soul, he wanted, wished, hoped such a thing wasn't true, but how could it not be?

James asked Nathaniel a question and he nodded in response to whatever it was. He dared a glance at Kitty and her tender expression nailed his heart to his ribs. The yearning in her fathomless eyes only pressed the agony deeper.

A bitter laugh surged upward but he killed it in his throat. Such irony. Thomas had nearly lost Eliza to a Redcoat, but in the end he'd won his prize. Now, Nathaniel had fallen in love with a woman who had turned him down to go running into the waiting arms of the enemy.

Chapter Thirty

Will he not return my smile?

Kitty did her best to capture Nathaniel's attention, but his eyes darted everywhere but near her own.

She cleared her throat and turned to James. "What business brings you here, James? I didn't know the army cared for such a small town."

"Our good king cares about every province, no matter its size, though there are many who choose to believe otherwise."

Kitty darted a look at Nathaniel, knowing full well what thoughts must be racing through his head, for the same thoughts also ran through hers. At one time, James's sentiments might have been strangely comforting, but now they burned, making her ache all the more to lay bare her soul to the man she loved.

But he didn't look at her. He only chewed the inside of his lip and stood motionless, his arms held rigid at his sides, fists tight. She'd never seen him so uncomfortable.

James continued, cupping her elbow. "Let us not talk of business, but center our attentions on something more pleasant." He nodded his chin in the direction of town. "Sandwich is lovely, Kitty, I can see now why you would want to trade Boston for this place." He winked and the teasing in his tone brought a smile to her lips, but did nothing to her heart.

Her cheeks heated and she lifted her lashes hoping Nathaniel would see the flush in her face, but he looked away, his chest lifting and lowering a bit too much. A biting twinge nipped at her conscience. This chance encounter would certainly not ease her forthcoming revelation.

In a swift move, Nathaniel bowed. "I must be going."

Mindless of the impropriety, Kitty lunged for Nathaniel and tugged on his arm. "Wait!" She turned to James. "If you'll excuse me for a moment, I must speak with Dr. Smith. I won't be long."

Nathaniel's glare hit Kitty like the back of his hand. She touched his arm, waiting for the tenderness she knew so well in his eyes, but it never surfaced. Swallowing, she pulled away and knit her fingers in front of her stomacher, trying to flood her voice with jesting. "You mustn't go yet, you promised to speak with me, or don't you remember?"

He looked behind her and nudged his chin upward. "'Twould seem you've already found someone else with whom to speak."

Kitty frowned. "What troubles you, Nathaniel, you are not yourself."

"Am I not?" The animosity ran thick and circled her neck. He tossed a cold glance over her shoulder before turning away.

All the strength left her limbs. She stepped forward and braved another tug on his sleeve as she filled her voice with as much weight as it would carry. "Nathaniel, please. There's something I *must* tell you and it cannot wait."

He stopped and stared at her over his broad shoulder. "I know what it is you wish to tell."

What? How? She shrunk back, her heart collapsing within her chest. "You do?"

His mouth pressed tight. "I do."

"Oh... I... I see." She looked away, her mind swimming. So he knew. Somehow he knew what she'd done.

She smiled and ached for him to hold her in his arms, tell her he knew it had all been forced upon her and that he loved her anyway.

But he didn't.

"'Tis time for me to return home." The finality of his words pushed her back.

Biting her cheek to keep from crying, she nodded. "But you will come for supper. I want to explain myself. I want to tell what I've just now come to understand—"

"Good day." He tipped his hat and turned away. She stared at his back as he left, her heart crawling after him. *Please don't hate me!*

Tears burned her eyes but she batted them away. After her actions, she deserved his disdain.

A warm hand came to her back and she quickly dotted her eyes before facing the man she knew had come to her side. "Forgive me James, I didn't mean to neglect you."

"No apology necessary." He took her hand. "Anyone could forgive you anything, Kitty."

She looked to where Nathaniel had gone. If only that were true.

His gaze trailed her face. "I'm heading down to New York. Uncle has provided me with a new assignment and I'm to be stationed there indefinitely.

When I found out I was to pass a message on to another solider here in Sandwich, I knew I had to find you." His grip on her fingers tightened and his voice dropped. "I couldn't go to New York without knowing your decision."

His features lifted in a hopeful smile and Kitty's lungs stilled. Poor James. She offered her most gentle grin and slid her hand from his grasp. "James, you are indeed generous in your affections for me, and you know I am honored by them. But, my feelings… I am… as much as I appreciate your friendship, my heart belongs to another."

James dropped his chin with a nod. His mouth tightened, and he looked away with a brave set to his jaw before looking back. "I cannot say that I am not disappointed, but I want the best for you and I respect your feelings." Silent, he motioned with his head toward the road. "Am I wrong to assume your heart leans toward a certain country doctor?"

Had her attentions been so obvious? She lowered her eyes. "Dr. Smith has been a good friend to me."

A wounded smile rested in James's eyes. "I wish you every happiness."

Just as she opened her mouth, another voice peeled from behind.

"Well, Kitty, what a pleasant surprise."

Kitty spun around as Henry Donaldson approached, his expression bright as a noon sun.

"Henry, what are you doing here?" She breathed easier, and her smile broke free as the discomforts from seconds ago eased thanks to the presence of one whom she cared for as a brother.

Henry looked at James before swooping off his hat and offering a generous bow. "I've come to see Lt. Higley as I pass through town." He winked. "I should have known he would have found the most delightful woman in Sandwich to fawn over."

James's mouth straightened in a tight smile and he cleared his throat. The sorrow in his expression sat heavy against her heart when his gaze shifted from her to Donaldson. "There is an urgent matter which I need to discuss with you privately."

"Aye." Donaldson turned to Kitty. "We'll not be a moment."

"Of course." Kitty glanced to the road where Nathaniel had gone, her mind rehearsing the revelation she must make to him this evening. Or at least, the revelation she must explain. He said he already knew. But how? Both her head and her heart began a dull ache. *I will trust in God. All will be well.*

She gazed across the vacant churchyard and squinted at the sky when a low rumble rolled inland from the sea. From behind, the men's voices floated toward her and she stepped forward, uncomfortable with overhearing the transaction, when an invisible hold held her back.

As the muted words trickled into her ears, the hairs on her neck stood on end.

"You have a message for me?" Donaldson questioned.

"Aye, sir." James's quiet tone thundered in her ears. "We have intercepted this message from a patriot courier. My uncle's orders are that it must not make it to Plymouth."

"I understand." Donaldson answered, his tone reflecting his rank.

"We believe there might still be another courier on his way. Tell your men to keep an eye out, and question anyone traveling north."

Kitty's arms went numb and her fingers tingled. A

message important enough for two couriers to deliver? What kind of message? What wasn't Plymouth to know?

The men cleared their throats and the sound of their steps grew louder. Kitty spun to face them.

James tapped his hat atop his head, his eyes trailing her face. With a forced smile, he bowed. "Miss Campbell."

Sorrow for having caused him such pain tightened the rise and fall of her chest. "James, I'm—"

"Say no more, Miss Campbell." He breathed out a rough sigh and stepped away. "I bid you farewell."

Kitty curtsied. "God's blessings upon you, James."

He offered another half-smile and tipped his hat and after a quick nod to Donaldson, exited the courtyard, leaving Kitty and Donaldson alone in front of the chapel.

"He cares for you a great deal." Donaldson peered at her then flung a quick look at Higley's retreating frame.

"Aye." She kept her eyes on James until he disappeared behind the trees on the corner. "Higley is a good man."

"But?"

She felt Donaldson's gaze though couldn't find the strength to meet it. "He is... his is simply not..." The answer formed, yet she couldn't speak it.

He hummed as if he had easily interpreted the tensions and tight-lipped smiles. "You do not love him."

Kitty snapped her gaze to him and gauged his knowing look before finally speaking. "'Tis true." She studied the far end of the churchyard. "I cannot commit my life to someone I do not love."

"Wise." Donaldson's chest rose as he inhaled a

long breath. "Not everyone would feel the same. But then again, you and your sister are more thoughtful and sensitive than many women in your station."

She smiled at him as a comfortable silence rested between them and suddenly the urge to expose her political shift became almost too much to restrain. What would he say? Surely he would not be surprised. She opened her mouth then snapped it shut again and formed a smile on her mouth to hide her near mistake. Nay, she should not tell him. 'Twould be Nathaniel who first learned of her change of heart. And how she longed to tell him! Her smile broadened. The thought alone bloomed in her soul like the very flower she still carried in the pocket of her skirt.

Straightening her shoulders she lifted her chin, found a familiar friendliness and latched on. "'Tis a great pleasure to see you here, Henry. Are you able to stay for supper? I know Thomas and Eliza would be so pleased to see you."

"I fear I cannot." He pointed with his hat to the road. "I am here on business. I regret I don't have the luxury to enjoy the company of friends." He repositioned his hat on his head. "Please give your sister and brother-in-law my regards and when I am next in town I promise to stay longer."

"I understand."

Placing his hat on his head, his eyes narrowed and Kitty's fears were realized. Henry fastened his stare on her face. "Are you all right?"

Kitty's eyes grew wide. "Me? Why of course."

Mercy! Must I always wear my feelings so? She shook her head and blinked, praying he would believe her mock surprise.

He quirked one brow. "I'll take your word, though

I have my doubts…"

With a playful giggle Kitty brushed him forward. "Safe travels, Henry. I do hope we will see you soon."

He nodded with a grin at one side of his mouth and took his leave when a small slip of white paper floated to the ground from the inside of his jacket.

"Henry…" Kitty's throat seized as if the words refused to come forth.

He turned. "Aye?"

She froze and pressed her hands to her stomach to hide the trembling of her fingers.

Kitty stepped forward, and brushed her foot over the note. "God be with you."

A smile lit his face. "God be with you, Kitty."

Her heart sputtered as he strode away.

Alone, she stood in front of the church. Clouds thickened and another rumble of thunder growled overhead. Fingers numb, she glanced behind her and scanned the surrounding trees beyond the road.

The woods were hushed. No movement, no rustling of leaves or hoof beats on the road. In a single movement she swooped down and plucked the paper from under her foot. Her breath raced. Her fingers quaked. After another swift skim of the empty space around her, she unfolded the note.

Absorbing the scribbled text, Kitty's pulse thundered like the threatening summer storm.

Lobsters planning a powder raid.
Hide munitions…

The rest of the note blurred as the weight of the words pressed on her mind like an anchor. Fighting the quiver in her spine she folded it again and stuffed it in her pocket.

No more secrets, no more silence.
This time, she knew exactly what to do.

Chapter Thirty-one

Nathaniel stormed into his house through the back door and slammed it shut. Higley's face loomed like a haunting nightmare.

He flung off his hat and threw it down on the desk, a roar building in his chest, but he kept it behind the cage of his ribs. His jaw ached from clenching. How could Kitty have chosen that man over him? Shutting his eyes, he growled. And yet, he had no more proof of it than the shy looks and *polite* words the two had shared in his presence. The fresh memories baited his anger. How could it not be true?

Reason tapped him on the shoulder. There was much still he didn't know, much to make clear before he latched so tight. With a grunt he brushed the irritating thought away. Kitty had been trying to tell him for weeks that she had chosen Higley, and he'd been too much of a fool to see it.

But what of that night when she was so sick and racked with fever? She revealed so much of her pain. A small voice tickled his ear and he jerked back, half expecting Thomas to be standing behind him. *What of the yearning in her eyes that she needed you?* Nathaniel glanced out the window at the sinister clouds. Could he dismiss her so easily?

As if responding to a physical adversary Nathaniel spoke to the empty room. "She couldn't trust me from the beginning. Why should I place any belief in her now?" He snatched his hat from the table and launched it across the room.

A censure rained from above. *You are better than this.*

The jealousy snickered back. *Perhaps, but without the anger how could one stand the pain?*

The thickening storm outside mimicked the sinister darkness that shadowed his soul as the rain began to flick against the windowpane.

A knock at the back door stole Nathaniel's attention.

Yanking open the door he froze, trying to bite back the inkling of disappointment that it wasn't Kitty, and the rage at who stared back at him.

"What do you want?"

Cyprian's gaunt eyes blinked. He extended his hand and offered Nathaniel a small bag of coins. He spoke as if the words slashed upward from his throat. "Camilla requested I give you this. For what you did for Jacob."

Nathaniel glared as the fat drops pelted against him. "I don't want payment."

Staring back, Cyprian's glare thinned. He lowered his arm and started away, but quickly stopped and faced Nathaniel again. "I must say I was quite surprised to see you speaking to Miss Campbell after services today."

Nathaniel stiffened. The sound of her name made his heart take flight and plummet in the same second. He wouldn't endure this.

Stepping back into the house he began to shut the door when Cyprian's volume rose.

"After what she did, and knowing your political sentiments, I was surprised indeed."

Nathaniel shoved the door open with a smack and stepped into the rain. "What are you talking about?"

Cyprian's expression grew wide. "You don't know? So she never told you... then of course, why would she?"

"Tell me what?" Nathaniel pulled at the rage that strained against the ropes of his composure.

Cyprian's words oozed from his tight mouth. "Your beloved Miss Campbell helped move the powder from the magazine. 'Twas why that Officer came to town—to check her progress. And from the look on his face, he seemed quite pleased with her."

Nathaniel's spine split and he bolted from the doorway. "How dare you speak such slander! You know nothing about her!"

"No, Doctor. *You* know nothing about her."

The rain continued to fall as a familiar pain strummed against the tight strings in Nathaniel's heart. Could *that* be the reason she'd been so quiet, secretive, reserved?

He shook his head and thrust the man backward.

Cyprian grinned as if the heated exchange was merely a child's game, and one that he was winning. A sickening laugh rumbled from his chest as another roll of thunder bounced among the clouds. His face twisted. "Ask her what she was *delivering* and see if she can deny it."

Nathaniel couldn't swallow, couldn't blink. It was not true. There was no possible way it could be true.

"Good day, Doctor." A nauseating grin crept up Cyprian's face as he stepped backward. With a quick turn he jogged to the road.

Nathaniel stomped inside and yanked his cloak

off the peg before charging into the storm.

It couldn't be true. There was *no way* it could be true.

But there was only one way to find out.

Cyprian stumbled toward home, hardly able to place his steps from the grief that flowed through his blood like hard ale. The rains descended and coated him with cold as if the clouds knew his sorrows and wept for him. He hadn't wanted to leave Camilla that morning, but this business with the powder and the money it provided was the only thing keeping her alive.

He stared at the ground as he walked, watching the drops splash into the dirt. A light chuckle bubbled. Why hadn't he thought of it before? The inspiration for placing the blame on the Campbell girl had served his purpose with even greater reward than he could have ever imagined.

With Miss Campbell's family, and now her lover blaming her for involvement, Cyprian could only hope it would allow him and Andrew enough time to discover the hidden munitions before next week's scheduled rendezvous.

Once at home, he tromped in and pulled his limbs from the sopping jacket and removed his mud-covered boots. He shut the door with a hard breath. Thank goodness Joseph had been willing to see to Jacob's care and recovery at his home in town. 'Twould have been impossible to keep the truth of Jacob's injury from Camilla with the boy at home. She didn't need the added grief. The ruse of offering of money in her behalf had been the perfect transition, a way to bring the news of Nathaniel's love's deception without appearing suspicious.

He snatched the amber-colored vial from the table, rolling it in his fingers as the pain in his tired muscles clawed deeper into his spirit. With every dose, her heart continued to beat. Every dose kept her eyes open, allowed her lips to speak his name. He would not give up now. *I will find that powder. I must!*

Slowly, he crept upstairs, and carefully opened the door. Nearing the bed, he whispered. "Camilla, 'tis time for your medicine."

She didn't stir. He quietly took his seat beside the bed and uncorked the vile. Gently he took her hand and his throat seized. She must be over tired today. He squeezed her limp fingers.

"Camilla, my love, you must wake."

Still, she didn't move.

He sat back, his quivering hands and lungs struggling. He touched her head, her face, her hair before he finally leaned forward and gripped the edge of the bed taking in quick, short bursts of air.

Nay. It could not be!

Tears stung his eyes. He blinked them away, shaking his head as her lifeless body whispered what he dared not allow his heart to hear.

This morning she'd spoken a few words, even smiled at him. She had lived.

But now...

His blood congealed and the room faded. His grip went limp and he dropped the bottle.

He'd promised her from the beginning he would be there when she passed. He'd promised Camilla that in her last moments he'd hold her hand and comfort her as she moved from this life to the next.

In that moment all his sorrows collected and molded into an iron rod of hatred in his stomach. If not for that patriot woman, he *would* have been with her.

Now more than ever, he would make the Campbell girl feel the levels of his rage. For because of her, his Camilla was gone forever.

Kitty burst through the front door, rivulets of water trickling down her neck and back. “Is Thomas here?”

Eliza whirled in front of the fireplace. Her eyes widened then narrowed and she rushed forward. “Whatever is the matter? You look pale.”

Thomas rushed in from the kitchen, his dark brow arched down. “Kitty?”

Struggling to calm her breath, she reached into her pocket and hurried toward Thomas. “I’ve just discovered something you need to know. I—”

“Kitty!” Nathaniel stormed in, his face a tangle of rage. Rain flooded in the open door as a gust of wind whipped at his coat. A flash of lightning illuminated the outline of his frame as he stomped forward.

Her limbs turned cold. “Nathaniel?”

He stomped forward, his stare staking her to the ground, as large drops plunked down from his tricorn. “Did you do it?”

“Did I... did I do what?” The fury in his eyes drained the blood from her face.

His jaw ticked. “Were you or were you not involved in the theft of the powder from the magazine?”

Her lungs started a desperate quest for air. What could she say? The ugly truth must be exposed, but didn't he already know?

Nathaniel stepped closer. "Deny it. I must hear you deny it."

Thomas neared, his own tone heavy. "What is he speaking of, Kitty?"

Eliza came to stand behind Kitty and held her shoulders. "Nathaniel, come now, you know she would never do any such thing."

Kitty reached out to grip the chair beside her as the room wavered. *Dear Lord, give me strength!*

Nathaniel stepped closer, looming only inches from her, his hazel eyes now darker than night. "Say it!"

"'Tis not what you think Nathaniel, if you'll only let me explain!"

Nathaniel's face contorted and he stepped back as if she were riddled with pox. The anger in his soft tone ripped the strength from her legs and she clutched the chair to stay erect. "You knew full well our desperation to keep the powder out of enemy hands and now I discover you were complicit!"

"Nay!"

"You are the enemy, Kitty."

"*Nay*!" She lunged forward, choking on her tears. "Nathaniel please, I didn't have a choice! If you will listen—"

"Enough!" A crack of thunder shook the house as he stormed to the door.

Kitty stumbled forward. "Wait!" She gripped his arm, her limbs unstable under the weight of his deadly glare. "Nathaniel, listen to me. This note was bound for Plymouth. James gave it to Henry, but he dropped it and I—"

"I refuse to listen to your lies."

"Lies? No, Nathaniel!" She thrust the paper toward him, but he shoved her hand aside.

Without a second look, Nathaniel charged into the rain, wrenching Kitty's heart from her chest as he left.

Tears burned and Kitty dared a glance at Thomas as Eliza rushed forward and gripped her around the shoulders. Kitty's throat ached as tears flooded her eyes. Surely he didn't believe she would be a willing accomplice. Thomas of all people would understand the terror of her enslavement and the ash that such blackmail left behind in its soul-destroying blaze.

Thomas's austere expression slashed her heart. After a nod to Eliza he jerked his cloak off the hook and charged after Nathaniel into the rain.

Kitty whirled around, speaking through the quiver in her voice. "'Tis not what they think!"

Eliza pulled Kitty into her embrace. Her warmth chased away a portion of the bitter cold in her spirit, but couldn't eliminate the chills. "I believe you."

Disbelief shook Kitty's frame like a dead leaf clinging to a branch in the wind. "He didn't even give me a chance to explain."

Another flash of light lit the heavens, followed by a clap of thunder that shook the ground. Eliza eased her sister away and pushed the door closed, never letting go of Kitty's hand. "I'll listen."

Kitty's chest strained and her throat ached until she feared her neck would burst. "I... I'm..." She cupped a hand over her mouth and dashed up the stairs to her bedchamber.

The walls swayed and the floor dipped beneath her feet. She fell onto the bed, her shoulders shaking. Painful regret curled around her bones and she tucked her knees to her chest.

What have I done, Lord?

Nathaniel's slicing words cut through her. *You are the enemy, Kitty!*

No matter how she tried to explain, no matter if or when the truth was told, Nathaniel would hate her the rest of his days.

Dropping her head to her knees, Kitty curled her body tighter, praying as she wept that somehow she might discover how she could make it right—for God, and for the man she loved. *Lord, I will do whatever thou dost ask of me to make right the wrongs I have done.*

Wiping her cheek with her hand, Kitty stilled as her vision focused on the note in her hand. Her tears retreated and she pushed up, staring at the folded message. Blinking, she cleared the remaining moisture from her vision as the doors of her mind were opened. She sucked in a choppy breath and pressed the paper to her chest.

'Tis the only way.

Leaping from the bed, she hurried to the armoire and found her winter cloak, slinging it around her shoulders before stuffing the folded paper into her stays.

Anxiety popped in her veins. Her palms sweat.

Moving to the bedchamber door, she stopped when another crash of thunder shook the house. What if she were caught? She might never have the chance to tell Eliza and Thomas—and Nathaniel—that she had come to prize freedom as they did.

Turning, she went to the small table and picked up the precious white flower that had sparked this mighty change. She reached for her Bible and turned to Second Corinthians, resting the now-wilted bloom on the verse that had come to mean so much to her. She stood back, feeling her pulse race, and her spirit calm. If she never returned, then God willing, the scripture by which the flower rested would tell them of her change of heart.

A smile lifted her mouth. Redemption didn't come without a price, but with her trust now firmly in God's hands she would prove to herself and to Him, that no matter what happened, she would not waver in the cause of liberty.

She was a patriot.

Chapter Thirty-Two

A pounding at the door echoed through the lonely house, but nothing could break Cyprian from the grief that encased him like a stone tomb. The pounding continued, followed by muted yells. He ignored it and closed his eyes, wishing he could as easily close his soul against the pain. The weight of Camilla's loss wrapped around his chest and crushed his ribs into his heart.

Suddenly the door burst open and a harried voice blasted up the staircase.

"Cyprian! *Cyprian*!"

Smith?

Anger exploded in Cyprian's chest and he leapt from his seat, charging down the stairs.

"Smith, I—" He jerked to a halt. "What do you want, Andrew?"

The umbra of hatred sat deep in Andrew's shadowed eyes as lightning flashed behind him. "I'm through."

"Through?

"I'm through being your pawn. I will no longer do your bidding."

Cyprian shouted from the depths of his pain. "You don't have a *choice*!"

Andrew stalked nearer, mouth hinged down, and pulled a weapon from his cloak as another angry flash of light glinted off the pistol.

Cyprian tipped his head back and peeled the air with a bitter laugh that attempted to purge a measure of his suffering. "You'll kill me?"

Andrew charged forward, slamming the point of the gun into Cyprian's chest. "I'm not a thief and I'm not a murderer!" He lowered his gun and stepped back. "I challenge you to a duel."

"A duel?" The man had always been daft. Cyprian glared, reading the resolve in Andrew's shifting jaw and unwavering eyes. "We have no second, no doctor present."

"I care not for such formalities." He stood straighter and widened his stance. "I would see this ended. Tonight."

Cyprian grinned.

So be it.

The storm outside raged as ferocious as the emotions that whipped inside Nathaniel's chest.

He paced in front of the blazing fire as another bone-rattling clap of thunder crashed in the heavens. "Do not try to persuade me of her innocence, Thomas. We both know she is complicit."

"I know I cannot persuade you to anything." Thomas pressed his forearm against the wood beside the mantel and gestured with his other. "But do not speak with such finality until you have all the facts, Nathaniel. It hardly seems like her to do such a thing. Do you not know Kitty at all?"

The question stabbed. "I thought I did."

Thomas continued his barrage, now using both hands as his features reddened. "You should have let her speak!"

Nathaniel pointed at the door, his volume ripping at his throat. "She betrayed us!"

Thomas lunged forward, his own tone matching Nathaniel's as his eyes darkened. "This is the first time I have seen you act the complete fool, Nathaniel. You, of all people, should be above such behavior." He stepped closer, only inches away. "Do you think you're better than she?"

"Do not turn this on me."

Thomas's eyes thinned. "Have you forgotten that night when she was ill? Have you forgotten her terror and how she pleaded with whoever-it-was she saw, not to hurt you or her family? Have you forgotten how you vowed to find whoever had treated her thus and bring them to justice?"

"She refused my continued offers of help."

"'Tis a sorry excuse and you know it." The accusation in his tone grated against Nathaniel's already raw interior.

Shifting his feet, Nathaniel glared at the ground, still gripping the chair. His breath turned heavy and he spoke through his teeth. "Higley was here."

"James Higley?" Thomas's expression went flat. "You jest."

Nathaniel shook his head. "He was here after church services." The memory stabbed him anew. "He was looking for Kitty. Said he had urgent business with her..."

He couldn't bring himself to speak the rest, though Thomas must have deciphered what he did not say for he tipped his head back and released a mocking laugh that shook the walls almost as much as the continuing thunder. "If you believe that Kitty had designs on that man you are truly daft. She only ever cared for you."

"She was working for him, Thomas, can you not see?" With a grimace, Nathaniel pulled back. "'Tis not only that. I am a patriot. Higley is a Tory, a man made of the same cloth as she." He released his grip on the chair and paced in brooding silence. Suddenly he stopped and pointed at Thomas. "You know, I should be pleased this happened. I should be pleased we discovered her treachery or I might have done something foolish."

Thomas's expression softened only slightly. "Marrying for love is never foolish."

"Kitty is a traitor to her family, friends and to the people of this town!"

"Take your share of the blame, Nathaniel. Your inability to love her despite her different political views—"

"Inability to love?" Nathaniel swung the chair aside, his pulse raging. "I have loved Kitty with every pulse of my heart. I have pleaded with her to allow me to share the burdens she carried, and she would not!" He panted as if he'd run for miles. "Higley's arrival today made everything clear. She refused to open her soul to me because she was working for the enemy, the man to whom she'd already given her heart."

Thomas yanked Nathaniel by the coat and shoved him away. "The only thing that has been made clear is the fact that you are too blinded by jealousy and fear that you cannot see what is clearly in front of you."

Nathaniel curled his fingers, grappling for a

proper response.

Staking Nathaniel to the floor with his iron stare, Thomas's words struck like a swinging fist. "Did you not vow you would never be with her because she believes different than you despite her devotion to you and to Christ? 'Tis you who could not trust, Nathaniel. At the first mention that something was amiss you rush to accuse her without insisting on knowing the facts she was plainly willing to tell."

Nathaniel turned away as silence loomed. He closed his eyes. The crack of the fire snapped between them. The continuous rain and intermittent thunderclaps pressed Thomas's words deeper and deeper.

Nathaniel's cravat coiled around his neck and a pain lodged deep. Could Thomas be right? He forced himself to hold tight to the anger, to keep from falling into the pit of regret that gaped behind him. "Cyprian told me Higley was here today to talk to her about the powder. He said she was involved."

"Who said she was involved?" Thomas's jaw dropped and his arms hung at his sides. "Cyprian? You would take the word of *that* man before you take the word of the woman you supposedly love?"

"Why wouldn't I?" Nathaniel flung his arms, his voice taut. "He knows all the Tories of this town, and I have seen him speaking with her on numerous occasions from the very time of her arrival." His mind whirled, desperate to find something to prove his veracity.

Breathing harder, Nathaniel strode forward. "The first night she arrived here, at the party, after she left the ballroom and I went to fetch her, I saw her speaking with Cyprian and—"

He stopped. The sound of the storm went mute.

Thomas grabbed his arm. "And?"

Nathaniel turned to his friend, eyes round. "'Twas Andrew."

"Make sense, Nathaniel."

Nathaniel tried to swallow but the vortex of his wrongs began to spiral upward until he almost couldn't speak. "'Twas Andrew who took the powder. He must have been working with Cyprian from the beginning."

Thomas's face turned crimson. "You have only now come to this conclusion?" His expression contorted. "You have accused the woman you love with something so wretched, and all the while it may have been for naught?"

"She didn't deny the accusations!"

"The evidence points to the truth that Kitty has been blackmailed. Need I tell you its horrors?" Thomas lunged, growling in Nathaniel's face. "It can destroy a man. And I can only begin to imagine what it would do to an *innocent* woman."

Pulse slowing, Nathaniel gazed across the room, his breathing shallow. Intermittent flashes of lightning illuminated the room, as the pieces of truth began to illuminate his mind. It couldn't be...

Thomas raked his hand over his head and turned to the fire. "How did I not see it until now? How could I have been so blind?"

Nathaniel blinked, his arms limp at his sides. The impact of the truth on his heart crashed through him like a ball from a cannon. *Lord, what have I done?*

"What else did Cyprian tell you?" Thomas's bellowed question jerked Nathaniel away from the pit of his sins. "Did it not occur to you that perhaps *he* had been the one who'd threatened her, had in fact attacked her those many weeks ago? Blast it,

Nathaniel! Even I can see that now!"

It had occurred to him. How had he so quickly forgotten what for so long had been so plain? Nathaniel gripped his hair at the root. Cyprian had used them both! He dropped his hands to his sides and stared motionless into the fire.

He had failed her.

Like a flailing sailor tossed among the waves, Nathaniel groped for anything that might save his drowning soul. How could he make her feel the depths of his regrets? Would she ever forgive him?

With a loud crack the front door burst open and three figures stepped in from the storm.

"We need Doctor Smith!"

"I'm Doctor Smith." Nathaniel rushed forward as two strangers carried a man between them, his body limp.

Rain trailed off them in little rivers, joining together on the floor in a large puddle. Thomas came behind and helped lay the victim on the rug in front of the fire.

Nathaniel snatched a glowing lamp from the table and crouched, scanning the man's body. "What happened?" No bleeding wound was immediately evident. "Who is this man? Who are you?"

He opened the victim's sopping jacket and searched for signs of injury along his chest.

The oldest man with a dripping beard spoke first. "I'm Jack Green and this is my son. We were going up to Boston when we found this fellow just a few miles west of here. West, wasn't it?" He looked at his son for affirmation, face crunched. "We thought he was dead, but he started babbling on about a message he had to get to Plymouth. Didn't say his name or where he was from."

Nathaniel exchanged a passing glance with Thomas who dipped his chin in agreement. These men were speaking the truth. "Help me remove his jacket. I need to find where he's hurt."

As they lifted him, the man roused and his eyes circled, round and white. He clutched onto Nathaniel's jacket, the urgency in his stare cutting Nathaniel clear through. "My note, my satchel, the British..." He dropped his head back, groaning as his eyes closed. "They took my satchel."

"Satchel? What satchel?" Nathaniel glanced at the two strangers before locking eyes with Thomas.

Thomas lowered to his knees and spoke up to be heard above the booming thunder. "He could have been a courier."

"That's what I gathered from his bumbling." The old man sat back on his heels, his white beard shining as another flash of lightning gleamed.

Lifting the man's limp head, Nathaniel ran his fingers gently against his neck and the base of his skull. Even with his soaking hair, the sticky lump behind the courier's ear made Nathaniel growl. He pointed to the surgery. "Help me carry him."

Once they hefted the man on the table Nathaniel fully stripped back the coat and scanned for other wounds. He ran his fingers along the man's ribs while Thomas lifted the lamp. So far he saw only the head wound.

Nathaniel pointed at Thomas. "Hand me some bandages."

Thomas tossed over empty baskets, and opened and closed drawers. "I don't see any."

Blast! "Upstairs you will find an extra sheet in my trunk—grab a quilt as well."

Thomas darted out of sight while the other two

men cowered in the corner, their dripping hats in their hands, looking more like frightened children than grown men.

"You've done enough." Nathaniel pointed toward the kitchen. "There's nothing more you can do here, go into the—"

The back door burst open.

"Blast it! What now?" Nathaniel swung round and instantly his brow plunged to his nose as worry slapped him. "Eliza, what are you doing here?"

Brown eyes wide, Eliza clutched her hands at her waist. Wet hair stuck to her face, and the cloak around her shoulders hung to her like a dark cloud. But it was the quivering of her chin that made his stomach turn.

Nathaniel motioned her forward, looking up toward where Thomas had gone. "Are you all right?"

"I can't find Ki—what's happened?" Eliza stared at the two strangers then at the man on the table.

Nathaniel gestured to the good Samaritans. "These gentlemen found this wounded man in the woods. We believe he may have been a patriot courier, but we can't be sure." He paused to glance again at the motionless figure on the table. "They say he was bumbling about the British taking his satchel, but there's no way of knowing—"

"Eliza, what are you doing here?" Thomas tromped down the stairs and tossed the sheet and quilt to Nathaniel before taking his wife by the elbow. "What are you doing out in this storm? You should never have left the house."

Nathaniel focused on his patient but stiffened when Eliza's trembling voice met his ears.

"Kitty's missing."

Missing? Nathaniel yanked a piece of cloth from

the sheet and quickly wrapped the man's head before going to Eliza.

Thomas's tone remained tranquil but the fervor behind his words matched Nathaniel's inner question. "What do you mean she's missing?"

Tears ran down her cheeks, getting lost in the remnants of rain still dripping down her face. "I thought she was still upstairs after..." she looked at Nathaniel, "after what happened, but when I went to check on her I couldn't find her. I've looked everywhere."

Nathaniel took her arm, straining to keep his touch light as his blood thickened. "Where do you think she's gone?" The guilt that had pricked moments ago now assailed him. If Cyprian had done anything to her...

"I don't know," Eliza answered, gripping Thomas's hands. "Please come with me."

With a strong nod, Thomas snatched his hat from the peg and flung his cloak around his shoulder before clutching his wife's hand and leading her into the rain. Another flash and rumble rattled Nathaniel's conscience.

"Thomas, wait." Nathaniel looked at the two strangers. "I have to go."

"What?" The oldest one protested. "We can't stay here, we need to make it to Boston."

Nathaniel swung his arms into his greatcoat. "You won't make it far in this weather." He nodded toward the unconscious man. "There's nothing more I can do for him. His wound is bound. We simply must wait." He tossed the large quilt at the man. "Put this over him and stay here until I get back."

He pressed his hat to his head and dashed into the rain, damning his earlier foolishness as he slammed the door shut.

Large drops flicked him in the face, castigating him with every step. His impetuous outburst—his rage—had led Kitty into unmentionable grief. And now, for reasons unknown, she'd disappeared and likely at the hands of an enemy.

The enemy.

"Thomas, Eliza!"

They turned in unison.

He rushed forward. "Continue your search in town. I've another place to look."

Thomas scowled. "Where?"

Nathaniel turned and ran, answering over his shoulder. "Newcomb!"

Chapter Thirty-Three

Kitty brushed her hand over her face, flicking the rain from her eyes. She leaned into her mount as it galloped across the rain-soaked ground and prayed this speed would take her to Plymouth within the hour. Without the fitful flashes that brought occasional light to her path, she could never have navigated the road in such blackness. Still, anxiety scratched in her chest but she ignored it, gripping harder to the reins of Thomas's mare.

Another enormous explosion rocked the skies like a mythical creature roaring down from the heavens. The deluge of rain fell harder, drenching the courage Kitty clung to as the insecurities drove deeper. If she made it to Plymouth, who would she tell? And would they believe her?

She shoved the thought from her mind at the next clap of thunder. Where was her faith? Leaning forward she focused on the strong, heaving breath of the horse as it ran. God would see her safely there.

Another flash lit the road and Kitty's stomach hurled to her throat at the illuminated silhouettes of two approaching riders. The glint of their weapons shined in the blackness.

Soldiers.

Kitty tugged on the reins and brought the horse

to a trot. Keeping her breath at even measures of in and out, she rallied her best skills of deception and prayed to God that the only thing the soldiers would find was an ignorant woman simply trying to get home.

Nathaniel didn't even think to knock. "Cyprian!"

Charging through the door, he jolted back as Cyprian and Andrew spun around, their features hard and shadowed in the dimly lit house.

"Get out, Smith!" Cyprian yelled, pointing at the door.

Nathaniel tried to keep the explosives in his voice from igniting the primed air. "I should have known it was you."

Andrew turned to him, gun in hand. His face knotted and he answered as if his skin were aflame. "You've arrived just in time. Someone is about to be shot." Andrew pointed a rigid finger at Cyprian. "We shall settle this now!" His rough voice shook as he yelled to be heard above the storm. "I can no longer be forced into such oppression. I can no longer be forced to go against the very cause I champion."

Nathaniel glanced between them, and suddenly the answers of the riddle he'd been unable to solve flooded his mind. He stepped forward, hand outstretched as compassion toward his fellow patriot filled his rigid muscles. "Andrew, you don't have to—"

"I do!" The more Andrew spoke the more his frenzy consumed him. His eyes grew wide and his voice scratched the air as he yelled. "I can stand the guilt no longer! He forced me, Nathaniel, he forced us both!"

Both. The raw lashes in Nathaniel's conscience throbbed. He'd seen that same terror before in Thomas's eyes. He'd seen it in Kitty's.

He turned to Cyprian. "What have you done with her?" He lunged, gripping him around the neck. "Where is she?"

Cyprian scratched at his throat, choking and sputtering. "I don't... know where she is!"

Nathaniel clutched harder. "Where is she? Tell me now!" With a shove Nathaniel released him, allowing the purple color to fade to red as Cyprian choked for breath.

Cyprian groped his throat. "I have no idea why your lover has left you. Didn't I tell you she couldn't be trusted?"

Andrew grabbed Nathaniel's raised arm. "This is my fight, Nathaniel, let me fight it!"

The anxieties exploding in Nathaniel's soul escaped through his voice. "The minute this man began taking our powder it became everyone's fight!"

He yanked Cyprian by the arm and thrust him into the chair by the table. Cyprian's small eyes thinned and in a single motion he launched from his seat and heaved the table across the room. "I needed that money!" He charged, waving his weapon. "But no amount of money will bring her back to me now!"

Nathaniel stilled. Had Camilla died? "What happened to Camilla, Cyprian?"

Cyprian stared, his mouth half open and his chest pumping. Slowly, his lips closed and face warped. His gaze didn't move from Nathaniel as he spoke to Andrew. "I accept your challenge, Mr. Cooper."

Shocked, Nathaniel almost laughed. "You cannot

fight a duel. Not like this."

Motionless, only Andrew's eyes blinked while his voice landed flat. "My honor is destroyed, Nathaniel. I care not for formalities."

Disbelief forged a frown on Nathaniel's brow. He stepped back, praying for guidance as the two men took their place at opposite sides of the room and raised their weapons. "This is madness!"

"Count for us, Nathaniel." Andrew's voice was calm as a spring breeze.

"Andrew—"

"If you will not, Nathaniel, I will," Andrew said. "On three. One!"

"Stop!" Nathaniel lunged for Andrew as the door burst open and Joseph rushed in.

"Nathaniel! I heard Miss Campbell is miss—what's going on?"

"Two!"

"Joseph, get out of here, now!" Nathaniel bellowed, his muscles cramping.

"Three!"

Time slowed as the ball entered Cyprian's chest. The fire cut through his flesh, consuming him body and soul. He stumbled backward and moaned as his mind flashed with memories of times past. Camilla's smiles, Jacob's childhood giggle.

He tripped and fell hard on his back, the cold floor breaking his fall as a warm liquid poured over his skin.

Voices and bodies drew near. Someone's hands felt around his chest. Another held his head.

Cyprian strained to revive his slowing mind. Where was Jacob? He must speak with him...

More yelling, more grabbing at his chest.

He blinked, and coughed, the searing pain flowing down to his feet.

His lungs seized and for a moment his thoughts cleared. So this was death. Had Camilla felt so cold, so afraid?

The sounds faded. The dim light dissolved to black, and he succumbed, praying Camilla waited to take his hand on the other side.

Hands covered in blood, Nathaniel sat back on his heels and rested his arm over his leg. With a heavy exhale he shook his head. "He's dead."

Joseph knelt beside him and closed Cyprian's eyelids before sending Nathaniel a look that screamed with unspoken questions.

Andrew stood at Cyprian's feet, his arms hanging heavy at his sides. He stepped back, his shoulders squaring. "'Tis over."

Nathaniel glanced between Andrew and the man he'd just killed. Somehow Andrew seemed taller, his face younger.

"So it is." Nathaniel pushed to his feet. "I must go. Joseph, take care of the body—and check on Camilla." He paused, and looked toward the stairs. "I fear she might be dead as well."

Joseph turned his head with a quick jerk. His round eyes widened. After a moment he nodded. "You are going to look for Miss Campbell?"

"Aye." He stomped to the door and charged into

the deluge, racing across the rain-soaked roads to the Watson's.

Nathaniel burst through the front door, praying somehow he'd find Kitty draped in a blanket by the fire. But the house was silent. Alarm scratched over him and he raced to the kitchen, then darted upstairs just as Thomas and Eliza entered from the back.

He halted on the middle step as his heart leapt in hope. "Well?"

Eliza rushed in, wringing her hands. "We alerted several in town, including Joseph and Roger."

"Did you find her?"

Thomas closed the door and shook his head. His tone sagged with dread. "Nay. But my horse is gone from the barn."

Nathaniel charged back down to the parlor. "Your horse is gone?"

"She must have taken it."

Nathaniel blinked, a scowl folding over his forehead as he strained to find function in his clouding mind. He must go after her, he must find her wherever she'd gone. But how was he to know where to begin?

"Did Cyprian know anything?" Thomas grabbed Nathaniel's arm. "You're covered in blood."

Nathaniel looked at his hands. "Cyprian is dead."

"What?" Thomas and Eliza spoke at the same time.

"There is much to tell, but naught that matters more than finding Kitty." He headed to the door when a tug on his conscious urged him to stop. He turned, and suddenly darted upstairs, unsure why, but praying that he might find the clue he needed to lead him to her. Thomas and Eliza followed close behind.

In Kitty's bedchamber, he halted at the foot of the bed, scanning the room from left to right, hoping for at least a hint of where she might have gone. "If she left on horseback she could be miles from here by now." He paused and turned to Eliza who stood in the doorway. "How long do you believe she's been gone?"

"She was so distressed after you left, she cried for I don't know how long." She glanced at Thomas behind her. "Some time later I brought her some warmed cider, and that's when I discovered her missing."

Nathaniel slammed his eyes shut. The image of Kitty weeping on account of his cruel actions slashed like a razor and he clenched his fists, praying she could find a way to forgive him, that it wasn't too late to repair the damage he'd done.

Thomas stepped in, his face drawn. "Do you think Cyprian had something to do with this?"

Nathaniel flicked his fingers against his leg, battling the inclination that wormed within. "Nay. I believe... I believe she acted alone."

"Alone?" Thomas turned toward the door. "I'm not so certain. I'll check in the barn again. Perhaps I can determine which way she left."

"I'll go with you." Eliza followed Thomas out and soon Nathaniel stood in painful silence in the empty room.

'Twas almost as if he could feel her presence; see her smile, hear her joyful laugh, smell the sweetness of her skin. Everything rested just how she'd left it. Peaceful, calm. A paradox to the turmoil that assailed him, like the storm that raged outside. *Kitty, my love, where have you gone?*

Nathaniel glanced about once more and stepped

toward the hall then stopped hard, as if a hand had yanked on the back of his coat. He scowled and spun, scouring the room he had already memorized when his gaze brushed against the open Bible on the table. His breathing slowed. As if an unseen person directed his movements he drew forward. His heart thumped hard against his ribs. There, resting on the open pages was the flower he'd given her. Carefully picking up the open book, he shifted the flower upward on the page. *Dear Lord!* His throat seized as his mind interpreted the meaning behind the clear message Kitty had left behind.

His heart stopped as he read the verse beside the wilted petals. *Where the Spirit of the Lord is, there is liberty.*

In a flash the rabid events of the day poured into his memory with frightening clarity. His mouth pressed tight and he breathed hard through his nose. He looked up and stared through the darkened window as Kitty's pain-filled voice pricked his ears. *This note was bound for Plymouth. James gave this note to Henry, but he dropped it...*

The Bible nearly fell from his hands and he stepped back, his mind swirling as more pieces of the mystery slammed against him. He rubbed his grinding jaw. The courier, who even now lay unconscious in Nathaniel's home seemed to yell from the pulpit of his memory. *My note—my satchel, the British... they took my satchel.*

He set the book on the bed and stumbled backward, his hands trembling as the horrid realization rose like a red moon in the sky. The old man's explanation boomed loudest. *He started babbling about a message he had to get to Plymouth...*

He lost his breath.

Kitty had named herself courier.

Nathaniel sprinted down the stairs and charged out the back door into the pelting rain, yelling against the storm. “Thomas! Eliza!”

They rushed from the barn and Nathaniel ushered Eliza inside, but kept an arm on Thomas.

Thomas frowned, as thunder roared through the skies. “What is it?”

The rain splashed Nathaniel’s face and his breath heaved. “She’s gone to Plymouth.”

Chapter Thirty-Four

Kitty's hands trembled as she gripped her dripping skirts. Rain smacked against the sides of the large officer's tent as she inhaled the tobacco filled air, trying to find strength to stand erect. She shivered and clenched her teeth to keep them from chattering.

Seated behind the desk, the officer stared back, expression lifeless but for the way the muscles around one eye twitched. The light from the solitary candle skirted around his face leaving haunting shadows beneath his dark eyes.

"You were traveling by night to visit family you say? Alone?" His tone was calm, like that of a father speaking to his daughter, but the tick of his eye spoke as much as his mouth did. "Come now, young lady, do you think me a fool?"

She swallowed and lifted her chin preparing to answer when from behind, another man entered. "Major Stockton. You sent for me?"

With a grunt the major pushed to standing and came around the table. "Yes, Donaldson, come in."

Kitty spun, her heart thrashing. Henry! She clamped her mouth shut, unsure whether to reveal that she knew him. *Thank you, Lord!* Surely God had sent him to set her free.

Stockton pointed to Kitty as he spoke to Henry. "This is the prisoner I told you about."

"Aye, sir, I—" Henry's face slackened the instant his gaze landed on her. He looked between Kitty and Stockton, blinking as if his mind raced to determine why and how she could be standing beside him.

The tender concern in his eyes stroked Kitty's ever-growing fears when he continued. "Sir, forgive me, *this* is your prisoner?"

The stout man bobbed his chin. "Hard to believe the patriots would send a woman to do their work."

Henry pulled his shoulders back and widened his stance. "Sir, if I may, I believe a mistake has been made. I have known this woman for—"

"You know this woman?"

Kitty clutched her stomacher, praying with every intake of breath. Surely Henry knew what he was doing. She pleaded with him through her eyes, but he stared only at his superior.

"Aye." Henry's fingers curled and uncurled. His tone darkened. "I've known Miss Campbell for some time and I *know* she would never betray King George." He turned to her and cupped her elbow. "Are you hurt?"

"Do not touch her!" Stockton roared and stomped forward, turning to speak to Kitty in the next breath. "If you are a Tory as he claims, then what, pray tell, were you doing traveling all alone in a storm such as this?"

Kitty swallowed and prayed God would steady her voice. "As I said, sir, I was on my way to visit my grandmother and—"

"Ha!" Stockton bellowed.

She flung a worried look to Donaldson, but his

stoic expression remained unchanged. He must know she lied, and yet he cared not. God bless him!

Stockton rounded back to his desk and pulled open a small drawer to retrieve a long white pipe. "No respectable woman travels alone." He fiddled with it in his fingers. "You are a fool to think we'd believe such a story. That is of course, unless you are *not* a respectable woman." His tone quieted, making Kitty's ears ring as if he'd screamed. He neared, his sour breath searing her face as he spoke only inches from her. "I know you have it. And you *will* give it to me."

He glared before stepping back and sighing with the hint of a smile. "Tell me the name of the rebel leader who gave you the note and I shall consider releasing you."

Donaldson stepped forward, gripping the hilt of the sword at his side. "Sir, I will vouch for Miss Campbell's honor, she is not—"

Stockton's arm sliced the air. "Another word from you, Donaldson, and I'll remove you from your post!" He stared at Kitty. "I know you are a patriot courier, *Miss Campbell*, and you shall be my prisoner until you develop enough wisdom to surrender the note into my hands." He neared. "If you choose not to comply, I will come searching for it."

She threw a frantic glance at Henry who gave a nearly imperceptible nod and took a step in front of her. "Sir, if you will allow me, I should be happy to oversee her imprisonment while in this camp."

Stockton's glare thinned and his eye twitched again. Only his gaze bobbed up to Henry then back to her. "I shall give you one last chance. Give me the note, or you will be a permanent fixture to our little encampment." The foul smell of bitter tobacco on his breath burned her nose almost as much as his words burned through her remaining resolve.

Her knees shook. She couldn't stay here. She had to get to Plymouth. "Sir, I speak the truth, I haven't any idea what you're talking about—"

"Then a stint in captivity might be just the thing to enlighten you."

Henry put a hand on his sword. "Major, I will gladly see to—"

"I'm sure you would." Stockton walked to the door of the tent and called into the rain before turning back to them. "Which is precisely why I have decided that Brown should oversee her time with us, instead of you."

The thin soldier staggered in. "You called for me, Sir?"

"Take this prisoner to our holding cell and keep watch until morning."

He bowed. "Aye, Sir."

The instant the stranger pulled Kitty from the tent her heart collapsed. Henry was her last hope. If he couldn't convince Stockton, they would search her and find the note. Then her desire to make right the wrongs she had done would be for naught.

The man shoved her into a tiny shack and she swung around just as the door smacked shut. The muddy ground seeped around her shoes and quick rhythmic drops of rain plunked down from the cracks in the roof.

The silence moaned around her as the lonely rains continued to fall. Her wet hair clung to her neck as remnants of the storm cried down on her head. She cupped her face in her hands to stifle a cry. Surely by now her family had noticed her absence. Did they think to tell Nathaniel? Did he care?

She retreated to the far corner and hugged her chest. None of that mattered. She must train her prayers and energies on the mission she'd started and desperately needed to execute.

Raising her eyes to the heavens, she gripped her arms tighter. *Lord, I know thou art over all. Please carry me from here, and let me help the people of Plymouth as I did not help the people of Sandwich.*

Muffled voices drew near and she pushed off the wall as a warm spray of courage trickled down her back. She stared at the locked door. No matter what lay ahead, she would not submit. As her father had proven, freedom was worth risking all.

Her fight had only just begun.

Chapter Thirty-Five

"I know she has the note! Find it!"

From the other side of the shack door, Stockton's voice boomed.

Kitty's pulse thrashed. She scanned the dark room, looking for possible escapes for the hundredth time. But her prison offered only four crooked walls, one door and no window.

More strange voices erupted from beyond the thin wood.

"She has nothing!"

Stockton's roar echoed the rumbling thunder. "That note is in her clothes and we will find it."

"Sir, if I may." Henry's voice massaged the cramping muscles in Kitty's neck. "'Tis improper for any of us to do such a thing. I suggest a woman be found who could search the prisoner."

Stockton cursed, singeing Kitty's ears. "Locate one. Now!"

Kitty clapped a hand over her mouth and breathed through her fingers. *Thank you, Henry.* His forethought had bought her a few moments at least, perhaps more.

Backing against the rough wood, she looked up through the slats in the roof. The continuous rains fell softer, when Nathaniel's unbidden memory consumed her mind, pulling hot tears from her eyes. She bit her lip and closed her eyes. *Nathaniel, forgive me.*

Without warning the door creaked open. She pushed off the wall and relaxed her hands at her sides, feigning a calm demeanor while inside her pulse exploded like cannon fire.

When Henry entered, a breath of hope filled her lungs. He closed the door and spoke in a deadly whisper. “Kitty, what has possessed you?”

Her gaze darted between his caring eyes as her tongue stuck to the roof of her mouth. She hated to lie, but she must. Keeping the truth from Henry would keep him safe. Just as she had hoped it would for the man she loved.

Praying he wouldn’t see through her thin charade, she pleaded. “Possessed me? This is foolishness, Henry, I have done nothing!”

He stepped close and gripped her arms, speaking through his teeth. “Stockton believes you hide a patriot message and that you intend to warn Plymouth of our plan to seize their powder.” He lowered his voice. “If you are, they *will* hang you.”

Kitty gasped, clutching her throat. “They would not.”

“They would. Your gender has no softening effect on their rage.” He glanced at the door. “Are you?”

She straightened. “Am I what?”

“Are you carrying that message?”

Kitty pulled away from his hold. “I cannot believe you would ask such a thing.” She wrapped her arms around her chest to stop the trembling. “Henry, you know me. You know I would never go against the king.”

The following silence taunted as Henry’s eyes

penetrated her. "Does Nathaniel know what you've done?"

Kitty clenched her teeth, throat swelling. "Of course not!"

The faint light that filtered through the walls rested on the twitching muscles in his jaw. "You *do* have it."

Kitty looked away, clutching the cloak at her chest. Why must he see through her?

Grabbing her by the shoulders, Henry gripped hard, his mouth a firm line. "This is no time for games. You know I will do anything for you and your family, but you *must* find a way to destroy that note. Now!"

"But—"

"Get rid of it!" He released her then turned to the door and spoke over his shoulder. "I'll keep them away as long as I can. God be with you." He left, slipping quietly out the door and leaving her in a silence that pounded in her ears with the same rhythmic pulsing of her heart.

Her hands quivered. *Lord, what do I do?* Without thinking she pulled the crumpled paper from within her stays and rubbed it between her fingers. Any moment the door would open, and the future she may have had would be decided with a rope around her neck.

Unless...

Kitty stilled. An impression sparked in her mind and she pushed away from the wall.

Thank you, Lord!

She unfolded the message and committed it to memory before ripping off a corner and shoving the sour tasting paper into her mouth. With a shudder she swallowed it down and quickly severed the remaining message into pieces. Her muscles trembled and she clutched the fragments to keep from dropping them. A mumble of voices grew louder and she stuffed in three pieces more, grinding the parchment between her teeth and praying enough moisture remained in her mouth to carry them down her throat.

Again she swallowed, and again she filled her mouth with more fragments. Pressing her back against the wall to anchor her quivering body, she grimaced as the last bite struggled down her dry throat.

The mumbled sounds cleared into distinguishable voices as the speakers neared the shack.

Nay!

Kitty lurched forward and shoved the last pieces in her mouth, chewed and swallowed just as the door smacked open.

A smile hinted at her lips.

They would never find it now.

Pulling back the reins, Nathaniel squinted against the heavy drops. A frown pulled against his mouth. He squinted to see through the spattering of trees, almost wishing he'd accepted Thomas's plea to join him. But the risk Kitty had taken was because of him. And the remedy, he vowed, would be as well.

Keeping a tight grip on the leather in his hands, he spoke quietly to Astor while holding his vision on the faint lights glowing in the forest ahead. *What could that—*

The rhythmic drumming of approaching hooves

rumbled like the rolling thunder. Coercing his blood to move at a normal rhythm, he urged his horse toward the edge of a small embankment on the other side of the road, finding cover moments before the riders appeared. Nathaniel's neck corded and his shoulders cramped as three riders came into view, moonlight glinting off their swords and brass buttons.

A string of curses coiled on his tongue. *Soldiers.*

"Donaldson won't be happy we're late." One of the soldiers pulled his horse off the road and continued toward the lights.

Donaldson? Nathaniel's lungs heaved.

"'Tis Stockton we must answer to," another one replied.

The last soldier spoke. "I would know if they still have that woman they captured on the road to Plymouth."

Alarm shoved up Nathaniel's spine. *They have her!* This nightmare he had not considered, though he should have, knowing what the British had done to the courier he'd bandaged only hours ago.

Nathaniel jumped to the ground never moving his gaze from the far-away camp. Surely God had led him here. He had to trust that the Lord had opened this path and that He would guide him to Kitty.

Astor side-stepped as if he sensed the impending danger. Nathaniel stroked the animal's neck before tying the reins around a tree. "Don't worry. I shall return for you."

He glanced up and down the road before darting to the woods on the opposite side. Like heavenly watchmen, the noble forest seemed to shield him from detection. Nathaniel didn't stop running. Trails of cold rain trickled down his neck as he neared the camp. The scent of smoke and the sound of men's voices grew stronger with every step. The closer he got to danger, the more his blood heated.

Around the perimeter, only feet from the camp, the conversation of a group of soldiers stung Nathaniel's ears and he skidded to a halt.

A soldier sidestepped back and forth as he talked. "Stockton is convinced she has it in her skirts."

"Had you not heard?" Another approached and the men turned to him. "They sent Ward's old lady to search her. She found the note easy as you please."

"Ha! I should have been the one to check her," another man said with a sickening laugh, "I would have found several other useful things, I'm sure."

The men erupted with hideous guffaws and Nathaniel clenched the tree beside him. If those men had done anything to Kitty he would destroy them with his bare hands.

Pushing away his violent thoughts, Nathaniel gritted his teeth and continued rounding the outer edge of the camp. As he moved over the sopping ground, he sent endless prayers to heaven. *Lead me, Lord. Help me carry her to safety.*

As he circled, Nathaniel measured the strength of the camp. Eight tents. Seven small and one large, with a shack on the opposite end. As he counted, the door to the shack opened and Donaldson appeared. Nathaniel halted and stopped breathing as the commotion in the camp quieted.

Donaldson stepped aside as a woman emerged. Dress covered in mud, hair hanging around her face and neck, hands tied in front of her. Another soldier yanked her by the arm and led her toward the largest tent.

Nathaniel lunged, his muscles tearing.

Kitty!

Nathaniel strained against the urge to break out of the trees and rush to pluck her from their grasp. He shook his head. He must wait, no matter how painful the delay. Though he couldn't stop his heart from running after her.

Donaldson neared Kitty and whispered something in her ear, but the other soldier tugged her away before she could even glance in response. Whoops and whistles from the men made Nathaniel's muscles twitch as Donaldson followed Kitty into the large tent and out of sight.

I must get to that tent.

Speeding through trees, Nathaniel cringed at every splash his feet made in the shadowed puddles. Stopping just behind the largest tent, he crouched low. The lights in the canvas made blurry silhouettes of the three men who surrounded her.

The darkened figure of a tall, robust man moved toward Kitty, then pointed to the door. "Donaldson, Ward, I would speak with Miss Campbell alone."

"Sir, I—"

"Leave us!"

The door of the tent flung open and Donaldson emerged, followed by the other soldier who quickly tromped toward the group in the center of the camp.

Nathaniel held his breath, watching. Donaldson rubbed the back of his neck and turned to glance again at the tent. The urge to call out became almost too much to contain. Nathaniel opened his mouth but snapped it shut when Donaldson spun toward him and glared into the trees.

"Who's there?" His loud whisper sent spikes down

Nathaniel's spine.

Nathaniel rose and moved a step forward. A twig snapped beneath his weight and his pulse stopped. Should he speak? Would his rush to trust a Redcoat leave him in more peril?

Donaldson frowned and placed a hand to his weapon, growling as he stepped forward. "Show yourself."

Raising his hands, Nathaniel emerged from the shadows, keeping his volume below a whisper. "Donaldson, 'tis I, Nathaniel. I've come to rescue Kitty."

Even in the blackness, Nathaniel could see Donaldson's features relax. He removed his hand from his sword and looked behind before marching farther into the trees.

Donaldson reached out and gripped Nathaniel's arm. He answered through barely audible words. "I've been praying someone would come." The sincerity in his tone massaged away the pinch in Nathaniel's back. Donaldson peered over his shoulder. "Kitty is in grave danger."

Nathaniel stepped forward. "Tell me all."

"They have framed her, claiming she had a message that I know she did not possess."

The truth stabbed Nathaniel's tongue. "But she did. She told me this evening she had found a note you had dropped in Sandwich. We know she was planning to take it to Plymouth herself."

"'Tis my fault then." Donaldson closed his eyes and growled under his breath. "Kitty what have you done?"

"So 'tis true." Nathaniel wiped a hand over his jaw. "She had it, as the man claims."

Shaking his head, Donaldson spoke fast. "But

she did not. The woman who searched her confided in me that she found nothing. Kitty must have destroyed it before it could be discovered." He looked back at the camp. "'Tis Stockton who claims a note was found. He wishes to use Kitty as an example in Boston and hang her for treason."

"Hang?" Nathaniel grabbed Donaldson's arm. "Tell me what to do. Tell me how I can take her from here."

Donaldson nodded. "Wait here. I shall return." He started toward the camp then stopped. "And be prepared, I'll be bringing a *friend*."

Chapter Thirty-six

"Ward?" Stockton yelled toward the door.

Kitty flung a look behind her, trying to remember how to pray.

Henry charged in, offering Kitty nothing more than a fleeting glance. "Aye, sir."

"Where's Ward?"

"I do not know, Sir."

Stockton growled then gestured to the door of the tent, focusing on the papers on his desk. "Miss Campbell has committed an act of treason." He sat in the chair, speaking as casual as if he were ordering a meal. "Our prisoner will be accompanying us to Boston. See her to the shack and guard her until we break camp in the morning."

Henry bowed. "Right away, sir."

The inkling of hope that had floated in Kitty's chest dropped to her feet, taking with it the blood in her head. Henry took Kitty's arm and his fingers gouged her elbow as he led her into the damp night air, away from the suffocating stench of stale tobacco. At least the rain had stopped, but the mud it left behind oozed around her shoes with every step.

Her throat tightened until the words almost refused to budge. "Henry, please you mustn't—"

"Shhh." He refused to meet her gaze as he opened the door and nudged her inside. "Don't say a word."

He hurried out and shut the door.

Kitty stared at the wet wooden slats, blinking as all feeling left her limbs. Could he so easily forget their friendship? Were her actions so terrible in his sight that he would do nothing to aid her?

"Fredericks!" Donaldson pointed to another soldier. "Guard this cell until I return. I have business to attend to."

The soldier took his post outside the door, and stood at attention, musket in hand.

As she stared through the slats in the wood, the reality she'd refused to believe wound round her neck like the noose that awaited her and she clapped her hands to her mouth. She inhaled a quick, shaky breath. This could not be! The cool night air moved through her wet clothes and chilled her very soul. She heard nothing, saw nothing. Nothing but the faces of Eliza and Thomas. And Nathaniel. *God forgive me!* Tears flooded her eyes and coursed over her cheeks as she raised her gaze to heaven. *Help them to forgive me, Lord.*

Sobs threatened. Stumbling backward, she turned and pressed her face into the corner. Cupping her face, she fought against the anguished cries that rallied for release, allowing only stifled whimpers. She could not appear weak, could not appear to be the foolish woman they believed her to be.

Tears spent, body drained of strength, Kitty turned her back to the wood and slumped to the muddy ground, pulling her legs to her chest. The sounds of the camp had long since died and the soldiers had retired to their tents. All but the one that waited outside her door.

She leaned her head back as exhaustion wove its heavy threads through her weary muscles. As sleep toyed with her mind, Nathaniel's face consumed her memory. His laugh when he teased her, the merriment in his eyes when he found her in the kitchen, his smile—

Footsteps neared and she flipped her head toward the sound. 'Twas Donaldson. She could tell from his height and the way he kept his hand on the hilt of his sword. "'Tis time," he whispered. "We must take her now."

The guard at her door grunted a response.

They will take me now? Nay!

The door opened and Kitty jerked free from the remaining bands of sleep, hurling back to the dank night that surrounded her. Struggling to her feet, she gripped her stomach as the soldier entered. Closing the door, he stalked forward. Fear raged through her like a rabid animal.

She pressed harder against the wood. "Don't touch me!"

He lunged and covered her mouth. "Quiet!"

Kitty writhed under his strong hands, struggling to get free. She tried to scream but his grasp was too tight.

"Be still, Kitty, please!"

All fight left her limbs in an instant and she dropped her arms to her sides. Blinking, she tried to clear the dream from her vision. *It couldn't be...*

He removed his hand from her mouth and stroked her cheek, his husky tone warm with concern. "Are you hurt?"

She could hardly breathe. "I... I don't believe it." Her words quivered as much as her body.

"Believe." Nathaniel studied her face and tucked a

lock of hair behind her ear. "'Tis I."

Kitty took in quick short bursts of air and her voice cracked as tears burned her eyes. "I thought... I thought..."

"I was a fool." He tugged her to him, holding her hard against his chest. His deep whisper caressed her heart. "Forgive me."

"Nay." She pushed away from him, gazing up into his shadowed face. The words she harbored for so many weeks suddenly poured from her mouth like a river surging beyond its banks. "'Tis I who must beg forgiveness—"

"Shhh." He placed a finger to her lips. "There isn't time, my love."

"But I must explain—"

"Later. Come, we must take you away from here." He tugged her toward the door.

"Not yet." Kitty tugged at his arm. "I must get to Plymouth. They must know what's coming."

"Nay, you mustn't worry about Plymouth." Nathaniel's tone dropped. "The British believe *you* are the second courier." A smile tilted one side of his mouth. "But you are not."

The meaning of his words settled upon her like dew. "So, the message has gotten through."

Nathaniel nodded and the solemn expression in his eyes softened to longing as his gaze lowered to her mouth.

Nathaniel dotted his lips to her forehead, fighting the urge to press his mouth against hers. "You have many questions, and I *will* answer them. Now, I must focus on bringing you home, so you may be my wife."

"Your wife?" she breathed. The sparkle in her eyes and the way her mouth bowed upward coated his heart like warm honey.

He smoothed his hand over her velvety cheek, yearning to hold her against him. "I—"

"Fredericks, why aren't you at your post?"

"That's Henry's voice." Kitty jumped and looked at the door, gripping her chest. "Who's Fredericks?"

Nathaniel squeezed her hand before going to the door. "Stay here, and follow our lead."

He peeked out of the shack as Donaldson approached. Like an actor resuming his character, Nathaniel closed the door and stood at attention, doing his best to appear normal in the ill-fitting clothes of the enemy.

"Fredericks, why weren't you at your post?" Donaldson neared until but a few inches separated their bodies. He continued as if nothing were amiss, and looked around before slipping Nathaniel a knife and pistol. "Don't tell me our prisoner tried to beguile you into freeing her."

Nathaniel tucked the weapons into the tight jacket. "She asked for water, sir, that is all."

Donaldson gave a slight nudge with his head to the side and spoke in a voice barely audible. "I've found your horse and relocated him in the trees behind the shack. I'll keep watch while you make your escape." His jaw hardened. "You must move quickly."

A thickness settled in Nathaniel's throat as he stared at the man who, for the second time, had saved their lives. He spoke no louder than the sound of the drops that fell from the roof of the shack. "We will forever be in your debt, Donaldson." He swallowed the lump in his throat and allowed a small grin to peek out from the side of his mouth. "I never thought I would put my life in the hands of a Redcoat. Twice."

Donaldson held his mouth together, wrestling a smile. "You—"

A rustling behind the shack jerked Donaldson around and he reached for his sword. Nathaniel gripped the pistol and widened his stance, his pulse thundering, but only an eerie stillness approached from the shadows.

"Go now." Donaldson turned and stood at attention as Nathaniel ducked inside the shack. He motioned for Kitty then put his finger to his mouth and spoke to her ear. "Stay with me."

Nathaniel put his arm around her shoulders and led her into the night. The urge to carry her to safety—and keep her there—sent jolts of fire through his legs. He bolted for the horse, but Donaldson yanked on his arm, halting him.

Nathaniel froze and pushed Kitty behind him. Questioning Donaldson through his eyes, Nathaniel scowled.

Donaldson shook his head and spoke over his shoulder. "Something isn't right."

All the blood in Nathaniel's body slowed.

"Someone's watching." Donaldson scanned the forest, as if he could see through the mists of darkness that veiled them. His voice scratched against a whisper. "Run. Now!"

Yanking Kitty beside him, Nathaniel fled to the forest. From behind the shack a soldier darted in front of him, his pistol pointed at Nathaniel's chest.

He flung Kitty behind, shielding her from the impending ball. Nathaniel glanced back and his chest turned to stone. Donaldson stood with his hands raised as another soldier aimed at Donaldson's head. "Stockton knew some foolish rogue would try to steal the wench."

Nathaniel spun to the man in front of him, planning the ways he might disarm the boyish soldier.

"How pleasant." From behind, the other Redcoat responded. "We shall witness three hangings, not one."

Nathaniel turned toward Donaldson as his muscles flexed. A spark flickered behind Donaldson's impassioned eyes and Nathaniel dipped his chin.

They must act. Now.

Donaldson nodded again and Nathaniel lunged forward. He bashed the pistol away from his chest and jammed his boot against the soldier's stomach. The man flew backward clutching his belly. From behind, a crack and a groan wailed toward the heavens.

Nathaniel shot a glance behind him to see Donaldson wrenching the pistol from the soldier's limp hand.

Donaldson motioned to the trees, his face wild.

Nathaniel snatched Kitty's hand and tugged her towards the woods as a shot rang out, flashing the forest with a burst of yellow light.

Pulling his weapon from his side, Nathaniel shoved Kitty away. "Get behind the shack!"

She dodged behind the building just as another soldier appeared from the dark. With barely enough time to think, Nathaniel fired and the soldier dropped to the ground.

Nathaniel spun around as Donaldson ran forward, snatched the ready gun from the dead man and shoved it at Nathaniel. Sounds of the camp—yelling, running, clanking of weapons grew louder with every second.

"You must leave. Now!" Donaldson turned to reload when a ball struck him in the arm and pushed him to the ground.

"No!" Kitty lunged from behind the shack, but Nathaniel waved her back.

"I won't have you killed," he yelled and pointed toward the trees. "Run to the horse. I'll meet you there!"

Kitty reeled backward then stumbled and obeyed his command.

As more soldiers rallied in the confusion of the camp, Nathaniel pulled under Donaldson's good arm and helped him to rise, but Donaldson grunted and pulled back. "Nay, go." He grimaced. "I shall be more help to you here. I can convince them you went north. Go!"

Nathaniel nodded and dashed into the woods as more voices and shouts erupted from the smoke.

Kitty waited astride Astor with the reins in her hands. "Hurry!"

A bullet whizzed past Nathaniel's ear. He launched himself onto the horse and secured one arm around Kitty's waist as he flicked the reins.

His legs corded as he kicked the horse into a run. Not daring to look back, Nathaniel kept Astor at a pace that would have them in safety's grasp in only minutes. *Lord, do not let them follow us.* The misty air coated his skin and hair as he leaned forward into the wind. Soon, the fearsome sounds faded and he braved a glance over his shoulder. He sighed, but still would not slow his mount. They were not followed, so it seemed, but 'twas too early to relax. Nay, they would need to prepare to make an even greater escape should the British come searching for them.

He tightened his grip around Kitty's waist. *Lord, be with Donaldson. Keep him safe and cause the other soldiers to believe his tale for our sakes. And for his.*

Chapter Thirty-seven

Kitty stared out the window of the Watson's parlor. It had been nearly two whole days since the ordeal and both Nathaniel and Thomas seemed certain if the soldiers hadn't followed them here already, they were likely safe. Forever. And yet, Kitty couldn't allow herself to believe it, no matter how much she yearned to do so. Their trunks were packed and ready should the need to flee prove paramount. Blessedly, the Lord had seen fit to protect them from further turmoil. At least for now.

A ripple of purple eased up toward the sky, heralding the coming night, but the first sprinkle of starlight was still hours away. She wrapped her arms tighter around her chest. Eliza had long since retired, the babe in her belly having stolen every strand of energy. Thomas had retired with her, leaving Kitty alone to ponder the events that had nearly changed her life in a way she dared not even consider.

Leaning her head against the window frame, Kitty peered at the road. The news of the deaths of Camilla and Cyprian had been nothing short of shocking. And with the horror and confusion of recent events, Kitty had hardly been able to speak more than a few words.

The pounding of an approaching horse stole

Kitty's attention and she pulled away from the window. A rider came into view, his black cloak floating behind him on the wind. She recoiled and hid in the shadow of the stairs.

Nathaniel rushed into the parlor from the kitchen and looked out the window before he quickly opened the door and raced to meet the rider.

The man stopped his horse only long enough to hand Nathaniel a note before he yanked the reins and raced back the way he'd come.

Nathaniel tugged the paper open and after a breathless moment, dropped his hands at his sides, his shoulders visibly drooping.

Lord, no!

Kitty turned toward the door at the sound of Nathaniel's steps.

He stopped just inside and glanced behind him. When he gazed back at her, the gentleness in his eyes brushed against her like a breeze on a field of wheat. He sighed and closed the door.

Handing her the note, he leaned his shoulder against the wall. "Read it."

Her fingers quaked. She resisted and he dipped his chin. "Read it, Kitty."

Carefully she took the note in her hands and exhaled a long breath out through pinched lips before scanning the words.

Friends,

All is well. Higley heard tell of the tragic events and has vouched for Miss Campbell's loyalty to King George. Stockton is subdued.

You are safe.

God be with you until we meet again,

Donaldson

Kitty's mouth hung open and she flung a look to Nathaniel. "I cannot believe it. 'Tis nearly too marvelous to be true."

"But it is." His mouth twitched upward in a half-smile. He looked out the window. "We will be indebted to Donaldson forever I believe."

"Aye." Relief, and a heavenly peace rested against her heart. They needn't hide. They needn't escape to find refuge from the king. *Lord, I thank thee!*

Kitty continued to gaze at the note, but Nathaniel's heated gaze warmed her cheeks. She swallowed, unable to bring herself to look at him.

He chuckled and pushed away from the wall. "I'd never have imagined Pigley would assist in saving our necks."

Peeking sideways, a grin bloomed on Kitty's face, and in her heart. "Nay, neither would I."

"He possesses wisdom," Nathaniel continued, "I'll allow him that, for falling in love with an extraordinary woman."

The warmth in his tone smoothed across her shoulders and down her arms like a loving caress. She wriggled to escape its alluring capture and shrugged, unable to structure a proper response. If she'd been brave enough in the beginning to place her trust in God, and even in Nathaniel, then all of this turmoil could have been avoided and all this heartache undone. The memories stabbed deeper as the vision of Donaldson's torn garments and bleeding arm expanded in her mind until she could see nothing else.

Nathaniel stepped closer. The soft inhale and exhale of his breath made Kitty's skin tickle with unbidden nerves. The urge to peek at him took control of her muscles and she dared a glance from the corner of her eye.

Time slowed.

That familiar look of desire and longing circled in his rugged features, melting her bones.

"You're avoiding me." His rich voice drew her closer, while the jest in his words tied her lips into a grin she attempted to crush.

"I am not."

"You are."

"I will neither confirm nor deny any such thing." She lifted her chin and tried not to laugh as she knit her fingers behind her back, avoiding his gaze. If she allowed herself to reveal the emotions that hid behind her threadbare curtain of strength, she might never recover.

He toyed with the lock of hair at her neck. His fingers tickled her skin and all she wanted to do was collapse against him and lose herself in his warm embrace.

"Kitty," he said, "I hardly know what to say. 'Tis clear that I'm the chief of fools. If you never forgive me, I will understand, though I will pray for your forgiveness every day for the rest of my life."

His words, like soft linen circled her wounded heart. She stared at him as a painful swelling threatened to close her throat.

She inhaled a ragged breath and her voice wobbled. "You have every right to think ill of me, after what I've done." She turned away and stared out the window. "'Tis true that I was involved with the powder, though I give you my word had I any other choice I would have gladly spoken of it." Returning to face him, she willed her tone to stay even. "I know I was wrong, but you must believe me when I say that I wanted nothing to do with it. I never wanted to—"

"I know." He smoothed his palm against her cheek, sending a spray of gooseflesh down her neck and arms. His eyes trailed over her face, robbing the breath from her lungs. "You are not to blame, and if I had been more astute, if I had had less pride and fear for my own heart, I would have seen that from the beginning." He stopped again, this time cupping her face with both hands and speaking so tenderly Kitty's heart swelled until it pushed tears from her eyes. "I love you, Kitty. I love your virtue, your passion for good, your kindness and strength. I love the fire in your spirit and your yearning for right. I want to spend the rest of my days with you. And more than anything I want you to know that you being a Tory—"

"Stop." Kitty placed a hand on his chest. A light from within glowed, warming her body with the brightness of truth. "Nathaniel, that's what I wanted to tell you—*one* of the things I wanted to tell you after church this past Sunday. God spoke to me. He showed me the errors of my thinking and I know now, without a grain of doubt remaining, that your cause, the cause of freedom, is God's cause." She paused, and lifted her chin. "I'm a patriot."

Nathaniel's dark brow narrowed and his head tipped slightly. He never moved his gaze and his mouth tightened.

Kitty licked her lips and shifted her feet. She smiled, hoping such would coax a response from him. "Are you not pleased?"

His expression didn't change and a surge of panic inched up her back. "I do hope you are not upset. Nathaniel, you must know I wouldn't jest about something like this to entice you to say you love me—"

Nathaniel swooped down, cutting off her words with a kiss that turned her knees to liquid. His warm breath on her face mixed with her own and she clung to his chest to keep from melting to the ground. He pressed her to him, smoothing his hands down her back and gripping her as if he wished to mold her to him forever.

He broke away, breathing heavy. The brightness in his eyes matched the glistening of his lips. "Nay, I am not upset. I'm delighted to the point of utter disbelief. Though I do believe you Kitty, completely." A deep, quiet chuckle rattled in his chest as he lowered his head. "And I must ask you to stop your bewitching ways, or I won't be able to resist you as I should." His eyes wandered to her mouth and he shook his head. "You never answered me."

"Never answered you?"

"I asked you to be my wife. Am I to believe my feelings are not returned?"

Kitty's heart grew wings. "Do you believe they are not?"

He stepped closer and nuzzled her ear with his nose as he whispered. "Marry me tomorrow, and let me begin to cherish you the way I desire to for the rest of my days. For I can no longer withhold my longing for you Kitty, not when I am consumed by so true a love."

Ever so slowly, he trailed kisses at the edge of her hair and down to her mouth. His warm, possessive kiss removed every other thought from her mind. He directed her face upward and continued sharing his passion until he finally pulled away, staring at her with parted lips and hooded eyes.

"Marry me?" His voice carried no louder than a

prayer.

She nodded, her throat too thick to make a sound.

He must have seen the unspoken answer in her tear-filled eyes. Tucking the stray hair around her ear he leaned closer. "Are you opposed to an afternoon wedding?"

"Nay," she whispered.

Trailing a finger around her ear and down her neck, Nathaniel's mouth twitched upward into a smile that whispered of delicious secrets to come. "I am glad to hear it. As of tomorrow night you will no longer be Miss Katherine Campbell. You will be my Mrs. Nathaniel Smith."

Epilogue

Nathaniel stood in the far corner of his parlor, watching his newly pronounced wife smile and giggle with her sister and several other women in the opposite corner. He hadn't expected the wedding to be such an occasion, though he should have known as much. It seemed women spent their entire youth planning such an event, and he wouldn't have it ruined for Kitty, no matter how he wished it were already over. 'Twas surprising what a few women could produce in less than a day when it came to such a thing.

A smile warmed his face as he glanced at the table in the center of the parlor. The only request Kitty had made for their sacred day was that a large vase of white flowers be placed in the room when they spoke their vows. The thought nestled in his heart and he loved her all the more.

Thomas approached, a cup of cider in his hand. "You name the moment, man, and I shall usher all from the house so you may enjoy your wife, as I can plainly see you wish to."

"Is such a thing so terrible?" Nathaniel chuckled. "All in good time."

Thomas took a sip. "I am very pleased."

"Pleased?"

"Aye." Thomas smirked. "'Tis no secret, I'm sure. You must know Eliza and I have always wished the two of you would marry."

"Did you?" Nathaniel tried to jest, but all humor remained subdued under the peaceful serenity of the moment. "Then I suppose I ought to thank you and your wife for hoping such, for I can assure you this union is more joyful than I could ever have imagined."

Thomas cupped his arm. "And may your joy be ever constant, my friend."

As if Eliza had heard her name, she tugged at Kitty's arm and pulled her away from the few others leading her in the direction of the men. Eliza stopped in front of them and winked at Thomas. "'Tis becoming late. We best be going."

Thomas cleared his throat and set his drink on the small table beside him. "Aye, I do believe you are right."

Eliza leaned in and whispered something in Kitty's ear that made the color in her face reach crimson, and the itch to ask what was said hovered on Nathaniel's tongue, but he bit it back. Kitty in turn whispered something to her sister. Eliza kissed her cheek and tugged on Thomas's arm.

Eliza turned to Nathaniel. "God is surely smiling this night." Then, she turned to Kitty and stroked her sister's face. "And so is Father."

Kitty glanced up at Nathaniel, her eyes wide as the horizon. "I believe he is, Liza."

Nathaniel gripped Kitty around the waist, grinning broad and warm from the depths of his spirit to the tips of his fingers. "'Tis true," he answered. "But I venture to suppose that no one in neither heaven nor earth is smiling more than I."

When the last of the revelers had stepped into the summer eve, Kitty peeked out the window and waved at Eliza who turned one last time to smile over her shoulder. Nerves danced both beneath and atop Kitty's skin. Her hands grew clammy and she hardly had the strength to turn around when she felt Nathaniel's breath on her hair.

"We are alone." His husky timbre tickled her heart.

Kitty swallowed and turned, praying at least this once her emotions wouldn't display on her face. "That we are." She smiled despite how her breath came in quick, short bursts.

He stepped nearer, producing a white flower in his fingers. "Are you not pleased?"

She could hardly speak for what his nearness did to her heart. "Aye, I am pleased."

His gaze narrowed on her mouth then skirted away and he studied her hair. Gently tugging against the pins that held her tresses in place, he all but whispered as he let her hair tumble around her shoulders. "I am glad to hear it." Gently, he brushed her hair behind her ear and tucked the flower in place. "Now, Kitty, I will kiss you."

He leaned near and Kitty could not resist him. Tilting her head back, she welcomed his descent and wrapped her arms around his neck, lifting on her toes to more fully return his passion. She plunged her fingers through his hair and felt his strong, warm fingers do the same to hers. His hot breath against her mouth weakened her limbs and she leaned against him as a quiet moan escaped her throat.

Still holding tight to her waist, he pulled back. "I love you, Kitty." Studying her face as if he had only just begun to treasure her the way he wished, he stroked his thumb against her cheek. "Shall we ascend to the bedchamber?"

Kitty's body suddenly grew hot with nerves both anxious and wanting, and she knew her face displayed her feelings as Nathaniel's unreserved gaze roamed her up and down. A smile lifted his mouth.

Releasing his hold, he trailed his hand down her arm and twined his fingers with hers. "Come, Kitty. Let me love you."

Kitty gripped his hand and stepped beside him. "Aye, Nathaniel. Forever."

Dear Reader,

I hope you enjoyed Kitty's and Nathaniel's story. I am thrilled to finally be able to share their romance with you.

Both characters are based roughly on real people's experiences during that time. Emily Geiger was a remarkable Revolutionary heroine who did in fact eat a note she carried to keep it out of enemy hands. And the doctor of Sandwich during the Revolution was indeed a strong patriot who did much for the cause of liberty.

The next installment in the series, So Rare a Gift, will feature Henry Donaldson and Anna Martin—sister of Samuel Martin. I hope you will enjoy their story as well.

Blessings to you, dear friends. You make this journey a joy.

Acknowledgements

It is difficult to know how to fully thank all those who have helped me along the way. Muzzy, what would I do without you? I am forever in your debt! To my family who is patient with my need to tell the stories that live inside of me, I love you more than I can ever express. Jennifer Major, thank you for all your support. You are a crit partner like no other!

And thank you, Lord in Heaven, for guiding me and for taking my hand as I strive to bring glory to Your name. I will love and serve You forever.

Amber Lynn Perry is a historical romance novelist, focusing on her favorite time in American history, the Revolutionary era. She received a Bachelor's degree from Portland State University and currently lives in Washington state with her husband and two daughters. She loves to hear from readers and you can contact her through her website, www.amberlynnperry.com or through her Facebook page, www.facebook.com/amberperrywrites.

Made in the USA
San Bernardino, CA
09 March 2015